Off Limits

Limits Series Book 1

Shayna Astor

From the Author

Off Limits is a full-length, stand alone that features strong language, mature situations, explicit sexual scenes, abandonment, alcohol use, promiscuous behavior, and death of a loved one. This book is intended for readers age 18 and up.

To some, Shay may be considered an annoying character. This is intentional in many ways as her relationship with Lochlyn is her first real relationship. Her growth is meant to be big and take place over multiple books.

Thank you so much for reading my novel! I hope you enjoy reading it, as much as I enjoyed writing it!

Other Books by Shayna Astor

Hot & Cold

Shattered Pieces

Own Me (A dark romance)

Off Limits (Book 1 in the Limits Series)

Setting Limits (Book 2 in the Limits Series. Coming December 20 2022)
Stay tuned for the last two books in the Limits series in early spring 2023.

Dedication

To every one who ends up with the one they
always knew they wanted.

Chapter 1

Lochlyn Reynolds is the one boy I want to date. But I can't, because he's my best friend's brother.

He's the guy I want to share my first kiss with. But I can't, because he's my best friend's brother.

He's who I want to be with. But I can't, because he's my best friend's brother.

Maybe if I repeat it enough times, I'll start to believe it. I'll stop dreaming about his hands on me. Stop drooling over him as I watch the rivulets of water flow down his impeccably toned chest and abs as he climbs out of the pool. So far, it hasn't worked. *Nothing can happen with Lochlyn. He's your best friend's brother. Her very, devastatingly handsome and sexy older brother.*

Already I'm on the cusp of losing my so-called resolve.

Humid July air wraps its thickness around us on this starlit night. Eyes glued to the crackling fire, Lochlyn slouches in his Adirondack chair to my right. He's been home from Cornell for eight weeks now, and though we see each other almost daily, this is the first time we've been able to get time alone together. Time I cherish.

Chelsea, my best friend and his sister, left for bed hours ago. She's never been a night owl; she's usually ready to go to sleep by ten o'clock, but wakes up at six every morning. I'm the opposite—staying up late, then wishing to sleep all day.

We'd spent the day at their house swimming and lounging by the pool, coming back to my house for Chinese food and a fire. I expected Lochlyn to leave when Chelsea did, but he's made no move to rise from his chair. I appreciate the company, especially *his.*

"So, how are you? Really?" His feet almost reach the fire pit as he stretches out his six-foot-two frame. I'm acutely aware of how close his chair is to mine, so much so that I could slide my hand and touch his. But I can't do that. Because of Chelsea. She's been my rock for the past year, and my best friend for fifteen. Not to mention, I'm sure he doesn't see me that way.

"I'm okay."

He tilts his head, frowning. One thin lock of his light brown hair falls into his eyes. The sides are still cut short, but the part on top looks like it's grown a little longer than he usually keeps it. "Shay. Come on."

I release a low breath as I pull at a string on the hem of my shirt. My lips curl down in a way that I try to fight around everybody else. "I don't know. Every day is different. I didn't just lose my dad. I lost my family. I basically never see or talk to my mom anymore. If I do, it's about the store, while at the store. We're like passing ships in the night. And I miss her, which I hate to even admit because what eighteen-year-old misses their mom? Especially because she's still here...she's just not *here.*"

Dad passed away a year ago come September. It was one week and four months before I turned eighteen. Lochlyn had come home from college for the funeral, staying six days instead of the one night I'd expected. He and Chelsea spent that time with me, keeping me from being alone. Lochlyn sat with me, talked to me, let me cry. Unlike Chelsea, he never tried to cheer me up or take my mind off it. He let me mourn.

Those few days he was home was when I started having *real* feelings for him. I'd always had a crush, always appreciated how gorgeous he is. That week changed things. We'd often spent a lot of time together since he and Chelsea have always had a close sibling bond. Close enough that she told both of us when she lost her virginity at sixteen, which, in hindsight, was a mistake because he got very protective and angry.

What changed things was his gentleness with me, his overwhelming sense of calm. It certainly helped when he pulled me against him after the funeral. Lochlyn and Chelsea had me sandwiched between them on the porch swing as I bawled. When she got up to get me a water, Lochlyn had pulled me into his toned chest and held me.

Tucking one of my dark brown curls behind my ear, I continue, "I haven't even heard from Logan in months, let alone seen her. It's not like we were that close, but she's my sister."

Shaking my head, willing away the tears, I go on, "I don't feel like I'm on a good path. I delayed Cornell. My dad had been so happy when I applied. 'My baby going to my alma mater—nothing would make me happier.' That's what he'd said when I'd filled out the application. And now? I should be packing my things and leaving in a couple weeks. Instead, I'm staying here, going to community college, and working at my parents' store. The one thing I swore I'd never do."

"You'll get to Cornell. It's temporary. You're doing it for your family."

I scoff, slouching in my seat. "What family?" How can what we've become constitute as a family anymore? I spend more time blocking out the pain of losing all my blood relations in one day than I care to admit. Especially because two of them are still alive, choosing not to be available.

Filling my lungs, I speak louder. "I'm just afraid I'll get stuck. That I'll get stuck here, working at the store, going to community college. That's not what I want for myself. And I'm dragging Chelsea down with me." I've never admitted that to anyone, let alone myself.

The feeling of Lochlyn's hand on mine startles me, and tingles ping through my entire body. When I turn to look at him, his blue eyes, which appear darker in the night, are fixed on me. "You'll get out, Shay. And Chelsea made her own choice. You didn't ask her to stay. She did that on her own."

"Yeah, but she did it for me. And your parents were so mad." Chelsea had delayed her acceptance to Cornell as I did. "She didn't have to. She could have kept on the straight and narrow. But Chelsea doesn't have a path. She zigs and zags. While she may be using you as an excuse to stay, I could have seen this happening without you. And my parents will get over it. If they wanted more say, they could be around more." He says the last part with a bite to his tone.

But he's right. Chelsea's grades almost weren't good enough to get her into Cornell. It's just another glaring reminder of how starkly different Chelsea and Lochlyn are. Aside from their looks, Chelsea being much fairer than Lochlyn, with hair so blonde it's almost white, Lochlyn's exceptionally smart. He graduated top of his class in high school, in a group of over two hundred, and from what he says, is doing very well at Cornell. He studies, but not nearly as much as Chelsea needs to. Things come easier to him.

It's just one more thing I find attractive about Lochlyn. Looking at him, you'd be sure he's just a pretty face with those piercing blue eyes and sharp cheekbones. But his intelligence shines through in a simple conversation.

"Aside from worrying about Cornell and Chelsea, how are you? How is Shay?" I must not have given him enough since he's pressing about *me.* It's something he does—checking in about me specifically. Always.

How do I answer that?

"Honestly? I don't know. I kind of feel lost. Like I don't have direction, like I don't know where I belong. Before my dad got sick, it was pretty clear cut. Get good grades, get into a good college, and leave. Now, though? It's not clear at all." I hesitate before treading further. "Sorry, I know that was more about college. I guess it's just at the forefront of my mind."

"It's okay. Whatever you're thinking, you can talk to me."

My eyes fall to my hem, where I start picking at my shirt again. "I don't know. My dad's death anniversary is coming up in two months. It sounds far away, but it's almost still surreal that he's gone at all. I can't explain this weird feeling.

"My mom's still so broken. I don't blame her really, because they'd been married almost thirty years. Suddenly, he's just...gone." Part of me feels like I should have more emotion behind this sentiment. Instead, I feel numb. "Thank God for Chelsea. I really don't know what I'd have done without her this past year."

Feeling a squeeze on my hand, I turn my dark brown eyes to him. "What do you say we have some fun the rest of the summer? Try to take your mind off things?"

My heart flutters when he says *we.* "Yeah, I'd like that."

"What are your thoughts on things like, I don't know, skydiving?"

My eyes widen. "Um, not so good."

He chuckles. "How about bungee jumping?"

"I'm sorry, have you met me?" My eyes narrow, the fingers of my free hand pressing against my chest as I lean forward slightly in my chair.

I've never known Lochlyn to be that much of a daredevil. In fact, I can't think of a time he's done anything he shouldn't do, aside from attending a party or two. Right now, I wouldn't be surprised if he was just aiming to make the conversation lighthearted.

His chuckle turns into a laugh. My pulse speeds up at the sound. "Okay, so no crazy stunts. How about the shore? Would you want to drive down to shore one day?"

"A beach day sounds great, but I'm not sure I should leave my mom. I told her I'd be at the store every day to help out."

He nods, running his fingertips along his bottom lip, drawing my attention to his mouth and how much I wish he'd press it against mine. Heat crawls through my body, and I just hope it doesn't reach my cheeks as I think about what his lips might feel like.

I shake my head at the thought. *Off limits*. There's also the glaring fact that he doesn't look at me that way.

Pulling his fingers away from his mouth, he throws his hand in the air. "Welp, I guess that just means we'll have to find things to do at home, like lounging by the pool. Maybe a few parties...?"

"Maybe. We'll see."

He nods. "I know, you're not much of the party girl. But it could be worth trying, at least this summer while you're feeling off."

"Lounging by the pool sounds nice." Especially because then I'll get to see him without his shirt on. The tattoos he's gotten since he turned eighteen make him even sexier. Especially the lyrics he has scrawled along the side of his left rib cage. It was the first tattoo he got, quickly adding other lyrics on his inner right bicep, and a sword down the back of his left forearm.

Damn it. I shake my head again, trying to disperse the thoughts, as though they'd tumble to the ground in chunks of words. "Okay, I don't want to talk about me anymore. Tell me about you, about school."

His hand pulls against mine slightly as his shoulder rises and falls. "Not much to tell, really."

"Oh, come on. You just finished your second year. What's it like?"

"It's fun. It's nice to have fewer responsibilities. My dad can't check every report card for grades or call the teachers. The freedom's nice, the parties are pretty awesome."

"And the girls?" I'm painfully aware of Lochlyn's reputation as being "a sex god," so even though I asked the question, I don't really wish to know his answer. According to the rumors, which he has neither confirmed nor denied, he slept his way through the entire girls' volleyball and field hockey teams, and *earned* this title from them at school. I'm sure college has been no different.

My insides twist as he smirks. "The girls are nice." He shoots me a sideways glance, causing heat to rise to my face. I'm not sure how much Chelsea has shared with him in terms of my entirely nonexistent sexual history. She'd told me she keeps me out of most conversations. But I don't believe her. Not wanting to know more, I don't press. Lochlyn and I are worlds apart in this area.

He can have any girl he wants, he knows it, and often does if the rumors are to be believed. And he doesn't want me. Why would he? I'm his little sister's best friend. She's also forbidden it. She's told us both, several times, that she is absolutely not at all okay with it.

But that doesn't mean I'm not going to enjoy his pres-ence—one that I'm acutely aware is missing when he's at col-lege—while I have it. He is the star of my dreams, after all.

We sit watching the flames for a few minutes, the only sounds the crackling of wood and the occasional distant chirp of a cricket.

"Can I tell you something I haven't told anybody?" My voice is so quiet I'm not quite sure he heard me until he intertwines our fingers. For a moment, I stop breathing and turn to look at him. His eyes are on me, waiting for me to share.

I take a deep breath, preparing myself. "I feel horrible for thinking this, but I almost feel like it's better my dad's gone. He was in so much pain, so miserable. It was awful seeing him like that."

"I remember." Lochlyn had come by every time he was home while my dad was sick. Since we'd grown up together, our families had always been close. He came to see him before he left for school, just a few weeks before my dad passed.

Tears spill from my eyes without warning. I reach up to wipe them away, but Lochlyn beats me to it, leaning over in his chair, keeping his hand in mine while also gently swiping a thumb across my cheek.

It may just be my imagination, but his hand hovers against my jaw for a moment before he settles back in his seat.

"I saw how broken my mom was, how broken she still is. Logan can't even bear to call. And somehow, I just feel at peace. I don't know, maybe I'm the one who's broken. I didn't even cry at the funeral. I mean, I did after, but that was kind of it. I know I'm crying right now, but it's more for feeling...guilty. That I'm not more upset. I kind of always sense it's right there, on the cusp of breaking free, but it never really does. And the times it does, it always just feels like it's something else." I shake my head, looking down at my lap. "I don't know, maybe there's something wrong with me."

"Shay. Shay, look at me." I turn my face to him, his blue eyes gentle. "There is *nothing* wrong with you. I was here with you after the funeral. You didn't shed a few tears. You cried, truly cried. Just because you weren't more upset then, that you aren't breaking down every day, doesn't mean you're broken. I know you miss your dad. He was a great man. And I'm sure you've been upset more often than you realize."

He pauses, looking pensive. "You're one of the most down to earth, mature, and intelligent people I have the pleasure of knowing. I think you look at the situation differently. I think you can look at it and see that your dad was suffering. That while you lost him and miss him, he's no longer miserable. That's not being broken, Shay. That doesn't mean you don't miss or didn't love your dad."

His words make tears pour faster from my eyes. I'm not sure if it's what he said or missing my dad. He's right, I *do* miss my dad, every day. My dad was always the first one up in the morning, making breakfast for everybody. Every morning he said the same thing, *"Breakfast is the most important meal of the day. It sets the tone for your entire day."*

I look up, wiping the tears and sniffling a little. Then, I break out into a small smile. "Ya know, after he died, I couldn't eat breakfast. For weeks. I just completely skipped it. I haven't had a real breakfast since then. I alternate between a piece of fruit, a handful of cereal, a granola bar. Anything quick and easy that doesn't require real cooking, since I never really learned the basics."

Glancing over at Lochlyn, I notice he's scowling, a look usually saved for Chelsea. "That's not healthy, Shay."

Self-consciousness picks at my chest, making my pulse flutter. "I just can't. For my whole life, he had always been the one to cook breakfast. By the time I get up in the morning, my mom's already gone. Seven days a week, she's at the store to open. She stays till close. The last day she took off was my graduation. And I'd wondered if she was even going to follow through with it."

"Well, I guess we'll have to teach you how to make yourself some breakfast."

I look over at him, brows furrowed. "You can cook?"

"I can, in fact."

"Huh. Who'd have known."

We sit in a comfortable silence for a little while longer, hands still linked as we stare into the low flames licking the charred wood.

When Lochlyn turns to me and smiles, my heart flutters as he says, "I'm full of surprises, Shay Sterling."

Chapter 2

It's a Tuesday in early August, and I'm sitting in the office going over some paperwork with Mom, while Chelsea's out on the floor, and Lochlyn is unloading some boxes in the stockroom. He's been helping out all summer and it's very appreciated, especially since he refuses to accept Mom's money.

"You know, I've always liked Lochlyn. He's a nice boy," Mom says as she signs some checks.

"Mom, you've *never* liked Lochlyn." I lean forward in my chair, uncrossing my legs and resting my fingers on the desk.

"Well, that's not true."

"Okay, maybe you didn't dislike him, but you also never thought very highly of him, either." Something I never really understood.

"I don't know what you're talking about."

"His tattoos? Do you not remember when he started getting them? You asked why somebody would modify their body so permanently and wondered what he was thinking."

She waves a hand at me like I'm crazy. "Oh, nonsense. It may have just been because they were so new. I've known the boy since he was five. I think they suit him and who he's grown up to be."

I agree. Though, I've always liked Lochlyn's tattoos. Felt they suited him. He looks tantalizing with them.

He's your best friend's brother. Nothing can happen. Deep breath.

"Well, whether you like him or not, it *is* nice of him to help out around here." So nice it makes me like him even more. Which makes me war with myself, because I can't. I shouldn't.

"It certainly is. The Reynolds raised those two right."

"Any chance you'll be home for dinner tonight?" Though I know the chances are slim, and I try not to get my hopes up, I had to take this opportunity to ask. This has been one of the few, albeit short, conversations we've had that hasn't been strained, or about Dad.

"I'm sorry, sweetie, I have too much to do." In reality, she doesn't. To avoid coming home, she'll rearrange things like folding towels that have already been folded once, straightening stacks of boxes, organizing her desk, and the list goes on. She basically stays until she's too tired to do anything but sleep. But I understand. It's the home she built with Dad that she's avoiding, their dream store that she's trying to perfect. She once told me nights are lonely without him, and it all but broke my heart all over again.

"It's alright. I'll just go over to Chelsea's or something." Like every other night. I shift in my seat and chew the inside of my lip.

"Oh, that sounds nice. I'm glad you two have been able to stay such good friends all these years." Another swipe of her pen across the paper.

"Yeah, it's been great having her. You good in here? I'm going to head out to the floor." Defeat weighs heavily in my chest and the room becomes more and more stifling by the second.

"Sure, sweetie, go ahead." It's not lost on me that my mom hasn't looked at me once.

I wander out to the floor to find Chelsea straightening up a few stacks of towels, grumbling to herself.

"Hey, Chels, something wrong?"

I catch the perfected Chelsea eye roll. "No, just another customer who decided they wanted to see exactly how big the towels are and proceeded to unfold about seven different ones, just in case each color was sized differently. And then...bought none." It's an alarmingly frequent incident.

I stifle a laugh. "I'm sorry. Can I help?"

She puffs some pin straight white-blonde hair out of her face. "No, I'm done."

"Okay. Do you mind if I join you guys for dinner tonight?" While it's basically an every night occurrence, I still like to ask. My parents put a lot of work into my manners.

"Sure! It's just me and Loch, anyway. My parents left today for who knows where. They'll be gone for a few weeks. Loch said something about a party or two, I don't know."

When Chelsea and I were fourteen, their parents started leaving them with a sitter for several days at a time to travel. Once Lochlyn turned eighteen, their parents had started leaving them alone for overnights, which quickly turned to a week at a time, asking my parents to check in on them. It slowed once my dad got sick and Lochlyn was at school, but when he's home for summer and breaks, they spend the majority of their time traveling.

"Oh, that sounds fine." Though the idea of a party sounds awful, I had told Lochlyn maybe I'd try one or two.

"Just come over when we leave. We'll all go together. Your mom would be cool if I left my car, right? At least for a few hours?"

"Yeah, I don't think she'd mind. I wouldn't suggest leaving it overnight, though."

"Loch and I can come back and get it after dinner. Go tell him you're coming, so we order enough pizza." This is such a Chelsea thing to do. She'll never ask Mom, leaving it to me to ask or be the bad guy. And then not asking Lochlyn, just assuming he'll be okay with getting it later on.

"I don't eat that much, Chels." I cross my arms against my chest at her suggestion.

"No, but he does."

It's true. I've seen him eat an entire pizza by himself. I don't understand how he's still in such amazing shape when he can eat the way he does. *He's your best friend's brother. Nothing can happen.*

"Sure. He still in the back?"

She turns back to the towels, angrily refolding one and smacking it on the top of the pile. "As far as I know, I haven't seen him on the floor."

When I get into the stockroom, I don't see Lochlyn. "Loch?" My voice echoes off the walls. It's a huge room, with shelves and boxes everywhere.

He pokes his head around one of the shelving units, a smile breaking across his face when he sees me, making my heart skip a beat. "Oh, hey." The words come out breathless, and it's just another reminder of how hard he's working back here. For free.

"Hey. Chels wanted me to let you know that I'm joining you guys for dinner tonight."

"Oh, okay, good. What do you like on your pizza?" Resting his elbow on a shelf above him causes his shirt to ride up the slightest bit, and my mouth feels parched as I try not to stare at the hard lines and angles.

"I'm not picky."

He narrows his eyes at me. "You most certainly are."

I sigh. He's right. I'm pretty picky. With food and boys. "I don't want to be a bother. Just get whatever you guys want and if I don't like it, I'll pick it off."

"You're not a bother. If you want something specific, let me know. Otherwise, we'll get one with just cheese."

"Just cheese is fine." I lean my back against the wall, the cool brick a welcome shock to my system, cooling me from the outside in and dousing the fire burning inside for the man in front of me.

"Shay. Come on."

"Alright. I like peppers and onions." Though I've known Lochlyn almost my whole life, these moments of being open and honest aren't common. He was there for me after Dad died, and I let my walls down then, but I don't need to be a burden on him when he already has Chelsea to deal with, who's no picnic. Something as simple as pizza is no biggie to me.

It's just another instance where Chelsea would chastise me for being a people pleaser. I can't help that I'd rather keep the peace than cause tension.

"See? That wasn't so hard, was it?"

"I don't want you to get a pizza just for what I like."

"Well, I happen to not be picky. So, it's fine. You driving back with Chelsea?"

"She actually said something about us all going together? You two coming to get her car later?" While I try to make it sound like a question and I'm not sure she said that, we both know that she did.

His face pulls into a scowl. "Of course she did. I love when she volunteers me for things." He sighs. "We'll figure it out when we leave."

"Do you need anything? Water? A break? I mean, you don't have to stay, you're not even getting paid. And it's a lot of heavy boxes to be moving, unpacking, and breaking down." A light sheen of sweat is visible on his forehead.

"Water would be great."

We keep a fridge in the stockroom for water and anybody who brings a lunch. The staff may be small, and mostly consist of our family, but it's still nice to have it. It's so far in the back, I'm not sure most people even know about it. I bring him a bottle of water, and when his fingers graze mine, it sends tingles through my body. *Nothing can happen. He's your best friend's brother.*

He uncaps it and takes a long drink, his Adam's apple bobbing repeatedly. "Thanks. Lots of boxes."

I can't help myself from glancing at his strong arms. Or prevent the heat that reignites in my chest.

"Seriously, though, you don't have to stay. You've been helping out for a few weeks already, and while it's extremely appreciated, it's really above and beyond." Not a single part of me wants him to leave, but I feel guilty, like we're taking advantage of his generosity by putting him to work day after day. He's a nice guy, maybe he feels bad refusing.

"I don't mind. It's nice to be doing something with myself. I'd just be sitting around otherwise, or doing something stupid with Jay and Heath. Plus, it keeps me from having to go to the gym."

I already know that he runs every morning. I've watched him as he runs past my window. What I didn't know is that he also goes to the gym. It makes sense. Taking a deep breath in, I try to settle my hormones.

"We really appreciate it. My mom was just saying how much she's always liked you."

"Ha! She has not. She thought I was trouble and was all too happy to tell me."

My eyes widen and my eyebrows reach my hairline. "She did?"

He nods, brow furrowed, while taking another sip of his water. "Oh, yeah. The second she saw my first tattoo, that was it. She had labeled me as trouble. She'd known me almost my whole life and my choice to get a tattoo changed her opinion of me." He shakes his head.

"I'm sorry." And also very shocked at my mother's audacity.

"Don't be. I knew what I was getting myself into."

"If it makes you feel any better, I did, in fact, point that out, and she said that she finds they suit you."

He quirks up an eyebrow. "Oh really? Now she thinks that? She probably takes me as someone who grew into the role she felt they gave me."

"I think she feels like you did the right thing. Followed the path set for you and all that. I do know she's talked highly about you going to Cornell and sticking with your parents' wishes for you."

"My path," he mumbles.

My brow furrows. "Hmm?"

"Oh, nothing. Thanks for the water. I wanted to try to get to a few more things before we leave. I hope you and your mom don't mind, but I'm sort of rearranging some things back here so they're easier to find and reach." Again, with the above and beyond. I really wish he'd take Mom's money. Or even merchandise for his time. Something to truly grasp how much we value what he's doing.

"Sure, no problem. That's very appreciated, being short and all. I'll uh, I'll see ya later."

I walk out of the stockroom, feeling like I hit a nerve. But I'm not sure Lochlyn and I are close enough for me to ask him something that personal since it's not my place to pry. So I leave it alone.

Chelsea and Lochlyn's company helps the summer go by much faster. And we have a lot of fun. I'm kind of surprised the summer is almost over, and a little upset since that means Lochlyn leaves again soon. We've gone to a few parties, both of them convincing me to tag along despite putting up a good fight to just stay home. We've hung out by the pool, spent many days at the store, and had a lot more nighttime fires.

One of the harder aspects with all of this is that Lochlyn flirts with me. A lot. He's always been on the flirtatious side. It's something I've seen him do with just about any girl he's been around. But after realizing that I like him, truly like him, it's harder to handle.

It's little things—a touch on my arm that makes warmth spread through my body. An overheated gaze that makes my heart race. His wide smile that makes me want to melt right where I stand.

Two weeks before college classes are set to start, Chelsea meets a guy at the store. Walking out of the backroom on one of the days Lochlyn isn't here, I find her unabashedly flirting. As we leave that night, she tells me that she invited him over to her house to swim the next day and that I absolutely have to be there.

That's how the next day we're all hanging out by the pool. Lochlyn is tense; his eyes trained on Brendan. It's a little awkward, with Chelsea and Brendan on some weird pseudo date, and then me and Lochlyn, who are, of course, not. I'd love to be here on a real date with him, though. The reminder that we can't be together seems moot at this point.

Chelsea and I are standing by the edge of the pool as Brendan tries to convince her to go in, but she keeps refusing, having spent too much time straightening her hair to ruin it.

I'm busy laughing at Chelsea when I'm suddenly falling into the water below, with strong arms wrapped tightly around my waist. As my head breaks the surface, I see Lochlyn treading water, eyes fixated on me. I can't seem to pull my gaze from his.

Until I hear Chelsea screaming, "What the hell, Lochlyn! That wasn't nice! And you got me soaked!"

"Sorry, Chels," he yells, eyes still locked in on me. Before I can think or feel anything, he turns away. "Just trying to get Shay to have some fun." Pushing himself up and out of the pool, he reaches a hand down for me. I take it, and with a hard tug, he's able to pull me out, one-handedly.

I stumble a bit, falling against his hard chest. His hands are gentle on my hips. When my eyes find his again, I'm stunned still, in awe of how he feels against me. Where my palm rests over his heart, I feel it hammering away, just like mine is.

Chelsea's next to us in a second, pushing us apart. "Hands off, Loch."

He lets go and takes a step back, running his fingers through his soaked locks, a few stray strands falling back in his face. "I don't know what you're talking about. I was just helping her out of the pool."

"Mhm, I bet that's what you say about all the girls before they fall into bed with you. Not my best friend. No way."

He rolls his eyes and sighs. "I'll go get us some towels." After stripping his shirt off, he walks inside.

Lochlyn pulling me into the pool isn't that abnormal. It happens at least once a summer. The part that's different this time is that he wrapped his arms around my waist. Normally, he gives me a shove, pulls me in from below, or takes my hand as he jumps in. It doesn't help my resolve that I can't have him.

I'm so lost in my thoughts that I don't notice he's returned until he's wrapping a towel around my shoulders. Sitting on the pool chair opposite me, he puts his knees on either side of mine.

"Sorry, Shay, just trying to have some fun."

"It's fine, I'm fine. I'm used to it." I smirk, pushing him gently against the shoulder. A smile lights up his entire face, causing mine to expand even further.

"I'm nothing if not traditional."

"Well, you got your pool toss in this summer. Cutting it close too. Don't you leave in a few days?" An ache settles in my chest at the thought.

"I do, yeah." He nods slowly as his face turns to the ground, using the towel to wipe under his nose.

"It must be nice, getting an apartment."

"I don't know. Campus has its perks. But it will be good to have some more space. You'll see next year."

"Yeah, I hope so," I say, nodding. One thing I've had to learn not to do is let that hope rise too far in my chest. It's not worth it. The loss of Dad taught me that nothing is guaranteed, and tomorrow isn't promised.

"You'll get there, Shay. You have to trust that." My face must not look convincing because he rests his hand on my knee, causing me to look up as warmth spreads from his fingertips through my body. "You will."

Nothing can happen. He's your best friend's brother. It doesn't matter how many times I reiterate this motto. It doesn't help. I still want Lochlyn Reynolds.

Chapter 3

C lasses start for me and Chelsea a few days after Lochlyn leaves. We're both a little nervous, not really sure what to expect. But we have our first class together, which helps.

A few weeks in, and we're sitting outside at a local café with two girls, Rachel and Eve, whom we met our first day. We like them enough that we decided to see them outside of school. They're nice and easy to get along with.

"So, why'd you two start at WCC?" Eve asks before taking a sip of her coffee.

It's a perfectly innocent question, one I'm curious to know about her myself. But for Chelsea and me, it's a little more complicated.

"Uh, well, my dad died." Any time the topic of Dad dying used to come up, I'd beat around the bush and avoid talking about it. But at a certain moment in time, I realized...what's the point? It doesn't change anything. Dad's still dead, and I've likely just rambled some other nonsense. So, now, I rip the Band-Aid off.

"I postponed so that I could help my mom at the store they opened together. Chelsea was sweet enough to stay with me." I turn to her with a tight smile while my fingers tap against my paper cup.That's when I get 'the look.' The one most people give me. The one full of pity. I've grown so used to 'the look' it hardly fazes me anymore.

After Dad died, 'the look' always made me want to shrink in on myself. There were only a few people who I didn't receive it from. Lochlyn was the main one, as his expressions never changed. Even Chelsea had it for a long while. I found that only other people who had experienced loss were able to talk to me without pity.

As with most, the pity fades to a gentle smile, a hushed *I'm so sorry* and a quick change of subject to take the attention off of me.

"What are your plans after WCC?" Rachel flips her straight brown hair over her shoulder. It's a few shades lighter than mine, but I've always been jealous of girls with naturally sleek straight hair. She could straighten it, but mine never came out that shiny.

"Cornell. For both of us. How about you two?" I answer without pause. It's just that easy for me. It's barely even something I have to think about.

"Cornell? Wow, you must both be pretty smart." Rachel seems truly awestruck.

Chelsea and I look at each other and shrug. For us, it's commonplace. Cornell holds a major role in both of our households.

"She definitely is," Chelsea says as she cocks her thumb at me. "Me? Not so much."

"Oh, come on, Chels, you got in, you're smart."

"Yeah, by the skin of my teeth." Although Chelsea would never admit it, I know it's a bit of a sore spot for her.

"I just study more than she does," I say as I motion my hand toward her, looking back at Rachel and Eve.

"It's just *easier* for you. I swear she's just like my brother. He definitely got the brains in the family."

"He also *studies*. A lot." When I notice the furrowed brow as Rachel and Eve look at each other, I realize they don't know much about us, so I rush to explain. "Chelsea has an older brother, Lochlyn. We've all been friends for fifteen years. Though I'm much closer to Chelsea."

Their eyes widen. "Your brother is Lochlyn Reynolds? Like, *the* Lochlyn Reynolds?"

Chelsea just purses her lips and nods. "Yup. So what brings you two to WCC?" She's always been good at dodging questions about Lochlyn. She loves him, but she doesn't love to talk about him. Well, to anybody else but me. With me, I never hear the end of it, but it's usually complaining, not praising.

"Oh well, my grades were shit. I didn't get in anywhere else." Rachel flicks her hand like it's nothing, but her face says otherwise; the disappointment that settles over her features impossible to miss.

"Couldn't afford anything else and don't really know what I want to do after school. I didn't want to get myself more in debt than I needed to while I figured things out." Eve seems a little smarter, or at the very least, more self-aware. It's possible she had the grades, just not the money.

I shrug while I fiddle with my coffee cup. "Not necessarily a bad plan. No point in putting yourself in debt to leave with a degree you may not use."

"Exactly." Rachel and Chelsea appear to have started their own conversation beside us. "So, what made you settle on Cornell? Kind of high sights, no?"

"I'm lucky that my parents were never stern about me going to college. It was expected I go, but they were okay with wherever I chose and whatever I wanted to major in. Cornell has always been *my* dream. My dad went there."

"That's a nice way to honor him."

"Yeah, I'm not sure how he'd feel about me postponing it, but...here I am." It's always been one of my biggest worries. What would he think of me? Of me risking my future and dreams of Cornell.

"I'm sorry if this is inconsiderate, but what made you decide to stay? Was it hard?"

My brows shoot up and I start playing with the lip of my coffee lid. "My parents own a household supply shop named Sterling's, in town. They opened it years ago. It had been their dream or something, I don't know. But my mom felt a little...overwhelmed. To say the least. So I stayed behind to help her as the dust settles and she gets used to running it alone. Staying was the hardest decision of my life."

"That's really noble of you. I don't know, well, anybody who would do that for their family. It's really nice of Chelsea to stay with you." Her green eyes dash to my right to see if Chelsea turned her attention toward her name.

"Chelsea's my best friend. She's really more like my sister, always been there for me. You know how sometimes in middle school and high school, new cliques form and you go different ways? That never happened with Chelsea. She always fell into the popular crowd and I, well, I didn't. But Chelsea never let me feel left out or behind for that matter. She made sure I was invited to the events, and if I wasn't, she'd avoid too, if possible." A slight shift in my seat and an adjustment of my shoulders allow me a second to gather my thoughts.

"I never asked her to stay behind with me. She did it to be supportive and believed we're going through life together. It's just that simple."

"You're really lucky to have a friend like that." Eve's voice is quiet as she runs a hand through her strawberry-blonde hair.

"I am. So, no thoughts on what you want to be when you finish school?" After the quick subject change to take the attention off myself, I take a sip of my hazelnut coffee, rendering myself incapable of speaking, so Eve has to.

I may be willing to talk about Dad's passing and my life choices, but that doesn't mean I want to *continue* to do so.

"Not really. I'm not super passionate about anything, I guess. I don't know I just can't see myself doing anything specific for the rest of my life." She picks at the cardboard sleeve of her cup.

"It's definitely intimidating. I mean, I know so many people who don't either. Chelsea has no idea."

"Really? She seems so confident and collected." Eve turns to take in Chelsea, who's talking excitedly with her hands, her blue eyes bright.

"Oh, she is. She's very sure of herself. Somebody who knows what she wants and goes after it. Aside from school. Cornell was sort of pushed on both of them."

"That's unfortunate."

"Her brother seems to have taken to it just fine. But Chelsea's a little more...difficult."

"I heard that." Chelsea turns to look at me.

"I said it nicely. I could have said you're a giant pain in the ass." I bump my shoulder into hers as I tease her.

"I guess you could say I like to push back, especially against those in charge of me."

"And set all the rules."

"Oh, well, of course." We all burst into fits of laughter.

A quick glance at my phone and I jump to stand. "I hate to break this up, but I have to get to the store. Chels, are you coming by today?"

"No, I'm going to go meet Brendan."

"Okay. Tell him I said hi. Rachel, Eve, it was really nice to talk to you guys. We should get together again soon." Chelsea swears up and down she's my only friend, but I've had a few outside of her that I mostly only saw when she was otherwise occupied. It didn't make me the greatest friend, but they understood.

They've all gone away to college in other states, so I don't hear from them anymore. Making new friends would be nice, and Eve definitely seems like somebody I could become close with.

"Mom, when was the last time you were home for dinner?" As usual, we're having a strained conversation in the office at the store.

"What are you talking about? I was home last night."

"Yeah, at like ten. That's not dinnertime."

"I have a lot to do here." Her tone is clipped and her lips press together, a sure sign she's lying, and knows it.

"You have wonderful employees and a great assistant manager. I think it'd be okay for you to leave and have dinner with me once in a while." My tone is bordering on angry, and acid rises in my stomach, though it's all pointless.

"Oh, but you're almost nineteen. You don't want to have dinner with your poor old mom."

"Actually, I *would* like to have dinner with you. We haven't had dinner together since my graduation. And it'd been months before that."

"It has not been that long, Shay. Stop being so dramatic." Part of me wants to tell her *exactly* how long it's been, that before my graduation it had been several months. But at the same time, I can't bring myself to call her out, to even risk bringing her more pain, shoving my own aside.

"Mom, you can't even look at me." Her eyes haven't left the book in front of her. It's a new catalog from one of our vendors, but there can only be so many new things she's looking at. Surely nothing that takes this much focus.

"What are you talking about? Of course I look at you. I'm just very focused on what I have in front of me right now."

I sigh, defeated and hurt. So much for getting used to it. "Okay, Mom. Should I leave?"

"Oh, honey, you're welcome to stay. How's school?" With a quick lick of her finger, she flips the page, but still keeps her face down.

Shock. I feel shock. Mom hasn't asked anything about me in over a year. "Um, school's good."

"Are you liking the college?"

"Yeah, it's not bad."

"Ever think of staying another year?" The way she asks is so nonchalant it takes me a moment to realize she's incredibly serious.

My stomach free-falls to my feet. This isn't her checking in on me, caring. This is her trying to ask me to stay, something I've been worried about.

"No, Mom. I don't. I'm going to Cornell next year."

"Are you sure, sweetie? It's just so far away. And you've been so helpful around here for the past year."

"I'm sure." Helpful. All she wants from me is my assistance to run the store.

"Maybe you can just think about it. Rethink your plans, you know."

"I'm sorry, I have to get out of here." My heart is hammering against my sternum and I'm not entirely sure I won't be sick.

Storming out of the office, I make a beeline to the backroom, crashing through the door and sliding to the floor, trying to catch my breath. I need something. I need to talk to somebody. But for some reason, the only person I feel could calm me down is the one who spent weeks in this stockroom out of the goodness of his heart.

I put my head between my knees and try to take deep breaths, thinking back to some of the conversations I'd had with Lochlyn in this room, not caring that he shouldn't be on my mind.

A few days after our conversation regarding my mom's thoughts on him, he expanded on his muttered comment.

"I know you were probably wondering what I meant when I grumbled about my path the other day." We were in the backroom again, a place that seemed to be somewhere we chatted openly.

"Oh, it's none of my business. You don't have to tell me."

"Simply put, my dad, in all his self-proclaimed wisdom on what's best for me, has decided that I will be going to Cornell, get into Cornell Law, where I will get my graduate degree, and then work for him. As a fucking lawyer."

"I take it you don't want to be a lawyer?"

A low laugh escaped him. "No, I definitely don't want to be a lawyer."

"What do you want to be?"

He looked up at me, eyes wide and brows high as his hair fell across his forehead. "You're the first person to ever ask me that. I've never put much thought into it. I was informed of this plan for my life a long time ago. But, I don't know, I've always liked music a lot. Maybe something in the music industry. I'm interested in business. Like, your parents opened this place themselves, ran it. I don't know, just...not a lawyer."

"Music, huh? You realize that's one of the first things we bonded over."

"You have good taste in music." I smiled, noticing as he absentmindedly scratched at his ribs, where he has the song lyrics tattooed. He's the only person I know that likes the same alternative music I do. "You know, my parents wouldn't even let me learn an instrument, aside from the one required for school? I wanted to learn guitar. They wouldn't let me. It didn't 'fit in' with their plan."

"I'm sorry." There were aspects of the lives of the Reynolds children that I knew, but much of this was a shock. What harm can learning an instrument cause?

"Did I ever tell you why I started getting the tattoos?"

I shook my head, mouth pressed into a line.

Lochlyn shifted his feet and leaned in closer, closing the two-foot gap between us. *"It was a tiny way to have control of my life. When I asked what would happen if I didn't follow through, didn't go to Cornell, or decided to go for something that was what I wanted, they said they'd cut me off. It's not like I have access to all the money in the world, but it's kind of hard to do anything with none."* A tick of his jaw showed the frustration his tone didn't.

"My dad flipped shit when he saw the first one. I told him I was eighteen, didn't need his permission, and it can be covered by a shirt. That if I wasn't wearing a shirt at work, I had bigger problems than a tattoo. The sword was a little harder. I just needed something that I was deciding."

"I had no idea." The lyrics on his ribs made sense suddenly; the song being about taking control of your life.

"I've never told anybody."

"Nobody? Not even Chelsea?"

He snorted. *"Definitely not Chelsea. As far as she's concerned, it's my 'rocker ways,' as she likes to call them. I like a certain type of music; it doesn't mean I lead a lifestyle or something."* I'd learned to read Lochlyn well enough to sense he was growing beyond frustrated. But I was hung up on the fact that he hadn't shared this with anybody, except me.

I wasn't quite sure what to say. *"You've really never told anybody?"*

His eyes locked on mine. *"Nobody."*

"Why me?"

"You're easy to talk to. You listen. I find you...soothing, calming. Why did you tell me some of the things you've told me?"

Because I'm pretty sure I'm in love with you. *"Same reasons. You're easy to talk to. I feel comfortable around you. Maybe for some of the elderly advice."*

Chelsea and I often teased him about being old and wise. Lochlyn was an old soul, who always had good advice, and his parents leaving him in charge made him grow up fast.

He smirked and rubbed a hand over the back of his neck while he looked at the ground. It made my insides turn to mush and a tingling settle between my thighs every time he did it. I loved it, especially when he used his right arm and the lyric poked out from his shirt sleeve, as it did that time.

A smile stretched across my own face. Until Lochlyn's eyes locked on mine with a look that took all the silliness away and made my heart race. We stood there, in some sort of staring contest, for a few minutes before he cleared his throat, turning to go back to work.

Sitting on the floor, thinking about that moment, that exchange and the comfort I felt around him, calms me enough for my heart rate to return to normal, for the feelings of nausea to subside. I would love nothing more than for him to be in this backroom at this very moment. His advice and the soothing tone of his voice would be incredibly welcome.

Instead, I try to think about what he'd suggest, what I think he'd tell me to do. Before he went back to school a few weeks ago, he gave me his number, said I could call him any time if I needed to talk to somebody, but I don't want to be a bother.

Later in the night, three days before the anniversary of my dad's passing, I fill out the paperwork I need to confirm that I want to end my deferment and start at Cornell the following fall. It's been my plan all along, and I'm not putting it off any longer. Some part of me hopes that Lochlyn would be proud of me. I know my dad would be.

Chapter 4

For Thanksgiving, the Reynolds invite my mom and I over for dinner. Logan had called to tell us she's not coming home, wanting to spend the day with her boyfriend instead. I'm not surprised, but Mom cried.

The Reynolds are gone a lot, but they come home for major holidays, putting on the face of a perfect family. Not knowing what else to do, we decide to go. Chelsea's been beside herself with excitement for days.

"We've never done a holiday together! It's going to be so fun." We're standing at the buffet table in her living room as our parents talk. "We see each other every day. We've always seen each other after Thanksgiving dinner."

"I know, but now we get all day!"

"What's Brendan doing?"

"He'll be with his family. I asked my parents if he could come for dessert, but, of course, they refused. They're barely around, but when they are, they want to play the responsible parents and have 'family time.' Whatever that means. He may swing by after."

"That'll be nice if he can." I hesitate, wanting to know about Lochlyn, but still manage to keep my voice casual. "What time does Lochlyn get home?"

"He'll probably be here any minute. He was supposed to come back yesterday, but Heath wanted to go to some party. My brother probably shacked up with some chick last night. Or two."

The thought sends ice trickling through my veins.

"I probably did what now?" We fail to notice Lochlyn sneaking up on us.

"Loch!" Chelsea throws herself at him. She isn't always the nicest to him, but she loves him.

"Baby sis. Now what exactly were you saying I did last night?"

"Oh, just that you probably hooked up with a chick or two at the party Heath took you to." Chelsea waves her hand in front of him like it's no big deal, instead of accusing her brother of being a manwhore.

"Nice, Chels." The irritation is easy to hear in his voice. He hates when Chelsea says things like that.

"Hey, Shay." He turns to me, leaning in for a hug.

"Oh, hey, Loch." I have to push up on my toes to reach around his neck, hoping he can't hear my heart pounding at his nearness.

"Your mom here?"

"Yeah, she's somewhere." I look around and notice she's not in the living room anymore. "Kitchen, maybe?"

"I'm going to go say hi." With a quick smile, he puts his hand on my lower back before walking away.

I turn on Chelsea. "He didn't seem too happy about you suggesting he was with a girl."

She waves me away, much like she did when she was talking to Lochlyn. "He likes to act like he's not a manwhore."

"I mean, is he, though? Do you guys actually talk about that?"

"You've heard the things people say about him, Shay."

"Yeah, I've heard what other people say but not from him or anybody who actually knows him. Very different." A part of me is wondering why I'm pushing. If she does have confirmation, do I want to hear it?

"Why do you care?" There's a heavy undercurrent of irritation in her words.

"I don't. I just feel like he was frustrated with you. I'm trying to avoid you guys getting in a fight. Again." A partial truth is acceptable in this situation, but to avoid any chance of her noticing something off, I pick at the tablecloth on the table next to us.

"We fight, we make up, we fight again. He's a pain in my ass, but I love him."

"Funny, I'm pretty sure he'd say the same thing about you." I tip my head sideways and kick gently at her foot.

"Yes, but I'm the baby. It's my job to be a pain in the ass."

"So, what's your excuse with me?"

She bumps her shoulder into mine as we both burst into giggles.

Dinner's a delicious affair. Which makes sense because the Reynolds hired a personal chef for the night. I'm not sure exactly how much money they have; I've never asked as it's none of my business, but *a lot* doesn't seem to quite cover it.

It was part of what threw me when Lochlyn told me he cooks. I know he and Chelsea eat real food while their parents are gone, but I've always just assumed they hire somebody to cook for them. Chelsea's parents have set up a meal company to deliver meals while they're away. And I've never actually seen Lochlyn cook, despite how frequently I'm at their house.

As we sit around the table sipping our coffees, bellies full, I keep catching Lochlyn's eye. I try not to look at him too often, but I can't help it. The thing that confuses me is that many times he'll look up at me, too, and I'll notice a smirk on his face as he watches me flush.

"Shay, honey, I'm leaving now." Mom's whisper startles me. I had been lost in a trance, holding Lochlyn's gaze, not sure what exactly is going on as he has a gentle smile on his face.

Tearing my eyes from him, I turn to Mom. "Oh, alright. You sure?"

"Yeah, I have to be up early to open the store in the morning."

"Okay. Do you want me to come with you?" *Please say no, please say no.*

"Oh no, you stay. Have fun with Chelsea."

"Alright. I'll be home later."

"Take your time, no rush. Just let me know if you decide to stay the night."

"I will."

She gives me a tight-lipped smile and walks away to say good-bye to the Reynolds. I glance around for a clock, wondering what time it is. How have I never taken note of the location of clocks? We had gotten to their house around three. I'm curious how many hours Mom had actually put in. Before we left, I begged her to just tough it out and put on a brave face.

Lochlyn's watch lands with a thud in front of me. Since he first started wearing it five years ago, I've never seen him take it off, not even to swim. I'm pretty sure he even sleeps in it. As I turn it over in my hands, I notice its weight for the first time. It's a quarter to seven. She made it almost four hours.

Standing and leaning across the table, I hand Lochlyn his watch. "Thank you." A shock shoots from my fingertips through my body as his fingers graze mine.

"You're welcome."

My offer to help clean up is denied. "We have people for that, dear," Mrs. Reynolds responds. In all my years of knowing the family, I've always continued to call her Mrs. Reynolds; it's never felt right to call her Veronica.

I've never been sure why they stayed in our neighborhood. It's definitely very middle class. Even though they had become upper middle class, if not upper class. When they bought the house, Mr. Reynolds had yet to really break out in his law firm. Since then, he'd become a partner and as his status and reputation climbed, along with his income. He had quickly become a valued employee, paving the way for him to be more of a figurehead than actual practicing attorney by the time Lochlyn turned sixteen.

But it also allowed for him to have a position ready and waiting for Lochlyn as soon as he finished school. Lochlyn's future was determined for him. There was no wiggle room. I'd been hearing about "the plan" for as long as I could remember. It wasn't until that day in the stockroom I learned that Lochlyn isn't for it.

The grades have always come easy to him. He scored a fifteen fifty on his SATs. By his guidance counselor's insistence, he applied to Harvard, Yale, Columbia, and Stanford in addition to Cornell. He got into all of them.

Chelsea's plan is a little less set. Cornell is again part of the equation. But once she gets there, she has choices. A list of certain choices set by her parents, but a choice nonetheless. Any time their plans were brought up, it made me ever thankful for my parents.

Breaking me from my reverie, Chelsea pulls on my arm. "Let's go in the living room."

Lochlyn follows, flopping onto the end of the couch, his feet on the coffee table, as he stretches his arm down the side. Grabbing the remote, he flips on the TV, finding a football game. The scene is familiar; it's the one I've always seen coming over after dessert. Most years, he has stayed until about nine and then left to see Heath and Jay, his best friends since childhood.

"Hey, Loch, you seeing Heath and Jay tonight?" For a second, I wonder if I said something out loud or if Chelsea can read my thoughts. If she can, I'm in big trouble.

"Not this year. Jay went to Bri's and Heath's crazy cousin came to visit." His attention doesn't leave the TV and his words come out low, as though he barely puts any effort into saying them.

"Mom and Dad won't let me leave to see Brendan." Chelsea's leaning around me as I sit in the middle.

His brows furrow. "Who?"

"Brendan. The boyfriend that you've met like a hundred times. Really, Lochlyn?" She looks at me like she thinks he's crazy. It's arguments like these that it's best for me to just sit here quietly.

"Or maybe I've met him a few times and didn't really think he'd still be around by Thanksgiving." He has a perfectly neutral tone to his voice.

"Either way. You act like you don't know who he is or that I ever mention him when we talk."

He sighs. I often don't understand his patience with Chelsea. I often don't understand *my* patience with Chelsea.

"I'm sorry you can't see him tonight. That must be disappointing." Lochlyn has this amazing way of making his voice sound sincere when it's very clear he does not care. His line of sight never strays from the screen.

Chelsea just rolls her eyes and turns to me, officially done talking to Lochlyn.

"So, are we shopping tomorrow?" There's pure excitement in her voice and she sits up straighter, her eyes wide.

"Chelsea, you're supposed to be at the store at six."

"Duh, I know. I meant after that."

"I have to be at the store longer. And you know I hate Black Friday shopping." Way too many people, far too few actual deals.

"You come with me every year."

"And every year I complain about it."

She huffs like a child. "Fine. I'll just get Brendan to take me."

Lochlyn scoffs next to me. She leans around me and shoots him a death glare. Sometimes I feel like I'm surrounded by children when I'm with them.

Chelsea rambles on for the next two hours. She doesn't require much input from either of us. Every so often, Lochlyn flinches or yells at the game. Any of the other friends I've made over the years, many of whom didn't stick around for long, wondered how I put up with Chelsea. She's demanding, makes all the decisions, and can talk for everybody in the room. But she's also kind and caring and will be there for you at the drop of a hat. It's just Chelsea. I'm also on the quieter side; I don't mind if she talks a lot, as I don't have as much to say.

She sighs. A change of topic, to something about me, ensues. "Shay, I just wish you'd find a boyfriend."

I stiffen next to her. My social life is not something I like to talk about in front of Lochlyn. Especially when I feel him adjust next to me. I'm sure he's as uncomfortable with possibly hearing about it as I am to talk about it.

"I'm fine, Chels. You date enough for the both of us." My voice wavers as we tread into territory I don't like to be in.

"Very funny. I'm serious. It'd be nice for you to have somebody. I worry about you when I'm spending my time with Brendan."

"Chelsea, you've had boyfriends for years. I've always been fine. I do have other friends, you know." I've hung out with Eve a few times since the day we had coffee.

"I know, but nobody's as awesome as I am."

I roll my eyes at her confidence, something I don't have. "That may be true, but they're good company. And I'm at the store a lot."

"Ugh, that store. I love working there, I love your parents, I love the store they built. But you're there too much. It's not your store, Shay, it's not your dream."

"You know it's not that simple." My gaze drops to my lap, fingers lacing together.

"I know. I do. But I see you sinking more and more time into it. I'm worried about you, for you. I want you to have *fun*. Find somebody who makes you happy, makes you laugh. That's not me, of course."

"I will, Chels. I'll get out of the store. I already sent my stuff back to Cornell for next year." Lochlyn adjusts in his seat again. I hadn't mentioned this to him yet. He may be the only person who semi-cares that I make it there, besides myself.

"I know. But it was so easy for you to defer."

"You did, too, ya know." My defense is weak, just like my emotional stability right now.

"Yeah, but Cornell's not *my* want, Shay. It's forced on me. I'd be happy staying here. You? You want Cornell. You always have." She's right. Chelsea would be happy doing anything, going anywhere. I even think she'd be content not going to college and just traveling the world. There's no way she'd get it past her parents.

I, on the other hand, have wanted to go to Cornell since I learned about college. One day when I was six or seven, Dad sat me on his lap and showed pictures and told me stories about his time there and ever since I've strived to wear the red and white.

"A boyfriend won't deter you from getting to Cornell. But it may make your time waiting more fun. And give you something else to do aside from spending all day at the store."

"I don't mind being at the store." My voice is barely above a whisper, filled with the lie I've been trying to tell myself for months.

"Do you hear yourself? You don't mind the store? Shay, all you've said for years was that you never, ever wanted to end up there. You worked your minimum hours over the summer and were out the door the second your shift was over. Now, you're basically *volunteering* to be there." Every time she speaks, she's louder; her words firmer.

"It's different, Chels. It's not what it used to be. Everything's changed." There's a meekness in my voice, a sense of defeat. Lochlyn is stiff as a board next to me.

"Yeah, everything did change. And you're the only one taking on the responsibility. You have a sister, you know. I mean, genetically speaking. Realistically, I'm not so sure since it's been, what, over a year since you last saw her? Why are you the only one taking on the added pressure, changing your life?" But Chelsea doesn't stop, she keeps going, pushing until I've had too much.

"I need some air." I'm on my feet, heading for the back door before she can even respond.

Lochlyn comes to find me on the back deck, sitting at the top of the stairs, lowering himself next to me. Chelsea went upstairs to call Brendan and go to bed, or at least that's what he says. He's so close I can feel his warmth, which I welcome on the chilly night.

"How are you doing, Shay?"

How am I doing? What a loaded question. He just stayed silent as he listened to the conversation with Chelsea. Lochlyn always asks the hard questions. I take a deep breath in and hold it for a beat before letting it out.

"I don't know. Fine, I guess. School isn't bad, but obviously not what I'd thought it would be, expecting to be at Cornell. But it's not bad. I'm doing well."

"I didn't ask about school. I asked about you." There's a terseness to his voice that isn't usually there.

"That's always harder to answer. I don't know. I'm hanging in, I suppose. This time of year has been really hard. My dad loved Thanksgiving and Christmas. The anniversary of his death was painful. Logan...she didn't even call. I don't understand how I'm related to her sometimes. Mom closed the store and spent the day in bed. I just went about my life, thankful that Chelsea was around to distract me." I pull at a string on my shirt, my fingers always needing to be busy when I'm nervous.

"I had wanted to come home for that; I just couldn't get away. I'm sorry." There's such sincerity in his voice, it makes my pulse increase.

"That would have been nice, but it's no big deal. Not much you could have done, anyway." I lift my head to look at him and notice the clench set in his jaw.

"Chels said something about you finding a boyfriend. What's she talking about?"

I give a small laugh, looking up at the stars twinkling above us. "Oh, Chelsea. She certainly doesn't help sometimes. She has it in her mind that I need to find a boyfriend, so that all my problems will go away. Just like that." I shake my head as I look back at the string I'm working between my fingers, my curls falling like a curtain on the side of my face.

"She just makes me feel pathetic at times. I'm eighteen and have never even kissed a boy. She gives me shit for it, but it's like, *I'm sorry I was a little preoccupied with my dad dying*. She doesn't understand why it didn't happen before that, but it's just not the type of person I am, you know? I'm not exactly thrilled that I'm eighteen and going away for school next fall and still haven't kissed a boy and have zero prospects."

"You're worried about kissing somebody?"

"I know, pathetic, right?"

"Well, I mean, I can help with that."

Before I know what's happening, he has my chin between his thumb and forefinger as he leans in to place a quick kiss on my lips. It's so fast I almost wonder if he did it accidentally, leaned in a bit too far and our lips happened to brush. Regardless, that single peck steals my breath.

As he pulls back, his eyes lock on mine. And then he leans in and closes his mouth over mine again, spreading his hand against my cheek.

All of my senses are completely overwhelmed with Lochlyn. His sandalwood scent filters through my nose, the warmth and pressure of his lips on mine making my emotions tumultuous. When he parts my mouth, peppermint swirls across my taste-buds as his tongue curls against mine. No sounds exist in the night except my racing heart.

Never having kissed somebody before, I have no idea if I'm doing it the right way. But Lochlyn intensifies the kiss, the pressure of his lips stronger, the pull against my cheek firmer, as he twists his fingers into the hair at the base of my head.

I don't know how long he kisses me—if it's thirty seconds or ten minutes, everything else completely disappears and time all but ceases to exist. But when we separate, I'm breathless. He keeps his palm against my cheek, looking at me intently, his blue eyes sparkling like the stars above us for another minute before he moves back.

"Well, now you can at least say you've accomplished that. So, how's the store?" He moves on like it's nothing, but to me, it's everything.

I want to melt into the floor beneath me. I want to kiss him again. And again. And again. But he's still my best friend's brother. He did me a favor, taking pity on the sad girl whose dad died and who hadn't kissed a boy yet, at eighteen. Whose best friend basically just called her life pathetic. It's not interest.

"Shay?"

"Huh? Oh, sorry. Uh, the store is good. I don't get over there as much with classes and studying, it's not as much time as Chelsea thinks. I don't know, it's just hard. That's basically the only time I see my mom. She's home so late, partially because she extended the hours. It's almost like she lives there.

"Essentially, nothing's changed. I still don't see her, still haven't heard a single word from Logan." I look over at him and see concern on his face. "I don't know why I'm complaining to you. At least my mom is here, if I really need her. Your parents started leaving years ago."

"Yeah, that was pretty rough. Especially because I was basically in charge of Chelsea too. Not exactly easy."

"No, it's not." A series of difficult moments due to Chelsea flash through my mind as I recall all the ways she gave Lochlyn a hard time over the years. He deserves some sort of award for all the things he's had to put up with and handle. It's not so much that Chelsea did anything more than a typical rebellious teenager, the issue is that Lochlyn is obviously *not* her parent, and therefore, not the one who should have been having to deal with it.

"I feel bad for Chels now, though, being on her own." There's a tinge of guilt, both hanging from his words and on his face. But none of this is his fault.

"I don't know. I mean, she's not really on her own."

"You're right, she has you."

"And Brendan."

He puts his head in his hand. "Ugh, don't remind me."

A smile breaks across my face. "He's a nice guy, Loch. Really."

"It doesn't mean I have to like him. She's my baby sister."

"Don't worry, I'm watching out for her."

"I know you are. But Shay, who's watching out for you?"

I'm taken aback. It's an interesting question. "Well, Chelsea is."

"Come on, Shay. I love her, but she's probably the most self-centered person I've ever met. I know she loves you, but is she really watching out for you? Has she ever?"

"I mean, yeah? I don't know. She has her ways and moments. I guess I've always looked out for myself. Maybe that's why I've never had a boyfriend. I don't want to just flit around from boy to boy like Chels does. I don't want to have meaningless sex." I turn to him quick, hands outstretched in defense. "No offense."

He rubs his fingers along his lower lip, drawing my attention to his wonderful mouth. "None taken."

"Maybe it's easier to watch out for myself by being alone." It's a sad reality, and a sad existence, but it's the hand life dealt me.

"But if you don't let anybody in, how are you going to find someone?" His curiosity strikes me as odd, but Lochlyn often takes the opposite side of Chelsea, and I'm sure he's just trying to point out all aspects of the situation.

"I don't know. I think once things calm down, maybe once I get away next year, I'll be able to let my guard down a bit. We'll be on the same campus, so Chelsea can be your problem again." I bump my shoulder against his, shock waves pulsing through my body. It's such a normal thing to happen between the two of us, yet something shifted with the kiss. Something I need to bury.

"Oh, great. Just what I need, to be responsible for Chels again." He shakes his head, running his hand through his hair as a few pieces fall in his eyes. It's been a while since he's had a haircut. It's sexy. *He's your best friend's brother, nothing can happen. The kiss doesn't count. It was pity.*

He flicks his wrist, looking at his watch. It's an analog watch with a leather band. Whenever Chelsea gives him a hard time about it, he says he prefers the analog, things are becoming too easy being all digital. And he's not glued to his phone like she is. I've always felt like it suits him.

"It's pretty late. Let me walk you home."

While I can walk myself, I want his company. "Sure." I stand, brushing at my butt, pulling my coat tighter around me, realizing how cold it truly is.

Part of how Chelsea and I had become such good friends is that our houses are only four apart. An easy walk—day or night, rain or shine.

Lochlyn and I shuffle down the road in silence, his hands in his pockets while I hold my coat against me. But we're close enough that our arms brush every so many steps.

When we get to my driveway, I pause, turning to face him. Sometimes I forget how tall he is and that I usually need to tilt my head slightly to see his face.

"Well, good night, Loch. Thanks for chatting."

"Anytime, Shay." Before he turns to walk away, he leans down, hand on my cheek, and presses his mouth to mine again. A million butterflies flutter in my stomach.

"Good night," he says against my lips.

Slowly, he pulls his hand from my face, lingering for an extra second, before turning and walking home. I stare after him, entirely unsure of what just happened between the two of us, but knowing that I want it to happen again.

Chapter 5

"I get out at six tonight," Chelsea says as she flips through a magazine.

"I know Chels. I help with the schedule."

"Oh, right. Well, either way, why don't you just come over from work?"

"I don't want to be a bother."

"Nonsense." Though she waves her hand at me, she doesn't glance up from the magazine in her lap.

"Chelsea, I've been at your house, like, every day this break. I'm sure Lochlyn's sick of me being there by now."

Lochlyn had left the day after Thanksgiving without a word about what had happened between us. I've tried pushing it to the back of my mind, reminding myself over and over that he's Chelsea's brother, that nothing can happen, that it was surely pity. But that doesn't I mean I don't *want* it to happen again.

He's been home for about a week, coming back on Christmas Eve. I've only seen him a few times since, and every time he's acted like nothing happened. It makes my head spin. The one thing I do know is that Chelsea has no idea. I certainly haven't told her. And I know Lochlyn hasn't either because she would lose her mind. First at him, then at *me*. Which hasn't happened yet.

"Who cares what he wants or who he's sick of. And you're so quiet there's no way he could be sick of you. You just kind of...exist." Great. Just what I want him to think of me. That I just kind of exist.

"Nice, Chels."

"You know what I mean. You don't make a fuss, you don't make things difficult, you just graciously accept whatever is offered and say thank you."

"You make enough fuss for the both of us."

We're sitting in the office at the store. Chelsea works extra over breaks to earn more money. While her parents are loaded, they weren't pleased with her decision to defer Cornell, not even sure she'd be approved. They don't see *my* loss as a reason for *her* to stay behind. They cut her off. They make sure all expenses are paid, that she eats, but she has no access to fun money. And if there's one thing Chelsea needs, it's fun money.

"You're impossible sometimes."

"Funny, I'm pretty sure I say that about you." I stick my tongue out at her as she swats at my leg.

"All I'm saying is that you don't have to just accept everything. Lochlyn can be an ass. But you'd never tell him."

I shrug and lean forward slightly, almost like I'm trying to keep her from hearing the sudden increased thumping of my heart. "I don't know, he's always been nice to me. And I'm not afraid to tell him off, Chelsea. I've known him almost my whole life."

"How about this summer when he pulled you into the pool?" My pulse flutters remembering how his arms felt around my waist, the way his eyes zeroed in on mine.

"He does that every year, Chels. For, like, the past ten years. I don't know why you got so upset about it. I honestly was surprised it hadn't happened already."

"And I don't understand how it doesn't bother you every year." She angrily flips a few more pages of her magazine.

"Because it's harmless, all in the name of fun. He's not doing anything to hurt me, he's pushing me in a pool. It's literally classic summertime fun."

"It just seems like he targets you." This time, her eyes lock on me. If she's trying to say something, I'm not sure what it is. Regardless, I fight the heat creeping up my neck so she doesn't press further.

"The only other option is you. He's not stupid. He knows better than to toss *you* into the pool. Plus, you're always telling me I need to have more fun. I bet that's all he's trying to do."

"Yeah, okay. But either way, you're not at all a bother and you're coming over from work. End of discussion. We'll grab food on the way home." The pressure in my chest deflates as she turns back to her magazine.

"Why aren't you going to be with Brendan again?" I'm thankful she's going to be around. It keeps me from having to spend the New Year home alone, which would be incredibly depressing.

"He's out of town. His family goes to his aunt's for New Year every year. The family has a handful of December and January birthdays, so they get together to celebrate."

"Oh. That actually sounds nice." I don't have a big family. My parents were both only children. I have no extended family. Chelsea's the closest thing I have to actual family these days.

"If you say so. I do miss him, though."

"When does he get back?" These nice, easy flowing conversations are one of my favorite things about having Chelsea as my best friend. She doesn't give me much opportunity to put my foot in my mouth, and if I do, she ignores it instead of calling attention to it, which others have done in the past.

"Oh, he'll be back tomorrow night. They just stay the one night because it's in Pennsylvania, like three hours away or something."

"So, I won't see you the day after?"

"Pretty much." A sly smile spreads across her face. I don't ask, because I don't want to know. "We'll be having sex all day."

"Ugh, Chelsea, I didn't need to know that." A prickly feeling inches up my spine. There are some things I just don't need to know about.

"Oh, grow up, Shay. Just because you choose not to have sex doesn't mean I have to."

"Yeah, but I don't need to hear about it." I swipe my clammy palms on my pant legs.

"Trust me, you're not. If I wanted you to hear about it, I could tell you how he makes me scream when he—"

"Girls! Break's over." I have never been so thankful for Mom's interruption.

"Be right there!" I yell back. "Saved by the mom." I smack her leg. "Let's go."

We both take a deep breath and plaster on our smiles before walking through the door to the floor. Only two more hours and we're free to enjoy our night.

We waltz into Chelsea's house at six thirty, two pizzas in hand, and go straight into the kitchen.

"Pizza? Really, Chels?" Lochlyn's voice is dripping with irritation.

"What?"

He points a knife at the cutting board and vegetables in front of him.

"How was I supposed to know you were going to cook?"

"When have you ever starved?"

"Never. But I wanted pizza." When he just glares at her, she drops her attitude. "Look, I'm sorry, okay? I didn't know you'd be making something. Or that you'd started yet. I thought it'd be nice if I brought something home, so you didn't *have* to cook. I was trying to be nice."

With a deep breath, he sets the knife down. "It's fine. I can save this stuff. Get plates, let's eat."

I often stay quiet during their exchanges, letting them work through it. While Lochlyn puts the vegetables he'd chopped into a storage container, Chelsea grabs plates, and I get napkins. We take the pizza over to the kitchen table, then set the plates and napkins at each place. Lochlyn comes to sit with three sodas in hand. We sit at the table for an hour, talking about the store when we finish eating.

Lochlyn's gaze keeps finding its way to me. I know because more often than not I'm—hopefully stealthily—looking at him.

After cleaning up, we make our way to the living room, flipping through many of the early New Year's celebrations. Lochlyn settles on *The Twilight Zone* marathon as Chelsea grumbles. It's become a yearly tradition. We usually get together to watch something before Lochlyn leaves for a party. He's taken us to one here and there.

"Do we have to? Again?" she asks, whining like a petulant child.

"Shay?" Lochlyn turns to ask me.

"Sorry, Chels. I vote yes." While it may be part of our annual New Year's Eve tradition, it's another interest that Lochlyn and I have in common, so another thing that I file away in the part of me that shouldn't care.

"There ya go. Majority wins." Lochlyn settles into the couch, a victorious smile on his face.

When we started spending a lot of time together as a trio, we found that we often didn't agree on things. We had started voting to end arguments. If we all had varying opinions, then we found something different.

"I swear, if you weren't my brother and best friend, I'd suggest you two get together. You'd make a perfect couple. Same taste in music and shows. You're both brainiacs." My heart speeds up at the suggestion, so loud I'm worried they can hear it, and I have to fight the urge to put my hand against my chest to try to contain the sound.

"Well, Chels, we do a little thing called studying," Lochlyn says mockingly.

"Yeah, yeah, so do I. It just comes easier for the two of you." She's lost in thought for a minute, staring at the far wall as though something's written on it, before picking up her phone.

We sit in silence watching the show for almost two hours. Every so often, Lochlyn shifts, usually the slightest bit closer to me, though I could be imagining it. At one point, I notice his hand seemingly reaching for me before he pulls it back and rests his arm across the back of the couch. All the while, Chelsea's on her phone oohing and ahhing.

"I'll be right back, guys." There must be something interesting that pulled her attention away, as she jumps up and sprints out of the room.

"So, how are you, Shay?"

After a lot of reflection on our kiss and time spent together in recent months, I've come to realize that Lochlyn asks me this question when we're alone together. He's never asked in front of Chelsea. I'm not entirely sure why that is, but I do have a feeling it has to do with our summer conversations, that I told him things I had never said aloud before.

"I'm alright." I nod resolutely, tucking a curl behind my ear.

"Yeah? How's school? I know you've been worried about that."

"School's fine. I, uh, I actually sent my paperwork in to end my deferment, starting in the fall." I turn to him and the giant smile that's spread across his face is infectious and causes one to stretch on mine. He clearly overheard me at Thanksgiving when I talked to Chelsea, before finding solace on the back deck. But there's something different about telling him directly. Probably the reaction he has.

"I'm really happy for you. I know that was a huge deal. That's great news."

I'm about to respond when Chelsea walks back in, stealing the words from the tip of my tongue.

"So, Loch, what's the social life like at Cornell?"

"You ask me this all the time. The answer is always the same."

"I'm not sure if that's your way of saying your bed is busy or not."

He sighs, tipping his head back to look at the ceiling. "That's it. I'm done. Good night, Shay, Happy New Year." Putting his hands on his knees, he rises to stand, and I shift with the loss of his weight on the couch, my body cooler without the heat emanating from his body.

It's a pretty regular occurrence. Chelsea knows exactly what buttons to push to get him to leave. It always irritates me, because I enjoy his presence. Which then makes me feel guilty because I shouldn't.

"Well, now that he's gone..." she says, taking the remote.

"You know, I was watching that too."

She waves me off. "You've seen them a hundred times."

A sigh pulls from deep in my chest as I slouch down on the couch. She flips through until she finds a song she likes, singing and bopping along. It's somewhat insufferable, not my kind of music. But one thing I learned a long time ago is that it's easier to just let her be happy.

So I stay and let her watch her show. She finds ways to make it fun, to make me laugh. Including running to her room and grabbing her hairbrush, singing into it like she's the star. Chelsea has little to no shame in doing anything. It's part of what makes me stay around. She can be selfish, but she's fun loving and knows how to put a smile on my face.

"Alright, my love. I'm going to go upstairs and call Brendan before I pass out."

"You're not going to stay up until midnight?" I'm not sure why I'm surprised. She never does.

"Nope. My pillow is calling."

One corner of my mouth tips down. What am I supposed to do now? "Okay. Good night, Chels. Happy New Year."

"Happy New Year, Shay. Don't feel like you have to leave. Stay the night even! We can have the first breakfast together."

"I'll probably just go home." The sting of dejection resides in my chest as she stands from the couch.

"Whatever you want, just don't feel like you have to. You're always welcome to stay!"

She drifts up the stairs. When I hear her door shut, I sigh again, looking around me. I feel awkward staying alone, sitting downstairs watching TV while Chelsea's asleep and Lochlyn's upstairs doing...something.

Before getting ready to leave, I clean up the mess we left in the living room, knowing Lochlyn will be the one to do it otherwise, and I don't want him having more on his plate.

I'm gathering my things to head out when he comes sauntering down the stairs. My breath catches in my throat as I take in his black t-shirt, tight across his chest. I'm not sure if I can really see the single line song lyric peeking out from under his sleeve or if I just know it so well.

I clear my throat and turn back to putting my things into my purse.

"Chels couldn't hang, huh?"

Spinning around, I notice just how close he is, his blue eyes sparkling.

"Nope. You know Chels, all talk. I was just about to leave—"

"Why don't you stay? Watch the ball drop with me?"

Stay? He wants me to stay? With *him?*

"I mean, unless you don't want to. I just figured since we're both up, before you leave, you may as well watch."

"Oh, uh, yeah, no, that sounds great." Turning back to my things, I take a quick glance at my phone, which tells me it's only eleven.

"You don't have to be scared of me, Shay." Shivers race down my spine as he whispers in my ear, his fingers lightly tracing down my arm.

Turning my head to the side, I'm acutely aware of how close his mouth is. "I'm not."

"Then why are you trembling?" His breath ghosts over my ear, hand hovering over mine. Am I trembling? I hadn't even noticed. His nearness has erased my ability to think, feel, or recognize anything except his proximity and his intoxicating smell.

I spin around to face him. His lips are less than an inch from mine. If I lean forward, just the slightest bit, I can feel them again. Something I've longed for since Thanksgiving.

I look up at him and notice a glint flash through his irises. He takes a step back, but not before giving me a once-over. Immediately, I want him back in my space.

"Come on, let's go watch whatever nonsense is on TV." He extends his hand out for me, and I take it willingly.

We sit on the floor, leaning back against the couch. I'm sitting stock-still, back straight, legs crossed, while he's sprawled out. He's slouched down and has his hand on my knee.

I'm not really sure what's going on, still convinced that what happened at Thanksgiving was pity. He felt sorry for me as I basically sat there and cried about never having kissed a boy and not wanting to go to college like that. But here he is, sitting close to me, touching me. It's making my hormones rage. I take what I hope is a secretive deep breath to steady myself.

We've spent time alone together over the years. But not like this. Though, I'm realizing I'm not really sure what *this* is.

"Shay. Shay, look at me." He pulls my attention from the singing and dancing we've been watching in silence for the past half hour. I was definitely spending more time in my head than I was paying attention to the show.

Reluctantly, I turn, sure he's going to tell me what I know, what I don't want to hear. *He's not interested in me, and Thanksgiving was a mistake. I'm his sister's best friend, after all.*

"What happened over Thanksgiving break..." Here it is. The moment I've been dreading. I build up a wall to protect my heart from the ambush about to happen. "I'd wanted to do that for a really long time."

And the wall crumbles around me with a whoosh through my mouth and a jumpstart to my heart. That was not at all what I was expecting to come out of his mouth.

"I know Chelsea tells you things...about me. I know you've heard things when we were in high school together. I don't expect anything from you. I won't ask you for anything you don't want to give me." He runs his tongue over his teeth. "But I want to do more than just kiss you."

My pulse flutters in my neck. He'd wanted to do that for a long time? How had I not known? Am I blind? He's always been a little touchy, but I'd just written it off as that being his character trait.

Before I know what's happening, his hand cups my cheek, and he leans in to kiss me. The moment his lips brush mine, something inside me snaps.

My hand slides around his neck as he smiles against my lips. He parts my mouth with his, tongue sliding to meet mine. Keeping one hand against my jaw, the other glides down to my lower back, pulling me to him.

The angle is awkward. My leg develops a cramp, but I don't want to lose the feeling of his lips on mine. As if hearing my thoughts, he slowly leans me backward onto the carpet.

Somewhere in the back of my mind, I know I should be feeling nervous that I'm lying on the floor with him, lips locked on one another's, as his hand makes its way up my shirt. But this is Lochlyn. I've known him for years. I've *longed* for him for years. If do something—*whatever we're doing*—with anybody, I want it to be with him.

As his hand slips farther up my shirt, cupping and gently massaging my breast, running a finger over my hardened nipple, I can't help but sigh, my body vibrating under his touch. His mouth finds my collarbone as he pushes aside the cup of my bra, and takes my pebbled nipple between his fingers, twiddling, tweaking, and pinching. A tiny whimper escapes my lips as an unmet need settles between my thighs.

Lochlyn groans as he slides his other hand to the waistband of my jeans. He pulls away from my neck, eyes locked on mine, fingers still working under my shirt as my breathing increases.

"Do you want me to stop?" I know what he's asking. Is it okay if he reaches into my pants, if he touches me where nobody has ever touched me.

I bite my lip and shake my head. *No.* The need to add the word is strong, as I don't want him having a shred of doubt in what I want. If what he's already doing feels good, I know that everything else has to feel even better.

I've never been unabashed around him. Not even at his subtle glances, his conversations, his gentle touch. Right now, I should be hiding in fear behind the couch. Instead, my body is thrumming with desire and my hands are everywhere on his. Not to mention, he's touching me wherever he wants. It's what I've always craved.

With a smile, his mouth claims mine again as his hand slides under my pants, rubbing over my panties. I start imagining doing more, what he'd feel like inside me, acutely aware of his hardness pressing into my thigh.

As my daydream intensifies, he pushes aside my panties. "Holy shit, Shay," he says as he feels me, the wetness of wanting him. His breath catches with a groan.

Then something changes in him. His kiss becomes hungrier, his hand flying to pull down the collar of my shirt, exposing my breast. As he closes his mouth around my nipple, he slowly slides one finger inside me, followed by another. He moves his tongue and fingers together, causing me to wrap my arms around his head, pulling him closer to me, as my back arches and a low moan escapes my throat.

Lochlyn reaches his free hand up and covers my mouth while he continues to use his tongue and fingers in unison. I can't even find the words to describe how incredible it feels. I'm pretty sure I could climax just from this alone. My breathing shallows and my toes curl. Why did I wait to do this again? Oh yeah, part of me has always been waiting for Lochlyn.

Right as the wave is about to crest over me, he stops, pulling away to look at me. I finally understand his reputation and we haven't even had sex yet.

Tenderly, he kisses my neck, along my jawbone, then lands on my lips. He hovers above me, so close it would take the slightest movement of my head to press my mouth to his.

Sighing, he runs a hand down the side of my body, stopping on my hip, thumb digging into the bone as he pulls me against him.

"I want to be your first. Please, will you let me?"

"Yes," I breathe. I don't even have to think about it. In my wildest dreams, it's what always happened. But never did I actually believe it would.

He smiles as he moves the slightest bit closer, locking his mouth over mine. His hands make quick work of our pants.

"Are you sure?" he asks, skeptical.

I nod. "Very."

There's a slight moment of pain as Lochlyn presses into me, causing me to gasp. But it's quickly forgotten as a much more pleasant feeling overtakes me. I'm not thinking about anything, not the fact that we're in the living room, that Chelsea is asleep upstairs. Only the amazingness of Lochlyn and I together.

In the distance, I'm vaguely aware of the countdown and ball drop, as I ring in the New Year, losing my virginity to my best friend's brother.

As I lie against Lochlyn's heaving chest, trying to catch my breath, I revel in the feeling of *us* together. It was amazing. I've heard from so many people that the first time can be terrible, awkward, painful. Outside of the brief pinch of pain at the very beginning, it was none of those things.

Lochlyn's arms are around me, one drawing tiny circles on my hip while the other holds my hand against his chest. His heart hammers beneath my fingertips. Somewhere in the recesses of my mind, I know I should be getting up, getting dressed, going home. But I can't tear myself away from him.

With a kiss to the top of my head and a squeeze, he gently pushes my shoulders back to look into my eyes. "How are you? Are you okay?"

I'm better than okay. "Yeah, yeah, I'm good. Really good."

A smile breaks across his face. But reality strikes, and I start to back away. I feel awkward lying here, not regretting a thing, but I'm sure that's all it was. A one-time sex episode between two...friends. Maybe he even just wanted to make sure I lost my virginity to somebody I feel safe with. Maybe he just always wanted to have sex with me and figured it was as good a time as any.

"I should probably get going." I move to sit up.

He grabs my arm and pulls me down to him. "Not yet." His arms tighten around me, holding me against his body.

While I don't want to be anywhere else, I know the longer we stay here, the more chance we have of being caught. "Loch, really, I have to go." I push away from him and sit up. The last thing I want to ruin an otherwise perfect ending to the night is for Chelsea to come downstairs and find us.

He sits up next to me, cupping my chin and pulling my lips against his. "Stay here tonight with me," he whispers as he leans his forehead against mine.

I close my eyes as I push my forehead firmly against his. Even if all he wants is more sex, I'm completely fine with that, even though I know I probably shouldn't be. "How? Chelsea."

He shakes his head. "I don't care. I don't care about Chelsea and her wants and wishes. What about us? What about what we want?"

I pull back, separating myself in case the answer is not what I'm wanting to hear. "What *do* you want?"

"You." He says it firmly, almost before I'm finished talking. Then he hesitates, wanting to say more. "I've always wanted you, Shay. And not just like this."

My heart falters, and I nod. I've slept in Lochlyn's room before. Sure, he slept on the floor or the couch and we hadn't just had sex in the living room, but I know there's a way we can figure it out.

We put our pants back on and clean up any evidence that something other than TV watching happened. A jolt shoots through me as Lochlyn takes my hand and leads me upstairs. Once inside his room, he closes and locks the door.

He starts pulling clothes out of his dresser, handing me a t-shirt. "Here, you can wear this if you want." I take the shirt from him, our fingers brushing, sending tingles through my entire body. I want his hands on me again.

My breath hitches as Lochlyn takes his shirt off. Somehow, his body is even better than when he left for school in August, stomach stronger and more toned. A defined six-pack and indent just above his pants, hinting its way to what lies beneath. His low chuckle catches my attention as I'm suddenly aware that I've been biting my lip and staring.

"Nothing you haven't seen before, Shay."

"Better than it used to be," I mumble absentmindedly.

He's across the room in two strides, taking my hand and running it down his chest, gliding gently over the light ridges. "And now you can touch."

I look up into his eyes quickly before my gaze settles on his lips. His mouth crashes on mine in a second, my arms lacing around his neck as I tug him down. His arms wrap around my waist, pulling me tightly against him.

As his tongue slides across mine, I trace my fingers along his shoulders. I'm surprised I know what to do. I don't have to think about where to put my hands, or if I'm doing the right thing. I can tell by his reactions that he likes everything that's been happening.

He breaks the kiss as his fingers slide under the hem of my shirt to lift it off, then his lips find mine the second it drops to the floor. With one flick of his wrist, he's unhooked my bra, pushing it gently off my shoulders. He leans back, eyes locking on my chest, as he licks his lower lip.

I'm amazed at how confident I feel under his scrutiny. Not an ounce of insecurity or self-consciousness left. I'd always shied away from his gaze, even when fully clothed. Here I am, half naked, not inching away. If anything, I crave it. So much has changed in just two short hours and the flip of the calendar year.

Lochlyn's hands slide into my back pockets, yanking me against him. I'm met with his warm and hard chest against mine. As I'm staring at his perfection, my finger tracing his defined collar bone, just feeling him against me, he tilts my chin up, lips meeting mine. He starts walking, pushing me backward toward the bed.

As my legs hit the mattress, he doesn't slow, sliding his hand up to hold me, gently leaning me down, coming to hover over me. Then he brushes some hair from my forehead as his eyes roam my face.

When his lips close over mine again, there's a new urgency behind them, his hands flying down to the button of my jeans. He hesitates, unsure if I want to do this again. I push my mouth harder against his, reaching for his pants, a hand sliding along the length of his erection. His breath hitches and his hesitation fades as he tears at my zipper, his mouth attaching on my neck.

He feverishly kisses down my chest, running his tongue over my nipple, kissing down to my navel before standing and removing my pants and panties in one quick tug, then pushing his off and kicking them across the room.

As he climbs back over me, he slides his open mouth along my skin, starting at my ankle and gliding, slowly, up my leg, over my hip bone, and up my stomach. When he reaches my breast, he breathes against my nipple, running his lips over it softly, before flicking it a few times with his tongue, causing my back to arch and a low moan to rise in my throat.

Gliding the rest of the way up my body, his lips lock on mine as he slides his hand between our bodies, slipping along my soaking entrance. Not one finger enters me before he eases his hardness inside me.

I tear my mouth from his as I suck in air, my nails digging into his shoulders. There's no way for me to control the sounds rising from my throat as he moves inside me.

As my volume increases, Lochlyn's mouth is right by my ear. "Shh, baby. You're going to get us caught."

"I can't...help it." I can barely get the breathless words out.

He smiles against my ear before giving my lobe a quick nip, slowly sliding his hand up to cover my mouth. "For the noise," he murmurs against my neck.

His eyes lock on mine as he holds himself above me, hand still on my mouth, as he begins to move faster. I understand the reason for the hand as I make noises I didn't know I could make, at a level that had his hand not been there, surely would awaken Chelsea, and maybe the neighbors.

When I start to tremble and my chest heaves, Lochlyn's lips find my neck, his hand pushing slightly firmer against my mouth as a loud cry escapes from my throat. He groans against my neck as his hand balls into a fist against the sheets, his teeth digging into my shoulder.

We lie like that for a few moments while we catch our breath, his hand slowly moving away from my mouth, thumb trailing along my bottom lip before leaning in and brushing his lips along mine.

Wrapping an arm around my waist as he turns to his side, he flips me to mine and pulls my back tightly against his chest.

His heart is hammering, much as mine is, his breathing heavy and shallow. He kisses along my shoulder to my neck, settling behind my ear. "Good night, Shay."

"Good night, Loch."

I fall asleep in Lochlyn's arms, realizing that my dreams have become reality.

Lochlyn's lips are on my shoulder as he trails a fingertip down my cheek. "Shay. Shay, wake up."

My eyes flutter open as warmth spreads through me, taking in his smiling face. At first, I'm not sure the night before had really happened, thinking maybe it was a wonderful, realistic dream. But here he is, shirtless, smiling at me, while I lie naked between his sheets.

"I really hate to even think about you putting clothes on, but you need to get dressed before Chelsea wakes up." His voice is low, barely above a whisper. He hands me the shirt he'd taken out earlier and a pair of his sweatpants. Leaning in, he tenderly brushes his lips against mine. "Here, put these on."

Slowly sitting up and sliding out of bed, I smile to myself when I hear him groan while I stand fully exposed. He hands me my panties from the floor as I slip his shirt over my head. It falls to my mid-thighs. I step into my panties and his pants, which require several rolls for them to not be falling off.

He grabs the pants at my waist, pulling me against him, and fusing our mouths together. Every time seems so urgent, like he can't keep his lips off of mine. I certainly don't mind, because I'd keep them connected if I could. When he breaks free, he rests his forehead against mine. "I'm going to go downstairs to sleep on the couch. It's early still, but I wanted to wake up before Chelsea, and get you dressed."

I don't want him to go; I want to curl into him, feel his warmth. But I know it's safest. Much easier to explain that I spent the night and he slept on the couch. It won't raise any suspicion since it's happened before. Normally, I borrow some of Chelsea's clothes, but it will be easy to just say we didn't want to wake her.

I climb back into bed, curling in on myself and pulling the collar of the shirt up to my nose. Sandalwood swirls through my nose and my body relaxes into the mattress below me. It smells like Lochlyn.

I'm rudely awoken by Chelsea bouncing onto the bed. "Oh! Shay. I wasn't expecting to see you here." Her brow knits together. "Why are you here? In Loch's bed?"

"I was getting ready to leave when he came down and invited me to stay to ring in the New Year. I didn't feel like going home, so he gave me clothes and let me stay," I groggily explain. Not entirely a lie. I just left out a few details. Significant ones. It gives me a bit of an icky feeling in my chest.

She shrugs it off. "I have to work. Let's go."

"Why do I have to get up because you have to work? You went to bed hours before I did."

"Because I said so! Let's go!"

She pulls the covers off me and yanks me out of bed.

"I hate you," I grumble at her.

"You love me. And you'll feel better once you have some coffee."

"Mm, coffee."

Walking into the kitchen, I'm greeted with a shirtless Lochlyn, lips pulling up at the corners as he scans my body, still dressed in his clothes. To hide his smile, he pulls his mug up to his mouth. Trying to fight my own smile, I bite the inside of my cheek, not wanting to tip Chelsea off to anything being different.

My gaze skims across his bare chest, my fingers twitching at the memory of how he feels. I quickly track each of his tattoos, the two spots where he has lyrics and the sword, which is visible as he holds his cup.

"Good morning, ladies. Sleep well?"

Heat floods my cheeks at the thought of how much I *didn't* sleep last night, and where I was when I did.

"Yeah, actually. What'd you guys do?" Chelsea asks, pouring herself coffee.

I cough, choking on air, suddenly nervous in his presence. Lochlyn raises an eyebrow at me. "We just watched the ball drop." He's so nonchalant, I almost wonder if I dreamed about it all. "Not too exciting." He hasn't taken his eyes off me since I walked into the kitchen until he turns to fill a teal mug.

"Here, Shay, have some coffee." Lochlyn pushes it across the island to me, his fingers brushing mine as I take it. The look in his eyes tells me he made sure they did, and that he both saw and knows why a shiver runs down my spine.

"Thanks." I'm sure even the one word sounds weird, different.

Chelsea sighs. "Loch, could you like, put a shirt on or something? Is it really necessary for you to be exposed all the time? We get it, you have muscles and tattoos."

He returns her sigh, grabbing a shirt off the counter and pulling it over his head, and disappointment fills my chest. "There, better?"

"Much." She gives him a forced smile.

I'm standing in the fridge, pulling out the half and half when Lochlyn's hand closes over the one I have holding the door. His whole front brushes against my back as he reaches into the fridge behind me. Every hair on my body stands at attention from his nearness.

"Excuse me, Shay. I'm just grabbing some eggs to make breakfast," he murmurs impossibly close to my ear.

Nothing about the exchange is different than it has been any other time, except his extreme closeness and our shared knowledge of what happened between us last night.

Chelsea starts talking about her plans for the day while I attentively watch Lochlyn prepare breakfast. My gaze is fixated on his hands—hands that were all over my body mere hours ago—while he chops a green pepper and mixes up some eggs.

Every so often, I'll catch his eye as he looks up at me intently. It makes me squirm as desire tears through my body.

Once Chelsea leaves the kitchen, I walk around the island to pour myself more coffee. Lochlyn is suddenly right behind me, his hands splitting. One slides around my waist to dip into the front of my pants ever so slightly, while the other wraps gently around my throat. He's breathing hard against my neck. My head tilts back against his shoulder on its own, and my eyes flutter closed. *Yes.*

When we hear Chelsea coming back into the kitchen, he steps away, leaning down in a cabinet to my right to pull out a pan. But Chelsea is on the move, chattering away as she walks through to the living room. Her voice is a beacon to her general location.

"Stop doing that!" I mutter under my breath.

"Doing what?"

"Looking at me like you've seen me naked."

Standing right in front of me, his hand brushes my cheek. "Oh, I've done much more than just see you naked. And I'll be doing it again, soon." He runs his thumb over my lower lip as he licks his.

A throb settles between my legs just thinking about it. I shake my head, regaining the ability to think. "Well, at least stop touching me."

He cocks his head to the side. "I thought you liked it when I touched you. You certainly seemed to last night."

My chest heaves, heat crawling up my face. "That's not the point. You're going to get us caught."

We hadn't exactly had an opportunity to discuss telling Chelsea or the ramifications of her finding out. He had said he doesn't care about her wishes anymore. But what does that really mean in the grand scheme of things?

"You didn't answer my question."

"You didn't ask one."

Caging me against the counter, he leans in, his mouth against my ear. "Did you like it? When I touched you?" As he asks, he runs his hand down my front, passing over my breast and sliding down the front of my pants.

A breathless "Yes" is all I can muster.

He smiles against my ear and pulls away, leaning back against the island, arms crossed at his chest, eyes fixed on me. "Hey, Chels!" he calls out, unsure of where exactly she's gone.

"Yeah?" Her voice carries from upstairs.

"What time are Mom and Dad getting back today?"

"Around four, five, I don't know, somewhere around there."

"And you'll be out for a while?"

"I'm heading to work as soon as I can find my damn ID badge!"

"Mind if Shay and I hang out?" Lochlyn raises an eyebrow, his gaze intense and dark.

My racing heart seems like it should be evident to the whole world, not just me. The look in his eyes gives away his intentions for what our time together will look like.

"Like she'd have any interest in spending time with you," Chelsea says, appearing on the other side of the island. Lochlyn still hasn't taken his eyes off me.

"I don't care what you do"—she turns to Lochlyn and points at him—"just keep your filthy hands off of her."

He holds his hands up, turning them back and forth. "These hands?" *Those hands*. Those magical, amazing hands. "They look pretty clean to me."

"Well, not knowing who they've been touching in the past several days, let's just say to keep them off her and her sacred body. 'Kay?"

If only she knew that a few hours ago, those hands had been touching me. All of me. And that I can't wait for them to touch me again.

Chelsea walks over and gives me a hug. "Don't be afraid to tell him to fuck off. I promise he can take it," she mutters before letting go. "Bye, loser." She smacks Lochlyn in the stomach on her way past him.

"Love you too, sis!" he calls after her. When he turns back to me, there's a potent hunger in his eyes. And it's all for me. He walks over to me, putting an arm around my waist and yanking me against him. "I'm going to make us some breakfast, and then I'm going to be taking my clothes back."

<h1 style="text-align:center">Chapter 6</h1>

L ochlyn and I find a way to have alone time every day in the two weeks he has left at home. I have no idea what will happen when he leaves, but I don't care. We can't get enough of each other. *I* can't get enough of *him*.

I let him bend and twist me any way he wants, leaving it to him and his...expertise. I'm never disappointed. He knows all the right places and ways to touch me to make me scream.

Chest down, ass up—per instructions—quickly became a favorite. Especially when I heard "Fuck, Shay," as he sank into me. I love the huskiness in his voice when he likes something.

We spend our time together in secrecy. Reading, watching TV, just being together. By the end of the day, we always end up in bed.

Our spending time together won't raise any flags. While before it wasn't usually just the two of us, it would be easy enough to write off. But we want to touch each other constantly. We can't hold hands in front of other people. And when we're together, we can't keep our hands off each other. When Chelsea's around, it practically hurts because I can't be as close to him as I want to be.

Two days before Lochlyn has to leave, we're lying in my bed, his arm around me drawing tiny circles on my lower back as I lie across his chest. Worry starts to weigh me down, filling my chest like a lead balloon. What happens in two days? Is it the end? We'll be on the same campus next year. Will it be a break until then?

"What's in your head, baby girl?"

I turn to face him, resting my cheek on his chest. His eyes are closed.

He opens them a slit, looking at me. "What?"

"How'd you know something was bothering me?"

"I've known you for a long time, Shay. I've paid attention, picked up on a thing or two. These past two weeks have only helped."

A frown spans my face as a sigh escapes, and I try to swallow around the lump forming in my throat as a burning settles behind my lids.

He opens his eyes completely, brushing his knuckles lovingly over my cheek. "Talk to me," he quietly urges.

I shake my head, my sight blurry, tears threatening to break free. He grabs a pillow from next to him and shoves it behind his head, pushing himself up higher. Putting his hands under my arms, he pulls me up, holding my chin between his fingers, eyes locked on mine. "Talk."

He swipes away the tears before I can.

"What happens when you leave?" My lip trembles as the words come out in a mere whisper.

Letting go of my chin, he pulls me against him as his chest rises and falls with a deep breath. "It's going to be really hard. I'm going to miss you, a lot."

"But are you...are we..." I don't know how to ask what's gnawing at my mind. Yet, somehow, he knows.

"I'm with you, Shay. Not just right here, right now. Not just this break. I'm with you. My leaving won't change that." The words I've wanted to hear for so long, yet they don't bring me the comfort they should.

"What about all the pretty college girls?" Surely there are several who throw themselves at him, who are far prettier than I am. For all I know, he's been talking with a few. Though he told me he was single, that doesn't mean there isn't somebody back at Cornell awaiting his return.

He takes my chin in his hand again, pressing a tiny kiss on my lower lip, and meeting my eyes. "They pale in comparison to you."

He holds me against him as I cry. At no point does he try to tell me it'll be okay, or try to talk me out of crying. He just holds me, kissing my head every so often, running his hand down my hair, knowing that at this moment, I just need to let it out and that his words would fall on deaf ears.

The last day he's home, he tells his family—parents having returned on the first—he'll be gone until dinner, wanting to see some friends. But he's coming over to spend the day with me.

It's the one time I'm thankful Mom has thrown herself into the store. She doesn't worry about me being alone. Not only is she too self-consumed in grief, but I'm the good daughter. The one who follows the rules. I ask permission instead of forgiveness.

I've never done anything that would make anybody unhappy with me or would make them disappointed in me. Except being with Lochlyn. And that I do for myself and my happiness.

Before he's even shut the door or had a chance to take off his coat, I'm pulling him against me. There's not a single second to waste.

Gently placing his hand on my shoulders, he pushes me back, brushing my cheek with his thumb. "Hey, slow down. We have time. This isn't goodbye, Shay."

I lean into his palm, biting the inside of my lip, as my foot tilts on its side. "It feels like it."

"Let's just spend the day together. See where it takes us."

My brow furrows. "You don't want to, we're not going to—" I can barely say the word *sex*, though we've had it every day since New Year's.

"Oh no, I do, and we will. But there's no rush. There's more here than sex, Shay." He looks lovingly into my eyes as he swoops some curls behind my ear. "So much more."

Taking off his coat, he slings it over the back of an armchair, leaving his shoes by the door and flopping onto the couch. He holds his arms out to me, and I walk over, leaning into his embrace. I'm okay if he just holds me for a while. It will give me time to memorize his scent, the rhythm of his heart, the heat of his body seeping into mine. All things I'm going to miss once he's gone.

Lochlyn's gone off to college before; he's been gone for two and a half years, but he wasn't mine then. But then, I wonder if he's even mine now. Absentmindedly, I start picking at his shirt.

"What's wrong, baby girl?" My stomach flutters every time he calls me that.

Mindlessly, I lift one shoulder. "Nothing."

He puts his hand over mine, stilling it. "If nothing's wrong, you wouldn't be fidgeting."

Sighing, I push myself up to look at him, but I can't meet his eye. My fingers wiggle under his grasp, too much running through my head to calm them. "Why did you kiss me?"

"What?"

"Over Thanksgiving break. Why did you kiss me?" I look up at him. His brow is furrowed, a mask of confusion in his eyes.

"Because I wanted to. I told you, I'd wanted to do that for a long time."

"But was it, like, some sort of challenge for you or something? You had to nail your sister's best friend?"

He straightens up, taking my hands in his. "Not even a little. The only reason I didn't try to be with you sooner was *because* you're Chelsea's best friend."

"Why now?"

"I got tired of delaying my happiness."

"I make you happy?" My head cocks to the side as I ask.

He looks shocked, even a little hurt. "Extremely. You don't see that?"

I shake my head.

He cups my cheek. "You make me extremely happy, baby girl."

"How did you know that I would?"

"I guess, I didn't know. I just had a very strong feeling you would. I'm glad I was right."

"Why?"

He knows me well enough that I don't need to elaborate. "Shay, look at me and listen."

I lift my gaze from my lap and sheepishly meet his.

"You are beautiful, sexy, and smart. You're funny and have good taste in music. You're a devoted and loyal friend, and I know it's eating you up inside keeping our secret from Chelsea. You love with your whole heart. You know more about household supplies and products than any girl your age should, including how to run a store. And you read more than anybody I know, you always have.

"You're the most selfless person I've ever met. You not only put hours and hours into the store on top of school, while still maintaining good enough grades to get into Cornell, might I add, but you also spent all that time with your dad. You put your whole life on hold to be there for your mom after he died. And I know you well enough to know that you're going to say that anybody would do that. But it's just not true. Your own sister isn't even around. It all fell to you, as a senior in high school."

He brushes hair off my face, tucking it gently behind my ear and leaving his hand cupping my jaw. "You're kind of incredible." He says it quietly as he leans in to kiss me.

Incredible? He thinks *I'm* incredible? How is that possible?

I lean into his kiss, intensifying it by slipping my tongue into his mouth. His hands slide down to my hips, pulling me onto his lap. His grip tightens as he digs his thumbs into the bone, then pulls me across his lap, his lips hungry against mine.

I whimper as his mouth moves down to my neck.

"Want to go upstairs?" he murmurs against my ear. All I can do is nod.

His hands slide down to support under my thighs as he stands. I wrap my legs around his waist, my mouth seeking his as he carries me upstairs to my room.

Laying me down gently on my bed, reaching behind his head and peeling off his shirt, his hands immediately dive to the hem of mine, leaning me up as he pulls it off, unhooking my bra. His open mouth grazes over my stomach, breathing gently as he works his way up to my breast. Pushing my bra to the side, he runs his lips over my nipple, sliding his tongue out to flick at it. That causes my back to arch in response and fire to rip through my veins.

He smiles against my breast, closing his mouth around my nipple as he slides his hand under the waistband of my pants. His breath catches as he slips his fingers against me, feeling the wetness that has pooled. It causes an eagerness to overtake Lochlyn.

Pushing two fingers into me, he starts moving his tongue faster. I moan, one arm wrapping around his head while the other grabs hold of his arm as the pressure builds in my lower belly. Every noise, every moan, every gasp, causes a change in him.

"Loch," I sigh. I can't hold back any longer, bucking against his hand. He groans against my chest, hands diving to the top of my pants, yanking them off before pushing his off.

As he climbs back over me, he trails his tongue along my skin, starting at my knee, tracing over my hip, running over to between my legs, giving a quick kiss before sliding up my chest, over my collarbone. He closes his mouth on my neck, licking and sucking. I yelp when his teeth dig in.

Hovering over me, he takes my chin firmly in his hands.

"Look at me," he growls as he presses into me.

His grip on my chin tightens as I try to tip my head back, a squeak seeping from my lips. My fingers dig into his shoulders as he starts moving inside me. Letting my chin go, his hand slides down my body to press down on my hip, thumb running over soft skin.

He leans down to my neck and his teeth graze my skin. The sensation causes me to tangle my fingers in his hair, needing more. Noises filter into the air from both of us. We're absolutely starving for each other. Hungrily, his lips find mine.

As his thrusts become hurried and harder, I whine and whimper with each one. Nothing has ever felt better than Lochlyn moving inside me, above me, touching me all over my body with his large hands and soft lips. It's worth every second of wait, every day of longing for him.

His mouth is pressed against my throat as my head tilts back, and I moan, shuddering underneath him. He slows as his breath falters and a low "Fuck" escapes his lips.

Kissing my collarbone, he rolls to his back, one arm flung over his eyes.

When I don't settle into him immediately, he blindly reaches his other hand to wrap around me and pull me against him, fingertips running gently against my hip.

I don't want to know how little time we have left together, but my self-control is nonexistent. I grab his wrist from his eyes and bring it in front of me so I can check the time.

"Shay," he says disapprovingly.

"I can't help it. I'm not ready to say goodbye." I just got him. How can I say goodbye after only a few days? Even if it's not forever, it's still too long. One day is too long.

"Stop looking. We have as much time as we have."

"But what if there's something else we want to do and we don't have time?"

"I'm keeping an eye on it. Please, just relax. Enjoy this time with me instead of worrying about it being over."

I sigh. "Okay. I'll try. What should we do?"

"Right now, I just want to lie here with you."

I bite my lip but nod. Taking a deep breath, I settle against him. I'm still holding his wrist, but he makes no move that he wants it back.

We rest in silence for a few minutes as his breathing slows. Though his fingers are still moving on my hip, I'm afraid he's falling asleep. I don't want to lose a second because we drifted off and when we wake up, it'll be time for him to go. But I don't want to disturb him.

"Shay. Relax." He's picked up on my uneasiness again.

"I just...I don't want you to fall asleep."

"I'm *not* falling asleep. I'm enjoying this moment here with you."

"Your breathing is slowing down." And his eyes are closed. How could he not fall asleep? It's just so cozy lying here together.

"Good, because if I was always breathing like that, there'd be something wrong with me. I just had some exertion, my breathing was elevated, so was my heart rate. Here, feel." He takes my hand and places it above his heart. "Much slower." He presses my hand against his chest and takes my chin between his fingers, turning my head to look at him. "I'm right here, baby."

I nod as tears well and my lip trembles. It's temporary. He's only home for a few more hours. He wants me at this moment. But what if, when he goes back, he changes his mind?

Sighing, he pushes himself up higher, pulling me into his lap as he wraps his arms around me. I lace my hand around his neck, pulling myself as close as I can, then cry against his chest.

"It's okay, Shay. I'm here. I don't want you crying for the rest of our time together. No more tears. Let's be happy."

"I'm trying. I'm just...I'm really going to miss you."

His arms tighten around me. "I know. I know, baby. I'm going to miss you too."

After a few minutes, I'm able to get control of myself and stop crying, breathing him in. Then I have a thought.

"How long?"

He sighs frustratedly, not that I can blame him. "Shay."

"No, not how long do we have left. How long had you wanted to kiss me for before Thanksgiving?"

"Years, Shay. Years."

Linking my hands behind his neck, I lean back to look at him, his arms loose around my waist. "Really? How'd you keep it hidden for so long?"

Shrugging, he says, "Honestly, I don't really feel like I did."

Something clicks into place for me. Something that maybe should have been obvious, or would have been if I paid a little more attention, or wasn't filled with low self-esteem. "Is that why you offered to help out at the store this summer? And stayed a week when my dad died?"

"Yeah. I mean, I like to think I'm a good person, but, man, that was some real manual labor moving those boxes. I just wanted to be near you, any way I could." He runs a finger along my eyebrow and down my cheek. "I knew you weren't okay. I wanted to try to help you be."

"I wish I had known."

"Honestly, sometimes I thought you did. I always hoped you did. But when you didn't reciprocate, I wasn't sure. I didn't want to make any assumptions. I just thought that if you didn't have the same feelings, maybe if I put in the time, the effort, one day you would."

"The feelings were definitely mutual. Are mutual. I sometimes thought maybe I was picking up on something. The way you'd look at me or prolong a touch. But then I'd think there was no way. No way you could ever possibly be interested in somebody like me." I laugh. "I was sure you were going to catch me staring at some point."

He chuckles deep in his chest. I love the sound. "I may have once or twice. I always hoped *you* wouldn't catch *me* staring." His hair grazes my skin as he drops his head and shakes it. "I *had* planned to take things a little bit slower. Of all the times I went over it in my head, it was never a kiss on the deck, disappearing for a month, then coming back and getting right to sex."

"I can definitely say that's not how I'd ever pictured it either. But I don't mind. If you think about it, we really built a lot of the background first, for years even. Especially with all those late-night chats we had over the last year."

"My very artfully designed conversations."

"You're revealing your secrets."

"I guess I am. It's okay, though. As long as you know now." His knuckles graze my cheek while his eyes search my face before he leans in to kiss my bottom lip.

Sleep is hard to come by, which leaves me awake in bed, wondering what Lochlyn's doing, if he's thinking about me, when my phone chirps.

Lochlyn: _Come outside and meet me._

I immediately text back.

_Me:_ _My mom._

While she may not pay much attention to me, she'd certainly notice the door, as quiet as I may be.

Lochlyn: _Sneak out or lie. I need to see you._

_Me:_ _Ok._

I've never lied to my parents. This secrecy between me and Lochlyn is causing me to do things I don't normally do. I'm lying to Chelsea and Mom. But it's all worth it.

As quietly as I can, I shut the heavy mahogany door behind me, pulling a long sweater duster tight against me to block out the chill in the air. I don't see Lochlyn anywhere as I move around the side of my house, thankful there isn't any snow on the ground since I threw on my slippers.

Suddenly, I feel his arm wrap around my waist, pressing against my back, his breath a gentle puff in my ear. He spins me around to face him, mouth claiming mine as he pushes me back against the house.

Reaching his hands down to my thighs, he lifts me up. I wrap my legs around his waist, tangling my fingers in his hair as he puts one hand against the side of my face. Ending the kiss, he rests his forehead against mine, our breath swirling tendrils of steam in the space between us. He lowers me to the ground, his hand settling against my chest, just below my neck.

"Hi," he whispers.

"Hi." I close my eyes, breathing him in.

"I just wanted to see you one last time before I leave tomorrow. I'm heading out early. I wish...I wish I could come see you. But you know I can't."

"I know," I whisper, keeping my eyes shut tight to keep the tears at bay. It doesn't work.

His thumbs brush the droplets before they reach my chin. "Hey now, no crying."

"I don't want you to forget about me." How much more pathetic can I sound?

"Impossible."

I choke out a sob.

"Shay, listen to me. I'll be back in March for the break, and we'll spend time together. It's not as far away as it seems. Maybe you can come visit me. We can figure something out." He takes a breath, swallowing audibly. "I'm not the sex-crazed monster my sister makes me out to be. Nor am I the guy my reputation says I am. I want *you*, Shay. I only want you. I've always wanted you."

I open my eyes for the first time and look up at him. His eyes are trained on mine, filled with sincerity. It only makes things worse.

My fists tangle into his shirt as I bury my face in his chest. He wraps his arms around me, pulling me closer and holding me as I cry. I hate that I spend so much time in tears around him. I'm not usually a crier.

After a few minutes, he takes my face between his hands and tilts it so that I look at him, then kisses me tenderly. "You know I'd love nothing more than to sleep wrapped around you tonight, but I have to go. I'll call you when I get there tomorrow."

I nod, my eyes filling with warm, salty liquid again as he presses a long kiss on my forehead, then another on my lips before backing away. My hand presses against my chest where his had rested a moment ago as I watch him walk away, hoping beyond all hope he won't forget about us, about me.

Chapter 7

"Chelsea, I'm turning nineteen. You don't get a big party at nineteen." She just sprung on me the fact that she wants to throw me a party, in true Chelsea fashion. I'm not exactly feeling in the party mood, as I'm not over missing Lochlyn yet.

"You didn't have a party at eighteen, so we're just celebrating a year late."

I catch myself sighing, though I know it's pointless. "Chels, come on. I don't want a party." The only thing I really want for my birthday is Lochlyn. He's been gone two weeks and the daily text messages and calls just aren't enough. I need to see him, to feel him.

Exasperation spreads across her face as she turns to look at me, rolling her eyes before they widen. "Shay, you've had a rough few years. Let's just have fun. It's your birthday. I just want you to let go. For *one* night."

"I'm not going to get drunk, Chels."

"Did I say you should? I said let go. That can have many meanings. Including just spending the night with some fun people."

"How big are you planning?"

She smirks, knowing she's wearing me down. "Nothing *huge*. Just us, Bren, some of the girls we've met at school. I told them they could invite their boyfriends if they have one."

"Wait, you already planned it all?" She just said she wants to, not that she already told a bunch of people.

Her shoulders and eyebrows raise in unison. "Oops." But a smile plays across her lips.

"What if I said no, Chels? Like adamantly said no?" It was a strong possibility. There have been many a party I've declined attending.

"I'd either have found a way to convince you or just had a party for myself."

I roll my eyes, knowing she would have. "What time?"

She claps her hands and bounces on my bed, giddy. "Eight."

"Why so late? You'll be tired by ten."

"I can make it until midnight, at least."

"New Year's Eve begs to differ." Not that I'm complaining; that was the best night of my life.

"Yeah, but that wasn't *fun*. This will be."

"Okay, I guess I'll be there at eight." Thankfully, she's hosting. One year, she tried to convince me to throw a party at *my* house. That was a big fat *no*.

"Let's get your outfit picked out now."

"My outfit? Can't I just wear what I'm wearing?" A quick glance down reminds me I'm wearing my ratty jeans and a holey sweater. Maybe not.

She gives me a once-over, making me shrink a bit. "You're joking, right?"

"Just pick something," I grumble as I wave her toward my closet, turning my attention back to my books.

We're supposed to be studying for a test we have coming up in our English class. She's set most of her schedule around Brendan this semester. It works for me. I've been able to meet a few new people and still see Eve every so often.

The alone time is the worst. It's when I miss Lochlyn the most. I loaded my schedule with five courses, filling the rest of my days with studying or at the store with Mom. My long days of classes are the opposite of Brendan's, which means on my less busy days, Chelsea and I get to hang out. But I still get far too much time to myself to miss Lochlyn. Especially at night as I climb into bed.

Some nights I'm kept up with worry. Am I over the top with my longing for him? Is his absence affecting me too much? Having never been in a relationship, I can't say for certain. But all I know is that my body and my heart miss his terribly.

"Here." An outfit lands with a thud a few inches from me. A pair of dark wash skinny jeans and a fitted teal sweater.

I glance up at her. "What about the shirt for under the sweater?" It has a relatively deep V for the neckline.

"You won't be wearing one."

"Why?"

"To attract any single guys."

"Are you inviting any single guys?" Not that it matters. I don't want anybody else.

"Brendan was going to bring a few friends."

"And you think a low-cut shirt is the way to go? That's the first impression I should make?" Clearly, our clothing choices are incredibly different. I wouldn't say she dresses provocatively. Lochlyn would lose his mind and throw all her clothes away, but I definitely dress more modestly than she does.

"It's *always* the first impression you should make. You're hot, Shay. Embrace it."

There's no point in arguing with her. I'll just grab a cami to throw on underneath when I change.

Plopping herself back on the bed, she picks up her phone. A quick scroll through must give her nothing of interest and she throws it back down, reaching for mine.

"Hey!" I lunge at her.

Her brow knits together. "Wow, since when can I not see your phone?"

"Just ask first." I have to check to make sure I don't have any new messages from Lochlyn. Knowing she'd be looking at my phone regularly, I wasn't sure what to put as his contact. Currently, he's in there as a musical note since we've always bonded over music.

A brief glance tells me there's nothing from him. "Here." Defeat steals the air from my lungs as I hand the phone over.

"Alright, spill. You met a guy, didn't you?"

My face burns. "Why would you say that?" I keep my head down, unable to look at her.

"Because you've never been like this before and you're checking your phone constantly. I see the little giggles as you read messages." Busted.

"He's just a guy I met in one of my classes." It's become far easier than I like to lie to her. Guilt tries to worm its way through my mind, but I raise my chin to push it away. One thing I keep trying to remind myself is that sometimes I deserve happiness too.

"You should invite him tonight! I'd like to meet him."

"Oh, I can't, he's busy."

"Too busy for your birthday? Did he even wish you a happy birthday today?" One brow ticks up and she looks at the screen with irritation.

Swiping open my phone, she jumps into my text messages. At this second, I'm nothing but thankful Lochlyn and I are always careful not to say anything that could even remotely identify him. Most of our messages are innocuous.

"Wait, are these song lyrics? You guys text song lyrics back and forth?"

"Yeah."

"That's weird, Shay."

"Have you read them? It's sweet." Normally, I'd care what she thinks, I'd let her thoughts make me second-guess something like this, but not here. It's something I've grown to love about my relationship with Lochlyn.

"Whatever." She scrolls some more. "At least he wished you a happy birthday."

He had. I woke up to a deliriously sweet message wishing me a happy birthday. We had a few exchanges after that, but he's been silent for a few hours. He has classes most of the day, but usually finds a way to send a little something. I've been trying not to let it bother me. It's not going well.

She tosses my phone down next to me. "I'm bored."

"We're supposed to be studying, Chels." While she's done almost anything *but* look at her books, I've had my nose in the pages and have been taking frivolous notes. Aside from standing to stretch, I haven't gotten up from my bed in hours.

"Studying is boring."

"It's not supposed to be fun. It's supposed to help you do well in class."

She checks her phone again. "It's five thirty. Let's get dinner."

With a sigh, I close my books, knowing I'm not going to be getting any more studying done tonight.

"What are you thinking?" I ask.

"For your birthday, where do you want to go?"

"Hana." I don't even need a second to decide.

"How did I know you were going to say that?"

Hana is a newer Japanese restaurant that opened in town, and I love it. Lochlyn had taken me and Chelsea while he'd been home—just friends having dinner. It made no difference that

Lochlyn's and my knees touched the whole time and then he took me home and we had sex. Twice.

"Get your stuff. Let's go. Your birthday, so it's my treat!"

I hate myself a little bit as I check my phone one last time before we leave for dinner. My chest collapses when it comes up blank.

Pathetic, party of one.

At seven forty-five, I open the door to Chelsea's house. Her parents are on yet another trip. She'd turned nineteen a few weeks before Thanksgiving, so they feel comfortable leaving her home alone. Her parents have always been a bit more hands off anyway.

"Chels?" When I walked in, I expected to find her setting up, but instead she's somewhere in the house.

"Hey!" She's breathless as she comes into the living room carrying a bowl of chips, Brendan not far behind her. I don't want to think about what they were or were not doing before I walked in.

There's a table off to the side filled with various snacks. Chips, pretzels, even pigs in a blanket. Then I notice the coolers, filled with beer and wine coolers, and I scowl. I knew she was planning for there to be some sort of alcohol, Brendan having turned twenty-one in December, but I hadn't been expecting this much.

"Chelsea, most of us are underage. Why is there so much alcohol?" The disapproval is clear in my voice, and it irks me that I have to act like the parent.

"It's a party, Shay!" She gives me a once-over and frowns. "You have a cami on."

"Yes, I do. It's a low one, though, so I partially appeased you." I'd chosen a white one that has a lacy top. It's still pretty low, but it covers most of my cleavage.

"I guess you don't need a guy, anyway. Why didn't you tell me?" Her voice is a mix between hurt and angry.

"Oh, uh, I guess it's just that it's so new."

"Doesn't seem new from the messages."

My face burns and I swallow audibly. If you really read the lyrics, they're filled with emotion. Longing, desire, even traces of love. "That honeymoon phase, you know. New and fun."

She nods as she pops a chip into her mouth. "What's his name?"

"John." It comes out faster than I'd like and before I can think of a better name.

"Well, I look forward to meeting him at some point in the near future."

"Oh, sure. I mean, he's pretty busy with school and work, but we'll try to set something up!"

Before she can respond, the doorbell rings. She runs over, yanking it open to let in a group of girls we'd met on campus, most of whose names I can't remember. They all hug before walking over to me. I'm feeling a little disheartened, not really wanting to be around people. I haven't heard from Lochlyn in hours.

But I plaster on the fake smile I'd perfected while Dad was sick and hug each of them as I thank them for coming. It's not their fault I'm not in the mood to celebrate.

Around eight-thirty, I'm still standing by the snack table, feeling a little sorry for myself, fingers playing with the tablecloth, when I hear some murmurs around the crowd.

A hand slides to my waist and there's a quiet whisper in my ear. "Happy birthday, baby girl." My chest seizes. Lochlyn.

I spin around to face him, and I throw my arms around his neck. He wraps his arms around me and pulls me close, melding our bodies together.

"Lochlyn!" Chelsea's voice cuts through the crowd. I start to pull away, but his grip tightens around me before slowly letting go. Still standing close to Lochlyn, I turn to face Chelsea. Nothing about it would seem odd; we're friends, except for his finger hooked through my back belt loop.

"Hey, sis." His voice is nonchalant, like nothing about this is strange, even though he drove four hours to be here for me. Even his stance, one hand leaning against the table, is relaxed and carefree.

"What are you doing here?" Her face says she's excited, but her tone is questioning.

"Are you serious? You told me I absolutely had to come and under no circumstances would it be okay if I didn't."

"I did?"

"You said that it was for Shay. That we all had to be here." When he says my name, he gives a little tug against my belt loop and there's a softness to his tone I never noticed before.

"Oh yeah, I guess I did. I just didn't really expect you to come."

"And face your wrath? No way."

"Smart man. Okay, well, now that I see Shay's in capable hands, I can wander." She gives one last glance at us before walking back into the crowd.

After she's out of earshot, he leans down, whispering in my ear, "Very capable hands indeed."

Heat creeps up my neck, a tingle flashing through my body. I so desperately want to grab his hand and drag him upstairs. But being the honoree, I know somebody will notice if I'm suddenly missing, even if Chelsea is the star.

I turn to face him again, his eyes on me. "What are you doing here?"

"I missed you."

"I was worried. I hadn't heard from you all day."

"Sorry, I wanted to surprise you, part of why I didn't tell you about this plan of Chelsea's. I had my morning classes and then packed a bag. I left straight from my afternoon class."

"This is so unnecessary. But I'm very happy you're here." *Elated* is a better word, but I don't want to seem too eager, too desperate. Though I'm absolutely both of those things.

"I really want to kiss you right now." The twitch of his hand tells me he wants to touch me as well.

"I want that too."

"So, how far do you think we can push this?"

"Hm, I don't know. Lots of eyes. I can't exactly disappear, being the birthday girl. Right now, it just looks like we're talking, standing close to hear over the noise." I take the tiniest step closer.

"So, I probably shouldn't slide my hand into your back pocket?"

"Probably not the best idea." Though it would be very welcome.

"And pulling you against me? Also bad?"

"Doing it here? Yes. The actual act itself? Never." Oh, what I wouldn't give for that right now.

"Are you staying with Chelsea tonight?"

"No, actually. She has Bren here. She so kindly offered me your room." With a quirk of my shoulder, I put my hands toward him, as though in offering.

His brow knits together, and he takes a step back. "She has Brendan staying, after *your* party?" He looks around for a moment, taking in the alcohol. "Did he buy all this?"

I nod. "Yeah."

"For your underage party?"

"I told Chelsea I didn't want it, but—"

"Excuse me." He cuts me off, putting his hand on my arm as he walks away. My gaze follows him as he tracks down Chelsea, grabbing her bicep, and spinning her around. They're a few feet away, but I can hear small bits and pieces. Looking at Lochlyn, anybody can see that he's *mad* with his clenched fists and puffed out chest. The scowl is just an added touch.

"The fuck, Chelsea?" One little blip.

"A party, Loch." Another one.

Somebody turns up the music and I can't hear anymore, but I see them both gesturing wildly. At one point, Lochlyn waves his hands at me, and for a second, I think we're in trouble, that Chelsea has figured things out.

It's not so much that Lochlyn's against underage parties. He's not even twenty-one himself and he's certainly taken us to our fair share, even hosted a few. I think it's more that it's a party for me and I don't drink. Or that Brendan's the one who bought the alcohol. Or that he didn't seem to know he'd be here to supervise. Possibly all of the above.

When he stands in front of me again, I can feel the anger rolling off him as he glares after Chelsea and Brendan. But when he turns back to me, his gaze softens, and his body loosens as he reaches down and takes my hand in his.

"I think I bought us the ability to sleep in the same room tonight." A smile graces his lips as he talks.

"Oh, really? How'd you do that?"

"First of all, I yelled at Chelsea for the alcohol. It's fucking moronic of her. Then I yelled at her for having Brendan staying on your birthday and making you sleep in the other room. I made it very clear to her that I'm *not* going to be sleeping on the couch and that if she's not going to send Brendan home, that she'll have to deal with us sleeping in the same room."

"Really? What'd she say to that?"

A mischievous smile spreads across his face. "She made me promise to keep my hands off of you." Looking around to see where Chelsea is and to make sure we're not being watched, he slips his fingers into my front pocket and pulls me closer. "I walked away before promising any such thing. Because I have absolutely every intention of putting my hands all over you." His mouth is right against my ear, and his words are coated with that huskiness I love.

I stifle a moan at the thought of his hands on me, a throb settling between my legs.

Looking into his eyes, I see the burning and desire I feel through my entire body. "Come outside with me. For five minutes." His voice is low and strained, a hint of gravel.

"What do I tell Chels?"

"I don't care. I don't care if you tell her nothing. I have to kiss you." My lips tingle at the thought.

"Okay. I'll meet you out there in a minute."

He pulls his hand from my pocket, squeezing my hip before he walks away.

I wind my way through the cluster of people to find Chelsea. There's a bigger crowd than she originally anticipated. It seems like of the ten or so people she invited, everybody brought at least a plus one.

"Hey, I need to get some air." After finally making my way across the room, I stand in front of her.

"You okay?"

"Mhm, just warm." I pull at the front of my shirt as though I'm fanning myself to prove my point.

"You sure?" She flips her hair over her shoulder with a stoic look.

"Yeah, I'll be quick. Just want some cool air." I'm trying to sound calm, but I'm not sure it's working.

"Want me to come with you?"

"No!" I say it a little too enthusiastically. "No, I'm fine. You stay, entertain."

Her narrowed gaze drifts over my body.

"I'll be fine, Chels. Five minutes."

"Okay. Let me know if you need something."

"I will." Before I walk away, I put my hand on her arm, grabbing my coat on the way out the front door.

The cold air slaps me in the face. It's been a few hours since I've been outside, and the temperature has dropped tremendously. I know Lochlyn's out here, but I'm not exactly sure where.

As I'm walking around the corner of the house, I find him leaning against the side. The second he sees me, he pushes off, wrapping his arms around me as his mouth crashes onto mine.

My mouth opens for his as he turns us around, pressing me up against the house. As his tongue seeks mine, his hands slide down to under my thighs, lifting me up. I hook my legs around his waist as his mouth finds my neck.

"Fuck, I missed you." I don't have a chance to answer before his lips are on mine again. Devouring me.

Far too soon, he pulls away and sets me down. We're both out of breath.

Every so often, I forget just how tall he is. His hands are resting against the house, boxing me in and surrounding me as he towers over me. Sometimes, nine inches doesn't feel like much, other times, it feels enormous.

"You go in first. I'll grab my bag and make it seem like I came to get my stuff."

I bite my lip, nodding. Air hisses through his teeth. "Please don't do that."

I furrow my brow, confused. "Do what?"

"Bite your lip like that."

"Why?"

"Because then all I can do is think about your perfect mouth." He runs his thumb over my bottom lip, making my breath hitch.

I can't help but smile. "Okay. Sorry. I'll see you inside?"

"Yeah. I, uh, I need a few minutes."

My brow furrows, confused again. "Why do you nee—" And then it dawns on me as he bounces and adjusts his pants. My eyes widen while my panties dampen. "Oh. Never mind."

I slink back inside, slipping onto the empty couch. Immediately, Rachel and Eve flank me.

"Happy birthday, Shay!" they sing-song in unison.

"Thanks, guys."

"It's really cool that Chelsea could throw this party. Where are her parents?" Rachel looks around with round eyes and a tenseness in her body, seemingly afraid we might get caught by the not present adults.

"Oh, they're not around much." I say this like it's completely normal. Though when I think about it, it's anything but.

"I wish my parents would go away for once," Eve grumbles to the right of me. She's complained about her parents a few times. Chelsea and I can't really commiserate. Hers are basically invisible. Mine's heartbroken and distracted, making me the invisible one.

Lochlyn walks in, making brief eye contact with me before walking upstairs, bag thrown over his shoulder.

"Oh my God, Chelsea's brother is so hot." Rachel's basically drooling at my side.

I bite the inside of my cheek. "Really? I've never noticed."

"You haven't noticed? How could you *not?*" Eve is just as awestruck, jaw hanging open slightly and eyes wide.

"I've known him for years." I shrug it off. While it may be true, it's impossible not to notice how gorgeous he is. I'd have to be blind. And deaf, because his voice is deep and smooth like velvet.

"What's he like?"

"Are the rumors true?"

Their questions come in rapid fire. It's like I'm holding candy above their heads. *My* candy.

"He's cool. He's into music, a junior at Cornell." The words come out like I'm reading off a list.

"And the rumors?" Ah, yes. The infamous rumors. Having met them at the community college, they were from a nearby district. The rumors about Lochlyn had stretched beyond our school.

I make a show of putting on a dramatic shrug. "I have no idea. I mean, they're just rumors. No way to know whether they're true or not." Though the one about him being good in bed is most definitely true.

As he comes bounding down the stairs, he catches Eve and Rachel's attention again. He's changed into a tight, black, long-sleeved shirt, the sleeves pushed up to just below his elbows, the blade of the sword on his arm sticking out.

"How could they not be? Look at him. He just oozes sex," Eve swoons.

"I wonder if he has plans for tonight. Or if maybe I can convince him to make *me* his plan." Rachel looks like she's a hungry tiger ready to pounce.

I bristle in annoyance. Neither of them has taken their eyes off of his perfection. I wonder how long I'll have to wait until at least one of them throws herself at him.

It turns out not long, as Rachel stands, pushing her breasts up before walking over to the cooler Lochlyn's reaching into for a beer. I watch as she saunters up to him and introduces herself. She subtly touches his arm. I feel helpless as I can't do anything, but I can't seem to tear my eyes away either.

By the way she's talking to him, I can tell she thinks she's being coy, but from my angle, she just looks desperate. Though I'm probably just being biased.

Lochlyn nods, smiling curtly, as he raises his beer and walks away. Eve has gotten up before he flops down to my left, leaning into the corner. He shakes his head and takes a sip of his drink before resting his arm on the couch.

"Happen to you often?" I ask, jutting my chin toward Rachel and Eve.

"What, desperate girls hitting on me?"

"Yup."

"All the time." He tips his head to the side briefly and takes a swig of his beer.

I nod, biting my cheek and looking at the floor. I shouldn't have asked; I don't want to think about it. "She's pretty." I don't know what else to say.

"Okay?"

"Prettier than me."

From the corner of my eye, I can see him look at me. "Shay. She is *not* prettier than you." I stare at Rachel for a minute. Her long straight brown hair shining, her blue eyes that seem like they see everything are bright and shimmery.

"Look at me." His voice is tight.

Reluctantly, I do. "You are the most beautiful woman in this room. By a long shot."

I take a quick glance around. The party has mostly girls. I see several that I think are better looking. But Lochlyn is only looking at me. I let out a low breath, wishing I could sink into him.

I'm sure he's thinking the same thing as he shifts closer to me, our legs touching. He reaches around the back of the couch so that when I lean back, his fingers graze my shoulder. It looks natural, like two friends sitting together on the couch. Not two people who are thinking of all the ways they want to touch each other. Or at least, that's what I'm thinking about.

"I'm pretty sure I know the answer, but do you want a drink?" His fingers press into my shoulder as he asks.

"No, no, I'm good."

"Doesn't really seem like a party for you."

"Never really is with Chelsea."

"I wish you'd stand up to her. Just once." There's a bite to his tone. I know some of it is because he wants to tell her about us. Whatever consequences I'm worried about, he thinks aren't important compared to us being happy together. But I also know it's because he thinks I let her walk all over me.

"I don't mind. She's happy. If she wants to think she threw this party for me, let her. I don't care right now. I'm happy just sitting on this couch with you."

He gives my shoulder a squeeze, lingering for a few seconds.

Lochlyn and I stay on the couch talking as the party wears on and slowly starts to wind down. A few other people stop by to chat with me, many giving glances at Lochlyn that make me think they only came over to be near him. When they realize he's not going to give them any of his attention, they usually walk away. Even Eve gives it a shot, probably thinking she may have better luck than Rachel. It's almost comical. Almost.

When only a few people are left, we start cleaning up, throwing away bottles, red cups, food. I watch his body tense as he glances over my shoulder and turn around to see what he's looking at. Chelsea is draped all over Brendan.

"He's a nice guy, Loch." "I don't like that he's sleeping with my sister." His fist clenches around the bag he's holding.

"Well, I guess that's something you two would agree on, then."

He looks back at me, scowling. "It's not the same."

"How?"

"You're her friend, and I'm her brother," he points at me, then rests his sprawled fingers against his chest. "We're not some stranger the other met somewhere."

"You knew she was going to be with somebody. She always is." Chelsea is rarely not with some guy in some way. Not always a relationship, but there's always some guy hanging around.

"Doesn't mean I have to like it." The words come through gritted teeth as he looks at the ground.

"Like it or not, he really is a nice guy. He treats her well."

"At least there's that."

Chelsea's ponytail bounces as she skips over, still bubbly and excited. "Oh, you guys didn't have to clean up. I would have done that."

"When, tomorrow?" Lochlyn spits out. I shoot him a look, my eyes narrowed and mouth in a hard line.

"It's fine, Loch, it can sit for a night." Chelsea sounds frustrated. Sometimes it's hard to tell.

"Whatever, we have this under control." He's calmer, but irritation still pricks at his words.

"You sure?"

"Yeah. Isn't it past your time to turn back into a pumpkin?"

"The carriage turns into a pumpkin, not the princess."

"Whatever. Same thing."

"Not at all. And yes, I'm exhausted." Putting her hand on my arm, she turns her attention to me. Her eyes are glassy, but I'm not sure if she's drunk. "I hope you had a good party."

"I did! I really did. Thank you." I don't need to tell her the only reason it was good is because Lochlyn's here.

"Oh, perfect. Okay, I'm going to bed. Good night, my loves!"

"Good night," we call after her in unison. Lochlyn's jaw is clenched as he watches Brendan follow her upstairs.

When they're out of sight, his eyes still trained on the stairs, he starts grumbling to himself. I only catch bits and pieces, but definitely get the gist of it being about Brendan and Chelsea. My intention is to let him work it out himself, but when he starts toward the stairs, I stop him.

"Lochlyn." My voice is low and gentle. I seem to catch him out of whatever trance he's in, and he softens as he looks at me.

Within two strides, he's in front of me, losing a hand in my hair as his lips close on mine and he pulls me flush against him. Dropping the cup in my hand, I wrap my hands around his neck.

"We give them five minutes and then we go upstairs." His voice is gravelly.

I nod, unable to make words. He pulls away and goes back to cleaning up.

As we finish clearing off the table, he flicks out his watch. "Five minutes are up. Let's go." Before I can answer, he grabs my hand and pulls me toward the stairs. We walk quietly and he peers around the corner before stepping onto the landing to make sure they're in Chelsea's room.

His hands are in my back pockets, lips on mine, before his door's even clicked shut. We move together, with me going backward, until my legs hit the bed and he slowly lays me down, lowering himself over me to rest on his forearms.

With his fingertips, he swipes some hair off my forehead and looks at me intently. "I'd love nothing more than to touch you and taste you right now, but I don't think it's such a good idea with Chelsea right down the hall."

"I can be quiet," I plead. I need to feel him.

He quirks up an eyebrow, asking an unvoiced question.

My whole body deflates. "Okay, no, I can't. But you should take that as a compliment."

"Oh, I do, trust me." The smirk that pulls at his mouth makes wetness pool between my thighs, increasing my need for him.

His lips meet mine again, tenderly at first, then turning hungrier. His hand starts to slide up the inside of my shirt, his touch scorching like fire against my skin.

"Did I tell you I really like this shirt?" he murmurs against my mouth.

"No."

"I do. I just wish you didn't wear anything under it." Maybe Chelsea was right after all.

He slips his tongue into my mouth again as his fingers rub against my nipple.

Just as things are ramping up between us, we hear a loud moan from down the hall. Lochlyn freezes. Turning his head from me, he groans into the pillow.

Before I realize what's happening, he's pushing himself off the bed. "Fuck this," he mutters under his breath.

I reach up and scramble to grab at his arm. "Loch, no."

Easily, he pulls out of my grasp.

I'm worried he's about to throw the door open and go bursting into Chelsea's room. Instead, he locks the door and turns on some music. Seether blasts for a second before he flips the dial down.

"I want to have sex with my girlfriend on her birthday." As he walks back over, he pulls his shirt over his head and tosses it on the floor before hovering over me again. "And I'm going to," he says against my neck. I love when Lochlyn takes control of the situation, knowing exactly what he wants, which is most of the time.

He has my clothes off in about three seconds, his pants coming off last. As he slides his fingers inside me, his lips are next to my ear. "Shh, baby, not too loud now."

His face moves away from mine, kissing down my chest as he pulls my nipple into his mouth. His tongue and fingers working in tandem have me writhing underneath him, fighting hard to keep the noises at bay. I twist my fingers into his hair as one squeak escapes my throat.

Immediately, his hand is over my mouth as he moves faster. Changing the tempo and hooking his fingers, I start to buck against him. Unable to control the noises, he releases my nipple, replacing his fingers with his hardness as he slides into me. My nails dig into his shoulders as I arch, my chest meeting his.

"I'm going to leave my hand here for a few minutes, Shay," he whispers, his breath in my ear making me shiver as I nod.

His hand remains in place as he moves inside me. Within minutes, my breathing increases and the pressure starts to build in my lower belly. Lochlyn's eyes lock on mine as he starts moving faster. The sounds are sticking in my chest. Every push in hits a spot inside me that makes my eyes want to roll back in my head and screams to burst from my mouth.

Still being newer to sex, I'm a little nervous to talk much, not that I'm able to at this very moment. If I could, I'd tell Lochlyn how good it feels, how close I'm getting. I hope he knows anyway.

Though my head tips back in ecstasy, he's able to keep my mouth covered. At the same time, I tighten around him, my nails scratching down his back as his breath hitches, a tiny groan slipping from his lips.

Dropping his head to my shoulder, he slowly pulls his hand away. I turn my mouth to follow, causing his fingers to trace along my lips. He kisses from my collarbone up to my ear. "Happy birthday, Shay," he whispers before rolling to his side.

Immediately, he's pushing his arm under my neck and pulling me against him. I rest against his heaving chest, reaching to hold his shoulder. One of his hands twirls a curl while the other runs gently up and down my arm. It's everything I've missed for two weeks, everything I wanted for my birthday.

"I still can't believe you drove all the way down here just for me. It's like four hours."

"I've never missed your birthday, Shay. I especially wouldn't this year." I take a second to think back. He's been at every celebration, big or small, for as long as I can remember. Even last year when I hadn't done anything but wallow in sadness, with it being my first birthday without my dad. He'd always gone big for birthdays, starting with my favorite breakfast of banana chocolate chip pancakes.

I crane my neck to look at him. "You said *girlfriend* before. Am I your girlfriend?"

His brow furrows as he looks down at me. "Well, yeah, Shay. I try not to make a habit of falling in love with girls I'm not in a relationship with." My already racing heart beats faster.

"You're falling in love with me?" It comes out as barely a whisper.

"No, Shay, not falling. Fell. Hard and fast. I love you. I'm in love with you." A warmth that starts in my chest slowly spreads through my entire body.

Best birthday present ever.

I push myself up to kiss him. "I love you, too," I whisper against his lips.

Before I can lie back down, his hand is at the back of my head, twisting into my hair and pulling my mouth to his, tongue claiming mine. His other hand moves to cover my breast, palm sliding gently along my nipple, sending a twinge through my body, settling between my thighs. I feel him harden against me.

Without hesitating, I throw my leg over him, pushing myself up to sitting, lowering myself slowly on top of him as he holds himself in place for me. My head falls back, and his breath catches as I take all of him inside me.

His hands slide down to grip my hips as I start moving on top of him. Pressing his thumbs into my hipbones, he grinds me against him, forward and back.

I don't know what I'm doing, running off intuition and what feels good. Which is all of it.

I alternate speeds, and momentum, changing from rising up and down to sliding my hips against his. When he tries to take over, I stop him, swatting his hands away. The smirk that crosses his face tells me he likes it.

My hips are starting to pinch, my thighs are getting tired, but the feeling is so amazing. The look on his face keeps me going. It's pure desire, he's completely lost in the experience, in me. I bite my lip to keep from crying out, the tiniest taste of metallic crossing my tastebuds, and I'm sure I'm bleeding.

As I begin to shudder, I reach down, grasping for his hand, holding it against my mouth, a scream rising in my throat, as his fingers dig into my thigh, and he groans.

A few more small grinds against him and I stop moving. Slowly, I lower his hand from my mouth, dragging it down my chest and breathing heavily. It takes me a moment to gather myself, to regain the ability to think and move as I tremble on top of him.

Climbing off him, I lie on my side, my head against his chest. He wraps his arm around my waist, squeezing my waist. "That was fucking hot, Shay."

I can't help but smirk. I reach my arm across his body to trace along the words written on his ribs. The words I know by heart, the song being one of my favorites. I still can't get over us together. After all those years of longing for him, and now he's mine. And he loves me.

"I know I'm really going to regret this, but we need to get dressed before we go to sleep. I don't want to run into a situation where we're scrambling in the morning."

I nod, avoiding pulling away from him. "I know."

He kisses the top of my head before sliding out from under me. Bending down, he pulls on his boxers, walking over to his dresser and pulling out a pair of pants and a shirt. He rifles through his bag to pull out another pair of pants.

"So, I'm going to make a recommendation." Somewhat clumsily, he yanks his pants on, coming over to sit next to me on the bed. "I think you should wear just this"—he hands me a shirt—"and keep the pants on the floor for the morning. I mean, it's just my suggestion."

"I think it's one I can get on board with."

I scramble to my knees, pulling the shirt over my head. "How do I look?"

He tackles me down to the pillows, holding my hands down under his. "Very sexy." His mouth is on my neck, giving a tiny nip before he rolls to his side.

I turn my back to him, snuggling down for sleep as he ropes his arm around me, pulling me tight against him. Kissing the top of my ear, he whispers, "Good night, baby girl. I love you."

"I love you too, Lochlyn." The words I've always wanted to say and never thought I'd be able to are finally a reality. I fall asleep the only way I want to for my birthday, wrapped up in Lochlyn.

Chapter 8

Lochlyn's birthday is two weeks after mine, a few days after Valentine's Day. He's turning twenty-one, and I'm somewhat heartbroken we can't spend it together.

"Come visit me," he suggests during one of our nightly phone calls.

"I can't." I twist my fingers into my bedspread as disappointment floods through me like a tidal wave.

"Why not?" It's a good question. There really isn't any reason.

"You know, I don't know. I guess I can. What do I tell Chelsea?" Hope starts to lighten the load that weighs me down daily.

"Tell her you're going away with *John* for Valentine's Day."

A small laugh escapes before I can stop it. He's not fond of the name John. I've had to assure him more than once it was just the first name to blurt out of my mouth.

"The *John* she still hasn't met?"

"Yeah, I'm not sure how much longer you'll be able to keep that going."

"I kind of have a plan. I was thinking of saying he transferred into a four-year school. Something like that. I don't know. I hate this."

"There are only two alternatives, Shay." We've had this discussion a lot. The only alternative is to tell her, which is Lochlyn's vote, but I have on good authority that it will not go well. The other is for us to break up, which neither of us sees as a valid option.

"I'll figure something out. I just want to be with you on your birthday."

"Okay. But I want you staying the whole weekend. I don't want you driving eight hours in two days."

"You did it for me."

"I know. And I know how hard it is. If you haven't noticed, I'm very protective of you. Plus, I want you here longer. One night wasn't enough." No, one night certainly wasn't enough.

"Okay. I'm not sure what to tell my mom. Though I don't even know if she'll notice if I'm not around."

"She'll notice, Shay. It may not seem like it, but I'm sure she misses you."

"Maybe. I don't know. Tell me about your day."

We spend the rest of our hour-long phone call talking about our days, how much we miss each other. We work out the logistics of my trip up to see him. His actual birthday is on Wednesday. I want to go up on that day, but he doesn't want either of us missing classes and wants me to stay as long as possible.

The next day, I decide to broach the subject with Mom.

"Hey, Mom. I was thinking of taking a weekend trip around Valentine's Day, if that's okay with you?" I start the conversation gently while having a snack in the office of the store.

"Where are you going?" Mom's eyes stay on her paperwork, pen hovering in the air.

"Up to Ithaca. Cornell's doing something for accepted students. I know I've seen the campus and stuff, but it was a long time ago, and I just want to refresh my memory before the fall." Lies, so many lies. They come way too easily, and with each one, I feel less and less guilty.

"Oh, that sounds nice. Do you need a hotel room?"

"No, they have some type of housing. Or Lochlyn offered me his couch."

"And you're comfortable to drive yourself up there? Why don't you bring Chelsea with you?"

"No!" I tense at her suggestion, but force a breath to calm myself. "Uh, no, that's okay. She's going to be with her boyfriend. I think she said he has to work on Valentine's Day. I'll be fine. It's good for me to practice the drive now anyway."

"Okay, if you're sure."

"Yeah, I am. I'd really like to go." Eagerness brings me to my toes and I bounce a few times before lowering to flat feet. While she could say no, it doesn't really cross my mind and I'm not sure she'd have a leg to stand on.

"Alright then. Let me know if you need anything for the trip."

"I will."

"I'm going to head back out to the floor now, if that's okay?"

"Sure, Mom." As she walks away from me, I realize I can't remember the last time I saw my mom at home. I know she's there, know she sleeps there at night, but I can't place when I last physically *saw* her in the house.

I knew the conversation with Mom would be easy. I'm not as confident about the one I have to have with Chelsea. She has a way of seeing through me. I feel like I've been lucky so far that she hasn't figured anything out. Her time is so prioritized with Brendan; I thank my lucky stars for him and his presence in her life, especially because it takes her attention from me.

We're studying in my room, which really means I'm studying and Chelsea's on her phone, a few days before I leave.

"Oh, I forgot to tell you. I'm going to be gone this weekend." I try to sound nonchalant, glancing sideways at her without lifting my face from the book.

"You're what? We're never apart! Where are you going?" Never being apart is a bit of a stretch, since we've spent many a weekend not together and she's always with Brendan these days, but I understand why she's being dramatic in this moment.

"John wants to take me somewhere for Valentine's Day."

"John? The same John that I've never met?" I don't need to look at her to know her arms are crossed against her chest.

"The very same."

"How are you going to let him take you away for the weekend when I haven't even met him yet?"

"Because you don't need to meet him for me to like him or go away with him." I finally pull my eyes from the book to look at her.

"If he's taking you away, you know what that means, right?" Her eyebrows dance across her forehead.

I play dumb. "No, what does it mean?"

"That he wants to have sex! Oh, Shay, might my pretty little virgin finally be deflowered?"

My cheeks burn before I have a chance to knock it down.

"OHMYGOD, it's already happened! Why didn't you tell me? How was it? When? Where? Tell me everything." She throws her phone down and hops closer to me on the bed, eyes wide and eager.

Damn my body's quick response to blush! It's going to be very uncomfortable to tell her the details while knowing it all happened with her brother and not imaginary John. But I know I'm not going to be able to get away with not telling her at least something. When Chelsea wants something, she's like a dog with a bone. I'll never get her off my back if I don't tell her now.

I take a deep breath to prepare myself. "Well, it was around New Year's and—"

"New Year's and you didn't fucking tell me? It's been over a month, Shay!"

"Do you want to hear or not?" I straighten up to look at her.

"Okay, okay, I'll be quiet." She points her finger at me. "You still should have told me."

"Hi, personal business."

"I always tell you!"

"That doesn't mean I want to know. Can I continue?"

"Please do." She motions with her hand that I may, in fact, continue.

"Okay, so around New Year's. We were at his house, watching TV, and he kissed me. He said he wanted to do more, I let him, and it led to sex." I keep my voice as neutral as possible.

"That's it? That's all I get?" She looks disappointed, as her stories are usually much longer and far more informative.

"I'm not giving you intimate details."

"At least tell me how it was. Or I guess, is."

"It's...incredible." So incredible.

"Aw, yay, Shay. I'm so happy for you. I knew you'd find somebody that makes you happy."

"I really am." Happy doesn't even feel strong enough to describe it. Happy is how you feel after eating ice cream or drinking a good cup of coffee. This is more in line with absolute, life-altering elation.

"Okay, so, do you want to go buy, like, lingerie before your trip?"

I hadn't thought about that. Is it something Lochlyn would like? Or expects at some point? It'd make a nice birthday present, I'm pretty sure. Isn't it something all guys want?

"I don't know. Should I?" I'm not sure it's right to trust Chelsea on this, but I'm going to, anyway. She'd never intentionally lead me down the wrong path, but the guys she's interested in and Lochlyn are so different.

"I mean, you know I love every and any excuse to shop. Is he the sort of guy that would like lingerie? Most do, so it's usually a safe bet."

"I'm not sure. It hasn't come up, not that it would, I guess. How do I know if he's the sort of guy?" Confusion swirls in my mind.

"Like I said, most guys do. But if he hasn't hinted at it or anything, maybe not? Why don't we run over to the mall and take a look around. Maybe you'll find something you like. I know it's probably a little uncomfortable and different for you. And if he seems happy and content with what's going on, then maybe don't go too crazy?" This is one of the times I'm so thankful for Chelsea. She knows how I feel about it, and isn't being pushy or eager.

"I guess I can do that. Mall sounds good."

She flips her books closed and hops off the bed. "Okay, good, let's go now."

"Chelsea. Studying? Does that mean *anything* to you?" Not that I can really concentrate right now, but I'd be able to power through. I think.

"Nope. Let's go."

Sighing, I close my books. I know I'll be fine, but I worry about Chelsea. I put it out of my mind as I let her lead me through the mall and help me pick out a few things to try on, leaving the ultimate decision up to me.

Trying on lingerie is such a foreign concept to me. Even bras and panties are more of a necessity than something I do thinking I want to look sexy. But being with Lochlyn, knowing he's going to see it, I want to find something that will amaze him. Looking at myself in the mirror, I *feel* sexy, for the first time ever.

That night, while I'm on the phone with Lochlyn, I feel a little giddy.

"What's going on, babe? You sound excited." There's a lilt in his tone that tells me he's smiling.

"I'm looking forward to this weekend. To seeing you." I'm so wired I can barely sit still, pacing my room and fiddling with things on my desk.

"I am too, but you sound almost...secretive."

"I may have bought one or two things at the mall today." I had decided on a lacy red bra and panty set and a tight lacy black bustier with matching panties.

"Oh, really?" His deepened voice sends shock waves through me.

"Yeah. I'm kind of excited for you to see them."

"I guess now I have an extra reason to be excited for you to come visit."

"I told Chelsea today."

"How'd that go?" His voice changes from fun and flirty to more serious.

"I think it went okay. I told her that John wanted to take me away for Valentine's Day and then she assumed we were having sex, so I kind of had to let her know. She was mad I hadn't told her."

"That's kind of awkward."

"Yeah. I mean, it was for me. As far as she's concerned, it was John. But knowing that I was telling her about our first time and that it was really you and not *John*, was kind of strange. Made me feel weird." I pick at some pilling on my comforter.

"I can imagine. I'm sorry, baby."

"It's okay. Nothing I can do about it. I knew at some point she'd figure it out or I'd have to tell her sex was involved. It's just a matter of who it's *actually* with."

"How much did you have to give her?"

"I tried to be as nonspecific as possible. Said around New Year's, that we were watching TV, and you, he, you...this is confusing. I'm going to say you, because obviously it was with you." I'm rambling from a mixture of excitement and leftover nerves from telling Chelsea. "Anyway, I said we were watching TV, you kissed me, and that one thing led to another." My fingers work a string loose from the stitching on my blanket. "That's it?"

"Yup."

"And she was okay with that?"

"I kind of gave her a hard time that it's personal. She was pissed I didn't tell her earlier, since it was over a month ago."

"I hate that she's so in your business," he grumbles.

"I mean, hello, she's in yours too."

"She *thinks* she's in mine, but she doesn't really know anything. I let her believe what she wants, correct her when it's important. I mean, shit, Shay, she reads your messages. I can't send you half of the things I want to in a text because she may see." Irritation hangs off his words, and I know it's because of the situation. If he had it his way, she'd already know.

"I like our cryptic messages. It's kind of our thing." My voice is mousier than I like, feeling less enthused about our way of communicating.

"I do too. It *is* our thing. But there are things I'd like to be able to say to you that I'm not sure I can because I'm worried about Chelsea seeing it." There's a softness to his tone as he reassures me.

"You can say them now."

"I know. It's just frustrating." It's disheartening, to say the least. My shoulders slump as I internally deflate. It's my fault he feels this way, my fault he's frustrated.

I bite my lip, not really sure what to say. There are tons of things I want to be able to tell him that I can't because it would be clear as day that I'm *not* talking to John.

"I'm just excited that I'll be able to hold you again in a few days." His voice is low and throaty. It sends a tingle through my whole body.

"Me too. I'm taking shirts home with me, so if you're going to be picky about what's missing, have some ready."

He chuckles, making my heart flutter. "Okay, I'll be sure to make you a pile. Should I wear them for a little bit first?"

"Oh, yes, please. Especially if you're wearing your cologne."

"I'll wear each one for about an hour before you come on Friday. What time do you think you're getting in?"

"My class ends at eleven thirty. I figured I'd leave from there. It's a little closer than home, so I'm thinking around three? Maybe three thirty? Chelsea said something about grabbing lunch and giving me some sort of pep talk first. For what, I have no idea. But if we do lunch, I'll make sure it's quick."

"Okay. Just make sure it doesn't get too late. I'll feel better if you're not driving in the dark."

Even before we started dating, he was protective of me. Then, I'd always assumed he was just being nice, looking out for his sister's best friend. Now, I know it was because he had feelings for me.

"I will. I'm far too eager to be there to waste even a second." I take a deep breath, looking at the time. It's getting late. I have an early class in the morning. But saying goodbye is the worst part of my day.

"You should be going to bed, baby girl. It's late." It's like he can read my mind.

"I know. I just, I don't want to say goodbye." That's always the most painful part. The moment silence fills my ear.

"I don't either, but you'll be here in a few days."

"It can't come soon enough."

"No, it certainly can't. Go to sleep, my beautiful girl." How does one not swoon over such sweet words? He's always saying something that makes me want to hug him, kiss him, adore him.

"Okay. Good night, baby. Happy early birthday. I'll call you after my class tomorrow. I love you."

"I love you, too. Dream of me."

"I always do." Pressing the end button is always the hardest part. I hate cutting the connection.

Climbing into bed, I'm worn down. This long-distance thing is for the birds. The shirt I'd made Lochlyn let me keep before he left from my birthday visit barely smells like him anymore. Even still, I slide the collar up over my nose as I close my eyes, hoping what little smell is left will trigger wonderful dreams.

Chapter 9

I get to Lochlyn's at four on Friday. Chelsea kept me longer than I wanted, but I'm happy I've eaten and gotten a coffee before hitting the road. The drive isn't as bad as I was anticipating, never really having done this far of a drive by myself before.

For some reason, I'm jittery as I stand in front of Lochlyn's door. I'm not really sure what to expect. It also could be the matching bra and panty set I have on under my clothes.

Taking a deep breath, I knock on the door. It flies open within seconds as Lochlyn's beaming face appears on the other side. He grabs me by the belt loops and pulls me into the apartment, my body crashing into his as my bag falls to the floor. His mouth is colliding with mine before I'm even across the threshold.

His hand slips up to cup my cheek as he pulls away. "I missed you."

"I missed you, too."

"So, this is the place. Nothing too exciting." I take in his apartment. It's a large rectangular room. The right half appears to be the living room with a dark brown sofa and loveseat, a huge flat screen TV hangs on one wall, two tall bookcases stand on the opposite one. To the left is the kitchen, which has an eat-at bar, granite counters, and stainless-steel appliances. There's a hallway straight across from the front door, down which I can see three doorknobs. There are hardwood floors as far as I can see. It's a much nicer apartment than I'd expect for college students, but I know Lochlyn's parents paid for it.

"Where's Weston?" Lochlyn's told me a lot about his roommate turned friend Weston, but I notice we're alone as I take off my coat.

"Oh, he, uh, graciously gave us the apartment for the weekend. His birthday present to me."

"Why would he do that?" I know exactly why, but part of me wants to hear Lochlyn say it. Or more so, I want him to show me.

He leans in and starts kissing my neck. "Well, because there are things I want to do to you that he knows would be a little awkward if he was still hanging around." His mouth is still against my neck as he speaks. He peppers gentle kisses across my shoulder, pushing my collar to the side, running his hands down my arms. My head tilts back, and a tiny moan escapes as his hands settle on my hips, thumbs rubbing against the bone as his mouth works up my neck.

When his mouth finds mine again, there's an urgency behind it. His hand wraps around the base of my skull, fingers tangling in my hair, pulling the slightest bit as he tips my head back. As my mouth parts for his, our tongues collide, and as the kiss intensifies, his free hand slips under the hem of my shirt.

I tilt back to look at him, but he pulls me against him, mouth latching just under my jaw and kissing down my neck. A moan is my only response.

"You really don't want to do anything for your birthday?" It all comes out breathless.

"Oh, I definitely do," he says against my neck. Then his eyes meet mine. "You."

His mouth crashes to mine again, his fingers still in my hair. My chest is pressed so firmly against his, there's pressure in my breasts. His tight grip makes it so I can feel his muscles cord. I wouldn't be able to move if I wanted to.

It's a new sort of urgency, borderline aggressive, but I like it. It just shows me how much he wants me.

His hands slide to under my thighs as he pulls me up, and I loop my legs around him, his mouth shifting to my throat.

"You're feisty today," I say as his fingers dig into my thighs.

"I've really fucking missed you."

Once we're in his room, he sets me down in front of the bed. His hands move the hem of my shirt when I stop him, grabbing his wrists. Our faces are so close, his warm breath puffs against my cheek with his heavy exhale.

"I have a surprise for you." I try to use the sexiest voice I can muster.

His eyebrow quirks up. "Oh, really?"

"You just have to unwrap it first." I take his hands in mine and put them on my hips. Hand over hand, I slide my pants down as far as I can reach while standing straight. He crouches down, pulling them the rest of the way, holding my calf as he pulls them off.

Standing back up slowly, his fingers trail one leg while his lips gently caress their way up the other. He doesn't stop once he gets to the hem of my shirt, fingers slipping underneath and pulling it off in one quick movement.

Taking a step back, his eyes slowly graze over my body, his breath catching, eyes widening, pants tightening around his bulge. When his eyes meet mine, there's a glint in them, quickly replaced by an insatiable hunger.

Reaching behind his head, he tears his shirt off and drops it to the floor. Every time I see his bare chest, my breath stalls in my chest. My fingers move on their own, starting at his shoulders and gently tracing down over the ridges, my right hand gliding over to his ribs to trace along the words scrawled there.

I pull my lip between my teeth as I continue to stare at his perfection, still in awe that he's mine. Lochlyn takes my chin between his fingers and pushes upward, tilting my face up as his mouth closes over mine.

With a gentle shove, I'm falling backward to the bed with a giggle as Lochlyn rips off his pants. He starts kissing at my ankle, slowly working his way up my leg, taking excruciatingly long. When he gets to my panties, he kisses along the waistband, hip to hip, before taking the material between his teeth. Fire rages through my body as he slowly starts to pull them off, still tightly between his teeth, fingers hooked under the sides.

The suspense is tantalizing. It's been two long weeks since he's touched me, since I've felt him inside me. Every single one of my nerve endings is lit like a fuse, ready to explode. I sigh as he slips my panties over my ankles, dropping them to the floor, along with his boxers, and slowly glides his body over mine.

His hands slide up my body, flat palms running over my breasts as he kisses along my bra line. Moving his mouth over one breast, he bites my nipple, causing me to yelp and peel my back off the mattress at the shock it sends through me. Lochlyn seizes the opportunity to reach behind me, flicking his wrist as he unclasps my red lace bra, pulling it off and throwing it across the room.

My knee bends, leg wrapping around his waist as his mouth closes around my nipple, his fingers trailing down my torso. His breathing halts and he leans his forehead against my chest, releasing my nipple, as he reaches between my legs.

"Fuck, Shay," he whispers against my chest.

All at once, his lips close around my nipple again as he pushes two fingers inside me. My back arches, fingers tangling in his hair, as he moves his tongue and fingers in sync with one an-other.

"Loch." I sigh his name as the pressure builds.

Before I can release, he pulls away, leaning over me, wiping my hair back from my face. He takes my chin in his hand, reaching with his thumb to pull my lower lip down as his mouth closes gently around mine as he pushes into me.

A low moan eases from my throat as he moves inside me. My fingers wrap around his shoulders, nails digging in.

He adjusts, taking my leg and lifting it up so my calf rests against his shoulder. At the change in position and all the points it hits inside me, I can't hold back anymore, tightening around him, clawing at his arms as I call out his name.

It only makes him go faster, harder, the sound of skin slapping skin flooding my ears. Until he stops, pulling out of me, lowering my leg. He grabs my waist and flips me to my stomach, pulling my hips into the air and sinking into me. My hands tighten into the sheets as I moan loudly. There's a reason this position became my favorite over the break.

Lochlyn's hands are at my hips, thumbs rubbing as low as they can, fingers digging into my bones. I push up on my hands, my head tipping back as I curse under my breath. As he wraps my hair around his hand, a smile works across my face. Everything about it feels so damn good. His hand on my hips and in my hair with a gentle tug, the feeling of him thrusting inside me. It's like he was built for me and my pleasure.

Through the flutter of my eyelids, I see Lochlyn's head tipping backward, his eyes closing. The tiny glimpse of him so clearly enjoying himself with me and my body brings me over the edge again as I start to shudder, hands pulling at the sheets as I scream and collapse my upper half against the bed. Air hisses through his teeth and I feel him pulsate inside me and his movements slow.

Trailing his hands up my back and down again, he pulls away, flopping to his back, breathing hard. I keep my eyes on him, peering through strands of my hair, as I let my legs fall to the bed.

He flips an arm over his eyes, showing the lyric on his bicep. It always makes my heart flutter, seeing his tattoos. They're such an integral and personal part of him. But only I know the meaning behind them.

Without uncovering his eyes, he reaches his other arm out to me, searching for my body. "Come here."

I slink over to him, putting my head on his chest, feeling his heart hammering beneath my cheek. Closing my eyes, I listen. It's a sound I've missed every day. The slow circles begin on my hip.

"Did you like your birthday present?" My fingers start swirling along his chest.

"I *loved* my birthday present. Very sexy." The way he speaks is slow and drawn out, clearly tired.

"Good. I'm glad."

He pulls his arm out from under me, turning on his side, propping up on his elbow. The hand that had been over his eyes starts running down my side and back up again.

"I just want you to know that I don't need anything like that. I don't expect you to start wearing that. Especially not for me. If you want to, that's one thing. But I don't expect it or need it."

I look down at the sheet, twiddling some fabric between my fingers. "Did you...did you not like it?"

Glancing up at him, I see his eyes widen as he tugs my hip closer to him. "No, no, baby, I *loved* it. Trust me. I just think you're plenty sexy without it."

I shrug. "It was kind of fun. Like I had a dirty little secret. It made me feel a little more confident, I guess? I don't know. It was fun, though, shopping with Chelsea."

"I should have known Chelsea was involved." There's a grumble to his tone, but not too intense.

"Her intentions were in the right place. She didn't say I had to, didn't push anything on me...much. She didn't even force herself into the dressing room while I tried things on."

"Wow, that *is* surprising."

"Are you sure you liked it?"

He leans in and kisses me, twirling a curl as he pulls away. "Baby, I loved it."

Whatever confidence the bra and panty set had brought me is now gone. "I, uh, I bought another one."

Lochlyn quirks up an eyebrow. "Oh, really?"

I just nod in response, having lost my voice.

"Do I get to see it?"

"If you want to."

"Oh, I definitely want to."

I bite my lip and slide off the bed, crouching by my suitcase and pulling it out. I hold the bustier up and watch as his eyes grow wide, and he hardens.

"I am very much looking forward to seeing that on you. Can you make it a surprise again? Don't tell me when you're going to wear it, just put it on under your shirt."

I giggle. "I wasn't expecting to do much getting dressed."

"I figure while you're here, I'll take you over to campus, out to dinner, maybe take you around Ithaca a bit."

"Really?"

"Yeah, of course. I have to show off my girl."

A giant smile spans my face as I climb back up next to him. We've never been able to go places and really be together, always having to sneak around. It'll be a nice change.

"I'm starving. Come on, I'm making you dinner." His hand squeezes my hip.

"Me? Dinner? Well, I feel very special."

Leaning in, he kisses me tenderly. "You are very special."

Lochlyn hops off the bed and pulls on a pair of sweatpants, leaving the room with a quick wink that makes me turn into jelly. I rifle through his drawers and pull out a t-shirt, slipping it over my head and pulling the collar to my nose. *Lochlyn*.

I pad out into the kitchen where he's already begun pulling out an assortment of vegetables. I lean against the doorframe, not really sure what to do with myself.

"Come here." His voice is deep, commanding.

I skip over to him. Putting his hands on my waist, he lifts me up, setting me on the granite. Even though I'm on the counter, his height makes him still stand about an inch taller than me.

"Now, I know you can't really help, but maybe watching me, you'll learn something. At the very least, you'll be close to me."

"What are you making?"

"I am making you pizza."

"Pizza?" I'm fairly certain I've never had homemade pizza before. On one hand, I'm shocked Lochlyn knows how to make it. On the other, there are few things he does and reveals that don't make sense. And this falls into that category.

"Mhm. With peppers and onions." He remembers. I said it once in passing over six months ago, but he remembers.

"Well, I'm just the luckiest girl in the world."

I watch as he kneads the dough. I love watching him work with his hands; it reminds me of how well he uses them on me. While he cuts the peppers and onions, I pay close attention, watching the way he works his knife, the caution but ease and speed while chopping. He's comfortable in the kitchen.

As he stretches the dough to fit a pizza pan, I reach over and grab a piece of pepper, popping it into my mouth. He shoots me a glance. I lean over and grab another, which receives a harsher glance and disapproving tsk as he puts the dough in the oven. When I reach over a third time, he playfully smacks my hand, which causes me to grab a small handful instead.

His fingers are digging into my waist before I can react. Holding my prize between my hands, I try to fold in on myself, leaning into Lochlyn's shoulder instead. I squeal and scream at the onslaught, trying to move away but also not fall off the counter at the same time.

"Had enough?" he asks, putting his hands on either side of me.

I nod, too breathless to answer. I'm acutely aware of how close his face is to mine. We stare at each other intently for a minute before our mouths are crashing against each other's.

The peppers fall around us with hollow plops as I rope my hands around his neck and into his hair, parting my mouth for his as his tongue sweeps across mine. His hands rest on my knees, sliding up my thighs, pushing my legs apart as he takes a step closer. As his hands reach my upper thigh, he digs his fingers in, pulling me closer to him.

He smirks as his hands glide the rest of the way up, and he notices I'm not wearing any panties.

Everything intensifies and speeds up. I reach for his pants as he pushes them down, tugging me to the edge of the counter as he pushes into me. His fingers dig into my upper thighs as I wrap my hand around the back of his neck.

As my upper body tips back, and my free hand grips the side edge of the counter, I'm vaguely aware of the voice in the back of my head. It's telling me I'm having sex, on the kitchen counter. Hard, fast, inappropriate location sex. Then I realize it's probably what Chelsea would consider fucking. Lochlyn's fucking me in his kitchen.

Who is this person? Where did she come from? I've gone from shy wallflower, shrinking at the gaze of guys, especially the gorgeous one inside me, to fucking on the counter and walking around his apartment basically naked.

The dreams I have about him have changed from sweet to sexy. Some sex had always been included, but I hadn't known what it felt like. The sweet still exists, since he's the sweetest man I know, but I can't imagine that sex can feel any better than it does with Lochlyn. Even if it does, I don't ever want to find out.

While the voice in my head is having a full monolog, my actual voice is making all kinds of pleasure sounds. Tiny beads of sweat are starting to accumulate on my forehead and chest.

Before I hear the voice tell me I shouldn't be doing what I'm so clearly enjoying, the pressure that has been building with every thrust releases as my nails dig into Lochlyn's neck, and I tighten around him, crying out loudly. Three more thrusts and a tiny moan rises from his throat.

He rests his forehead against my chest, my hand still around the back of his neck, as our breathing slows. I tilt my head up as he kisses along my neck and jawbone, ending on my lips.

"Who knew my girl could get a little freaky?" he asks with a smile on his face as he presses his forehead to mine.

All I can do is smile in return. In all the times I've imagined having sex, even with Lochlyn, I've never thought about anywhere other than a bed. But after that, I'm pretty sure I'd let him fuck me anywhere.

With one last kiss, he pulls away, smoothing down my shirt and adjusting his pants, checking on the dough in the oven.

"And look at that, the dough's not even burned."

I watch as he spreads the sauce on the cooked dough, sprinkling veggies on top.

"I can't stay in here," I say as I hop off the counter. His proximity and the way he looks while he cooks is too much for me.

"Why not?"

"Because I am *not* having sex on that counter again."

All I hear is him chuckling behind me as I walk into his room. Pulling on a pair of panties, I dig my book out of my bag. Not really being sure what the weekend was going to look like, I tossed two in, just in case.

I flop onto the couch, leaning against the arm as I stretch my legs down the middle, crossed at the ankle. Sounds of more chopping come from the kitchen, but the pizza smells amazing.

Sometime later, I'm not sure exactly how long having gotten lost in my book, Lochlyn comes to sit with me. He lifts my legs, placing them over his lap. His fingers trace absentmindedly up and down my calves.

Glancing up at him, I notice he's staring at me, a tiny smile on his face.

"What?" I ask, smiling in return.

He hooks some curls behind my ear. "Nothing. You're just so beautiful."

I never know what to say when he says that. Lochlyn is the first boy to compliment me. The first *person* really, aside from my parents, but I never really counted that, as parents should build their children up. All I know is that it makes my heart flutter.

"I love you."

He leans his head back against the couch, eyes still on me. "I love you, too."

That night, as we lie in bed, I can barely keep my eyes open. I didn't sleep much the night before in anticipation, and the drive took a lot out of me. Dinner had been so good. I gushed several times over how amazing it is that Lochlyn can cook, thanked him profusely, especially for remembering my favorite toppings.

I'm curled into his chest, his arm flung over my waist drawing tiny circles on my back where he's lifted my shirt. Any time I feel like I'm about to fall asleep, I force my eyes back open.

"You can go to sleep, baby. I know that drive is tiring."

"It's still early. I don't want to waste any extra time with you on sleep." My voice is low, and my words are almost slurred together.

"But you're tired. And I'll be right here, all night." My eyelids have already fluttered closed again.

"Mm, okay."

Sleep overtakes me. But not before I feel Lochlyn kiss my forehead and tell me he loves me.

When I wake up the next morning, I'm alone in bed. The scent of coffee brewing wafts in to greet me. I stretch on the large bed, a smile spreading widely across my face. For the first time in months, I'm not waking up to go to the store or class. I don't have to be anywhere. And I'm with Lochlyn. *Alone* with him, without having to hide.

I pad down the hall, hearing something sizzling from the kitchen.

"Well, good morning, sleepyhead." He looks up and smiles briefly when he sees me.

"Why are you up so early? Aren't college students supposed to sleep until, like, one?"

He chuckles. "I've always been a bit of an early riser and night owl. I can do a lot on little sleep. Plus, I slept really well." His eyes meet mine. I'd slept really well too. The comfort he brings me allowed any tension to seep out of my body and to fully relax into the bed.

"So, what are we doing today?"

"Whatever you want. I plan to take you over to campus. But other than that, it's entirely up to you."

"Got any good bookstores?"

A laugh erupts from deep in his chest. "Only you would want to find a bookstore and not a party."

"Is that a good thing or a bad thing?"

Walking away from the stove and over to me, he wraps an arm around my waist, pulling me against him and sealing his mouth over mine. "It's a *very* good thing." With a tiny kiss on my nose, he walks back into the kitchen.

The apartment isn't quite what I'd been imagining. For some reason, when I thought about an apartment two college guys shared, I'd expected it to be a disaster. Ratty, dirty. But it's nothing like that. It's a nice apartment, kept neat. I can tell it wasn't just cleaned for my benefit. Though when I really think about it, I expect no less from Lochlyn. He likes things to be neat and orderly. Not overly so, just in a way where things aren't all over the place. It's a big reason why Chelsea drives him crazy.

We eat at the counter, sipping coffee and talking about what to do with our day. Lochlyn keeps his hand on my knee the whole time. When we finish, he insists on clearing the plates, though I put up a good fight.

"I'm going to take a shower." He's already taking off his shirt as he walks out of the kitchen. "Come with me," he whispers in my ear as he passes. My body won't let me say no, and I hop out of my chair and follow him into the bathroom.

I'm up against the tiled wall, steam filling the bathroom with my legs locked around his waist as he supports me under my thighs while he pistons into me. His mouth is latched to my throat as I moan loudly when the curtain rod comes crashing down.

I shriek in terror, which causes him to laugh. Putting me down, he guides me under the stream to rinse, tipping his head into the water over mine, then shaking it out of his eyes before reaching around me to shut it off.

After wrapping a towel around his waist, he holds one out for me. I sit on the toilet seat and observe as he picks the rod up and starts putting it back against the wall. Watching his muscles ripple makes me bite my lip, hard.

"This damn thing falls like once a week," he grumbles as he twists one side.

"You have girls in your shower once a week?"

He turns over his shoulder to look at me; anger blazing in his blue irises. "That's not even a little funny."

"You're right. I'm sorry. Though maybe Weston has girls in the shower once a week."

"I have no idea what he does or doesn't do in here, but I'm getting sick of fixing this damn thing."

"That may be so, but I'm certainly enjoying watching you fix it."

Smirk planted on his face, he spins around, and puts one hand on the wall, the other on the vanity, and leans in so his lips are against mine. "Oh, really?" His muscles strain as they support his weight. It sends tingles through my body, a shiver racing down my spine and a throb settling between my legs.

"I think we should finish what we started in the shower," he says against my ear.

Before I can answer, one of his hands swoops under my legs while the other hooks around my back and he scoops me up, carrying me out of the bathroom, leaving our towels behind.

Cornell's campus is just as beautiful as I remember it from when I was younger. Gorgeous buildings with sprawling areas of greenery, though covered in snow in February, bring back all the joy it had when I first toured it. The architecture is simply stunning. It had taken my breath away the first time, and it doesn't fail to do that again.

Lochlyn holds my hand as we walk around campus. At first, I pulled away, looking around us. Then I remembered nobody here will care. I keep my fingers linked with his, leaning into him. It's a cold day, so I cling to his arm to steal his warmth.

"I can't believe you wore your Converse." He looks pointedly at my shoes.

"What? I love them!"

"Shay, it's winter. You need boots."

"I don't like boots. I like my Converse." Though, I will say, on long walks like this, my toes do freeze a bit by the end. And encountering snow or ice could result in disaster, as I've fallen more than once. But I adore the shoes too much to toss them, even just for the season.

"You grew up and live in New York. We get snow. A lot of snow. You need boots." His tone is nothing but disapproving.

I shrug. "I'll be okay."

"I'm buying you boots before next winter."

"No, you're not! I'm fine. And if I need boots, I can get them myself."

"Nope, I've already decided. I'm not taking any chances with you."

As we walk around campus, he tells me about his classes, the buildings, anything he can think of. Heads turn to follow him everywhere. It doesn't matter if we're inside the campus center or out in the cold, he's watched. I also notice a few angry glares from women, and a man or two, as we walk hand in hand. He's completely immune to it.

It's not until we run into a very attractive brunette that he takes note of how he's looked at.

"Lochlyn, hi," she says as she tucks some of her long brown hair behind her ear. She has the biggest puppy dog eyes I've ever seen, clearly very smitten with *my boyfriend.*

He has a tight-lipped smile and gives her a nod. "Leslie."

"It's nice to see you. I don't see you much around campus anymore." She hasn't even glanced over at me even though my fingers are connected with his and I'm hanging on to his arm.

"I live off campus now."

"Oh. That sounds nice. I was thinking, if you're ever free for—"

"Leslie, I'd like to introduce you to my girlfriend." He pulls his hand from mine, sliding it around my waist, his thumb hooking into my belt loop. "This is Shay."

When her eyes finally turn to me, they're filled with hatred. The old phrase *if looks could kill* immediately comes to mind. I'd assuredly be dead, right here in the middle of campus.

"Hi, nice to meet you." I extend a hand, but all she does is glare at me before storming off.

"Friend of yours?" I ask, turning my head up to look at Lochlyn.

He runs his hand down his face and starts walking again, leaving his thumb in my belt loop. "Leslie. She and I had a history class together freshman year. We talked in class, if we saw each other outside of it. Very minimal, hi, how are you type stuff. I knew she had a crush on me early on. She asked me out for coffee like once a week. I always turned her down."

"Did you guys ever..." I can't finish the sentence.

"No. God, no. She's pretty, but no. I've always turned her down. We just had that one class together one semester. But every time she sees me, she tries."

"Why was she shooting daggers at me? I mean, aside from the fact that we're together and she's very clearly jealous." Maybe it's naïve of me, but I don't think that's the best reason to look at somebody like you'd love nothing more than slowly watch all the air leave their body.

"At the end of the semester, it came to a head. Every week she invited me for coffee, and every week I turned her down. So she asked me what my deal was. I told her I don't do relationships. She said she wasn't looking for anything like that, but with how desperate she'd been just for a coffee, I knew there was no way." His eyes lock on mine. "She wasn't who I wanted to be with."

"I almost feel bad for her."

"Really?" His face scrunches as he says it.

"I do. I mean, look at you. Everywhere we go, you turn heads, girls, *and* guys. You always have. Remember my birthday? And you said you don't do girlfriends, and now here you are, with a girlfriend." Things about the look are a little clearer now. Still seems a bit extreme to me, but for Lochlyn, I get it.

"How do you know the guys aren't looking at you?"

"Trust me, when you're around, nobody's looking at me."

"I am." He stops suddenly, pulling me against him, holding my face in his hands as he kisses me. Smiling as he separates from me, he takes my hand and starts jogging toward a large building. "Come on, I think this is going to be your favorite place."

When we're outside the door, he puts his hands on my shoulders as he stands behind me. "This is Uris Library," he whispers against my ear. There's an air of mystique to his voice.

The building itself is beautiful, but once we get inside and through an interior door, my eyes widen and my jaw drops. I take slow steps into the room. There are three floors of wrought-iron shelves, filled with books upon books. You can see through the whole room and all the volumes it contains. It's a magnificent sight.

"You like it?"

All I can do is nod in response, causing a chuckle to come from Lochlyn. He wraps his arms around my waist and rests his chin on my shoulder as I continue to look around the room, completely awestruck. I hadn't toured campus before applying. The only time I had seen it before was with my parents when I was younger. If I've seen the library before, I surely didn't appreciate it.

After a few minutes and a kiss to the neck, I'm able to come to. I spin around in his arms to face him, hands resting on his chest. "Thank you for bringing me here. It's amazing."

He smiles and pulls a curl straight, grazing my breast with his hand. "You're welcome. I knew you'd appreciate it."

"Can I just live here next year?"

"Trust me, there will be times you'll feel like you do."

"That will be okay with me."

"At least I'll always know where to find you." It's not lost on me that we've only been together for a little over two months, but that he's already talking about things more than six months away. Repeatedly.

"Now we leave campus. You ready?"

"Just one more look." Both hands wrap around his forearm as I take one last glance around the room, even more excited than I already have been to be coming to Cornell in the fall.

Lochlyn takes me on a drive through Ithaca, showing me some of his favorite spots, like where he thinks the good Chinese and pizza places are. He explains that the town has a lot to offer and if it had been warmer, we'd be walking.

Finding a parking spot along the street, he takes me into a bookstore. Lochlyn stands close behind me, fingers through my belt loop, thumb under the waistband of my pants as I browse through the shelves.

He doesn't rush me. Keeping pace with me, hand at my hip the whole time, chest pressed to my back. Every so often, he'll pick something up with his free hand and give a quick flip through. I've started to collect a small pile that he takes from me and holds under his arm.

"Okay, let me go through my stack and decide which ones I'm going to get." I reach out for the books, but he pulls them away, walking toward the checkout and placing them at the register.

"Lochlyn, no. I can't let you buy my books." I try to reach for them, but he puts a hand on my chest, holding me in place.

"Yes, you can."

I point at him. "You're an enabler."

"At least it's a good habit."

"Seriously, let me pay for them." I extend my hand toward the stack again, which he lowers back to my side.

"No. Consider it a late birthday present." This time, he leans against the counter, effectively blocking me from them.

"You came home for my birthday. That was my present."

"Then consider it a boyfriend buying something for his girl-friend. That happens, you know. I can't do these things for you when we're home. Let me do them this weekend."

I sigh, but finally acquiesce.

"Besides, I like that you read. It's just another thing to love about you."

We spend the rest of the day around town. He buys me a few more things, including a Cornell t-shirt, in his size, that he promises to wear before giving to me. He even takes me to Wegmans, a grocery store that seems to be some sort of religious experience for those who frequent it. He says I'll understand when I live here.

That night, he takes me to dinner at a Japanese restaurant, knowing that I never refuse sushi. As we sit waiting for our food, a tiny laugh bubbles up from my chest.

"What's so funny?" he asks with narrowed eyes but a smile on his face.

"We've been together for, I don't know, anywhere from one and a half to two and a half months, depending on when you'd say we started this, and this is our first date."

His face drops. "I know. I'm sorry."

"No! Don't be sorry. God, maybe I said that wrong. I don't want you to feel bad. Our situation doesn't exactly lend to dating. Or being in public."

His mouth presses into a hard line. I notice his hand on the table and take it in mine, linking our fingers. "Hey. I had a really great day today. It was nice to be able to be a normal couple for once. No hiding, no secrets, no lies. Don't feel bad because you can't give that to me every day. I knew what I was getting myself into."

Fingers tightening around mine, he brings my hand to his mouth and kisses my knuckles. "You deserve so much more."

When we get back to the apartment, lips fused as our hands are roaming over each other's bodies in the hallway, we open the door to quite a surprise.

Weston is sitting on the couch, causing us to jump apart.

"Hey, Lochlyn. Uh, sorry, I know you weren't expecting me." He turns to me. "Hi, you must be Shay. I'm Wes." I take Weston in quickly. He has a head of thick black hair, cobalt blue eyes, and is almost as tall as Lochlyn. Good looking in his own right, but nobody comes close to Lochlyn.

"Wes, what the fuck are you doing here?" There's no denying the irritation in Lochlyn's voice.

"Claire kicked me out." He shoves his hands in his pockets and tips up on his toes.

"What? Why?" He turns to me. "Claire is his on-and-off girl-friend. Who he was *supposed to be* with this weekend."

"Yeah, about that. She found out I slept with her roommate. Threw me out." He runs a hand through his hair.

"Shit."

"Yeah. Anyway, Shay, it's nice to finally meet you. Lochlyn talks about you constantly." I tilt my head to look up at Lochlyn and find his cheeks tinged pink, running a hand up and down the back of his head. I'm not sure I've ever seen him embarrassed before.

"Well, that's very nice to hear. I'm sorry about your girl...trou-bles." Before I let an opportunity slip through my hands, I speak up again. "So, do you have any embarrassing stories about Loch?"

Wes's face lights up as I hear Lochlyn groan behind me. "Oh, tons. Come sit."

I make my way over to the couch, grabbing Lochlyn's hand. He huffs and drags his feet behind me. Sitting next to Wes on the couch, upright and perky, ready to hear some juicy stories,

Lochlyn sits slouched low in his seat next to me. I move myself closer to him, so my back is touching his arm, which he then wraps around my middle, pulling me against his side and hooking his thumb under the band of my jeans. His head is hung, his other hand rubbing his eyes. He's not looking forward to the conversation about to happen. I'm just happy he's allowing me to indulge.

Pulling my feet under me, I'm ready.

Wes jumps right in. He spares no detail. There are so many stories I can't keep them straight. He goes on and on with drunken stories, once finding Lochlyn on the bathroom floor in the dorm. He tells me about the first impression he'd had of Lochlyn, thinking he'd never get laid with a roommate like him who was sure to get all the girls, which Wes assured me he could have. That earns a glare from Lochlyn. But Weston doesn't falter.

In the end, I'm in stitches, as is Wes. Lochlyn isn't quite as happy, though. He hasn't said a word and I've felt him tense more than once, and groan at least ten times. I lean back, across his chest, running my hand down his cheek. His eyes meet mine, but they're strained. I lean up and kiss him, which makes him soften a little.

"That's cute." Wes pulls me out of my trance with Lochlyn, causing me to sit up again.

"So, I didn't hear any stories about girls." I haven't broached the subject with Lochlyn. I'm not sure he'd actually tell me the truth. He tries to spare my feelings with anything he thinks may upset me. But I knew he had a lot more experience than I did when we got into everything.

Wes's eyes flash to Lochlyn's, which I'm sure are very strictly saying *no way in hell*, but Wes turns back to me. "Honestly? He can have any girl he wants. Like, literally any girl."

"Yes, we ran into Leslie today."

"Oh, well, she's a little cuckoo. But I've known Loch for over two years now. One thing I can say for certain is that he has *never* talked about a girl the way he talks about you. Not even close. He's never brought a girl back to this apartment." That means he hadn't slept with anybody since a few months before he kissed me.

"And before that?"

"Let's just say it's been a while. A long while. And that he talked about you before you got together."

I hear Lochlyn sigh behind me. I'm not sure if he's upset because Wes is lying, which by looking at him, I don't think he is, or if it's because Wes has divulged information Lochlyn wanted to keep hidden. He's already told me he's wanted to be with me for years. But Wes made it known that he talked about me, thought about me. He insinuated that Lochlyn hadn't slept with other girls because of me.

Leaning back over my boyfriend's chest, I pull his hand from his eyes. His jaw is clenched. I adjust myself on the couch so I can sit with my head against his shoulder, my legs thrown over his.

After I sit curled into him for a minute or two, he sighs again and puts his arms around me, fingers lacing together at my waist as he kisses my forehead. I dip my fingertip under the collar of his shirt and run it back and forth across his warm skin.

"You guys are cute together. So, how is this working? You sneak around, right?"

I try to turn around to talk to Wes, but Lochlyn won't let me, tightening his arms around me.

"Yeah, it's not a great situation to be in. We basically just see each other when Chelsea's otherwise occupied, whether at work or with her boyfriend," Lochlyn answers for me.

"That sounds...tricky."

"It is. And I don't exactly like lying to my sister. Shay's lying to her best friend, but it's worth it. To me, at least." I'm happy he leaves out the part about wanting to tell Chelsea and that I've repeatedly and emphatically said no. There's enough blame that I place on myself for that one and how it affects Lochlyn.

I tilt my head up to look at him. "Me too." As much as I hate lying to Chelsea, having to hide to be together, being with Lochlyn is worth it. Every lie, every secret meeting, it's all worth it.

Chapter 10

Only two weeks had separated the times Lochlyn and I were away from each other after New Year's. Two weeks after he went back until my birthday, two weeks until his. Yet after that, we have a longer wait. The time between his birthday and the break in March is an excruciatingly long six weeks.

I cry more than once on the phone about how much I miss him, hearing his strained voice as he tries to tell me it'll be okay, that he loves me, that it isn't as long as it seems. Every day feels both better and worse. We're one day closer, but the feeling of him being gone is more and more real as each day wears on.

"What's wrong with you? You've been in such an awful mood lately," Chelsea asks me one day after class.

"Huh? Oh, nothing." I barely hear her over my own thoughts.

"Did something happen with you and John?"

"No, we're fine." I've gotten so used to her saying John, that I don't hesitate anymore. For a little while, it was awkward when she'd ask after him and I'd respond with a blank stare.

"I know it's been hard since he transferred." I had told Chelsea yet another lie, saying that John transferred to a different school at the start of the semester. She gave me a little bit of a hard time that I hadn't mentioned him earlier, but thankfully, let it go quickly.

"Yeah, you could say that. I miss him." Hiding behind the guise of John allows me to share feelings, like longing.

"He'll be home soon, though, right? Only two or so more weeks." My heart flutters as the date Lochlyn will be home grows ever closer. But it also aches.

"Yeah, something like that. I don't like to think about it."

"You're so strung out on him! I can't even believe it."

Strung out barely covers it. I love Lochlyn more than I ever thought possible. And in only a few months.

"I'm just excited I'll be able to see him again soon." See him, touch him, kiss him, feel him. It's all the same.

Over a week later, I'm gushing on the phone as I bounce on the edge of my bed. "You'll be home in three days!"

"I know. I wish you were more excited."

"Stop. Don't make fun of me," I whine as I outwardly pout.

"I'm sorry, I'm not. It's cute that you're so excited." It's clear he's smiling from his intonation.

"Are you not excited?" I work my lip between my teeth.

"Oh no, I'm plenty excited."

"You have a funny way of showing it," I grumble.

"I'm sorry it doesn't sound like it, but trust me, I'm counting down the hours to hold you again."

It feels like I have a balloon filling in my chest. Then I hear clicks in the background. *Pop.*

"You're typing." The clicking stops.

"No." It almost sounds more like a question, and he's not at all convincing.

"You were. You were typing." We have a strict "no school work or outside conversation" rule during our phone calls. And that agitation is not left out of my tone.

"I'm sorry, I was talking to somebody about my econ midterm."

"They're *all* econ midterms."

The sound of his exhale fills my ear. "I'm sorry."

"You owe me extra time."

"I can agree to those terms."

"So, somebody..." I can't quite ask the question on my tongue. Does this somebody have breasts?

"It's not a girl, Shay. And even if it was, it doesn't mean I'm going to invite her over and have crazy, wild sex with her." His voice is clipped and tight. He's frustrated with me.

"Okay." I can't get my voice to be level, and it raises at the end with unsaid disbelief.

"Shay. It's you, and only you. There is nobody else, there are no thoughts or considerations of anybody else."

"Six weeks is a long time."

"You're right, it is. Do you really think so little of me that you think in six weeks I'm going to be so sex hungry that I'd cheat on you?" Anger and disgust drip from his words and anxiety bubbles in my stomach.

"What? No, I don't—"

"Look, I think I should go. I'll...I'll give you extra time tomorrow. I'm stressed, I have a midterm in the morning. I don't want to fight."

"Oh. Okay." We haven't had many fights in the few months we've been dating. Mostly just simple disagreements or arguments. And he's never jumped off the phone. Everything inside me feels like it's twisting.

"I love you, Shay."

"I love you too."

"I just—" I'm about to hang up when I hear him talking again.

"What? You just what?"

"I just wish you understood. Trusted my feelings."

My eyes fill to the brim. I bite my cheek to keep from crying as my stomach slides from my body. He'll hear it in my voice instantly, and he'll stay on, even if he doesn't want to.

"I do."

"It doesn't seem like it." Disappointment and hurt fill my ear and shoot straight to my heart. "Good night, baby girl. Dream about me."

"Good night, Loch. I always do." It's become our routine good-bye, and I'm happy he sticks with it, even tonight.

I stare at the dark phone in my hands. What just happened? Why did I have to say that? Do I really not trust him?

I fall asleep feeling confused, sad, and a little less excited for him to come home.

On Friday, I'm a ball of anxiety, tense and jittery. The phone calls between Lochlyn and I have been...strained...since that night, mostly cut short. He has a morning midterm and then will be on his way home. I have midterms until three. He'll be at Chelsea's by the time I get back from class.

Trying to focus on my tests is nearly impossible. But I'm doing well in my classes and understand the material, so I'm fairly confident I can swing at least a decent grade.

Friday classes are just me. Chelsea has some but a different schedule, and she'll be finished by noon. After going home and changing my clothes into something a little more...attractive, I find myself standing at the front door to the Reynolds' house. I've never been nervous about letting myself in before. Yet here I stand, butterflies in my stomach and heart in my throat.

Taking a deep breath and shaking out my arms, I push the door open. Nobody's around.

"Hello?" I call out to the emptiness.

"Upstairs!" Chelsea yells down.

Before I can do more than throw my jacket on the coat hook, Lochlyn walks down the stairs.

I open my mouth to say something, but before I can, he takes my face between his palms and closes his mouth over mine, tongue sweeping through my lips. Six weeks of missing him culminates in this one kiss. Somewhere in the back of my mind there are alarms going off that Chelsea is upstairs, can come down at any minute and see us, but in this moment, I don't care. All I want is Lochlyn's lips on mine.

Far too soon, he pulls away and rests his forehead against mine, hands still on my cheeks. "I love you," he whispers.

I close my eyes as my heart hammers against my sternum. "I love you too."

He pulls me against him tightly, arms around my waist. It's my favorite kind of hug from him. His arms are so long that they can wrap completely around me, crossing my body so his hands rest against the opposite hip. It locks me in so tight I can barely move.

Breathing him in, my nerves settle, a peace washing over me and working through my extremities. The hug is nowhere near long enough as we slowly slide apart, hearing Chelsea walking down the stairs. A hug is one thing, but being bound so tightly is very different.

"Oh, well, I guess you see Loch's home. I was asking if he wanted to do anything tonight as a welcome home, but I guess he has other plans." I have a pretty strong feeling the other plans involve me, though based on how things had been before he came home, I'm not entirely sure.

"Yup, just said hi. It's okay. I have some stuff around the house to catch up on anyway." I'm giving myself the out I hope I need.

"I guess that's good, because I just got off with Bren. We're going away for a few days, leaving in about an hour."

My heart jumps. Chelsea will be gone? For a few *days?* I'm not sure what I've done to deserve the good fortune. I just hope I'll have a chance to make use of it.

"Where are you going?" Lochlyn tries to sound calm, but I hear the edge in his voice.

"Skiing." Chelsea doesn't ski.

If Lochlyn wants to say anything to discourage her, he keeps it to himself. I'm hoping that's a good sign because if Chelsea is gone, we can be together, uninterrupted. I already told Mom I need a few days off from the store to reset after midterms.

"Do you need any help packing?" Chelsea and I lock eyes on each other, hers filled with shock at Lochlyn's words.

"You're...you're not going to try to talk me out of it?"

"Is there a point?" Lochlyn's voice is dripping with disinterest and exhaustion.

"I mean, no, not really."

"I figured as much."

"I'm just surprised, is all. Usually, you give me a hard time, argue, something."

Lochlyn pushes up his sleeves and runs his hand through his hair, several things hitting me all at once. He has new tattoos, and as he runs his hand through his hair, it lifts his shirt slightly, showing off the deep v at the top of his jeans, causing desire to tear through my body.

"I don't have it in me to fight with you, Chels. It's been a rough week, midterms were tough, and I had a long drive today. So go, have fun, and be careful."

It all happens at the same time; his movements and his words are one. I'm speechless, but not Chelsea.

"Lochlyn! Your arm! What is that?" She points at him with wide eyes.

He holds his right arm out in front of him, pushing his shirt sleeve up a little more. "It's a hawk." Looking at it closely, I see the bird, wings outstretched.

"Why a hawk?" She sounds disgusted.

He rubs his fingertips along his lower lip, which draws my attention to his mouth, and a small tattoo above the base knuckle of his middle finger. He lowers his hand too quickly for me to see what it is. "Because I see everything."

I know he gets the tattoos for his birthday, but he didn't have them when I went to visit him. I wonder how new they are.

"Shay." Chelsea pulls my attention to her.

"Hm?" It takes a moment for my eyes and mind to truly focus on her.

"What do you think?"

"Of what?"

She rolls her eyes at me. "Of the tattoo! Duh!"

"Oh, uh, I like it." I hope it was nonchalant enough for her, but not too weak for Lochlyn. I don't want him to think I hate it.

"I swear I don't understand the two of you sometimes." Chelsea has never liked Lochlyn's tattoos, and she makes it well known. Frequently, I think it helps fuel his want to get more. She stomps back up the stairs.

I turn to him immediately, taking his hand to examine his finger. Delicately placed is an infinity symbol, but it has some extra lines around it, almost framing it. All black. Except for one part that has the slightest hint of red. A perfect S.

When I look up at him, his face is strained. For the first time since we started being together, I can't read him. He's not pulling his hand away, but he's not trying to touch me either. Was the kiss hello not really a hello?

"You don't really have chores to do tonight, do you?"

"No. I was just making sure I had something as a reason to not hang out. Do you really have plans?"

"I was hoping I would." He's not specific about what they are or who they're with.

"Shay! Get up here and help me!" Chelsea's voice bellows from upstairs.

Giving him one last inspection, I let his hand go and walk slowly upstairs. He watches me the whole way, and I hold eye contact until I'm behind the wall. The anxiety has returned, knotting my muscles, not knowing his mood or his thoughts.

"What's up?" I ask as calmly as I can. My brain is a mess. My heart can't decide if it wants to pound out of my chest or stop completely. My insides are going crazy. But I need to show control in front of Chelsea.

"Help me. I don't know what to pack." She sits on her bed surrounded by clothes as she whines at me.

"Okay, level with me here. Are you *really* going skiing?"

"Yes, I am really going skiing."

I just stare at her for a second, tight-lipped.

"Shay. I'm going skiing. Brendan likes to ski and snowboard. He wants to take me. I agreed to do something nice for him. I have no idea if I'll be able to actually do it, but he wants to take me, so I'm going. Now help."

"Well, obviously sweaters. Do you even own snow gear?"

"He said we can buy some? I don't know. Am I supposed to wear something specific underneath?"

"Long underwear?" We both burst out laughing. It helps distract me from the uncertainty sitting downstairs.

"I've never been nervous to go somewhere with a guy before." She almost whispers it, and I pick up a slight tremor in her words.

"Have you ever gone away with a guy? I mean, I see you basically every day."

"Not really. Day trips, sure. Not overnight. I'm not really nervous about being alone or anything. We're obviously having sex, it's not that. I don't know...what if he snores?"

"Chels, you've spent the night with him. Many times." I'm thankful for those nights because it also gave me the opportunity to spend the night with Lochlyn.

"I know."

"So you'd know if he snored."

"I guess. Ack! Why am I nervous?" Sometimes it's nice to have a reminder that Chelsea is, in fact, like the rest of us.

"Maybe it's more about the trip itself than who it's with?"

"Yeah, maybe."

"Leggings, bring leggings."

"Good thought."

After tearing out a few more articles of clothing, Chelsea's bag is packed, complete with a hat and scarf that she had in the back of her closet. She's not great at dressing weather-appropriately.

We make our way downstairs, Chelsea dropping her bag at the front door, and go into the kitchen to find Lochlyn working on something for dinner.

Chelsea scowls. "You're making dinner?"

"Just because you're leaving doesn't mean I don't have to eat, and I was going to ask Shay if she'd like to stay. I'm sure her mom is still at work." He doesn't even lift his gaze from the meal he's preparing to talk to us.

Chelsea huffs, about to argue with him, but is distracted when the doorbell rings and goes running to answer the door.

Lochlyn and I stand in awkward silence while we wait for Chelsea to return. In all the years I've known him, it's the most uncomfortable I've ever been in his presence.

Chelsea comes bounding back into the kitchen, Brendan trying to keep up as she pulls his hand. "Okay, we're off."

"Where are you going?" There's the sternness I've come to know from Lochlyn when Chelsea's going somewhere with a boy.

"Killington," Brendan answers. If he's nervous, he doesn't show it.

"You ski?"

"I'm more of a snowboarder, but yeah."

"You know she doesn't?" Lochlyn points the knife in his hands at Chelsea.

"I do. I'm planning to take her to bunny slope and try to teach her. At least a little bit."

Chelsea and I stay silent as they talk, my eyes ping-ponging back and forth.

"Keep an eye on her. If she comes back broken, I'll return the favor."

"Don't worry, I won't let her out of my sight."

While this conversation is tense, it's the *overly enforced, ready to pound him into the wall* attitude that Lochlyn usually has with Brendan. Either he's given up caring, or he's just that drained.

"Drive very carefully. That's my sister."

"I will."

"Chelsea, let me know when you get there, please." It's my turn to speak up.

"Okay, Mom." She's always said I'm like the group mother, asking people to be safe and call when they get places. Lochlyn's not much better.

She walks around the island, giving Lochlyn a hug and a kiss. "Behave yourself. And be nice to Shay."

"I'm *always* nice to Shay." Nicer than Chelsea could possibly realize. Though what lies ahead for the night, I'm worried may end up not quite as nice.

Giving me a giant hug, she pushes my curls behind my shoulders as she pulls away. "Try to have some fun. And remember, you can always tell him to fuck off."

I hear Lochlyn's heavy exhale behind me, sure he's also rolling his eyes before I hear an angry chop.

We watch them leave in silence. After the door shuts, I still hesitate to even glance in his direction. I feel like I'm being an idiot. I love him, immensely.

Taking a deep breath, I turn around. His eyes are trained on me, but his expression is still unreadable. At a loss for words, I wait for him to speak first. When he makes it clear he's not going to, I sit down at a barstool, nails tapping against the granite, looking around.

Warmth settles over my hand, stilling it, causing me to look up to find Lochlyn's hand over mine, his eyes on me. He has a look of irritation, with maybe disappointment mixed in.

"Are we going to talk, or are we just going to sit in uncomfortable silence for the rest of the night?" I blurt out. I just can't hold it in anymore.

"I need ten minutes to get this in the oven. You don't have to stay in here if you don't want to, but please don't leave the house."

Biting my lip, I slide off the barstool and go into the living room, flopping onto the couch. The house doesn't have the most open floor plan—you can't see from the kitchen into the living room.

I look around the room, biting my nails and cuticles. This house is a second home to me. Sometimes it feels like I've spent more time in their house than I have my own, especially in recent years.

Lost in anxiety and my own head, I don't hear Lochlyn come out of the kitchen, startling me as he takes my hand from my mouth and takes a seat on the couch next to me. He has a scowl on his face as he looks at my hand. He hates when I chew my cuticles.

Keeping my hand in his, he takes a deep breath. I'm afraid I'm going to explode, waiting for him to say something.

"Are you going to break up with me?" Boom.

His brow knits together. "What? Shay, no, of course not. I'm feeling...hurt."

My chin hits my chest. Hurting him is the last thing I ever want to do.

"When you say things about me having girls in my shower or worry that the person I'm talking to is a girl and that because I haven't seen you in six weeks, I'm going to sleep with somebody else...it hurts me. It makes me feel like you don't trust me. I've tried to tell you, more than once, there's nobody else. No other thoughts, no regrets, no questions. I just don't know how to make you understand it."

"I'm sorry." It comes out as a whisper as I try to push back the tears.

"I need you to talk to me, Shay. I need to understand what happens in your head. The good, the bad, the scary, the ugly. All of it. Being apart for so long, it's fucking hard. For me too. I'm not sitting there enjoying my life, living it up while my girlfriend is four hours away. I miss you, every damn day. Texting all day and talking for an hour or two at night, to then come home and have to hide. It's not enough. It hurts that you don't know that." The hurt is evident in his tone, and it's like a thousand needles poking into my heart that I put it there.

"I do. I do know that. It's just..." I can't say it, can't voice it.

"It's just what? *Talk to me.*" There's so much desperation coating his words.

"What's so special about me? I know you told me why you loved me. I remember. But...I don't know. I guess, I just don't feel like I'm anything special. And that you'll wake up one day and realize that. Especially not seeing each other for weeks at a time. That instead of you missing me more, you'll realize you're happier without me." He brushes some tears from my cheek before pulling me against him.

"Do you love me?" His voice is muffled as I lean against his chest.

I jerk my head away from him. "What? Of course I—"

He holds a hand up to stop me. "Just...answer the question."

"Yes."

"Do you believe that I love you?"

"Yes."

"We've known each other a long time, Shay. I feel like you should know me well enough to know that when I tell you I love you, it *means* something. It's not something I tell people. In fact, I've never told anybody else, besides my family. But if you can really think that I'd profess my feelings to you and then sleep with somebody else just because I can't be with you, or haven't seen you in a few weeks, then...I don't know.

"I understand maybe you have some insecurities about your-self, even about the relationship because you've never been in one, I've hardly been in one, and we're apart more than we're together. But if you don't trust me, don't believe me, that's a much bigger problem. One that I don't know how to fix."

I'm so confused. He's talking about problems, being unfixable, yet saying he doesn't want to break up. He also didn't answer my question. What am I supposed to say? How do I respond to that? It certainly sounds like he wants to break up.

"I have to go check on dinner. Don't...don't leave."

My mind is being pulled in a million different directions. Do I trust him? If not, why? In all the years I've known Lochlyn, he's never done or said anything to make me not trust him, to not feel safe with him. He's told me things he'd never told anybody else, has always made me feel like I could tell him anything and everything. So where is my concern coming from? Is it really just a lack of self-confidence? Is it Chelsea getting in my head that he's most assuredly living it up in Ithaca?

Or does some part of me doubt him? Doubt his feelings for me. It all boils down to my own insecurities in myself. He's told me, and shown me, in a million ways, how he truly feels about me. What is wrong with me?

Lochlyn finds me on the couch, knees pulled as close to my chest as they can be with my arms pressed in between, heels of my hand pressing into my eyes.

Sighing at my pathetic sight, he sits down, pulling my legs straight across his lap and wrapping his fingers around my wrists to pull them away. Even fighting him slightly, he peels me apart with ease. I can't look at him, can't talk to him. Everything I've wanted for so long feels like it's slipping through my fingertips.

Tilting my chin up to meet his eyes, I find sadness. It rips through me. "Come eat."

Following him into the kitchen, I try to steel my emotions. If I don't, I'll be a blubbering ball of tears before I even sit down.

Lochlyn made chicken parmesan, a favorite of mine. Just another example of the little things he does to show me he loves me. Why am I being so stupid?

"So, how were your midterms today?" He's making conversation, trying to be normal. It feels off, though.

"Um, they were fine. Not too hard, I feel pretty confident. I was a little distracted. How was yours?"

"Good, fine."

"This is really yummy, thank you." The whole conversation feels scripted, like we're actors who are saying what we're supposed to instead of two people in a committed relationship.

"You're welcome. I wasn't expecting Chelsea to not be here, so there will be leftovers; probably will make a good lunch tomorrow. I could run to the store and grab sub rolls or something, change it a little." He's talking about tomorrow in regards to being together. I take it as a good sign.

"That sounds nice. Do you want me to come back around lunch?"

His eyes dart up to mine. "Come back? Where would you be going?"

"I, uh, figured I'd be going home."

"I want you to stay, Shay. If you don't want to. that's fine. But *I* want you here." Another good sign.

"Okay. I wasn't sure. I'll stay."

Strained. It's the only word that comes to mind when I think about dinner, the way we're acting around each other, the atmosphere.

He lets me help clean up after dinner, standing so close to each other our arms brush every so often. Tension is not a strong enough word to describe what's existing between us.

Not sure what to say, I choose silence, assuming he's doing the same. Maybe I'm being a chicken by not talking first, but I figure so is he.

After we finish cleaning up, he takes my hand and leads me upstairs. I'm sure he's not expecting to just get naked and have sex. That won't solve any of our problems, but I certainly wouldn't say no.

When we get in the room, he doesn't kiss me, doesn't start tearing my clothes off. He leads me over to the bed, flops down, and pulls me down to lie against him. Arranging me how he wants me, head on his chest, arm draped over him, so my hand reaches his far shoulder, he runs his fingers up and down my arm while the other draws small circles on my back.

Lying in his arms was all I've wanted for six weeks, yet now it feels different, it feels off. It's not bringing the comfort I thought it would.

When Lochlyn clears his throat, I nearly jump out of my skin. "I need you to talk to me. I need to know where your head's at. For some reason, you seem to think it's going to be so easy for me to just forget about you and move on, because we're not physically together every day. Is it me? Have I done or said something that makes you feel that way?"

I sit up so I can look at him. He needs to be able to read my face as I say this. "No. No, you've been nothing short of amazing."

He pushes himself up to sit in front of me. "Then why? What is it?"

"Because I'm replaceable! Forgettable!" The words tumble out before I realize that's exactly what I've been feeling.

"How could you think that?" His voice is low but pained, which matches the look on his face.

"Look at my life! My own family has forgotten about me. My sister, my *mother*. My own mother, the woman who gave me life, barely even looks at me. And she hasn't for over a year. At first, I understood, it made sense, she was hurt, struggling. I have a lot of my dad's features, so I'm sure I remind her of him. But it's been over a year, and when we talk, it's only about the store. She still won't look at me. I could not even let her know that I'm going to be here for tonight or a few days or however long you want me to stay, and I doubt she'll even notice I'm gone.

"My sister left and never looked back. I haven't even heard a word from her since the funeral. Not once. Not even a happy birthday. She didn't check in on the anniversary. She's my fucking sister, and she's acting like she's the only one who lost somebody.

"And Chelsea. I love her, I do, but she gets a new boy and I go to the back burner. It's convenient that I'm around when said boy is unavailable, but I'm not the focus, the priority. I feel like for the right boy, it'd be the same thing as anybody else." The words gush out of me faster than I can process what they are and what I've been feeling, which is a lot of sadness based on the look on Lochlyn's face.

I take a deep breath, fighting back the tears. "I'm worried it's going to be the same for you someday." My gaze is anywhere but at Lochlyn, mostly down at the bed. I hadn't realized I was wringing my hands until he takes them in one of his, the other tilting my chin to look at him, swiping the tears that I didn't even realize were streaming down my face.

Before he says anything, he leans in and kisses me tenderly, pressing his forehead against mine. "I could never, ever, replace you or forget about you."

I choke out a sob as he lies back on the bed, bringing me down with him. He holds my hand in his against his chest, just under his chin. While I think I may be hysterical until I pass out, I'm not.

Instead, I let the steadiness of Lochlyn's breathing, the beating of his heart, the feel of his fingers on my skin calm me. Releasing my hand from his, I start running my fingertips along his new tattoo, the hawk. I lean on my chin against his chest and look at the tattoo on his finger, tracing along the infinity over and over.

"Why a hawk?" I know what he told Chelsea. I'm curious if it's true.

"Did you know that Shay means hawk in Irish?" My breath halts, my whole body stilling.

"And...and this one?" My finger, being the only thing that can move, traces along the symbol on his finger.

"It's a tribal infinity symbol."

"With an S."

"Yes. With an S."

"You really love me, don't you?"

"Yeah, Shay, I *really* fucking love you. You are completely unforgettable and irreplaceable to me. I understand you have some shit that makes you feel that way. I haven't come out completely unscathed either. But you are *everything* to me."

His words, his tone, they're my undoing. I don't cry, no, my undoing is physical. I slide my body up to lie over him, my mouth closing on his. He doesn't hesitate for a second as one hand reaches into my hair, the other wrapping tightly around my waist, his tongue slipping across mine.

He flips me to my back like it's nothing as we tear at our clothing. Climbing back over me after removing both of our pants, he slides his tongue along my leg, stopping at my breast, mouth closing over my nipple. I arch toward him as he pushes two fingers inside me, and mine twist into his hair.

"Loch." I sigh as his fingers and tongue move in sync.

Groaning against my chest, he releases my nipple, replacing his fingers, easing into me. A moan catches in my throat as my fingers tighten into his back.

"Fuck," Lochlyn groans, head against my clavicle.

His mouth crashes on mine as he starts moving inside me. Six weeks is way too long to go without feeling him.

Everything around me starts to disappear. Any worries, fears, concerns, they all fall away. It's just me and Lochlyn, together in this moment.

As I lie with Lochlyn, head on his chest while his fingers graze up and down my back, I still don't feel right.

Flipping to my stomach, turning my head to look at him, I speak quietly, "I'm sorry."

He smiles gently, tracing one finger along my cheek and wrapping some hair around it. "Nobody said relationships are easy."

"Is that why you haven't had one in a long time?" What the hell is wrong with me? We're finally somewhat back to normal, or at least on the path, and I'm still saying stupid nonsense.

Thankfully, he doesn't hesitate. "Maybe. I guess part of me felt like it wasn't worth putting in the work with the wrong person. Sex, it's easy. It's quick, it's over. It's all physical, no feelings. There was never a doubt here. I didn't want to have sex with you. I mean, I did...sheesh, this is coming out wrong."

The giggle that escapes me feels good, and I tilt my head to kiss his chest as he continues. "I knew I wanted the relationship with you. I wanted, *want*, to put in the work. Because there have always been feelings."

I press my hand against his jaw, running my thumb across his cheek. "I love you."

The scratch of stubble brushes my hand as he turns to kiss my palm. "I love you too."

"Are we...are we okay?"

Before answering, he wraps his hands around my upper arms and pulls me up, turning me on my side so I'm curled into him. He places my head on his chest, leaning his chin against my forehead and wrapping his arms tightly around my waist.

"Yeah, yeah, we're okay." Kissing my forehead and giving me a squeeze, I relax for the first time since I had walked into the house hours earlier.

"You really got two tattoos? For me?"

"I really did."

"You don't have any doubts that this won't work out?"

"None." Melting, right here. I'm melting. "And let's just pretend I did, a hawk is still a cool-as-hell tattoo."

We both laugh softly. Lochlyn always has a way to ease the tension. But it settles quickly. It was our first fight, and it rocked me to my core.

"How are we going to make it through another six weeks?" I ask quietly.

"We won't have to. That reminds me. There's going to be a concert in April. You should come up for it."

"Really?"

"Yeah. They've had a couple of good ones. Taking Back Sunday, All Time Low. I'm not sure who it's going to be yet, but I heard it might be Yellowcard."

"Yellowcard?! You know I love them!"

I shake as he chuckles under me. "I know. I had a feeling you'd be excited. I'm not one hundred percent sure it will be them, but if that's who they're talking about, it will at least be a similar type of concert."

"This is awesome." Daydreams start to filter through my mind of what going to a concert with him may be like.

"Man, I wish you were looking forward to it. Oh well, maybe you just shouldn't come."

He flinches as I pinch his waist. "Not funny. Not only am I insanely excited about the concert, but I get to see you without having to go *six weeks* again. It was hard. Too hard."

"It's only a couple of weeks. I don't know the exact date yet, and then you'll come for the show, and then just a few more weeks until summer. And before you know it, we'll both be up in Ithaca."

A smile spreads across my face. I can't wait to be at Cornell with Lochlyn. Not just because I'll get to see him all the time, but because I'm finally getting to where I want to be.

"Don't you usually get your tattoos for your birthday?"

"I do."

"But I saw you after your birthday. You didn't have them."

"I pushed it a week. I needed you to be genuinely surprised in front of Chelsea. I wasn't expecting for us to, uh, not be on the best terms."

"Oh. Yeah, yeah, that makes sense." My voice betrays me and comes out low and sad.

"Shay, it's okay. Couples fight, people fight. We just, we have to *talk* to each other."

All I can do is nod, which causes him to sigh and squeeze me. How does he expect me to talk to him when I've gotten so used to keeping it all bottled up inside, having had nobody to talk to besides Chelsea for years? And with all of this, I'm not willing to tell her and face the ramifications. Not yet.

"Let's sleep. Maybe you'll feel better after some sleep."

"I don't know if I can."

"You can. You will. I'm right here. I'm not going anywhere. Just relax."

Lochlyn starts twisting some of my hair around his fingers, slowly straightening the curl and trailing his finger down my spine as he lets go, then starting over in a slow rhythmic movement. As my muscles start to loosen, his other hand starts grazing up and down the arm that's draped over his chest. Within minutes, my eyes flutter closed.

Chapter 11

He was right. By the time I wake up in the morning, I feel better. Waking up next to the person you love has a way to make your worries fade.

The first thing I do when we get downstairs is check my phone. I hadn't let Mom know I'd be spending the night, and part of me hopes for a message wondering where I am. But...nothing.

"I'm sure she just knew you were spending the night here," Lochlyn says as he wraps his arms around my waist. I hadn't even told him what I was doing. As usual, he just knows.

We spend the next two days together, mostly at his house, mostly in bed. When I go home to get some clothes, I leave Mom a note. She may not be wondering where I am, but I feel like I need to tell her. Ever the responsible daughter. Lochlyn is my shadow the whole time we're at my house. Standing right behind me as I shift through the rooms, trying to convince me I don't need clothes, then trying to pick them out when I insist I do.

All the while, he makes me laugh, reminding me that we're happy together.

Two days after Chelsea left, I get a text message from her.

On my way home. Be at my house in twenty minutes. Need to talk to you.

Lochlyn and I are on the couch watching a movie, my legs draped over his lap, when the message comes in. We read it cheek to cheek, looking at each other with pinched brows and tight lips once we finish.

My mouth is arid, and for a minute, I think I've forgotten how to breathe. I'm so sure we've been made, and that she's coming back to fully express her feelings.

When she storms through the door twenty minutes later, I'm able to take the first real breath since I read her message. It's very clearly *not* about me and Lochlyn.

"I told you to go away, Brendan. Just leave!" she shouts as she marches into the house and starts up the stairs.

"Chelsea, we need to talk about this!"

"I said, GO AWAY!"

Lochlyn and I lock eyes on each other before glancing over at Brendan, standing at the bottom of the stairs as Chelsea storms up them. We'd gotten up from the couch and are standing behind it, watching the scene unfold in front of us. A quick look at Lochlyn, and I just know things are not going to go well in the next few minutes.

"What did you do to my sister?" His voice is filled with rage.

"I didn't do anything, we go into a fight and—"

"She's storming up the stairs telling you to leave! What the fuck was the fight about?"

"It's none of your business what happens between me and Chelsea."

That's the wrong thing to say. And Brendan realizes it the second Lochlyn's eyes widen, and he starts making a beeline for Brendan.

I put my arms out and press against Lochlyn's chest, but he keeps walking. I have to apply some force in pushing him back. "Lochlyn, stop."

His eyes flash to mine. "Are you serious? He did something to Chelsea!"

"I didn't *do* anything to her," Brendan immediately defends himself.

I whip my head around to look at Brendan, hands still against Lochlyn's chest, giving a firm push as he tries to move again.

"Then why the hell are you back a day early and she's racing up the stairs?" I seethe.

"I don't know. You know she can be crazy sometimes." He waves his hand toward the stairs while his face scrunches.

Big mistake, Brendan. I have to dig my heels in as Lochlyn attempts another push. It's the first time I've ever wished he wasn't so strong.

"What did you fucking say about my sister?" He's screaming and pushing toward Brendan. I'm pretty sure as mad as Chelsea is, she doesn't want Lochlyn beating Brendan to a pulp, which he's absolutely ready to do.

So I push back, hard. "Okay, kitchen, now. Go!" I shove him as hard as I can, which won't actually move him as he's built like a brick wall, but he at least stops trying to get to Brendan, meeting my eyes for the first time. "Kitchen." My voice is lower.

His shoulders lower and his muscles relax the slightest bit, and he turns to walk into the other room. My hands remain at his back in case he changes his mind. Just before we're out of sight, he flips around and points at Brendan. "I'm not through with you."

"Lochlyn!" I push him into the kitchen.

Flipping around, running a hand down his face, he slams his hands on the counter. A light bead of sweat drips down my back and my breaths are shallow from pushing against him, glad he's in my corner if I ever need protection. "What the hell happened in Killington?" His voice is quiet, strained.

"I don't know. I'll find out. *Stay here.* Do not, and I mean it, do *not* go back into the living room. I'm not fucking around, Lochlyn. Stay here." My tone is very firm—he needs to know I'm not messing around.

"I'm going to kill him."

"You're going to let me talk to Chelsea and find out what happened. Then I'll let you know if you can kill him."

"Promise?"

I wrap my arms around his waist, pressing myself to his back. "I promise that if I deem it's bad enough, I will let you at him."

He sighs, putting his hand over mine. "I need a drink."

"I'm going upstairs. If I have to come back down and break up a fight, it's not going to be good for you."

"I will stay here. Be fast."

Kissing his back, I walk out as he opens the fridge.

I barely look at Brendan as I walk past him, but I'm happy he's still here. "Do not leave this spot," I say to him through gritted teeth while pointing at him. I may be relatively meek with Chelsea, but other people know I don't mess around when I mean business.

After taking the stairs two at a time, I find Chelsea on her bed hugging a pillow, tears silently running down her face. Whatever happened, it was big. Chelsea rarely cries.

"Hey. What happened?"

She sniffles. "We had a fight."

When she's upset, she's almost like a wild animal, easily startled. I move very slowly through the room to sit at the foot of her bed. "About what?"

"Stuff." Helpful.

"Chelsea. What happened?" I try again.

She sighs and sits up, pillow falling to her lap. "I thought I was pregnant."

I have to control my reaction, not wanting to startle her or have her shut down on me. But on the inside, I'm having a conniption. "Okay. Are you?"

"No, Shay, I said I thought I *was*," she snaps at me.

"Hey, calm down. I'm just checking. So, you thought you were pregnant. How did things escalate?" And why didn't you tell me?

She takes a deep breath. "We were in our room after we'd had dinner. There were kids next door being loud, and he got frustrated. Said something about how they're annoying, and he hates when parents let their kids ruin it for everyone. And I got mad. I started yelling at him. And it just came out."

"Okay, take a step back for me. Tell me about the scare."

"A few weeks ago." A few *weeks*? And she hadn't told me? Ouch. She twists the knife she stabbed me with a few minutes ago when I realized she hadn't told me. "I was late. I'm *never* late. Like clockwork. Not to mention, ya know, the pill. But I had forgotten to take it a few times that month. It had been five days when I was going to suck it up and get a test, when my period started. But I was so scared for those five days that I was pregnant."

"Why didn't you tell me?" My voice comes out low. Hurt.

"I didn't tell anybody, Shay. I was scared. You'd want to be there for me, do anything you could, be supportive. I didn't want that at that moment. It would have been a mistake, a stupid mistake. I needed to feel bad and stupid about it. Plus, I was worried you'd tell Lochlyn and then he'd make sure Brendan never touched me again."

I freeze. Does she know? "Why would I tell Lochlyn?" There's a tremble in my voice that I hope she doesn't pick up on.

"Because you two are friends and have always talked about me. You'd tell him."

She's right, I probably would have, even if we weren't dating. "Okay, so you had your scare, but you're *not* pregnant. What happened at the resort?"

"When he was complaining about the kids, I got mad. If things had gone differently, I could have been pregnant at that very moment. So I said something about it. I don't even remember exactly what I said. I was furious and just blurted something out. But he turned *white*. Shay, I thought he was going to pass out. Now, I'm not saying I plan to, or even necessarily *want* to be with him forever, but it did not exactly give me the vote of confidence that if something were to accidentally happen that he'd be able to stick around."

The whole thing sounds messy. I know she wants to have kids someday. But how can you even contemplate that with somebody whose stance is that of Brendan's?

"Did he say anything?"

"Not for a while. He sat and put his head in his hands. Then when he did, he said, 'but you're not, right?'"

"Oh."

"Yeah. So I told him the truth. But the way he reacted. His whole body relaxed. I thought he was going to melt into the floor. And he goes, 'oh, thank God.' Like, what? I mean, yeah, I was happy about it too; I'm nineteen, I don't want a baby, but like, really? So, then he starts going on and on about how it's fine, it's great, we'll be more careful, that kids are *so* not something he's ready for right now, if ever." She's so worked up, the words pour right out of her with barely a breath between sentences.

"Eek." At the moment, I know I'm not here for much more than emotional support and for her to get it all out. My words are not necessary.

"Mhm. But at no point does he check on me, ask how I'm feeling, ask how I'm doing, ask my opinions. I mean, I want kids. Obviously not now, but someday. I mean, like I said, I don't know that I want to be with Brendan forever, but what if I do? What if I do love him enough for that? How can I be with somebody who doesn't want kids if I do?"

She looks off to the side of the room, squeezing the pillow against her chest.

"I told him I wanted to leave. I even started packing. He was shocked. Didn't understand. We drove most of the way in silence before I burst. I basically told him I didn't think we should be together if he didn't want kids, that I did some day. He said we aren't getting married now, what does it matter. It was a mess."

Filling my lungs with air, I hold it for a beat and nod. A pregnancy scare. If I'm being completely honest, I'm kind of surprised it hadn't already happened at some point.

"Have you actually spoken about it? In a calm manner?" I'm pretty sure I know the answer is no.

"I don't think I can right now."

"Do you want me to make him leave?"

"He's still here?" Her brows shoot to her hairline.

"Yeah. He's downstairs. Or he was when I came up. I told him not to leave."

Her eyes widen, to almost all pupil, and I know fear is overtaking her. "Oh, God. Lochlyn." She knows if left to his own devices, he'd happily end Brendan.

"I calmed him down, sort of. When I came up, he was in the kitchen, about to get a drink. I told him he better stay put until I talked to you." If he knows what's good for him, he better still be in the kitchen.

"You're always so good with him. Both of us. You're the calm in the storm."

"Thanks, Chels. So, do you want me to make him leave?"

"I just don't think I can talk to him right now. Can you let him know I'll call him tomorrow?" As though exhausted, her eyelids droop and she lies back down.

"Sure. You okay?"

"Yeah. I will be. I just...I want to be alone."

"Okay. Are you sure? I can stay." Though I'd definitely prefer not to, my body aching to be downstairs and in Lochlyn's proximity.

"I'm sure."

I stand to leave, giving her hand a squeeze. "I'll ask him to go, then."

"Will you tell Lochlyn for me?"

"Really? You want me to tell him?"

"I think he'll take it better from you. He'll just tell me I'm stupid and I don't want him to make me feel worse right now." While he wouldn't intentionally want to make her feel bad about it, that is what would happen. His emotions would get in the way, and he'd surely end up yelling at her.

"Okay. Yeah, okay, I'll tell him."

Just before I walk out the door, her voice stops me. "Shay, you're being careful, right? With John?"

Ice shoots through my veins. "Yeah, Chels. You made me go on the pill with you. Remember?" She said we needed to do it together, even though I wasn't having sex and had no plans to at the time. The way things had happened between me and Lochlyn, I was extremely thankful I did, because condoms were not even on either of our radars, which we both cursed ourselves for after the fact.

"I know, but I'm on it too."

Sensing this is going to be a little bit longer than just a few words, I turn around to face her. My hand lingers on the doorknob. "Yeah, but I take mine every day. Of the two of us, who do you think is more responsible to take it as directed?"

"Oh, absolutely you. I just don't want you to have to deal with this yourself."

"I appreciate that. You rest. I'll stay the night."

"I don't think I want company." The whine is in full effect.

"That's okay. I'll stay in Lochlyn's room. That way, I'm here if you need me." I try to sound as neutral about it as possible.

"With him on the couch." She's firm. It's comments like this that are what make me stand my ground with Lochlyn about not telling her. It's one night, while she's in a vulnerable place, and she can't even put aside her thoughts on it for one second to be comfortable with us. Right now, in secrecy, it may be hard on Lochlyn. And me if I'm being honest, but at least we get to be together and be happy. There's no lashing out against us.

"I'm not going to kick him out of his bed *and* his room. I've slept in there before with him in there. It's not a big deal. He's not a monster."

"He is actually—a sex-crazed one."

"So what, he's so sex-crazed, he's going to attack me while I'm sleeping?" He actually does, frequently. But it's different when I want him to than what Chelsea is worried about. Which is him somehow coercing me into falling in bed with him and then never calling again.

"No, no, I guess not. Fine, sleep in the same room." She gives in faster than I thought she would.

"I'm going to go talk to the guys. I'll be downstairs if you need me." I leave before she can say anything else, closing her door behind me.

Brendan's exactly where I left him. And in one piece.

"Is she...is she okay?" His voice is strained. I'd like to think Brendan is actually upset, but I don't really know him well enough to read him or his tone. The fact that he's asking and seems genuine is a good sign in my book.

"No. But she will be. She doesn't want to talk to you or see you right now, though, so please leave. She said she'll call you tomorrow."

"Shay, I didn't, I don't know what happened."

"Brendan, I can't talk about this with you right now. I just found out my best friend kept something pretty big from me." It doesn't feel so good being on the receiving end.

"I need to talk to her." Standing here, he must have had time to reflect. When they came in, it was clear he was trying to talk to her, but now he's practically begging.

"You need to wait. She'll call in the morning."

"Shay, ple—"

"Brendan." I use the sternest tone I have. "Leave. She doesn't want to see you. I'm about to walk into the kitchen to talk to Lochlyn. I suggest you not be here when I do. I guarantee he won't be nearly calm as I am."

That does it. With one last glance upstairs, Brendan leaves.

"Did I just hear the front door?" Lochlyn asks as I walk into the kitchen, not turning around to look at me. He's seated, hunched over the counter.

"You did."

"You let him leave." There's a deep annoyance in his tone.

"Chelsea doesn't want to see him. She asked me to send him home."

"Maybe I wasn't done talking to him yet." His voice is clipped and low, angry. I'm not sure if it's at me or the situation. Glancing at the counter, I can see he's gone from one beer to the next, two bottles in front him and one in his hand as he picks at the label.

Taking a deep breath and walking over to him, I prepare myself for him to fall into a worse mood. Brushing my fingers along his back, I slide into the barstool next to him, keeping my hand on his arm, hoping my touch will calm him and ground him a little.

"We need to talk." I try to keep my voice level.

His head drops. "That's never a good thing."

"First, you need to promise me that you're going to stay *in this seat* and not go storming upstairs or after Brendan."

One of his eyebrows quirks up as he looks at me. "That bad?"

"In reality? No. To you? Maybe."

He grumbles, "Get it over with."

"Chelsea had a pregnancy scare." I'm usually blunt. I like to rip off the Band-Aid instead of beating around the bush.

He turns and drops his head to my shoulder, hands moving to my upper thighs. "You're joking."

"I'm not." He hasn't moved except to wrap his hands around my waist, thumbs sliding into my belt loops. Even though Chelsea is in the house, I have zero concern she's going to be coming downstairs anytime soon.

"Is she?"

"No. She thought she was, for a few days."

"Why didn't you tell me?" There's a hint of accusation in his tone that I don't exactly appreciate but understand.

"I didn't know. She didn't tell me until just now. Said she thought I'd make her feel like it was okay because I'm calm and she wanted to feel stupid for a little bit."

"Good, she was stupid." His voice is rising. "And what was his deal? Why did they fight? Did he know about it beforehand?" He tilts his head up, hands still at my waist, voice loud. "Does she ever think about anything?"

"Lochlyn. Calm down. She feels bad enough. Lower your voice." My voice is low as I try to draw his to my level.

"Lower my vo—" One look at me is all it takes for him to freeze. "Okay, fine. Can I go kill him now?" His voice is at a normal octave again.

"No. You don't even know what happened."

"Do I need to? My baby sister came home crying over the guy she's with and then you tell me she had a pregnancy scare. What more do I need to know?" Angry Lochlyn is something I've seen before, but this is a situation where I'm not sure I can control his reaction like I usually can.

"She just needs time to cool down. He didn't do anything except act like having kids was the worst possible thing in the world. He said he doesn't even know if he wants kids someday."

"She wants to have kids with that asshole?" He practically shouts it.

"Lower. Your. Voice. I'm not joking. We just got over a fight. Want to jump into another one already?" My tone is as forceful and stern as I can make it.

Noticeably clenching his jaw and digging his fingers into my hip a little, he sighs. "So, she's upset because he doesn't want kids?"

"I think she's just upset because she doesn't feel supported. She doesn't feel like *if* something were to happen, he'd be there for her. Or be happy. She's not sure she does want kids with him, or to even stay with him for long enough to find out. But she wanted him to be supportive. I can't blame her for that."

Tightening his hands on my waist, he pulls me into his lap, resting his forehead against my temple and wrapping his arms around me. "I failed her," he mumbles against my ear.

"Lochlyn, you are *not* her parent. You're her brother, and you're at college. Chelsea and I are basically orphans doing the best we can. She just missed a few pills."

"I let her have sex in the first place." His self-deprecation is a new side of him. But I will not let him feel bad about this.

"You did not *let* her. Chelsea is always going to do whatever she's going to do. Nobody's going to stop her. You, of *all* people, should know that. It is absolutely, in no way, your fault. If you want to blame somebody, blame your parents. I mean, where the hell are they? I haven't seen them in weeks." Anger is rising like hot lava in my body and my voice. My poor, sweet, overly caring man is sitting here blaming himself for something his parents should have been on top of.

"They typically book their trips a year in advance now. They expected Chelsea to be at Cornell."

I can't help the eye roll and lava continuing to rise in me. His parents just choose to be gone. They should change their plans for their child.

"Regardless, it's not your fault." I run my fingers through his hair as I try to calm him.

"Why are you telling me instead of her?" He pulls his face back to look at me, but his eyes aren't focusing on mine, looking down at my lips instead.

"She asked me to. She thought you'd take it better from me. I'm worried she's seeing a shift in our relationship. Though, she did say you've always taken things better from me."

"You're calmer. The calm in the storm."

A smile pulls my lips up. "She said the same thing."

His arms tighten around me as he tilts his head to kiss my jaw. "Do you have to leave now that she's home?"

"Nope. You're sleeping 'on the floor' tonight." I use my fingers for air quotes to emphasize the statement.

"You're shitting me." He's completely baffled.

"I told her I wanted to stay, in case she needs me. That I'd sleep in your room and make sure you slept on the floor. I almost tried to convince her that the bed is big enough that we can easily sleep in it together and *not* be touching, but I figured it's too risky."

"You're amazing. I'm not sleeping on the floor."

"Oh no, you're definitely not."

He starts kissing along my jaw, down my neck, and across my shoulders. "How far do you think we can push it?"

"Not far enough," I moan. While we've had sex with Chelsea in the house before, on more than one occasion, this time, I don't trust her to not wake up, seeking a hug or a pint of ice cream.

Taking my chin in his fingers, Lochlyn turns my face to his as his mouth presses over mine, tongue barging in. My hand wraps to the back of his neck as I turn to face him more. His hand slides to my ear, fingers tangling in my hair.

I know we're taking a huge risk, that Chelsea could walk down the stairs at any moment, but I don't care. It had been six long weeks and one fight since I'd been with Lochlyn before two nights ago. I need him like I need oxygen.

Pulling away far too soon, he rests his forehead against mine, brushing his knuckles down my cheek. "We should get dinner. What would Chelsea want?"

"Pizza," we say in unison, laughing. I'm convinced Chelsea would eat pizza for every single meal.

We wait for dinner on the couch, watching TV, kissing a lot, and jumping apart at any sound we hear. When the doorbell rings, I nearly shriek.

We check on Chelsea together, tiptoeing into her dark room.

"Chels," I try in a low voice.

Sniffle.

Lochlyn and I frown as we look at each other. I sit near her head while Lochlyn sits near the foot of her bed. "Chels, we ordered pizza," I try gently.

She flips over and wraps her arms around my shoulders, crying. When I glance at Lochlyn, I see anger and hurt pull at his features. Instead of reacting to the anger and leaving to find Brendan, which I have no doubt he wants to do, he reaches out and rubs Chelsea's back.

"Chels, let's eat. You'll feel better after you have some food." There's strain in his voice. It's different than the one he gets with me. This is one I've heard over the years and that I always associate with how much he cares for his sister, how much he wants to protect her from every bad aspect of life.

Lochlyn's right, pizza does help her feel better. We let her pick a show to watch after we eat, which neither one of us like, but it makes her happy, so it makes us happy. Sitting next to him on the couch and not leaning into him takes a lot of focus and self-restraint, so it's good the show isn't captivating me.

When Chelsea goes up to bed early at nine instead of ten, we take full advantage. Once she's upstairs, Lochlyn pulls my legs over his lap and slides his hand up my thigh as he leans over me.

The second we hear her door close, his lips lock on mine as he leans me backward onto the couch, readjusting my legs so they wrap around his waist.

We stay like that until my lips are swollen, and my chin is raw from his stubble.

Lying in bed, my head on his chest as he runs his fingers along my arm, we're shrouded in silence. I know he's thinking over something heavy.

"Can you imagine Chelsea as a mother?" I almost jump at his voice, even though it's barely above a whisper.

"I think there'd be a lot of Uncle Lochlyn and Auntie Shay time."

"I can't believe she was so irresponsible."

"Yes, you can." I tilt my face towards his.

He sighs. "I guess I can. God, it sucks to have a younger sister."

"Would it be easier if you had a younger brother?"

"Probably."

"Really think on that. Think about what *you* were like at nineteen." My eyes narrow as I look at him, but I'm not sure he can see me.

"You mean, pining for a girl I thought I'd never have?"

"Be serious."

"I am." My heart flutters at his sincerity.

"Okay, maybe so. But think about the *other* things you did. With other girls. You're telling me you wouldn't be worried that possibly said brother could get somebody pregnant?" While Lochlyn told me he had always, *always* been safe in the past, there's a chance every time you have sex.

"I changed my mind. It's being the older sibling that sucks."

"Only when you're caring and interested. I'm sure Logan's not at all concerned with what I do." I pause for a minute. "I, uh, I just, I want you to know I'm still...we're being safe."

"I know."

"How?"

"I trust you. You're responsible."

"Sometimes I get tired of the pressure to be perfect," I mumble, frustration settling in my tone.

"You're the closest thing to perfection on this planet, Shay. But it's not about being perfect. You're a responsible person. You always have been. And if you make a mistake, it's not the end of the world."

My entire body freezes. Does he mean make a mistake with my birth control or in general?

"Uh, are you, do you mean...what do you mean exactly?" It's probably easier to let him tell me than to try to decipher it.

"I mean that you've always lived wanting to make other people happy. Your parents, Chelsea, even Logan, when she was around. And yeah, you do a lot that makes you happy as long as it's not going to upset somebody else. Being with me is the first thing you've probably ever done for yourself, right?"

"Right."

"I'm just saying that, that's part of who you are. You care about other people's thoughts and opinions. And you do what needs to be done. You're not taking care of things around the house and at the store because you want to take it over. You're doing it because it needs to be done and you step up. Making a mistake doesn't change who you are; it just means that you made a mistake, like the rest of us mere mortals." There's a melodic tone to his voice, one he uses when he's sincere.

"I think you put me on too high a pedestal."

"I think you don't put yourself on a high enough one."

I snuggle into him.

"And," he starts hesitantly, "if something were to...happen...we'd be okay. I'm not saying we should have kids now or anything. I mean, you're nineteen, I'm twenty-one, we have a lot of life to live before then. But, I don't know, I'd be okay with it, on some level."

"So, you're saying that if I make a mistake, forget my pill for a day or two, and accidentally get pregnant, you'll be *okay* with it? You won't be, I don't know, mad? Panicked?" All feelings I'm pretty sure he'd feel.

"I mean, yeah, I'd for sure be panicked. But mad? No."

"Okay. Good to know."

I rise and fall with his chest. "I'm not really explaining myself well. I guess I'm just trying to say that I don't want you to be scared to come to me. Chelsea didn't tell Brendan at first, and she spent five days worrying alone. I don't want that to be you if it ever comes to that."

"You want to worry with me?"

My body shakes as he laughs. "Yeah, I guess I do."

"I appreciate that. But I'm not scared to talk to you about anything, so it wouldn't be an issue." We haven't ever really talked about kids before. It's never really seemed like a good time or something worth bringing up since we haven't been dating for terribly long. "So, does that mean you want kids?"

Frozen. He has completely frozen beneath me. I'm not entirely sure he's even breathing. "This conversation took a turn I wasn't expecting."

"I just mean we haven't talked about it. Like you said, we're young still. I just, I don't know, maybe it doesn't matter." Maybe I got ahead of myself thinking he loves me enough to see that far into the future, or to discuss it with me.

"Yeah, yeah, someday, I want kids." He tightens his hold on me as he says it.

"Me too. Someday." Some far away day when I've graduated from college. That's my priority. And hopefully starting my career. Kids can come after that.

"Sorry, that conversation got a little...weird."

"No, no, it's good to know. I appreciate that you'd want to be there for me. I feel bad Chelsea was alone, that she didn't feel like she could come to me. And worse that she didn't feel like she could go to Brendan."

Every muscle in Lochlyn's body tightens. "Don't remind me. I don't understand what she's doing with him if she can't talk to him about something like that."

"I don't think he's permanent. He's just fun until we leave in the fall."

"One can only hope."

"So, do you think we need to set an alarm? I don't want her to come bursting in and we're like snuggled up or something."

"I'll risk it." He has his eyes closed and his sleepy voice. Who am I to argue? Squeezing into him, I let sleep consume me.

Saying goodbye doesn't get any easier. Lochlyn says it should only be a few weeks until the concert, but it feels like an eternity.

"We're in the home stretch, baby girl." He says it with his forehead pressed against mine as he wipes the tears from my eyes the day he leaves.

"Concert. Find out the details, let me know immediately."

"I promise."

"Can I just come with you?" Very wishful thinking on my part. If things had gone according to plan, I *would* be going with him.

"Sure. Pack a bag. Let's go." His shoulder hikes up and then he waves his arm toward the door as he speaks.

"I wish you were being serious."

"I am."

I jerk back. "I can't go with you, Lochlyn."

"Why not?"

"Because I have school. And the store. Chelsea, my mom." The weight of responsibility makes my shoulders slump.

"I know. I just wish you could too."

"For a minute, I thought you'd lost your mind."

"Not quite yet. I'm just going to miss you."

"How long until the concert?" My eyes are closed and I'm bouncing on the balls of my feet.

"Only a few weeks."

"Okay. More text messages and late-night phone calls until then, I guess."

"But then it's only another three or so weeks until it's over. And I'll be home." *Home.*

"I think I can handle that."

"You can." He sighs. "I have to go. I'll call you as soon as I get there."

We spent the day at my house, while Mom's at work and Chelsea had gone to Brendan's. Being with each other is always nice, but the last day together always has something heavy hanging in the air. It's always so much by the end of the day I feel like I can't breathe.

"I love you, Shay."

"I love you too." Mine always comes out as a whisper.

With one more big kiss, he's gone. The countdown to the concert has begun.

Chapter 12

"So, the concert's going to be the last weekend in April." Lochlyn's voice fills my ear.

"Who?"

"It'll be that Saturday. Starts at seven."

"Who?"

"I think you should come up after classes on Friday."

"Who?!" I'm bouncing on the balls of my feet in front of my bed, too eager to keep still.

"And we can go to dinner before the show."

I heave a frustrated breath. He's intentionally ignoring me.

"Oh, I'm sorry, had you asked who?" I can hear the smile in his voice as he teases me.

"Nope, must have been somebody else. Don't care. Not even sure I'm coming anymore."

"Oh. Well, then I'll guess I'll have to find somebody else to take to The Starting Line, Yellowcard, and Dashboard concert." The fake disappointment hangs from his words. I've come to recognize all of his different tones, voices, intonations. I'm not sure one exists that I don't know.

"No."

"Yes."

"All three?"

"All three."

"AHH!" I scream. Loudly. "Ohmygod, ohmygod, ohmygod!"

"Wow. I am so happy I had the forethought to pull the phone away from my ear. I think my neighbors heard you."

"How? How are they having all three?" My pulse is fluttering.

I can see his shrug in my mind. "It happens sometimes. You happy?"

"*So* happy. It's like my dream concert!"

His deep chuckle works through the phone straight to my heart. "I know. I had a feeling you'd be happy regardless, with the thoughts going around of who it would be, but when I saw the official announcement, I knew you were going to flip."

"Aren't you excited? Music's like the first thing we bonded over." For some reason, I feel a need to remind him of this often.

"I'm screaming on the inside."

"It's going to be so fun! Oh, I have to figure out what to wear." *Chelsea can help*.

"Can I make some suggestions?" His voice is low and taunting.

"I have to be *clothed*, Lochlyn." It's not hard to know exactly where his mind goes.

"Oh, okay. Never mind, then."

"Your suggestions are welcome after the concert."

"Even better."

"Maybe I'll go shopping with Chels."

"What are you going to tell her?"

"The truth."

"You're going to tell her we're dating?" He just won't stop teasing me tonight, and I can tell he's not serious by the lilt in his voice. While I know he's planted firmly in camp tell Chelsea, he understands I'm not and respects my decision. One of my arguments is that he's her brother, and they *have* to have a relationship even if it all blows up. She and I don't.

"No. I'm going to tell her that you told me about an epic concert and invited me to come up for it. She knows we like the same music. She won't think anything of it." I walk over to my desk and start fidgeting with the various trinkets. Now that I've seen Lochlyn's apartment, I can imagine him sitting in his chair, feet on his desk as he leans back.

"What about when you tell her you're staying the whole weekend?"

"I figured I'd just tell her I wanted to see campus again and that the concert is late Saturday, so I'd need to stay the night."

"And when she asks about sleeping arrangements?"

"Your ass is on the couch, babe." I make a small clicking noise with my mouth to give my sentence more emphasis.

"Why do I always have to end up on the couch?" he huffs out teasingly

"You really think Chelsea wouldn't call and scream at you for having me sleep on the couch when Wes is around?" I freeze on my trek around my room and look out the window in the direction of the Reynolds' house. I can't really see it from my room.

"Wes is a nice guy."

"Yes, he is. And you're her brother and she barely lets you be in the same room as me." Overdramatic barely covers it, but there's only so much to be done or said. Once Chelsea is set, it's futile to try to change her mind.

"Ah yes, but I'm her handsy, sex-crazed brother whose only goal is to corrupt girls."

"Well, you are handsy and sex-crazed. And you did a pretty good job at corrupting me. So, I guess she's not wrong."

"These hands are certainly missing you."

"I'm missing those hands more." The conversation has taken a very sharp turn and I have to clench my thighs together.

"Two and a half weeks seems really far away right now." There's tightness in his voice, and I can image the widening of his eyes, how the blue iris all but disappears as his pupils dilate.

"Yeah, it really does."

Clearing his throat, he changes the conversation. "So, come up that Friday after your class."

"Yeah, yeah, that sounds good. I'll want a pile of your shirts again."

"No, you're banned."

"What? Why?" It barely comes out as two distinct words as shock filters through me at the lunacy of his statement.

"You never gave me back that gray one with the guitar on it! I love that shirt."

"More than me?"

"Of course not."

"Then you're okay if I keep it." My tongue sticks out of the corner of my mouth as though he can see the face I'm making. Only in my wildest dreams.He sighs heavily into the phone. "It can't possibly still have any remnant of me on it."

"It doesn't. But it's comfy."

"That's why I like it!"

"Okay, tell ya what. Make me a pile, include that blue one I like, and I'll return your precious guitar shirt." It seems like a fair compromise to me.

"I like the blue one too. You're taking all of my shirts."

"I return them. Eventually. Besides, they're happy with me."

"Mhm. Fine, I'll make a pile of shirts, in exchange for my guitar shirt *and* you have to agree to wear them with nothing on underneath."

"Deal. Though if you're not around, how do you benefit?"

"Because I can just think about it next time I wear it."

"Oh. Well, that's not that hard to agree to since I do that anyway." Guess we're both in a teasing mood.

"Stop," he groans. "You're so mean."

"How am I being mean?" I have to play innocent, though, of course I know exactly what I'm doing.

"You're teasing me. It's so mean. Now all I can think about is you wearing my shirt."

"Oh. I'm wearing one right now, in fact. It's kind of cold with no pants on. Very drafty. I think this one probably wouldn't fit you anymore. It seems to have shrunk the last time you washed it because it hits me right at the upper thigh, just below my a—"

"Don't. Please. You're killing me." His voice is clipped and tight, the gravelly texture that he gets before we fall into bed.

I bite into my lip, trying not to laugh. "I'm sorry. I won't tease you anymore. Much."

"I need to take a cold shower when we hang up."

"Maybe I'll join you when I come up for the concert. We didn't exactly get to finish last time."

"Okay, if you're just going to keep torturing me, I'm going to go."

"No, no, no! I'm sorry. I'll stop. I promise." I reach my hand out to stop him as though he can see me. If only.

"Next one, I hang up on you."

"You'd never."

"You're right, I wouldn't. But you're being mean."

"I miss you."

"I miss you too. I really do have to go, though."

"Okay."

"Don't be sad. I'll talk to you tomorrow. Countdown is on for the concert! Only 15 days to go. I love you." Tomorrow seems so far away when we have to say goodbye.

"I love you too."

"Good night, baby girl. Dream about me."

"Good night, Loch. I always do."

I decide telling Chelsea sooner as opposed to later is the best approach. Then she can get any objections out of her system early and come to terms with it.

"I'm going to a concert in a few weeks at Cornell with Lochlyn." Spitting it right out seems like the best way.

She spins to look at me, pausing while bringing a pretzel to her mouth. "I'm sorry, what?"

"Lochlyn, your brother, he called me to tell me about a concert they're having that I'd like. Asked if I wanted to go. I said yes. I'm going up in two weeks, spending the weekend." The words come out slowly, almost like I'm talking to a child. It's probably better this way.

"With Lochlyn?"

"He offered to let me stay at his apartment so I don't have to get a hotel. Said he'd sleep on the couch or whatever." The 'or whatever' is really in bed wrapped around me.

"I want to go."

"I'm sorry?" I'm stunned. No, stunned isn't a strong enough word.

"I want to go. To the concert. Yeah, yeah! It'll be fun!" Her face is bright and cheery.

"I'm sorry, say that again. You want to go? To the concert? You don't like the same kind of music we do. Is this something about me staying with Lochlyn? Because if it's really a problem, I'll get a hotel."

"What? No, that's fine, you've been sleeping at our house for years, you just did last week. I just think it'd be fun!" If she's so *fine* with it, why does she basically throw a temper tantrum every time we're in the same room?

"To go to a concert...of bands...that you don't like." I'm still having a hard time putting together the pieces of this puzzle.

"Yes."

"Okay, help me connect the dots here 'cause I'm still confused." And incredibly so. I *know* Chelsea has zero interest in attending this concert. Something else is clearly going on here. It's just a matter of figuring out what.

"I just want to go, okay?"

Narrowing my eyes, I look at her. "Are you up to something? Do you not trust me?"

"Jeez, Shay, I just want to get away for the weekend."

"You just went away. To Killington." I absolutely, under no circumstance, want Chelsea coming to the concert with me. It would ruin my entire weekend with Lochlyn.

"Don't remind me. I haven't been to campus in forever." She looks nostalgic.

"And whose fault is that? You can go whenever you want." My tone is a little snippier than normal as frustration takes over.

"What is your deal? Why are you so against me going?"

"Because I'm not going to leave early or not go because you decide you don't like it." I'm fighting bouncing my knee in anxiety as we sit across from each other at the desk in the office.

"It's fine, Shay. I'll be fine."

"You have to get it past Lochlyn. I'm not asking him for you." Surely, he can convince her not to come.

"Fine, fine. I want to bring Brendan too." She's killing my weekend.

"Then you are *definitely* asking him." I'm ready to jump out of my chair, but she'll suspect something's up.

"I don't know why he hates him so much."

"Um, pregnancy scare? Ring any bells?"

"He hated him way before that."

"He's just protective. You know that."

"Yeah, I know. 'Kay, break's over. You coming?" She stands, wiping her hands and running them down her pants, tossing any crumbs to the floor.

"I'll be there in a minute."

As soon as she's through the doors, I whip out my phone, dialing as fast as I can, bouncing on the balls of my feet while it rings.

"Hey, why are you calling during the da—"

"Chelsea wants to come to the concert," I blurt out.

"She *what?*" He sounds as shocked as I feel. My heart is hammering so loudly I'm sure he can hear it through the phone.

"She wants to come to the concert. I tried to talk her out of it. I couldn't. I told her she has to call you to talk about it. I wasn't going to."

"Does she know something?"

"I don't think so."

"Fuck. *Fuck.*" My sentiments exactly.

"Yeah." Our conversation is moving briskly, one answering almost before the other finishes. It's not the sort of midday chat I'd like to be having, but at least it's a little extra time to hear his voice.

"I mean, I'll make a good argument, but ultimately I can't tell her no."

"I know."

"Which means..."

"Oh, I know. It gets worse. She wants to bring Brendan." Standing on my toes, I peer through the small window in the door to make sure Chelsea's not returning since I wasn't on her heels.

"No way. No fucking way."

"I say let him come. An extra distraction for her. And I guess have Wes stay too. At least then we can make the argument for you sleeping in your room with me versus on the couch, since everywhere will be taken."

"Good thinking."

"Yeah, I don't like how good I'm getting at both lying to her and coming up with ways to be sneaky."

"There is an alternative, ya know." He always brings it back to that. I understand his reasoning and thought process, but I know Chelsea well enough to know that it will be nothing short of a cataclysmic event.

"Sure, you say that since you're safe far, far away in Ithaca. Let's see how you feel when you're home all summer. I'd love to talk more, but I have to get back out on the floor before she comes looking for me. Wait for her to call you."

"Okay, I will. I'll call you tonight. I love you."

"I love you too."

After sliding my phone into my pocket, I make my way to the floor. I'm not sure what their conversation is going to be like, but I definitely want to be there for it.

I walk into Chelsea's house the next day to her screaming into her phone. When I had spoken to Lochlyn last night, she hadn't called him yet. I assume it's him. Sitting quietly on the couch, I perk my ears up.

"Because I want to!"

"Because I do!"

"I don't care that I don't like the music! I want to come." She's pacing behind the couch, and I have to keep turning my head from side to side to follow her trek.

"I know the point of a concert is to enjoy what's being played. I want a weekend away."

"Killington wasn't fun." Her hand moves up to her mouth and she starts chewing her cuticles, a sure sign that the thought of her trip still upsets her.

"Brendan is absolutely coming with me."

"No, I don't mind driving." She isn't yelling anymore. And apparently is driving. I guess he gave in. Seemed to put up a good fight, though.

"You're the best! Love you, big brother." She hops over the back of the couch to sit with me. "Sorry. Yay, we're going to a concert!"

"Yay." I try to fake excitement. "To make things even more fun, I wanted to go shopping, get something to wear to the show."

"Oh, even better! Tomorrow?"

"Sure."

"Anything in particular?"

"No, just wanted to look around. I'm just wearing jeans and Converse. Thought maybe a new shirt or something." Something tight that will make Lochlyn lose his mind.

"How's John taking this news about you going?"

"Huh? Oh, he's fine. I told him about it, but he's busy. Told me to go, have fun. He knows Lochlyn and I are friends." Very, *very* good friends.

"He doesn't want to go?"

"He does, but he can't get away." I'm beginning to think it's time to break up with *John*. I'm not sure what I'll do about the text messages besides hide my phone from Chelsea.

"You two don't seem to see each other much." She sounds a little sad as she says it.

"We don't, it's tough. We talk a lot. That's about all we can do."

"Makes me feel happy Bren is right here."

"Yeah, you're definitely lucky." I'd give anything for Lochlyn to be so close.

"Okay, shopping tomorrow. We'll both get something awesome. Now I may regret this, but play some of the music so I know what to expect."

A devious smile spreads across my face. "Gladly." I take her hand and drag her to her room. Maybe she'll listen, hate it, and change her mind, leaving me and Lochlyn to a weekend alone like I had hoped.

I've had no such luck with getting Chelsea not to want to come. A half hour away from Cornell, I'm feeling antsy and fidgeting my fingers nonstop. I'm not going to get the greeting I've been waiting for, dreaming of. In my dreams, I jump into his arms and he brings me straight to his room and tears off my clothes. The reality I'm faced with will be a quick, friendly hug.

She'd also made me drive part of the way, saying she'd promised Lochlyn that Brendan wouldn't drive but had said nothing about me. It made me tired, more tired than I want to be.

Brendan had grumbled something about not understanding why Lochlyn hated him so much, but I'm pretty sure as we get closer, he's thankful he wasn't allowed to drive. It truly is exhausting.

Lochlyn had insisted that we get in at four so we could go to dinner at a reasonable time. I had heard him telling Chelsea, as he'd asked her to put it on speaker so he 'had a witness.' Which, of course, means it's already almost five by the time we're knocking on his door.

"You're late." There's a deep set scowl on his face as he opens the door.

"Oh stop, it's fine. We're here. Yes, the drive was fine, thanks for asking," Chelsea says as she breezes past him into the apartment, Brendan on her heels.

Our eyes lock as I brush past him, making sure to slide my chest against his as though there isn't any room for me to pass. He responds by grabbing my ass. It's going to be a long weekend of secret flirting.

"Where can we put our stuff?" Chelsea already seems bored as she stops and glances around the room.

"Wes said you and Brendan can have his room." Lochlyn points down the hall.

"Oh, that's nice of him. What about Shay?"

"She'll be in my room."

"And you'll be on the couch?"

"Actually, no, Wes is going to be here."

Her face hardens and her mouth presses into a line. "So, what, you'll both be in there?"

"Yes."

"Chels, it's not a big deal. They're both adults." Brendan is trying to reason with her, putting a hand on her arm that she quickly shrugs off. Silly boy.

"I don't like it." She shakes her head once like that's all she needs to do to get everybody to jump at her command.

"Well, Chels, it's either she sleeps in my room or she sleeps on the couch with Wes. Take your pick." Utter irritation rips through Lochlyn's words and I'm sure if I turned around, it'd be written all over his face. As it is, he's still standing behind me, close enough that his sandalwood scent swirls in my nose and his warmth radiates against my back.

She chews her cheek for a minute before Lochlyn speaks up again. "Oh my God, are you actually thinking about it? She's sleeping in my room. That's the decision."

Before she can argue more, I interject, "Chels, it's fine. I've known Lochlyn forever."

"I'm not comfortable with it." It's so matter of fact and like it's all she needs to say to get us to change things. Part of me wants to yell at her, but this weekend doesn't need to be any more tense or complicated.

"Well, you're not the one who's going to be sleeping in there. I am. And I'm fine with it. I'm not sure what you're so worried about, but I highly doubt he'll try anything with you being just down the hall. Not to mention, I doubt he sees me that way." Lying has become so easy; it slides off my tongue like butter and barely requires any thought. As somebody who had never lied in the past, it's a little unnerving at how readily I picked up the habit.

She looks between us quickly. My body is thrumming, knowing he's only a few inches away and hope she can't see it. "Fine. Guess I don't have a choice." She points her finger at Lochlyn. "I swear you better not touch her."

"Chels, come on. You're going to be right there and Wes will be on the couch. I'm not sure what sort of thing you're worried about, but it needs to stop." Lochlyn puts a lot of emphasis on "stop."

I see the conversation going around in circles for the foreseeable future. While I usually let them battle it out, I decide to speak up. "Chelsea, calm down. I have no problem telling him off if I need to. But he's always been respectful when we've needed to share a room. You forget, I just slept in his room a few weeks ago. He was very kind and respectful. He didn't try anything." That I didn't want, that is.

"Whatever, I said it's fine. Which one is Wes's room?"

"Down to the right." Lochlyn points as though he's giving detailed directions, but the apartment isn't that big.

"We're going to drop this stuff in there, get ready for dinner. I'm hungry. Let's go eat."

"Sure thing."

The second they're out of sight, his mouth crashes on mine, arm wrapping around my waist and pulling me against him as his hand slides to the back of my head. I hold my bag as he walks me backward to his room, pushing me against the wall once we're inside.

I stifle a moan as he kisses across my jaw and down my neck.

"I missed you," he murmurs against my collarbone.

His lips are on mine again, and I feel like he's trying to devour me. At this very moment, I'm furious with Chelsea for crashing my weekend. All too soon, he ends the kiss, both of us breathless, as he rests his forehead against mine.

"I'm stealing every possible tiny second I can with you this weekend." His voice is quiet and strained.

"Please do."

"Nice job with Chelsea. I know lying is still a hard pill for you to swallow sometimes." As he speaks, he drags his palm down my chest to squeeze my waist before knotting my hair.

"It's getting easier and easier, and while this is probably a bad thing, I don't feel as bad about it anymore. And that's mostly because all I want is you. Please try *all* of the things with her just down the hall."

"Already planning on it." He bites his lip as his hand slides from behind my head to press gently against my breastbone.

Backing away, he tears his shirt off over his head. With a quick peek around the corner, I notice that Weston's door is still closed. I shut Lochlyn's most of the way.

Facing his dresser to get a new shirt, he's not paying to attention to what I'm doing. I flip him around, standing on my toes, to press my mouth to his. Sliding his hands under my thighs, he lifts me up and I hold on tightly. Turning, he pushes me up against the wall again.

When we hear the door open down the hall, he almost drops me. "Where are you guys?" Chelsea's voice has a way of carrying, even when she's talking relatively quietly.

Lochlyn grabs a shirt from the open drawer and pulls it over his head, adjusting his pants, and stepping out in the hallway, closing the door behind him. "Just changing my shirt. Shay's going to change."

"She was in there while you changed?"

"Relax, Chels, I only changed my shirt. We've all been swimming before, no different. It took me two seconds." It had. The other fifteen minutes he had his tongue in my mouth.

"What took you so long? You've had fifteen minutes."

"We were talking about the concert tomorrow and dinner. I told her if it'd make her more comfortable, we can get some extra pillows or something and make a barrier. It's a pretty big bed."

Tearing through my bag, I grab a red shirt that I know Lochlyn especially likes, and change as quickly as I can. I take his shirts from under all my packed clothes and toss them into his hamper before Chelsea can possibly see that I had them.

"Okay, sorry guys, I'm ready." I watch Lochlyn's eyes grow bigger the second I walk out of his room. Looking around, I notice Brendan isn't with us. "Where's Brendan?"

"Hiding," Chelsea responds as she bites at her nail like it isn't a crazy answer.

"What? Why is he hiding?" Am I the only one confused?

"He's scared of Lochlyn." Apparently, this brings great joy to Lochlyn, who bursts out laughing.

"Okay, well, you said you wanted to go to dinner, so we're all ready."

Sighing, she walks back down the hallway to get him.

Lochlyn is in front of me, fingers dipping into the waistband of my jeans, pulling me against him. "Mean."

"Me? Sweet innocent me?" I ask as coyly as I can, my fingertips grazing my chest.

"You know I love this shirt on you." His finger trails along the swoop neckline.

"I do, in fact."

"Mean."

"Oh, come on, isn't a little teasing fun?"

"Not when I don't get to act on it." His voice is low and gravelly, causing heat to course through my whole body.

"Who said you don't get to?"

"The fact that my sister, the only block in us being able to be together in public, will be right down the hall." He stretches his arm toward Wes's room.

"Yeah, but she's a deep sleeper." I trail my finger along his collarbone. I'm really pushing my luck. And his limits.

"You're killing me. Be nice. I can't have you, *and* I have to deal with Chelsea. And Brendan. Be nice."

Sighing, I push up on my toes and give him a quick peck on the lips before stepping back. "Fine. I put your shirts in your hamper."

"Thank you."

"Where are we going for dinner?" Chelsea asks distractedly as she walks down the hallway, phone in her hand. We both take another tiny step backward.

"I was thinking Japanese?" He glances at me to catch my smile.

"Sure." Brendan still hasn't said a word. He almost looks like he's cowering behind Chelsea.

As we walk out the door, I let Brendan and Chelsea go first, Lochlyn holding the door open for everybody. Thinking we're right behind them, Brendan and Chelsea start walking down the hall, giving me the chance to push on my toes and give Lochlyn a quick kiss before we walk out. As we follow them down the hallway, he loops his finger into my back pocket. Sometimes the tiny moments can be fun.

Friday went relatively smoothly. Chelsea isn't a huge fan of Japanese food but ate it without complaint. Until this morning. Which is how we find ourselves eating pizza, per her request, at five on Saturday. Lochlyn and I decide it's best to keep her happy, especially since we had a close call last night when we heard a noise in the hallway, jumping apart so fast I bit my tongue.

We had decided it was probably best to keep things tame the first night. Tame turned into a heavy make-out session with our hands all over each other and barely any clothes on. As soon as I squeaked out a moan, we stopped.

Lochlyn can't keep himself from me, not that I mind. Any time Chelsea and Brendan are out of sight, his mouth and hands are on me. When he took a shower, eyes dashing to me before closing the bathroom door, I itched to join him.

It's the one weekend we have together between the break in March and the end of school. While it's great to see him and just be close to him, it's not exactly what I've been hoping for.

Chelsea is, of course, making things hard on Lochlyn. Thankfully, the rest of us, Brendan included, are trying to help take the burden off him. Wes is surprisingly great with her. Better than Brendan, if I'm being fully honest. He's able to make her laugh, distract her, and will interject when Chelsea is about to explode all over Lochlyn for whatever unknown reason comes to her mind. They have a strong bond, but Chelsea takes most of her anger and frustration out on him, even if it has nothing to do with him. I think it's because he's the person she feels safest with. Maybe a little because she's mad at her parents, but he's the one who's around.

It's become apparent she's not happy that better arrangements hadn't been made in terms of sleeping. Lochlyn has made it exceptionally clear that he had *not* intended for Chelsea to be here, which is why other arrangements weren't made. That he's not going to kick Weston out of his own apartment just for her comfort.

One fight earlier today got particularly heated, and I had to push Lochlyn into his room while Weston and Brendan took Chelsea for a walk.

"Why is she pushing me so hard this weekend?" His hands gripped the edge of the mattress.

"She's not happy about this."

"Obviously. But what did she expect? It's a two-bedroom apartment."

"You know Chelsea, she always expects people to bend over backwards for her. Especially you."

Pulling me close, wrapping an arm around my waist while his other hand rested against my cheek, he kissed me tenderly. "All I wanted was to spend this weekend with you. How did it turn into this mess?"

It was how we had decided on pizza. When they returned to the apartment, Lochlyn offered to order, whatever kind Chelsea wanted, as an olive branch.

After eating, we all start to get dressed, Brendan and Chelsea locking themselves in Weston's room, and Weston hopping in the shower and taking some clothes with him. He's been a real trooper with having his home invaded and room taken over.

"She's trying to break me." Lochlyn has his head resting against my shoulder, hands on my hips.

"I know. She's in rare form this weekend." I run one hand through his hair while the other tips into his pocket. "Think she's suspicious?"

"I don't know. I think she's regretting having come for something she's not going to enjoy."

"Wes, he wouldn't...he wouldn't say anything, right?" There's a moment of fear that seizes my lungs in a vice. Of all the ways for Chelsea to find out, that's probably the least favorable.

"No. We had a very extensive conversation about it. He doesn't agree with it, but he understands and promised not to say anything."

"Doesn't agree with what? Us being together?"

"The lying part." There's a bite to his tone, and I know it's because he agrees.

"Yeah. That's kind of hard to swallow."

Twirling a few curls through his fingers, he exhales so heavily my hair flutters. "We should get dressed."

"Yeah, probably." Really, all I want in this moment is to stay like this, with his breath caressing my face, his hands on me, and us being so close that I can feel the heat emanating from his body.

"Can I watch?" One corner of his mouth ticks up in a devious smirk.

Giggling, I push against his shoulder. Before I can walk away, he grabs my wrist and pulls me against him, mouth melding to mine.

I sit on the bed while Lochlyn changes his shirt. It takes every ounce of self-control to not run my hands all over his chest. Kissing my temple, he walks out to let me change.

When Chelsea and I had gone shopping for the concert, I'd wanted to get something that would make it impossible for Lochlyn to keep his hands off of me. I'd figured Chelsea would have decided not to come, as had he, waiting until the last minute to buy her tickets. I almost feel a little bad because I know what I'm going to be doing to him. Almost.

Slipping on my jeans, I already feel good. They're Lochlyn's favorite. The black top I bought has a solid body with fishnet long sleeves. It's skin-tight. I've already refreshed my curls, which are bouncy and round, my make-up dark around my eyes, a light sheen of gloss shining on my lips.

After complaining I couldn't see how I looked when I visited for his birthday, Lochlyn hung a full-length mirror in his closet for me. Taking a look, I impress even myself, which is a hard task. It's not how I normally dress, tighter than the shirts I usually wear, but I look good. Chelsea's going to be proud, Lochlyn's going to go crazy.

Completing my look by pulling on my black Converse, I walk out of Lochlyn's room. All eyes fall to me. I watch as my boyfriend's widen and his lips part.

"Holy shit, Shay, you look *hot*!" Chelsea is, of course, the first to say anything, being the only one who really can. Noticing Brendan also staring, she smacks him on the chest. "Hey! Stop staring at my best friend."

"Sorry, you called my attention to her." If Lochlyn wasn't trapped in such a tunnel, I'm sure he'd be furious that Brendan was looking at me, but I don't even think he hears anything going on around him.

"Well, stop. Sheesh, all three of you. She has a boyfriend." I do. And he's one of the people staring at me with fire in his eyes.

"I don't want to be distracting. Should I change?" I hook my thumb over my shoulder to Lochlyn's room.

"NO!" all four voices yell at once. I'm thankful everybody says it and not just Lochlyn.

"Okay, then. Can we go?"

As everybody files out of the apartment, Lochlyn grabs my back belt loop and pulls me right up against him, his lips meeting mine immediately.

"You look so fucking sexy. Why are you doing this to me?" His voice is low and gravelly. It sends a stirring through my body, settling between my thighs.

"I picked it, hoping Chelsea would change her mind. You like?"

"To say the least."

"It'll be dark at the concert. We'll get close to the band."

"Mhm." I'm sure his mind is thinking of anything but words.

"Guys! What the hell, let's go!" Chelsea's voice echoes from down the hall.

Tipping up to give him one more quick kiss, I slide away. Groaning and grumbling, he follows me out, locking the door behind him.

The concert is amazing. Lochlyn and I try to break away as soon as we get there, but Chelsea isn't having it. Thankfully, before the first band is even finished, she's had enough and decides she and Brendan are going to leave. Lochlyn doesn't even care where they go or what they do, as long as they leave, asking Wes to give them his key. We'd driven over, but their apartment is close enough to walk.

As soon as they're gone, his arms are around me as we move to the beat. His chest vibrates against my back as he sings the songs we both know so well.

Somewhere through the concert, he spins me to face him, taking my hands in his and wrapping them around his neck as his slide into my back pockets. The way he looks at me as some songs play, the words dancing across his lips, it's like he's singing to me. And if he's not, I pretend he is.

When I reach my limit, I pull him down, crashing his mouth to mine as he slides his tongue across the crease of my lips. As my tongue seeks his, he moves his hands to my thighs, lifting me up.

I'm always in awe at how strong Lochlyn is. He picks me up like he's lifting a feather from the ground and holds me like it's nothing. It always seems like he can do it for hours.

Somewhere in the back of my mind, I'm conscious of the fact that we are surrounded by people, that Chelsea could decide to come back, and that I'm engaging in a level of PDA I'm not entirely sure I'm comfortable with. But in this moment, all I want is the alone time with Lochlyn that I've been longing for, surrounded by my favorite music.

"You have fun at your concert, baby girl?" Lochlyn asks between hurried kisses along my neck.

"Uh, huh," is all I can muster as I run my fingers through his hair, desire building in me like a quickly inflating balloon.

When we had gotten back to his apartment, Chelsea and Brendan were already asleep. Weston had left before the ending too, but stayed up until we got back. He had decided to do some digging on our behalf. They aren't suspicious at all; Chelsea is just frustrated with things not being what she expected and is having some trouble at school, which she's kept to herself. She had wanted to come to get away, but it isn't helping.

Since everybody's asleep, I let Lochlyn peel the clothes from my body. I've missed his warmth against me. I feel like I'm vibrating at his nearness, sure he can feel it where he touches me.

I'd put a shirt on, just in case. But it's one of Lochlyn's and long and loose, easy to lift and slide hands under. I'd tossed a pair of pants by my side of the bed, the far side, in case Chelsea starts pounding on the door.

It's somewhere around one in the morning and Lochlyn's tongue is sweeping across mine, his hand up my shirt, thumb resting just under my breast. Before I know what's happening, he pulls away, dropping a pillow on my face.

I'm about to push it away and ask what the hell he's thinking when his thumb moves from under my breast to graze across my nipple, the other sliding down to push aside my panties. Suddenly, the pillow makes sense, as he slips along my wetness and two fingers tweak and rub my nipple as it pebbles against his touch.

My back arches off the bed and my arm wraps around the pillow, pulling it against my face as his fingers slide inside me. The expert use of his fingers has me squeezing the pillow to the point where I almost can't breathe, trying to be sure to drown out the noises I can't control.

When Lochlyn touches me, my body is lit on fire. I lose complete control of my brain and just let some other urge or force take over. I hand my body over to him willingly, each and every time. He knows exactly what to do to bring me unimaginable pleasure, how to touch me, how to use his body.

As he flicks and slips along my nipple, his fingers hooking inside me, my toes curl, and I start to shudder beneath him. My teeth dig into the pillow still over my face, my hands searching blindly for any part of him I can reach, needing to touch him.

My fingers find his hair, twisting in and tugging, while at the same time pulling him against me. I'm close, so close...

He stops and pulls the pillow from my face. "Tell me what you want," he growls.

"You. All of you."

He pushes away from me and scrambles out of his pants, leaning back over me and brushing my matted hair from my face. As his mouth closes on mine, he eases into me. I pull away from him as my head tips back, trying to keep the noise as low as possible, as his lips lock on my throat.

The time away has heightened my senses and need for him. It also means my voice level is too loud for having other people around.

"Shh, baby. You *need* to be quiet." He draws out the shush and his voice appears strained, proving to me that he missed my body at least almost as much as I've missed his.

"I...can't..." I breathe. Silly man. He should know better by now.

I reach around for the pillow.

"No," he growls as I start to pull it over my face again. "I want to be able to watch you. It's been too long since I've seen your face twisted in ecstasy."

His hand finds its way to cover my mouth. It all happens as he keeps moving inside me and over me.

He has good timing, as the pressure in my lower belly is building and the sounds are growing more frequent. Knowing what's about to happen, he presses his hand firmer against my mouth and follows as my head tips back, my back arching, chest meeting his.

"Shh." It's drawn out and choppy as his breath becomes ragged.

All at once, I start to shudder, tightening around him. A sound I can't identify rises in my chest, causing a low grunt to escape his lips as he hisses through his teeth, slowing his movement to a stop.

As he rests his head next to mine, kissing my ear, he slowly pulls away his hand, trailing his fingers along my lips. I can't move, can't think, riding the orgasm high. I often feel like I'm floating when we're finished, unable to do much more than lie there. Lochlyn likes to tease me about it.

At this moment, he seems to have a bit of an inability to do much more himself. His breathing is heavy in my ear. I'm slowly regaining my ability to think and I'm becoming more aware that he's slightly crushing me.

With a kiss to my jaw, he rolls to his side, breaths evening out.

I roll to mine as well, a smile spreading across his face. He tries to tamp down and tuck away some of my hair. I don't even want to think about the rat's nest I'm sure to have in the morning.

"A little risky, don't you think?" I say as I run my fingertip down the center of his chest and through the gathered dampness.

"Baby girl, when you walked out of my room wearing that outfit, there was absolutely no way we were not having sex tonight. You're lucky I was able to control myself until we got home."

"This definitely is not the weekend I was expecting or hoping for." Because if it was, we would be gearing up for round two, at least.

"Me either. You're going to have to figure how to get your tears out without Chelsea seeing."

I groan as I lean into his shoulder. "I have no idea how I'll do that. I'm not going to feel sad until tomorrow. And I'm sure she'll want to leave before I do."

"Maybe we can get out alone. Or get her to leave alone. Maybe I can convince Wes to take her somewhere." The gears are working in his head, trying to come up with anything he can, knowing I need it.

"Think she'd really leave us alone?"

"Probably not," he grumbles.

"I'll have to just hold it in. Or come up with something. I don't know."

"I wish you could stay," he murmurs as he brushes his fingers down my cheek.

"Me too," I whisper, snuggling into his chest. Pulling my shirt back down to a respectable place and sliding my panties on, I lean up to kiss him.

"Good night, baby girl. I love you. Dream about me."

"Good night, Loch. I love you too. I always do."

When we wake up in the morning, we hear voices in the kitchen, but we can't tear ourselves away from each other. We just lie in bed, looking at each other, his arm around my waist as he draws little circles on my back.

I know we should get up, that Chelsea is bound to start pounding on the door, but I can't. The one time I made the slightest move to get out of bed, Lochlyn's arm tightened around me, so I settled in.

Chelsea's voice is rising above, closer to the door. If not for Wes, we may have been in trouble, but he steps in. "They got in really late, woke me up. I'm sure they're just still sleeping."

The reality of the day, and likely how soon we'll be leaving, hits me like a freight train and my eyes overflow. Lochlyn's face twists in pain, his lips tipping down and his brows scrunching, as he kisses away my tears, leaving his forehead pressed against mine. As they start to get worse, I press my face against his chest, pulling at his shirt, breathing him in.

Three weeks, three weeks, three weeks.

If I think it over and over, maybe it will make it go faster.

Tears slowing, we pull apart, ready to face the day. I wipe furiously at my eyes, trying to make sure Chelsea doesn't see the salty trails left behind. My plan is to make a beeline for the bathroom to give my face a quick splash of water.

Lochlyn has a better idea, though. "I'll go out first, say you're still sleeping. Take a few minutes, collect yourself. I'll distract them so you can sneak into the bathroom." He brushes his thumb down my cheek, causing the tears to threaten again.

"Hey, hey, hey. No more tears. It's only three more weeks, then I'm *home*. And after that, we'll be here, together." He must have noticed my lip beginning to tremble.

All I can do is nod. Kissing my forehead, he gets out of bed and walks out the door. I take a few deep breaths, burying my face in the sheets, before sliding out of bed and putting on my own clothes. One more quick swipe of my eyes and I'm on my way out the door, taking a deep breath to steel my nerves.

Somebody had gone out to get some breakfast, fresh bagels complete with cream cheese, lox, and other various toppings. There's a mostly full pot of coffee in the kitchen. After a quick rinse of my face, I head straight for the coffee, Lochlyn coming up behind me and pressing his chest against my back and resting a hand on my hip as he reaches up to grab a mug.

My breath catches as he brushes his hand down my back. The look that passes between us is filled with so much emotion. A tiny shake of his head tells me to hold it together.

Closing my eyes and taking a deep breath, I steady myself, pulling my full mug to my lips and tearing my eyes from his. I don't know how long until Chelsea will want to leave, but I know it's going to be torturous.

We leave two hours later, about four hours earlier than I want to. The weekend took an opposite turn from what I wanted it to be. It was the one chance to see each other to break up the six-week stretch, and it had been hijacked by Chelsea.

Not crying while I say goodbye is nearly impossible. I give Lochlyn a hug that's possibly too long for just friends, but nowhere near as long as I need. When we're halfway down the hall, I stop, dropping my bag.

"I, uh, I think I forgot something. I'll be right back."

"Do you want us to wait?" Chelsea also stops, turning to look at me.

"No, it's fine. I'll meet you down at the car."

"You sure?"

"Yeah. I'll be two seconds."

Chelsea narrows her eyes at me but doesn't argue, turning on her heel and heading toward the stairs.

Lochlyn opens the door on the second knock, pulling me against him and through the door, lips locking on mine quickly before resting his forehead against mine. "I love you."

"I love you too."

"Let me know when you get home."

"I will."

Biting my lip, I push up on my toes and kiss him again. I walk out backward, unwilling to turn away from him, fighting the tears with every step.

Once I get to the car, I slide into the backseat. "Sorry, Chels, I'm too tired to drive right now."

Leaning against the door, I look longingly up at the apartment as she gets into the driver's seat.

"What's wrong with you, Shay?"

"I'm just tired. Late night." If she doesn't buy it, she doesn't say anything. How can she know my heart hurts? That I left part of it upstairs in that apartment. I'm asleep before we even hit the highway.

Chapter 13

As we walk across the parking lot to leave our last final, I see Chelsea perk up, taking off at a sprint. I don't realize what she's running toward until I see him.

"Lochlyn! What are you doing here?" I can hear her as I get closer.

"I came to surprise my baby sister after her final!" His eyes are locked on mine. He didn't come to surprise her, he came to surprise *me*.

Chelsea's standing next to him, leaning against his shiny black Acura. "Shay, aren't you going to say hi to Loch?"

"Oh, of course." I lean in to give him a hug. He strategically leans to the side of me where Chelsea can't see him lick my earlobe. The wriggle his touch causes me brings a smile to his face. I can already tell he's going to make it very difficult to keep our relationship hidden all summer.

"So, what are your plans, Loch? I wasn't expecting you home until this weekend."

Finally, he breaks his gaze from mine, looking at Chelsea. "I finished my exams and figured I'd rather be home. More people I'd prefer to see here." His eyes dash over to me again. Chelsea's so absorbed in her phone, she doesn't notice. He could have his hands in my back pockets, and she probably wouldn't notice. Part of me wishes he'd try.

"I'm pretty free until Saturday. Heath and Jay are coming back Friday. They're talking about a party of some sort. You two are welcome to tag along." We've already talked about the party. We're going to try to convince Chelsea to go, not that it'll be too difficult. Chelsea loves a good party.

"Yeah, sure. If I can convince this one over here." She juts her chin toward me. I'm the one who's harder to convince. But I'm on the inside now.

I shrug. "I don't know, sounds like it could be fun. May be good to get used to some parties before we leave in August."

Chelsea glances up at me, her mouth slightly open. "Have you been replaced by a clone or something?"

"What? No. I thought you'd be happy. You're not having to pull my arm for once."

"I am. I'm just shocked. What's gotten into you?"

I notice Lochlyn smirk, catching my attention, as he mouths *me.* I grit my teeth to try to bite down the heat snaking up my spine.

Chelsea turns her head to look up at him. "Can I bring my boyfriend?"

"Uh, I guess. Brian? Or something." I know he's just giving her a hard time and is fully aware of his real name.

She rolls her eyes. "Brendan."

"Right. Brendan. Um, yeah, I don't see why not. You know the guys, always thinking the more, the better."

"Where is this party going to be, exactly?"

"I don't know. Not our house. That was my only requirement. They said something about the woods? I don't plan, I just attend." Lochlyn raises his hands in peace.

I feel slightly awkward as we stand around the parking lot. My body is longing to be against Lochlyn, but Chelsea's right here. She's making small talk, eating at my time to be close to him. I'm more interested in spending time with him than with her.

Our reunion isn't what I had built up in my mind. I'd had fantasies about him coming back, me running into his arms as he kissed me. I know how silly it seems, and unlikely since there's nowhere we can be public about it, but as it actually happened, it seems so anticlimactic. There's no grand reunion, just stealing glances and touches while making small talk in a parking lot.

I want her to go away and leave us alone. And I hate myself for it. In sixteen years of friendship, I had never lied or hid anything from Chelsea. Until the night Lochlyn kissed me. I've been lying to her ever since. It would ruffle my insides and eat away at me more if I wasn't so happy.

"This is perfect. I was going to head over to Brendan's after dropping Shay off at home. Loch, would you mind?" She turns to me. "That okay?"

I raise my eyebrows. Have I willed this into existence? "Yeah, that's fine."

"Not a problem, Chels. Have fun."

Chelsea puts her hand on Lochlyn's arm and skips off. We watch her golden ponytail bob away until she's out of sight. I'm in his arms in seconds, my cheek pressed against his chest.

"I missed you," he murmurs against my hair.

"I missed you too." I can't pull myself away to even look at him. In this moment, all I want is to feel him against me, to hear his heart beating, to breathe him in.

He gently pushes my shoulders back, tilts my chin up, and kisses me softly. My eyes widen. "What if somebody sees and tells Chelsea?"

One shoulder lifts as if it's no big deal. "We'll lie. Or, ya know, actually tell her the truth. We're running out of time for that."

I frown back at him. "We've been doing enough of that, don't you think?" I choose to ignore his ludicrous suggestion of telling her the truth. I know time's not on my side, but now that I'm so deep in it, I can't see a safe way out.

"Let's get out of here so I can kiss you how and where I want to." The familiar sensation of wanting stirs between my thighs.

He opens the door for me, fingers grazing my lower back as I slide into the seat. Once he's in the car, he leans across the middle and kisses me again, hand reaching behind my head to pull me closer, mouth parting mine.

Separating with a smile on his face as he adjusts his pants, he starts the car. Once we're out of the parking lot, he laces his fingers through mine, bringing my hand to his lips.

"Hey, turn this up." He juts his chin toward the radio.

My eyebrows scrunch. "Why can't you?"

He holds up our hands. "I'm not letting go anytime soon. Come on, hurry up."

Reaching forward, I spin the dial, cranking the radio, a Breaking Benjamin song filling the car. Lochlyn's fingers drum against the steering wheel.

His fun, easy-going personality shines through and makes me smile. I'd always watched from the sidelines, not sure how he lived that way when I analyzed everything I did both before and after I did it. But now I'm part of it. I'm part of his fun, carefree life. He's shown me how to let go, at least a little. To enjoy the moments for what they are.

When Chelsea had noticed the shift in me, she'd questioned it. I just told her I was getting ready for college, that I wanted to be more fun and embrace the experience, like she's always telling me. She'd let it go, not asking more questions. But what I'm really embracing is Lochlyn and his influence on me.

His carefree attitude is surface level, though. People think he just breezes through his life, not taking anything seriously. But he works hard and studies a lot. It absolutely astounds me how whip smart he is. Sometimes I'm convinced he knows everything. And just like anybody else, he overthinks and worries about a lot of things, but he just doesn't let it bother him on the surface. It's because he wants to make the most of his life, and that includes having fun.

For years, he'd made Chelsea his priority, taking care of her while their parents were gone. Then there's the whole path ordeal, the plan for his life that's laid out for him. In between those things, he's striving for happiness, for joy. If that means blasting music while cruising down the highway, he's going to do it. If that means getting tattoos, he's going to do it. If that means lying to his sister to be with me, he's going to do it.

His parents don't care anymore. As long as he stays the course, gets good grades, they feel like he can do whatever he wants.

"Hey, where are we going?" We just drove past the turnoff to head home.

"Somewhere special." As he looks at me with raised eyebrows and a smile on his face, I melt into my leather seat.

We drive with the music blaring for close to twenty minutes before Lochlyn turns onto a gravel driveway. On both sides of the car are sprawling fields, green and lush, that seem to go on for miles. What appear to be tennis courts and a playground are off to one side. The river is right ahead of us, sun shining and reflecting off the gentle waves. It's clearly a park of some sort, but one I've never been to.

He parks under some trees, car pointing toward the river. It's breathtakingly beautiful; the greenery mixed with the sparkling sunlight, especially as it peeks through the trees, sending glints of light in every direction.

"Nice spot. Bring a lot of girls here?" I tease with a smile. It's the perfect make-out spot. At least.

"Ha. No. Actually, I've never brought anybody here." His eyes lock on mine as he rubs his fingers across his lower lip.

"Why are you nervous?"

He drops his hand immediately. "I'm not."

I huff, tilting my head to the side.

"Okay, maybe a little. I don't know. This place, it's...special to me. It's really calming and quiet, peaceful. I come here a lot when I just need to be alone or need to think."

"I don't know why that makes you nervous. Do you not want to show me?"

"No, of course I do. I don't know, maybe it's because I know what I've thought about here."

For a moment, I wonder if I should question what he thought about or let it lie. I choose the latter.

After another minute of hesitation, Lochlyn gets out of the car. With no instructions or invitation, I do the same, but slowly, unsure if he wants me to join him. When he walks to my side of the car and loops his arm around my waist, I know I made the right choice.

I immediately sense what he means about it being calming and peaceful. Even though the playground is full of children, you really can't hear them here. Puffing some hair out of my eyes as it floats around my face in the gentle breeze off the river, my muscles start to loosen, my shoulders lowering.

Lochlyn hasn't said anything. It's not until he sits on the grass, pulling me to sit between his knees, my back against his chest, that he does.

Reaching around me to pick some grass, he speaks for the first time since we got out of the car. "I found this park about three years ago. My parents had left on another trip and Chelsea was driving me nuts. I felt stuck and lost. I was really mad at my parents for leaving me home, again, with her. I was a teenager, that was their job. At first, I'd been happy they trusted me enough. That was when I thought it'd be the one trip. Or maybe once a year. Not once a month.

"I think I had just found out Chelsea lost her virginity or something. I felt like I'd failed. That it was my fault because I was the one home with her. On some level, I think I knew that she was just rebelling because our parents weren't around. Which just made me even angrier at them. What was so wrong with us? Why didn't they want to be around? I know Chelsea's a pain in the ass, and I certainly have my flaws. My dad was less than pleased when the rumors reached his ears." I shift slightly at the mention of those rumors.

"He had said that I was painting the family in a bad light, that it wouldn't reflect well for me and certainly didn't reflect well on him. He didn't even ask me if they were true. Though, really, I knew what he would say. '*If enough people say the same thing, it may as well be true.*' He'd always said that about the firm's reviews." He tears at the grass in his hands. If I could see his face right now, I know it would be drawn, brows cinched together and jaw tight.

"I remember sitting here and trying to find some light. Something to make things easier, less difficult. I mean, I was eighteen and in charge of a wild sixteen-year-old. Instead of being thanked for the things I did to take care of her, I was condemned for the things I did to live my life." Angrily, he rips the rest of the grass apart. I haven't said a word as he talks, knowing he needs to get it all out, but I don't want to let the anger build. I tilt my head and kiss his jaw, getting a tight smile in return.

"I was never able to stay for long, not trusting Chelsea to leave her for more than an hour or two. Your parents were great then, a huge help, but they worked late. I'll never forget when I got back. You and Chelsea were in her room and you were arguing, sort of. It was that quiet arguing you've always done with her, where you make your points known firmly but don't actually raise your voice. How you keep your patience with her, I'll never know.

"But I heard you chastising her. Telling her she was way too young, she was being stupid, she wasn't really in love. All the things I'd thought of saying to her, you already were. That was when I realized, you are the light." My eyes flutter shut as warmth floods my chest, making my pulse race. His lips find the spot at my neck and graze against it lightly.

"I'd wanted to be with you for a little while at that point, often in ways I'm not proud of, though I wouldn't have acted on. But that was when I decided I *needed* you to be a bigger part of my life. More than just my sister's best friend and my...I don't know, sort of friend?" His inability to define what we had before makes me feel better, as I've never quite known what to call it either.

"I know there's all those stories, rumors, whatever. I'm not going to deny I had my share of...fun. But you know me. You've always known me. I hope you can know that they're not true. I need you to understand that I'm serious about you, about being with you. I don't know, I guess I just feel like it's important to remind you before going into the summer. It's going to be really hard trying to be together with everything going on and everybody being home. A week here, a weekend there, is one thing. A whole summer is very different."

"I mean, one rumor is pretty true." He tilts his head down to look at me. "You are *amazing* in bed." I shake against his chest as he smiles and laughs. Bending down, he presses his lips to mine.

I keep my head back against his shoulder as we stare out at the shimmering river, my forehead resting against his jaw.

"I'm worried about summer. I'm not going to lie." Not sure where I'm taking this, I start hesitantly, just speaking what's on my mind. "I know it's going to be hard. Ten weeks is a long time to keep a secret. It's not as new now, we're even more comfortable with each other. There are going to be so many times we want to just be close and sit, maybe even just like this, but can't." A heavy breath heaves from my chest as I try to wrap my head around the reality of it.

"Chelsea asked for reduced hours at the store too."

He hangs his head, sighing.

"I know. She did say she wants to spend a lot of the time with Brendan since she'll be leaving at the end of summer, but it will be harder to know exactly where she is or what time she'll be finished. Since I get to make the schedule, I'll know some hours for sure, but she'll get suspicious if I have a lot of those times opposite her."

"We'll certainly have our work cut out for us. But that was why I wanted to tell you all that. You're worth it. I'll figure out anything I have to, to have that time with you. And just be prepared that I'm going to sneak as many little touches as I can." His nose is in my hair as he speaks low in my ear.

I curl into him as need twists through me. "I'm okay with that."

Staring straight ahead, he rests his cheek against my temple. "Ever change your mind about telling her?"

"We've been over this. I'd love to tell her, stop hiding, stop *lying*. But she'll flip out. I don't even want to think about what she'd say or do. I can't risk it. I know it's foolish of me, cowardly even, but I'm too far down this road now. I have to keep going, there is no U-turn." The mere thought causes my limbs to tremble. However it comes out, as I know it will, it's going to be messy.

"Well, we can't do this forever. You'll be in the same room next year. You're welcome at my place all the time. In fact, I'll insist, but she'll wonder why you're not in your room."

"I know. I know we have to say something. I just, I don't know how. I don't know what to say. I'm certainly not prepared for the inevitable fallout."

"Why do we let her control our lives? Control this?"

Pressing my mouth into a hard line, I think for a moment. I've asked myself the same thing more than a dozen times, especially recently. "Because she's Chelsea. It's easier to give her what she wants. As frustrating and annoying and selfish as she can be, she has a good heart, and it's in the right place. She's always been there for me. Maybe she doesn't do things for me or the way I'd prefer them, if you remember my party, but she didn't hesitate to put her life on hold for me. And while it was still a party she appreciated, she had the thought to give me one, to take some time to celebrate *me*. She sat with me every day when my dad was sick. She's even offered to drive me to the cemetery, to sit with me. She's just...she's Chelsea."

"Yeah, yeah. I guess she is. Do you remember when I was a junior, so you would have been a freshman, and I was really sick for a week? I could barely get out of bed, I was so weak. High fever, body aches. Chelsea brought me soup, juice, and Advil every day when she got home from school. I know she hadn't made the soup herself since she could barely boil water, but she brought it to me. Sat with me and made sure I ate, told me stories about school and how her day was. Talked about you. Mostly she just kept me company, made sure I was okay." His voice is wistful as he thinks back on the memory.

"She may be a pain in the ass, but she's a good person. And a lot of that has to do with you."

His brows are knit together, eyes scrunched in confusion as he looks down at me. "Me? How?"

"Lochlyn, look at everything you did for her. I mean, those are some pretty formative years and your parents basically just decided they didn't want to be parents anymore. She could have fallen way off the deep end. But she didn't. You're her older brother. Who you are helped shape who she is just by showing her how to be. You've always been a good person. Kind, generous, caring. Protective. You're smart as hell, which obviously didn't translate *quite* as much, but Chelsea's still smart. She just doesn't have the same drive you do. Studying with her this year was a nightmare."

Does he really not see the influence he's had on her? How much he's affected her life in the best ways?

"I can only imagine. She still thinks I didn't do much while our parents were gone." Though he tries to hide it, I sense the hurt in his tone.

"That's her problem. And I've always told her that. She's always kind of put herself first, but things really changed when your parents started traveling. I think she took it harder than we realize."

"Has she ever said anything?"

"Not a thing. Which is kind of surprising because we know how much she loves to talk about herself. But even if I bring it up, she changes the subject. Quickly. That's how I know there's more to it. There are deep feelings there."

Silence overtakes us again as we let our thoughts on Chelsea linger.

"God, I so don't want to turn into my dad." His voice comes out just above a whisper.

"Lochlyn. Are you serious?" My voice is soft and shrouded in shock.

He hangs his head so his forehead rests against my shoulder. "I'm set up for that life, Shay. Cornell, law school, place at his firm. He wasn't always how he is now. We used to do stuff together as a family, families even."

"I remember."

"Then one day, they stopped caring, stopped being interested. It was like they finally had money to be able to do what *they* wanted and make sure we were taken care of. The first time they left for a week, Chelsea cried. She thought they weren't coming back."

Wrapping my arms around one of his, I pull it tightly to my chest, squeezing. I can't imagine how hard it must have been for both of them. My parents are gone in different ways. But they didn't choose that, it chose them.

"Lochlyn, you're *nothing* like your dad."

"I just don't want to harden like he did."

"Look at me." He complies and there's a sadness in his features. "You are a good person. You are caring and sweet and giving. You don't want that life, you're being pushed into it. And you push back." As I say it, I trail my fingers along any tattoo they can reach. "Please don't worry about becoming him."

He leans his forehead against mine, speaking quietly, "Promise me you won't let me become somebody I don't want to become."

"I promise."

Lochlyn keeps his arm over my shoulder, across my chest, pulling one of my hands down and linking his fingers through mine to rest in my lap. We sit there, a tangle of our bodies, not knowing where he ends and I begin, until the sky fills with vibrant shades of pink, purple, and orange.

Chapter 14

Heath decides to throw a party for the Fourth of July, having to cancel the first of the summer that we had planned to attend. It's at his parents' house, as they're out of town. His backyard is huge, complete with a pool and bar, for which he hired a bartender.

Things between Lochlyn and I have been tense. The sneaking around and lying is starting to take a toll. It's harder several weeks put together with many more ahead. More than once, he's begged me to tell Chelsea. But I just can't. I want to at least wait until the fall when we're all at school together, when I have a place to go, a way out. We've had a few close calls. It's destroying his confidence.

Lochlyn has been in a foul mood since this morning. He's been quiet the whole way over, music turned up loud enough that we can't talk. Though he holds my hand on the drive, he won't look at me.

We're sitting in the Acura in front of Heath's house, but Lochlyn makes no move to get out.

I chew on my lip, often stealing glances at him as he has his hand against his mouth, staring out the windshield. Looking at him makes me anxious. Looking away from him also makes me anxious. I don't know where to point my eyes.

He solves the problem for me, taking my chin firmly in his fingers and turning my face to his as he leans across the console, mouth closing over mine, tongue forcing its way to curl between my lips.

The tension I've been holding eases out of me as his hand slides to the back of my neck, keeping me against him.

When he pulls away, he's stolen all of my oxygen, but he still doesn't say anything as he gets out of the car.

Lochlyn opens my door and waits for me to step out, linking his fingers with mine as soon as I stand next to him. The grip he has on my hand tells me not to argue, not to point out that it isn't a *friends only* thing. It also doesn't scream relationship. The kiss he gives me before we walk through the back gate does, though.

I sigh as he smirks. He likes to do that, skate the thin line. Slipping his hand from mine, he opens the gate, pinching my ass as I walk through. Spinning around, I point a finger at him, a warning.

The party is in full swing, a huge crowd having gathered, including a lot of people Lochlyn, Heath, and Jay had gone to high school with. Most assuredly some girls that have either been with Lochlyn, or want to be. Taking a look around, we see Chelsea isn't here yet.

"So where's the line here, Shay? Chelsea's not here. How much can I get away with?" His mouth against my ear sends shivers down my spine. A low chuckle rumbles from his chest and straight through me as he notes my reaction.

Before I can respond, his hand is on my lower back, pinky dipping below my waistband. Hand on my back, not so crazy for friends. Finger dipping into my pants, not such a friends thing.

I shoot him a warning look but don't move away. Growing up with Chelsea and Lochlyn, I know Heath and Jay pretty well. They're Lochlyn's two best friends since the age of eight. Even going to college in different states, they still get together over breaks and spend a good chunk of the summer together. Until the past year, at least, when Lochlyn decided he'd rather spend his time in hiding with me. We have to lie to them too, since they'd be all too quick to let Chelsea know, even if by accident.

As we move farther into the throng of people, eyes start turning to Lochlyn. I'm used to it; he's always attracted attention. But it's harder being his girlfriend, his *secret* girlfriend, and around people we know. Before, I was just another set of eyes turning to him. Now, I feel a need to defend against them, but can't.

Lochlyn's so good at being secretive, it's a little scary. I hadn't really noticed before. He gently pushes me forward until we're so close to the music he has no choice but to lean down to talk against my ear, standing strategically behind me where his hand rubbing gently against my lower back won't be noticed.

"I'm going to get a drink. Why don't you go sit on that couch and I'll join you in a few minutes." He points to one of the patio couches on the opposite side of the pool, away from the music, in full sight of the bar.

I nod as he starts to walk away, sliding to my other side while trailing his hand along my back. He's toying with me, and it's working, as my body temperature rises and desire races through me.

Making my way over to the couch, I keep my eye on him, each of us stopping to say hi to a few people along the way. Not being with him and not seeing him was hard. But being in the same place as him and not being able to touch him is almost impossible. My body aches for his nearness, my fingers twitch with the need to touch him. We've spent the better part of the past five weeks together, even if just chatting while he helps at the store again.

Two hands suddenly wrap around my biceps, making me gasp. Turning, I take in Jay's smiling face.

"Oh, sorry, Jay. I wasn't watching where I was going." I'd almost walked straight into him.

"It's okay. How are you, Shay?" I can't help but notice as his eyes scan up and down my body, taking their time at my hips and breasts.

"I'm pretty good. How about you? How's Penn State?"

"It's good. Lonely." His shoulders tip up briefly.

"Oh?"

"Yeah, nobody to keep me company." I take a step back as he reaches out to grab a curl. My gaze flashes over to Lochlyn, who tenses and downs the amber liquid in his glass, tapping the bar for a refill, eyes locked on me and filled with fire.

I try to smile. "Yeah, I bet it can be. But you've been there a while. I bet you have some good friends."

"Not quite the company I was referring to." A smirk spreads across his face and I'm sure he thinks he's being coy instead of creepy.

"I'm sure there are plenty of pretty girls at school."

"Not any I've had my eye on." He's starting to make me uncomfortable. In this moment, I'd love for Lochlyn to just say fuck it all and come wrap his arm around my waist. Maybe punch Jay in the face, something I know he wants to do right now, childhood friend or not.

"Oh, that's unfortunate. It's too bad my boyfriend can't be here today. I was hoping he could meet some of my friends."

His face drops, and he takes a step backward, giving me some breathing room. "Yo-you have a boyfriend?"

"Yeah, for a few months now. We're really happy. He has to work tonight." It has gotten way too easy for me to lie, weaving them from nothing. What's worse is I don't feel bad about it anymore. And not that I've ever heard of Jay being opposed to cheating, but I do know he prefers to be the center of attention. And because I have a boyfriend, he clearly wouldn't be.

"Well, that sounds nice. I, uh, hope to meet him this summer. See ya around, Shay."

Once Jay's out of sight, I let go of the breath I've been holding since he stepped in front of me. Looking over at Lochlyn, I can see he is *not* happy.

Once I get to the sitting area, I notice that the atmosphere is much quieter on this side of the year, and flop down onto the couch. I'm sure it's strategic, a place for people to be able to sit and talk. Though Heath always wants "action" at his parties, as he likes to call it, so maybe he wants it quieter for people to hook up. Heath has a strange sense of what a party should be.

I take in Lochlyn's tall frame as he sits at the bar, legs sideways as he leans one elbow on the wood, the other arm thrown over the back of his seat. There's a toothpick hanging out of his mouth as he chews on it absentmindedly, glancing over at me every few minutes. He's already downed another drink, more of the amber liquid, and is slowly nursing the third as he waits for a refill. The bartender is busy at the other end with a group of girls in bikinis. It could be a while.

With so many girls walking around in skimpy bikinis, older and surely more experienced, I keep my gaze on Lochlyn, and he doesn't even glance at a single one. His eyes stay trained on the bottles of liquor behind the bar or me.

Out of my peripheral vision, I see a tall, skinny blonde in a red bikini walking toward the bar, making a beeline for Lochlyn. Before I can blink, she's standing between his legs, a finger tracing down his thigh. With bated breath, I watch the exchange. His eyes stay fixed on hers, gently pushing her hand off his thigh.

But blondie doesn't get it and tries again, trailing her finger along his shoulder, getting closer. This time he's more forceful, his hands on her upper arms as he pushes her away. She throws a hand up and walks away, looking upset.

I'm on my feet before I realize what I'm doing. Sliding into the barstool next to him, I turn so my legs are between his. Though he isn't looking at me, his legs inch closer to mine so we're touching. With my elbow propped on the bar, I lean my cheek against my fist, my other hand resting on my knee. He still hasn't looked at me, but rests his hand on his thigh, fingertips grazing mine.

"I don't know that I can ever be okay with that. I worry about what it's like when you're at school."

When he turns to me, I shrink under the intensity of his gaze. There's something there I haven't seen before; it steals the air from my lungs as my heart plummets to the ground.

He's on his feet in a second, grabbing my hand and pulling me to the back of the yard, through a gate that leads to the woods behind the house. When we've walked a few feet into the trees, he spins me around, then pushes me against a wide trunk, hand at my throat, mouth forceful on mine. For some reason, it makes me want to tear my clothes off, and a whimper rises in my chest.

As he pulls away, he lowers his hand to rest firmly against my chest. His breath is warm against my cheek. "I want you to listen to me, right now, and very carefully. I want you, and only you. I didn't turn that girl down for your benefit because you're watching me. I turned her down because I don't want her. I turn them all down because I don't want them. I want you. End of story. Understand?"

I try to move away from the tree, but Lochlyn pushes against my chest, pinning me to it. In the seven months we've been together, he's never been aggressive with me. Fire rips through his eyes.

I glare up at him. "You're mean when you drink." Red hot blood courses through my veins.

"I'm not being mean, Shay. I'm frustrated my girlfriend doesn't know or understand how much I love her and that other girls are just annoyances, not temptations. That I have to explain this to you *again."* His mouth is suddenly at my ear. "If I wanted to be mean, I'd let you watch me take them around the corner where you'd know exactly what I was doing with them. But I have no interest in doing that with anybody but you."

I don't like the side of Lochlyn that he's showing me right now. I'm not sure what it is; he barely drank anything. His mood has been foul, but this behavior is different. I scowl at him. Now I'm not only angry, but hurt.

His mouth claims mine before I can say anything, even more forceful than before, his hand still firm against my breastbone, keeping me glued to the tree. With strong hands against his chest, I push him away. A smirk flashes across his face before his lips are against mine again, his other hand sliding to my hip.

I twist away from him. "Loch. Loch, no."

"Come on, baby, I know you want to," he murmurs against my neck.

I do, but not like this. "No, Loch," I say, pushing against him again. "I don't like this version of you."

He runs his nose along mine before pushing against the trunk, hands on either side of my head, flipping away as his palm swipes down his face. Taking big strides to the tree next to me, he punches the bark. It's not even hard enough to crunch the flakes off. My flinch is so minuscule, I doubt he saw it. Lochlyn doesn't scare me, not in the slightest, but right now, he is making me anxious about the state of our relationship.

"Lochlyn, talk to me. *What* is going on with you today?"

Before I can blink or move, he spins around and is back against me, hands tight on my waist, head tilting down so his hair brushes along the top of mine. He's making me dizzy with the back and forth.

"I hate this. I hate this so much. The hiding, the lying. I hate that there's even an ability for other girls to come over to me because you're not there, where you belong. I hate that *Jay* felt like he could get that close to you. I wanted to jump up and punch him for even looking at you. I'm just tired of it. And I'm *very* frustrated I have to tell you, again, that I have no interest in anybody but you." His hands tighten against my hips, thumbs digging into the bones. He's grounding himself to me, me to him.

Guilt wraps its icy tendrils around my chest, squeezing. I did this. I brought him to his breaking point. My insecurities and unwillingness to tell Chelsea about us pushed him too far. I loop my arms around his neck, leaning on my toes to pull myself in as close as I can.

His hands rope around my waist as he nuzzles into my neck. "I love you, Shay. I love you so much. I just want to be able to be together. For all to see."

"I know, baby. I love you too. We just need to be patient." My fingers twist into his hair as I try to close any fiber's worth of space that exists between us.

"I don't like that I needed to remind you that I don't care about other girls."

"I'm sorry. It's hard to watch."

"You think it was easy for me to see the exchange between you and Jay? I know how he is with women. I know what he's said about you. But I know you're not interested in anybody else, especially Jay."

"Well, that's certainly true. I just know there's possibly girls here you've...been with. And definitely girls who would like to be added to the list."

He hangs his head against my shoulder. "It's not fair for you to hold the things I did years ago against me. And I can't control the thoughts or actions of others, just my response to them. My response will never be anything but rejection."

"I know. I'm sorry." I hesitate, not sure I really want to do what I'm about to suggest. "Maybe we should just tell her."

"We have to eventually, right? We'll have to figure out what we want to say. But not tonight."

Taking his face between my hands, I push up on my toes and fuse my lips to his before pressing my forehead into his. "Let's go back to the party." Having calmed down, noticeably relaxed, I feel comfortable that he'll keep it together.

Breathing deep, he gives my hips one final squeeze, lacing his fingers through mine as he pulls me back toward the fence.

Before walking through the gate, he brings my hand to his lips. "Come on, let's go and try to make the most of this."

Chelsea is holding court when we get back, having shown up sometime in the twenty minutes we were in the woods. If she's noticed we were gone, she doesn't mention it as she comes running over to throw her arms around my neck, Lochlyn having let go of my hand the second he saw her.

"I'm going to get a drink. Anybody want anything?" Lochlyn has his hand on my lower back, gently, a perfectly appropriate level for two people who have known each other for a long time.

I shake my head, glancing at him. Even though I'm off to Cornell in a few weeks, drinking still doesn't appeal to me. While I've had a few here and there, it's very atypical.

"I'm good. Bren's getting me something."

Lochlyn tenses before he walks away grumbling, still not overly fond of Chelsea's boyfriend even though they've been together for about a year now and we've all been together a lot this summer.

"How's the party so far?" Chelsea's very bubbly, overly so. Is she already drunk?

"Oh, you know, good." If you don't count other girls trying to hook up with my boyfriend and Jay being creepy.

She rolls her eyes at me. "You need to lighten up, Shay. It's a party. You're supposed to be having fun, getting drunk."

"Why do I need to get drunk to have fun?"

"It just makes you freer." That's what I'm worried about. I don't want to get drunk and start spilling secrets. Or worse, put on a show for her to see exactly how together Lochlyn and I are. It's safer to stay sober.

"I'm having fun without it."

"Whatever you say." She leans around me and waves to somebody enthusiastically. Being more outgoing and many of the people here being those Lochlyn knew, she's spent more time with them than I have. She's bound to know them. "I'm going to go say hi to Jane. You okay?"

"Mhm, totally fine."

She narrows her eyes at me, and I plaster my fake smile on. "Good, see?"

I can tell she doesn't believe me, but she bounces off anyway, yelling something at me over her shoulder.

Spinning around to search for Lochlyn, I find him sitting on the same couch I'd been planted on earlier, a glass with amber liquid in his hand stretched over the arm of the sofa. His other arm is stretched across the top of the back. It looks warm and inviting. His gaze is zeroed in on me.

My feet move of their own volition. I plop down next to him, inching closer until our legs are touching, my arm against his side. I lean my head back as he slides his arm forward the tiniest bit, my neck resting against the tattoo on his bicep. He brings his glass up to take a sip, trying to hide the smile that spreads across his face.

Though the stars are shining above us, the backyard is still bright, lights everywhere. Glancing around, I notice Chelsea on the other side of the yard with Brendan and a gaggle of girls. I decide to take a chance and lean into Lochlyn, resting my head on his chest as his breath stills below me.

There's no hesitation as his arm wraps around me, resting for a moment at my hip before moving higher, tracing circles on my arm. I close my eyes, enjoying the closeness and breathing him in. It may not be something friends do, but I don't care in this moment. I know Lochlyn will be able to come up with something to write it off as nothing if Chelsea says anything.

Which she does mere moments later.

"What exactly is going on here, Lochlyn?"

"Shh, I think she may be asleep."

"Why is she on you?"

"She decided to have a drink before. I think it hit her harder than she thought. She said she isn't feeling well. She doesn't really know anybody else here." I let my body flow with the natural shift as he holds up his other arm. "I've been drinking, didn't really think I should drive her home. It was this or letting her lie alone on the couch with all these other guys here. I saw Jay corner her earlier."

I can picture Chelsea's face in my mind, lips pressed into a line, arms crossed against her chest. "Just keep your hands in a respectable place. Let me know if she needs something." I'm surprised she glazed over the drink. Clearly, her priority is about Lochlyn and I being close instead of my supposed drinking.

"You got it, sis."

Her wedges slap on the concrete as she walks away. "Nice play, baby girl."

I smile against him, tilting my head slightly to kiss his chest. He gives me the gentlest kiss against the top of my head, and I stay right where I am, curled into Lochlyn, in front of everybody.

A few hours later, Lochlyn gently shakes me awake, whispering near my ear, "Shay. Baby, it's time to wake up."

My eyes flip open, and I grab his wrist. It's midnight. "Fuck, my mom." Though I'm sure she wouldn't care or notice, guilt still pangs my chest at the thought of even possible worry.

"Hey, relax. You told her you were going to be out late tonight, remember?"

I shake away the haze of sleep. "Yeah, yeah, I do."

"But we should get going."

I sit up to look at him as his hand slides down my back to rest on my hip. "I don't want to. I like being here with you."

"I know, I did too. But we can't stay."

Just then, Chelsea comes stumbling over. "Well, good morning, sleeping beauty!"

"You're still awake?"

"I am! And I feel great!" She sways on her feet as she reaches her arms out wide.

My eyebrows reach high as I turn to Lochlyn, whose mouth is pressed into a line, jaw tight. I'm aware of his hand still resting at my hip, but I know Chelsea is too drunk to notice, or remember.

"I guess we did a bit of a switch tonight since I'm the one who was asleep before midnight." Lying and hiding is exhausting.

Brendan is suddenly at her side, slipping his arm around her waist. "Come on, babe, time to get you home and in bed."

"Alone," Lochlyn growls next to me, shooting daggers at Brendan.

"Of course." The flush that rushes his cheeks tells me that hadn't been his intention.

Lochlyn tenses next to me, noticing it too. "I think she's a little too drunk for that. Don't you? Or are you interested in taking advantage of my sister in her inebriated state?" Shielded by my body, I slide my fingers under the hem of his shirt to try to calm him. The last thing we need is for them to come to blows. He doesn't look at me, but his fingers dig into my hip.

Brendan holds up his hands. "I have to be at work at six. I'm just making sure she gets in bed safely. You're welcome to take her home yourself."

"No, I want *you* to take me!" Chelsea whines at his side.

I can see the internal struggle going on in Lochlyn's mind. If he takes Chelsea home, he won't have any time with me. If he lets Brendan take her home, he can't be sure nothing will happen.

"If I find out anything happens between you and my sister tonight, I promise you I'm coming for you." He doesn't move his hand from my hip, the other gripping the armrest, but his eyes say he's ready to strangle Brendan with his bare hands.

"Understood." Even though Brendan and Lochlyn are the same age, Lochlyn stands a few inches taller and is noticeably stronger. He's scared away other guys by doing less. Though he looks intimidating, has a sharp tongue, and can be a little overly protective, he's a teddy bear. My teddy bear.

They turn and walk away, Brendan supporting her as she stumbles.

"He better keep his fucking hands off her."

I wonder what would happen if I just climbed on his lap at this very moment. There's barely anyone still at the party. Heath is *his* friend, so surely Lochlyn could convince him not to say anything, make sure he doesn't let it slip. But I decide it's not worth the risk, taking a less blatant approach.

With my fingers on his jaw, I turn his face to mine. "Take me home." Ever so gently, I lay the tiniest kiss on his lips.

He closes his eyes, fighting the same urge I have. "I wish I could put my hands on you tonight."

"Why don't you stay? At my house?"

"What about your mom?" Mom wouldn't have any issue with us being together. Her feelings about Lochlyn, as changed as they may be from years earlier, won't matter to her if I'm happy. But in her state of mind, I can't be sure she won't accidentally tell Chelsea, especially since they spend so many hours at the store together.

"I don't care. We can set an alarm, make sure you're up and out before she gets up. It's not ideal, but I'd rather have a few hours than none." While we've been spending a lot of time together, in the five weeks he's been home, we've only been able to sneak in a few nights at his house when Chelsea's at Brendan's. This will be the first night we attempt to sleep at my house.

"I need to keep an eye on Chelsea."

I pull back, my voice solid. "Chelsea's a big girl, Loch. She can take care of herself. She's just with her boyfriend."

"Who may try to take advantage of her when she's drunk."

"Okay, humor me. Let's, for a second, say I actually drank. If I was that drunk, and invited you back to my house, and wanted to have sex, would you consider it taking advantage of me? I can tell you I wouldn't in the morning. Because you're my boyfriend and I want to be with you, drunk or not."

"I see what you're saying. I'm her big brother. That protection doesn't go away."

"I know, but you need to loosen up a bit. You're not here all year. She'll be in college in a few months with a dorm room that I hope to rarely be frequenting. You can't protect her forever. Besides, wouldn't you rather be with me tonight than babysitting her?"

His eyes flip up to mine. "You're right. Let's go."

An hour later, we're lying in my bed, Lochlyn in just a pair of boxers while I wear a t-shirt of his that I'd stolen, making out, his hands exploring my body, when he pulls away.

"What's wrong?" We'd decided having sex is too risky, that kissing would have to do, and my lips feel plump and bruised in the most glorious way.

"I just...I'm sorry."

Confusion spreads through my mind and face. "For what?"

"I didn't mean to scare you earlier."

"Scare me?" What on earth is he talking about?

"In the woods? Against the tree? I was a little...aggressive."

"I know you'd never hurt me, Lochlyn. I wasn't scared."

His eyes flip up to mine. "You weren't?"

With pinched lips, I shake my head. Should I tell him it kind of turned me on? "I mean, it wasn't exactly your best moment, but I like when you take the initiative, are dominant."

A smirk pulls at his mouth. "So, some part of you liked it? Maybe a little?"

I laugh, very lightly. "Maybe just a little. Listen, I'm not saying, like, choke me or anything but, I don't know, it wasn't the worst thing. Mixed with your mood, though, a little too much. While I wasn't scared, I'm not interested in you being in a shitty mood all day and then throwing me up against a tree with your hand around my throat while you tell me that you could take any girl and go fuck her while I watch you walk away."

He winces at the crassness of the statement and my tone. "Yeah. I'm not proud of that. It wasn't the drinking though, Shay. It's that I'm just so tired, so frustrated. They're my friends and I can't tell them about you. I can't let them know how happy I am with you."

"Maybe we shouldn't go to more parties, and stay away from alcohol."

"Everything just got to be too much today, and the alcohol lowered my ability to tamp it down." He swoops some hair behind my ear, leaving his hand cupping my jaw. "I'm sorry."

"It's okay."

"It's really not. Not even a little bit. But I appreciate you saying that. I need you to understand, though, there is nobody else. I would never do...that. Shay, I couldn't imagine hurting you at all, mentally, and, God, physically doesn't even register because it's the furthest thing from reality. And if for any reason I ever slipped up and made a mistake that hurt your heart, it still wouldn't be cheating. I have no thoughts about others, no regrets. Not a single one. I can't control the actions of others. I can't change what people have said about me or think they know about me. I just feel like you still don't trust me."

I'm quiet for a minute, thinking of the best way to answer. "It's hard for me. I see eyes turning to you everywhere. At parties, when I visited on your birthday, at the concert, anywhere in public. And I'm so inexperienced. What if you get bored?"

"Bored? Shay, this isn't like a vacation or something. I'm not trying to change my 'wild ways' and just seeing how it goes. I am in love with you, wholly and completely."

"But you've never had a girlfriend before. What if you realize it's not for you?"

The bed shakes as he jerks back. "Who said I've never had a girlfriend?"

My finger twirls anxiously on his chest. "Chelsea. The rumors."

He chuckles, low in his chest. "God, those fucking rumors. I don't know where this shit comes from. First things first, I never slept with an entire team for any sport, not even half. And I lost my virginity *to my girlfriend,* who happened to be one of the players on the field hockey team. We didn't stay together, but she was my girlfriend at the time. I maybe haven't had many, or really any since, but I'm fully capable. When I want to. Which I do. With you."

On the outside, I try to show confidence. On the inside, I question how long he'll feel that way before he's done with me. I've been through enough difficult and heartbreaking situations in the past few years. I don't need to add being cast aside by the man I love to the pile. It's easier to hold on to the doubt.

Instead of answering, I snuggle into him. His arms tighten around me without hesitation.

Just before I fall asleep, I hear him whispering, "Good night, Shay. I love you, so damn much."

"I love you too," I murmur into his chest as I fall asleep.

The summer is proving to be increasingly difficult. Chelsea questions me extensively about resting against Lochlyn at the party. It doesn't help that the day after, he pulls me into the pool again, arms tight around my waist and then lets his hands linger on me the rest of the night.

"I just don't understand why you were lying on him. Do you like him or something?" No, I don't like him at all. I love him.

"He's my friend, Chelsea. I've known him for over sixteen years. Am I not allowed to be comforted by him?"

"I didn't say that. It just seems more like boyfriend and girlfriend than friend."

"Chelsea, I wasn't feeling well. Come on, when have you ever known me to be asleep before eleven? And even that's a pretty early night for me." Really, I had just felt so comfortable and at peace with Lochlyn, I drifted off.

"True. I don't know, I just feel icky thinking of you and Lochlyn together."

"We've spent a lot of time together, especially in recent years. He's been there for me through tough times. I trust him. I didn't drive myself, he'd been drinking, and you were off having fun. And I was pretty sure you'd shown up already tipsy. Jay had creeped me out earlier in the night. I asked him to sit with me because I was afraid of being alone on the couch. I didn't want to be cornered again." Frustration is creeping into my voice and words, and I need to be careful before it all goes to hell.

"Just remember, I wouldn't like it if you two got together. No part of me is okay with it."

"Why?" Exhaustion with the situation, with the constant reminders, has brought me to this point.

"Excuse me?" Her voice is angry, eyes filled with fire.

"Why are you not okay with it?" I'm walking a thin line here, and I know it.

"Because he's my brother and you're my best friend. He's a manwhore, and you're a virginal angel. It would make me uncomfortable."

"What about it would make you uncomfortable?"

"It just would, okay! Sheesh, why do you even care? Do you want to be with him?" Disgust hangs off her words.

"I just want to know why it's so forbidden in your eyes." I intentionally avoid her last question.

"Shay, he's not boyfriend material. And you're definitely not the sleep around type. I love him, he's my brother, but he's not fit for anything more than a string of one-night stands."

To make sure I don't fly off the handle, I have to bite my tongue. I don't understand how she can be so blatantly disrespectful in what she says about him. He's none of the things she says he is. Maybe at one point he had been, but he's also done so much for her, and he's a wonderful person.

"I don't think you give him enough credit."

"Shay, trust me, I'm doing you a favor."

"If you say so."

"Okay, I don't understand what all this argument is about. I'm not okay with it. End of discussion." To show she means it, she turns away from me.

"Sure, Chels. I'm going to go check on my mom."

I'd been avoiding Chelsea for a few days when Lochlyn told me she'd questioned him as well. It seems she was a bit nicer to him about it, thanking him for taking care of me and making sure I was okay. She had to corner me on the floor at the store to have the conversation.

Trying to keep my temper in check, I walk to the office, straightening and organizing on my way, taking my anger out on the stacks of garbage cans and drawer organizers.

Bursting through the office door, startling Mom, I pace the room for a few minutes before grasping the back of a chair and taking a few deep breaths.

"Everything okay, sweetheart?"

"Yup. All good."

"Tough customer?"

"Mom, would you risk a friendship for love?" I turn to her, blurting it out. I don't know why I'm asking her of all people.

For the first time in months, Mom looks at me. Really looks at me, her eyes penetrating mine. "I'm not sure love is worth risking anything for."

My heart slides down to the floor and I want to go right along with it. Possibly stupidly, I was hoping for some motherly advice. I know it's asking a lot with how things have been for almost two years. But I so desperately need my mom to be my mom again. I don't know who else I can turn to.

"Oh. Okay. Thanks. I guess I'll just—"

"It's Lochlyn, isn't it?" My eyes widen as I look at her.

"How did you..."

"I know I'm not around a lot anymore, I know I'm...distracted. But I still see you and notice you, Shay. You're my daughter, I love you. I still pay attention to you. To what's going on with you. I can see the way you look at him, the way he looks at you. And that's just in the confines of this store." She opens her arms wide.

"I know you've had him over more than once recently, and he's spent the night. I'm not mad. I'm not going to tell you he can't. You're nineteen; I trust you to make good choices, to be safe. Don't feel like you have to hide it from me. He doesn't have to sneak out in the morning." My heart is racing and my breaths are shallow. She knows?

"Chelsea doesn't know."

"I assumed as much. I've been careful not to tell her."

"How long have you known?"

"I had an inkling around Christmas that something had happened. He watched you very closely at Thanksgiving. I had a feeling when you went to visit in February. I've known him for sixteen years, so I know when his birthday is. I truly knew in March.

"You know your father—" Choking up, she stops, putting a hand to her mouth. Almost two years later and she can still barely talk about him. Tears in her eyes, she clears her throat. "Your father always thought that Lochlyn held a torch for you. I brushed him off, told him he was seeing things. I guess he was right."

"Yeah, yeah, he definitely was." My voice has grown quiet. "I miss him."

"I do too, honey. I do too."

"I don't know what to do, Mom. Chelsea is so against Lochlyn and I being together. But I'm so in love with him." The last words come out in a gust of air, as though they're coming from the very depths of my soul.

"You haven't been together very long." There's a disapproving tone in her voice.

"Maybe not. But we've known each other for most of our lives."

"The only thing I can tell you is that it needs to be worth it. To love at all. I was with your father for almost thirty years and suddenly he was gone. It's not the sort of pain I'd wish on you."

"Was it worth it? To love Daddy, knowing how it ended?"

The deafening silence says way more than her words could have. "I need to get back to this." She hasn't answered. It stings in a way I didn't think possible.

"Okay."

"Shay, just be careful. I won't say anything to Chelsea, but she's going to be hurt and mad when she finds out, especially since it's been so long. You need to decide if you really think he's worth it." Her words stop me before I make it out the door. But I don't look back at her as I walk through it.

I'm left with the difficult process of having to reconcile how to make my relationship work with Chelsea's knowledge it exists. Yet all I can think is that at some point I'm going to have to make an impossible choice between two very different kinds of love. The love of my best friend, who is more like a sister, or who I'm pretty sure is the love of my life.

Chapter 16

Lochlyn and I are always careful to not get caught. Mom is always busy, nobody else suspects anything, and it's going great. Until the day it isn't.

We're in my room, Mom's at work, Chelsea's with Brendan. I took the day off from work, claiming I was worn out. Really, I just feel like Lochlyn and I haven't been getting any real alone time together all summer and I need a day with just him.

Though he spent the night, he left early and comes over after breakfast. Even though Mom said he doesn't have to sneak out, which he doesn't anymore, he wants to avoid answering Chelsea's questions. So he usually leaves before she'll be up. It's pretty easy for him to slip out once Chelsea's asleep; she wouldn't notice he was gone until morning.

Walking in the door, he cups my cheek and claims my mouth with his. He kisses me like he hasn't seen me in days instead of it being a few hours. "Good morning, baby girl," he says as he rests his forehead against mine and twirls a curl around his finger.

"Good morning."

"What do you want to do today?"

"I don't know." I twist my fingers into his shirt because the only thing I really want to do is *him.* But he likes to spend our time together doing real things, not just having sex. Which is probably good because if we always did what I wanted, we'd never leave the bedroom.

The one time I asked him about it, worried he didn't want to be with me as much as I want to be with him, he assured me he absolutely does and would be naked every single second of the day with me. He went on to explain that he thinks it's important that we do normal couple things too, even if we stay hidden while we do them.

"Okay, so let's pretend I wasn't here. What would you do on a day off if we weren't together?"

I stare at him blankly and blink a handful of times.

He laughs as he drops his head and rubs the back of his neck. "You wouldn't be taking a day off, would you?" The shake of my head answers his question. "Well, we can do what we usually do, read, TV, whatever. Or maybe we could go somewhere?"

My face scrunches as I shake my head. Apparently, I've lost the ability to speak.

"Okay. Wait a second." He snaps his fingers and points at me. "You just got that new book, right? The one you preordered from your favorite author?"

I bite my lip as I look away and nod.

"Shay. If you want to read, just say so."

"I want to read."

He rolls his eyes and shakes his head. "Sometimes, baby girl, I just don't know what to do with you." Flinging an arm around my shoulder, he pulls me against him and kisses the top of my head as he walks me toward the couch and tugs me down with him. "Was that really so hard for you to tell me? After all this time?"

One shoulder tips up quickly. "I don't know. I just feel bad that this is all we do."

Hooking some hair behind my ear and trailing his fingers down my jaw, he turns my face to meet his eyes. "I'm just happy to spend the whole day with you, alone and uninterrupted. It's a rare treat. I don't care what we do." He leans in and presses a small kiss to my lower lip. "Actually, that's not true. I *do* care what we do. But not leading up to that."

My body burns with a deep-seated inferno, and I rub my thighs together at his words.

When he laughs, the corners of my mouth tip up as I look at him.

"What's so funny?"

He brushes his knuckles down my cheek as he answers. "I'm just happy I still have that effect on you, even after seven months."

"I don't see it going away any time soon." I lean in and brush my lips against his. "I love you."

"I love you too."

Clapping his hands and rubbing them together, Lochlyn's ready to go. "Okay, so where is this book? And the one I've been reading?"

"My room. I can get them." When I move to get off the couch, he stops me with a hand on my thigh.

"I got it."

I don't have to tell him what the right book is. He'll know, because he pays close enough attention to me and what I say.

Sauntering back down the stairs, he makes his way over to the couch, silently handing me my book and putting my legs over his lap.

We fall into a comfortable silence, reading our respective books, Lochlyn trailing his fingers up and down my bare calves.

I'm so engrossed in my book that I don't realize Lochlyn has closed his until his hands start rubbing up my thighs and dipping under the hem of my shorts. Adjusting my legs, he leans in between them, hovering over me as he kisses along my neck.

My arms reach around him, holding my book in the air as I try to keep reading, despite his hungry mouth scorching my skin.

Taking the book from my hands, he tosses it onto the coffee table as his lips connect with mine. I protest as he pulls away.

"Hey, I was into that."

"Would you really rather read right now?" He presses his erection right between my thighs as he asks.

"No."

A smirk stretches his lips as he crashes his mouth to mine. Hands start moving around bodies, into hair, under garments of clothing.

Climbing off me and standing, Lochlyn closes his hand around my wrist and yanks me off the couch. Looping his arm under my knees, he scoops me off the floor as I wrap my arms around his neck.

Practically running, he takes the stairs two at a time, while I giggle the whole way. Once we get into my room, it becomes a well-practiced dance of tearing off clothes and falling onto the bed.

Our mouths connect with whatever skin available. It's frenzied and hungry, desperate. My legs part for him instantly as he moves between them, hovering over me. The feeling of him there, paired with the need and desire whirling in his eyes, is heady.

I tangle my fingers in his hair and pull his face down to mine. I don't think there's any way I could ever get enough Lochlyn.

Gliding a hand between our bodies, he slides two fingers into me as my head tips back and I arch up toward him, a moan flying from my mouth. When he starts moving them inside me, I grip at his back, eyes locking on his and filling me with more of that sweet intoxication.

"Come for me, baby."

I get a little nibble of self-consciousness every time Lochlyn talks to me in bed. I never know how to respond. What sounds sexy in response to something like that?

But with a few more strokes inside me, I do as he says and mutter a fuck as my back peels off the bed.

Peppering gentle kisses along my neck, Lochlyn eases himself into me, making my breath catch in my throat. He has a similar reaction as he rests his forehead against my shoulder.

After being still for a minute, with him pressed all the way inside me, he starts moving and the whole world starts to twirl.

"Fuck, Shay. God, you're perfect. I'm so lucky you're mine." He runs his thumb along my lower lip before pulling it down and closing his mouth over it as his tongue seeks mine. Every time it's like we're searching for our companion, our other half, and it's only until we're completely together that we can calm the pull.

Keeping his lips moving against mine, he starts thrusting hard and fast. I pull my mouth from his to gasp for air as my fingers dig into the muscles straining in his shoulders.

Lochlyn runs parted lips along my neck to my shoulder as he continues moving inside me. I'm starting to make noises with every thrust when he sinks his teeth into my sensitive skin. It sends a thrill through my body and throws me over the edge as my voice fills the air and I tighten around him, dragging my nails down his back.

Smiling against my ear, a low growl eases from his chest as he licks down to my collarbone. With a few more hurried pumps, his head tips back as he moans and his hands fist into the sheets.

Collapsing against me, he breathes heavily for a minute before kissing from my shoulder to my ear, giving extra attention to where his teeth struck.

That's how the rest of our day in bed starts. We talk, kiss a lot, rest. At one point, Lochlyn runs downstairs to grab our books, stripping off the boxers he threw on the minute he's back in the room.

A naked Lochlyn is exceptionally distracting. After a few too many side glances at his chest, I set my book next to me and prop up on my elbow. He quirks an eyebrow at me as I run my hand down his chest, rolling over the ripples of his muscles, and sliding under the sheet to wrap around him.

I get a few glides up and down his length and a groan of satisfaction before he flips me to my back, holding my hands above my head as he kisses along my neck.

After a late lunch of a shared peanut butter and jelly sandwich in my bed, we're well into our third session of the day.

I'm moaning so loudly as Lochlyn thrusts into me that there's zero acknowledgment of the outside world.

Until my bedroom door is suddenly and unceremoniously thrown open. "What in the *hell* is going on in here?" Chelsea screams.

"Get out!" Lochlyn bellows, still on top of me. I try to sink farther under him, but Chelsea zeroes in on me, and the look of pain and anger in her eyes makes me want to disappear.

She turns on her heel and storms out, slamming the door behind her.

Lochlyn sighs, slamming his fist into the mattress before he hangs his head on my shoulder, kissing my collarbone. He still hasn't removed himself from me.

It's only when he puts his hand on the side of my cheek and turns my face to his that I realize I'm shaking.

"Hey. Shay, look at me." My eyes meet his. They're soft, calming. He leans in and kisses me tenderly. "It's going to be okay. I'll deal with Chelsea. Don't worry."

With another kiss on my temple, he pulls away, getting off the bed and sliding his shorts on. He yanks the door open as he pulls his shirt over his head, jumping back slightly. "Fuck, Chels, you seriously just stood here?"

I'm in the middle of buttoning my pants, wearing just a bra for a top, when she pushes past him and into my room.

Frantically she looks between the two of us, eyes wild, nostrils flaring. "*What* is going on here?" She doesn't give us time to answer, turning on Lochlyn, finger in his face. "Are you fucking her? My *best friend?*"

She spins on me. "And you. How many times have I told you? Lochlyn's my fucking brother, Shay. My *brother*. You can have any guy you want, they all come around you." Lochlyn tenses at her words, knowing some inside details he has yet to share with me. "And you go after my brother?"

"Chels, I—" She holds up her hand to stop me, her eyes filled to the brim, ready to spill over with the next blink.

"I've told you. I've told both of you, that *this*"—she waves her hands wildly between us—"was not something I was okay with. Not ever."

We all stand in silence. I catch Lochlyn's eyes across the room. His jaw is clenched, cheekbones sharp, eyes dark.

"How long?"

We both turn our eyes to Chelsea.

"Huh?"

"How long?" she asks again through gritted teeth.

I swallow, my mouth arid, a lump stuck in my throat.

"Since Thanksgiving," Lochlyn answers for me, seeing my struggle.

Eyes searing, she turns to Lochlyn. "You've been hiding this from me since Thanksgiving? You've been screwing her since then?"

"No!" we both yell in unison.

She turns to me, eyes pleading. "Shay, you've been lying to me for almost a year? How could you do that?" The pain etched in her voice slices through me, every word like a shard of glass.

"Leave her alone, Chels. I did this. I went after her." Why? Why would he take this all on himself? Yes, he made the first move, but everything after was completely mutual. The lying, keeping the secret for all this time, was *my* fault.

Chelsea throws her hands up as she turns on her brother. "Oh, poor, sweet Lochlyn. What, you couldn't get enough sluts at college? You had to turn my best friend into just another one of your conquests?"

Lochlyn tenses, hands balling into fists, as he points a finger at her. "Watch it," he says through gritted teeth.

"Really, though, Loch, have you told her about all the girls at school?"

Everything inside me twists into knots as his chest rises and falls. He has told me. I know all about what he's done at college, and before. As well as how wrong Chelsea is, and yet she throws it in his face constantly.

"I have not been with anybody since well before Thanksgiving. I have been faithful to Shay."

"Oh bullshit, Lochlyn. You couldn't keep it in your pants if a million dollars was on the line." She shakes her head. "It doesn't matter. I don't even care about that. I told both of you, time and time again, that I would never be okay if you two got together. I never thought I'd have to worry about it. You barely noticed each other. But I started seeing little things here and there this summer. I thought I was crazy. Guess not."

"Say what you want about me, Chelsea, but I have not, nor would I ever, cheat on Shay."

"To cheat on her, you'd have to be in a relationship, not just screwing around." She practically spits the words out.

When neither one of us says anything, eyes locked on each other, she picks up on the change in the room and looks between us.

"Ohmygod. You're in a relationship? Like officially boyfriend and girlfriend?" The words are a whisper of air and I know she doesn't want to believe it, yet has all pieces of the puzzle, she just has to assemble them.

She turns to me. "The messages. John. It was Lochlyn the whole time, wasn't it?" My heart drops at the look on her face. Betrayal. I hang my head, unable to hold her gaze. "That's why you never let me meet him. Because you were *lying* to me."

Lochlyn nervously rubs the tattoo on his middle finger. What will happen if Chelsea puts that together too?

"Chelsea, I'm—" I start quietly, not really sure where I'm going with my thought, but knowing I need to say *something*.

"You need to choose," she interrupts me.

The wind is knocked from my lungs, forcing me backward a step. "What? I—What?"

"You need to choose. Me or him."

"Chelsea, cut the crap. You can't make her choose between us."

She turns on him. "I can't be friends with somebody fucking my brother."

He glowers at her in response. "I won't let you do this."

Unfortunately, she takes it as a challenge, turning to me, shoulders squared and standing taller than before. "Here's the deal, Shay. I can't force you two to break up. But I also don't have to keep talking to you. It's him or me."

Without giving me a chance to say anything, she turns on her heel and walks out of my room, Lochlyn calling her name after her from where he stands.

When we hear the front door slam, he puts his hands on the back of my desk chair, anger plastered across his face. His whole body is tight, jaw clenched. A few books fall from the hutch as he slams the chair into the desk.

"Loch." I can't get my voice to be above a whisper.

He turns, his face changing to concern as he notices I'm trembling. He makes it to me in two strides, wrapping his arms around me in just enough time to catch me as my knees give out.

Choose. How do I choose? How has this become my life? The only thing I've ever done for myself and it's blown up in my face.

I can't help but wonder if we'd been honest with Chelsea from the beginning, if things might've been different. Or maybe Lochlyn and I would have just continued to deny our happiness and wouldn't have had all these months together, which were by far the best months of my life.

Lochlyn comes over every day. He spends hours at my house, spends the night with me. At no point does he try to convince me to choose him; he doesn't even talk about it. But he knows there's a battle raging in my head. Quietly he holds me, lets me cry, just spends time with me.

I don't know if he thinks it's goodbye and wants to be with me as much as possible or if he's trying to comfort me, thinking I'm saying goodbye to Chelsea.

Three days later, and I still have no idea. I don't want to choose, but I don't see any way out.

"What's wrong, baby girl?"

"What's wrong? Are you really asking me that?" There's an irritation in my voice that I don't want to be using on Lochlyn, but I can't help it. It's not his fault.

"I mean, what specifically are you thinking about."

"I'm mad. I'm really fucking mad."

"At me?"

"No, God, no. None of this is your fault." We're lying in my bed as I twist my fingers into his shirt. I can't meet his eye. "I can't believe she did this. I can't believe she's serious."

We've both tried to talk to her. She barely looks at me, let alone talks to me. Lochlyn says it's not much better at home, when she's there, which he says she hasn't been. Though he hasn't really been either. They're either passing ships or both gone. It's hard to know.

"I can't even find her to try to talk to her. She knows exactly what she did, what she's doing." His voice is low, but anger seeps through.

"Why is she so against this? Does she hate us that much?"

"Me, maybe. Not you. As far as she's concerned, I'm a horrible evil monster and you're an angel sent from heaven. She's right about that one, though." I know he's just trying to make me feel better, and if the situation were any different, I'm sure his words would set off a reaction in my heart, but right now, I'm lucky it's even beating since I'm sure it senses the impending doom and breakage.

"I'm no angel, Lochlyn."

"Either way, I'll never understand her motives. It's cruel. What is she hoping to gain from this? She really can't see us all just being together? It's not really that different than it used to be, except we touch and come home and have crazy wild sex." Though I'm still not looking at more than his clothed chest, I know there's a smirk on his face.

He's trying to make light of the situation, but I don't laugh. I can't.

Pressing his forehead to mine, our noses brushing, he speaks so quietly. "I miss your laugh." I haven't so much as smiled since Chelsea stormed out.

"Nothing's funny."

His hand tangles in my hair at the back of my head. He pulls me so close, it's like he's trying to fuse us together. If only it were so easy.

In all the times I'd thought about how Chelsea would react, what she really meant when she said she wasn't okay with it, I never expected her to do this. Chelsea's never been cruel before. This, making me choose, is beyond cruel.

"Lochlyn. I need you to leave." My throat hurts as I talk around the lump there.

"What?" He either isn't trying to hide the shock in his voice or just isn't doing a very good job.

"I can't...I can't think when you're here. I need to think about everything and if you're here, you're all I want." The past several weeks together have made me forget all about the many weeks we spent apart over the year.

"Wait, are you serious?" He leans back to look at me, hurt rippling across his features.

"Please don't make this harder for me."

"If you really want me to go, I'll go. Is that really what you want?"

No. "Yes." It comes out in the slightest hint of a whisper, one of the hardest syllables I've ever had to say.

As he tilts my head up, his lips meet mine tenderly, his fingers gentle on my chin. We haven't had sex in three days and my body is begging to feel him again, but my mind can't get there. I know he doesn't want to leave, and in reality, I don't want him to. But I need to think, and I can't do it with him near me.

"I love you, Shay. No matter what, I love you."

"I love you too." I have to close my eyes to fight against the tears. The bed shifts as he moves to leave, then he hesitates, knowing the second he's out the door, I'll be a blubbering mess. I'm sure it's tearing him apart inside to know that he won't be here to comfort me. But he's not leaving by choice; he's leaving because I asked him to.

The bed shifts as his weight is removed, and I bite back a sob. I don't need him feeling worse than I know he already does by falling apart before he's gone. Warmth touches my hip as he rests his hand on it and leans down to give me a kiss on my temple. I fight the urge to turn to him and pull him back down in bed with me, keeping my eyes closed tightly, hands curled under my head.

At the click of the door, my eyes overflow, then the sobs start. Grabbing the pillow that has become Lochlyn's, I hug it against myself and bawl into it. Then something changes and I start yelling into it. There are too many strong emotions coursing through me that I'm screaming as tears pour from my eyes, soaking the bedding below me.

I'm mad at the situation, at Chelsea, and even mad at Lochlyn for not fixing it like he said he would.

I'm mad at Dad. For leaving us, for destroying Mom.

I'm mad at Mom. For still being so broken.

For the first time, I really just feel angry at the world. I have nobody to turn to, nobody to help me. The last time I talked to Mom about Lochlyn, she basically said I wasn't worth it to lose my father. That the life they had wasn't worth the pain she feels. She won't be of any help except to say *I told you so*.

I'm alone, to make the hardest decision of my life, all on my own. Do I choose familiarity, comfort, history, or do I choose happiness?

Chapter 17

I spend two days utterly alone. Chelsea won't talk to me, and I ignore Lochlyn. It kills me, but I can't have his voice in my head as I work through things. I don't leave him completely in the dark, though. He seems to understand that while I love him, I need some space. The hardest part is when I ask him to leave me alone until I come find him. My heart breaks a little when he listens.

It's been five days since Chelsea walked out of my room, and in that time, I've barely slept, spending most of my time crying. My eyes are puffy, red, and tired. I text both the siblings and tell them to meet me at their house.

Standing outside, I take a deep breath and let myself in. Chelsea's not here yet, and that may be a good thing.

The second Lochlyn sees me, his arms wrap around me and pulls me close, making the conversation we're about to have so much more difficult.

"I missed you," he says against my hair.

"I missed you too." He's holding me so tightly I can barely breathe, which may be a good thing since it keeps that sandalwood scent I love so much from filtering into my nose and overpowering my senses.

I'm going to crush him. He's going to hate me and I'm going to lose the only thing that has ever made me really and truly happy.

"What did you want to talk about?" There's no hiding his nerves.

"I need to let you both know where my head is at."

"Oh." He knows. He knows I'm about to break his heart, and mine along with it.

"Chelsea messaged me after you left the other day, said she wants an answer, so…" There's a slight lift of my shoulder, but my body is too tired and sore to put any real oomph behind it.

"What do *you* want, Shay?"

"You know what I want doesn't matter here. It's Chelsea. You know she's serious."

"What you want has to matter."

"I want both of you."

"So make that happen."

"How!? How am I supposed to do that? I don't get what I want." I turn away from him, resting my hand on the back of the couch as I try to hold myself together. I've thought over the possibilities, as many as I could think of in as many different variations, including telling her we broke up and hiding more. After rolling it over and over, I came up empty-handed, with not a single way to convince Chelsea that nothing has to change if Lochlyn and I are together. I can barely find her now after her bomb drop. If I choose Lochlyn, I'm sure I'd never see her again.

"Maybe it's time you start."

I release a tired breath. "You don't get it. Chelsea may be selfish, but she was here for me and went through some of the worst times of my life with me. And it's not your fault that you weren't here. We weren't together, you were at school. But

Chelsea was. That counts for something. She stayed here for *me* this year. And as selfish as she may otherwise be, I love her."

"So, you're choosing Chelsea?"

"She's my best friend."

"You're going away to college in a few weeks. You'll make new friends."

"I can't lose her, Loch."

"But you can lose me?"

Tears well in my eyes as I bite the inside of my lip and my heart cracks.

"Wow. That's fucked up, Shay. I thought we had something here. I thought you loved me." There's no hint of hurt in his voice now, only irritation. On some level, I know it's for self-preservation, but it slices through me like nothing ever has.

"I do love you!"

"Then why are you choosing her over me?" His raised voice causes my eyes to overflow. He's at my side in an instant, hands cupping my chin and thumbs swiping away the tears. His voice is low when he speaks again. "I love you, Shay. I'm *in* love with you. I'd lose her before I lost you."

I look up at him, my eyes pleading. How can he not understand what a difficult decision this is for me? Chelsea has put me in an impossible position. I'm having to choose between the man I love and the girl I consider my sister.

But I had spent years longing for Lochlyn with those feelings going unanswered, weeks where we only talked once a day and I had survived. These few days without Chelsea have been unbearable. I know losing Lochlyn will be excruciating and difficult. Losing Chelsea would be impossible.

"I'm sorry," I whisper. He drops his head. We stand there for a few minutes, tears pouring from my eyes, before he tilts my chin up and kisses me deeply, his tongue sweeping across mine with desperation.

But it's not passion, it's not resolve. No, this kiss...this kiss is goodbye.

He pulls away before I can even wrap my arms around him, storming through the living room, passing Chelsea as she walks in.

"You win, Chels, she's all yours," he says angrily as he walks out the front door, slamming it behind him.

Chelsea looks at me, a frown on her face. But she drops her things and walks over to wrap me in her arms. I collapse against her, pulling her down to the ground with me as my knees give out and my heart shatters.

Chapter 18

I don't see Lochlyn again after that day. The next day, he's gone, leaving early to go back to Ithaca. Weston had been at the apartment most of the summer. Lochlyn had only stayed home to be with me. Now that we aren't together, there's nothing keeping him here.

Every single one of my senses is aware of Lochlyn's absence. The deep timber of his voice always had a way to calm me, soothe me.

Seeing his smile made my heart flutter, every single time. Now it's just a pulse, a mostly lifeless one at that.

My body misses his physical contact, even just his hand on my lower back, but especially his forehead against mine. It always felt so intimate to me, like it could somehow connect us even more. What if I never feel that again? Just the thought makes my eyes brim with tears and ice run through my body.

There's the slightest hint of his cologne, still left on the pillow he'd started using when he stayed with me. Every day I have an internal battle with wanting to hold it and being afraid to make it go away by overusing it.

His mouth always had the slightest taste of mint. The thought reminds me of the one time he tried to be funny and chewed Big Red gum before coming over. I immediately pushed him away as he laughed, knowing I hate anything even the littlest bit spicy. I'd give anything for that again.

I miss him so much my chest aches and my bones feel too weak to support me. Whatever comfort and calm his presence brought me is gone, replaced with tension. We always joked that we fit together like puzzle pieces—the way he could curl around me, how my head fell perfectly against his collarbone, that when he leaned down to rest on my shoulder, he just...fit. Now I feel alone, like the one piece that goes missing, lost forever and unable to fit into any full picture.

The time we spent alone together was always unparalleled to any I spent with somebody else, even if we were hiding out. Reading was easy since we both enjoyed it and we could split apart if we were surprised by unexpected company. I can't even look at a book now.

I miss his hands on me. Anywhere, everywhere. Aside from the sheer pleasure they'd bring me, fire always spread through me anywhere he touched me. Now it's like there's a ghostly flickering of a flame, the remembrance of what had been, but no longer is a fire doused while the embers still glint, trying to reignite but missing their spark.

Our conversations were never dull; Lochlyn could talk about anything. What hurts the most is how much he brought up the future, being on campus together, even what he could see happening after graduation.

Listening to music makes me sad, reading makes me sad. Everything makes my eyes sting with a hint of fresh tears.

Am I always going to feel this way? Did I make the right decision? Will I be able to see him and not feel like my heart was ripped out and stomped on? He's Chelsea's brother, so I'm bound to be around him at some point. I'm pretty sure if I saw him right now, I'd die. Worse, what if I see him on campus with another girl? I wouldn't be able to handle it.

I'm even more eager to leave home. Everywhere I go is filled with memories. My room, Chelsea's house, the store. Nowhere is safe.

I worry about things that don't matter anymore. How will I make my own way in the world without him? His carefree attitude, his want to embrace the good things in life, all helped me want to do the same. Now all I see is how that comes back to bite you in the ass.

Who's going to stop him from becoming his dad if I'm not around to keep an eye on him? I'm the only one who knows he's worried about that.

"I don't even understand why you're so upset. I mean, it's Lochlyn." The way Chelsea says his name is like it's the most absurd thought that somebody could possibly have interest in him for more than his body.

But how can I explain to her that he was all I had wanted for so long? That I finally had him and lost him, because of her. That I love him, really and truly love him, more than I ever thought was even possible.

It's only been two days when she asks me that. I've spent those two days crying.

I haven't been back to Chelsea's house since Lochlyn stormed out. I can't. It hurts too much. I meet her out or she comes to my house, though I'm not very good company.

I'm thankful we only have three weeks until we leave for school. It makes avoiding their house easier. I can avoid Chelsea a bit too, claiming I need to get things together before we leave. Busying myself packing and buying new things helps take my mind off the big part of what's missing from my equation.

When I'm at the store, I'm a zombie, going where I need to, doing what needs to be done, straightening in silence. I find myself in the backroom more than once, mostly by accident, not even sure how I got here. It's like some part of me is wandering there hoping it's a dream and I'll walk in to his warming smile. But it gets too hard when the memories flood back. The conversations, the time we snuck in a make-out session in the back corner. Not even the place my mother has used as her escape is safe for me. There *is* no escape.

The one time Mom found me in tears, all she said was: "I tried to warn you." Five words. None of which were comforting. None of which were something that should come from a mother to a distraught child.

Moving into the dorms contains none of the excitement it should. Mom doesn't take off work, which I had anticipated, planned for. Lochlyn and I were going to drive up together. We'd planned to leave my car behind, claiming I didn't need it. He was going to help carry Chelsea's and my things up to our room, help us get settled. Now, it's just Chelsea and myself, and we're both on edge still. I'm miserable, my chest aching at Lochlyn's nonexistence, knowing he's only minutes away yet completely unreachable. It pours into every action and conversation.

I hold resentment toward Chelsea and it shows in every exchange we have. Even sitting in silence, it rolls off me in waves. But I don't know anybody else, and I don't have it in me to try to meet new people.

Lochlyn was going to help me find all of my classes, get my books, anything he needed to do to help me be as ready for the first day as I could be. He knows I like to be prepared as far ahead of time as possible. Wandering around campus aimlessly, I'm struck with a flip of my stomach at every turn, hoping I both do and don't see Lochlyn.

Part of me desperately wants to see him, to just be able to lay my eyes on him, but I don't know what I'd do if I did. It's not like I can go running into his arms. The pull to be near him and knowing I can't would be too much. Right now, I'm not strong enough to resist, and that would only hurt both of us more.

I don't even enjoy the library. The first time I stop in, tears spring to my eyes and I have to leave, unable to appreciate the wonder I had once so clearly seen. I feel his absence like a ghost, haunting me with every breath.

Any time Chelsea brings up his name, I flinch. Three weeks into classes, she's had enough. "Come on, Shay, seriously. You made your choice."

"A choice I shouldn't have had to make. What's so wrong with him, Chelsea? He's your brother." I glance up from my books to look at her. We're sitting on her bed studying after class one day.

"And you're my best friend."

"So? Shouldn't you just want us to be happy? Why does it matter if that's with each other?"

"Because it's weird for me, okay?"

"So we're supposed to not be with each other, be broken and hurting and not with the person we love because it's *weird* for you? How is that fair?" My heart rate is rising the more we get into this conversation. Several weeks' worth of pain, frustration, and anger all bubbling under my skin, ready to explode.

She rolls her eyes and looks at the ceiling. "Oh please, Shay, don't fool yourself. He doesn't love you. You're just another conquest for him. That's what Lochlyn does."

Angry tears flood my eyes as I shake my head. "You're wrong, Chelsea. You are so fucking wrong, it's disgusting." I practically spit the words at her.

She jerks back at my tone. I rarely talk back to her, letting her have her way. Any time I have, I've been gentle, making my case in the least confrontational way I can. And I had chosen her in all of this. But at a cost. A really big one. Maybe too big.

She reaches over to take my hand. "Shay, listen, I know you think you know him, but you don't. His reputation exists for a reason. It's no different at college."

I rip my hand out from under her grasp, getting off her bed. "You're wrong. I do know him. I know him in ways you never could. I know things he's never told you. You think you have this great, strong, brother-sister bond that nobody can penetrate, but guess what. I did. Did you know he was willing to choose me? He wanted me to choose him. But I couldn't. And now you sit here and put down what we had? Telling me I don't *know* him? Fuck that." I surprise even myself with both my tone and my words. I'm not sure I've ever talked to *anybody* this way.

With a deep breath, I try to steady myself, swiping my hands hastily across my cheeks as the tears start to fall.

"I'm sorry." She's so quiet I'm sure I haven't heard her correctly. Chelsea never apologizes. She slides off her bed, walking to the door. "I'm, uh, I'm going to get some air."

Chelsea and I decided to room together last fall, well before Lochlyn and I got together. There was no way to pull out of it once we started dating without telling her. Then, as we were figuring out what we'd say and how we'd handle the ramifications, she found us.

I take a few deep breaths and climb up onto my bed, hugging my pillow to myself and sobbing. I've spent a lot of my time alone in the six weeks since I last talked to Lochlyn doing this very thing. At first, my pillow still smelled like him. When the scent faded, I cried harder.

I'm not sure how long I lie here for. My tears run dry and I'm trying to catch my breath, feeling how swollen my eyes are, my cheeks sticky with tears, when there's a knock at the door.

At first, I ignore it, not wanting to talk to anybody. But they're persistent, knocking harder. I throw my pillow down, hopping off the bed, giving a quick swipe at my face, knowing there's not much I can do.

When I throw open the door, I freeze.

"Hey, Shay." *Lochlyn.* My heart, which had momentarily stopped, hammers against my rib cage.

"Wha-what are you doing here?"

"I told him to come." Chelsea pokes her head out from the side of the doorframe. "I left to walk a little, think about what I'd done, why it bothered me if you two were together. I had some things I needed to clear up first. You were right, Shay. I was wrong, I was *so* wrong. After wandering a little, I found my way to Lochlyn's apartment, where I talked to Weston."

"Wait, you talked to Weston?" I interrupt her, shock filtering through my words.

"Shh. I talked to Weston. And he told me that Lochlyn didn't have a single girl at his place last year and was in his room every single night. That the only girl he saw with Loch, or heard him even talk about...was you. So I waited for Loch to get back from class and I talked to him."

I look up at Lochlyn, who's been standing there patiently, hands in his pockets. I'm aching to be in his arms, my whole body humming, finally in front of him for the first time in six weeks. But I'm not really sure what Chelsea is thinking. She didn't bring him to be mean; she wouldn't do anything like that, cruel as she's been lately, but I'm not sure she's accepting it either.

She takes a deep breath, ready to continue. "I asked him how he feels about you. And he told me he loves you. Plain and simple, not a second of hesitation. I've never, ever heard him say he loves anyone or anything, except that damn car."

His brow furrows as he looks down at her. "Hey, it's a good car, don't kno—" She cuts him off with a glare. "You're right, sorry, continue."

"So after hearing that, I was surprised. I wasn't expecting him to say that." She sighs and looks at the ceiling, almost like she's fighting something in herself. "I'm not super proud to admit this, but I honestly just thought he was saying that because he liked fucking you. I thought for sure he was here, living it up. When Weston again said he wasn't, I figured he just really likes it with you. So I asked why he loves you."

Her eyes shimmer in the light as they fill. "Shay, the things he said. I'd kill for a guy to say that about me. We've all known each other a long time. I never really thought he was paying much attention. I was wrong. And it's clear you've learned a lot about each other over the years and the time you've had together."

Though I'm afraid it's going to hurt, I turn to Lochlyn, who has his face tilted toward the ground, hand running up the back of his neck, gaze locked on me.

"I'm sorry. I'm so sorry, both of you. I realized that the reason I'd always been so against you two was two-fold and selfish. First, I was afraid I wouldn't be important to either of you anymore. And I was afraid I'd lose you if you two broke up. That it'd be too hard for you to be near me after. There's the *slightest* chance I have some abandonment issues. But I gave you an unfair choice, and you chose me. You gave up love for me. And while you haven't exactly been pleasant since then, you've been here.

"I guess this is my long-winded way of saying that I give my blessing or whatever. I'm okay if you two are together. It'll be *super* weird knowing that you're sleeping together, so we for sure will need a system so I don't walk in on anything again, but I want you two to be happy. You're my two favorite people in the world, and I'm honestly glad you found happiness with each other."

The second her speech ends, I'm pressed up against Lochlyn's chest. He folds his arms around me as he kisses the top of my head. And the tears start flowing again. He cups my chin with his hands and brushes the tears away with his thumbs, leaning down to kiss me.

I see Chelsea out of the corner of my eye, a smile on her face, wiping a tear from her own cheek.

"I missed you. So much." It comes out just above a whisper around the lump in my throat.

Lochlyn rests his forehead against mine, hands on my cheeks. "You have no idea, baby, no idea." His lips are on mine again. As my arms lace around his neck and my eyes drift closed, I notice Chelsea backing away.

I pull him into my room, closing the door behind us. We shuffle over the bed. When my tailbone hits the frame, Lochlyn ends the kiss, but stays against me. Putting his hands on my waist, he lifts me to the bed, kicking off his shoes and climbing up next to me, moving to lie against the wall, pillow under his head. He holds his arms out and I curl into him.

As much as I want his hands on me, I want to be close to him more. I nuzzle my head into his chest as he wraps his arms around me, pulling me so tightly against him there's no space between us. He runs his hand over my hair, the soothing motion calming me to steady my breathing for the first time since Chelsea left the room. Possibly even for the first time in six weeks.

There are so many things to say, so many things to do. But Lochlyn knows me well, and he knows in this moment, all I need is to be here, in his arms.

I'm awoken by the door opening and Chelsea talking loudly. "Hello! I'm coming in, I don't want to see anybody nake—"

"Shh!" Lochlyn is louder, cutting her off. I stay still, keeping my eyes closed, listening carefully.

"Shit, sorry." Her voice is lower now, just above a whisper. "It's been almost two hours. Has she been asleep the whole time?"

"Pretty much."

"She hasn't been sleeping well," she murmurs, almost as an afterthought.

"I hope it was worth it." His voice is quiet but dripping with anger.

"So, you really just sat here for almost two hours? Like that?"

"Yes, Chelsea, I really just sat here for two hours. Do you know why? Because it's what she needs right now. It's what I need."

"Were you really willing to give me up for her? I'm your sister."

"I was. You would too. She's worth it, and you know it." I hope Lochlyn can't feel my heart as it hammers erratically. It will surely give away the fact that I'm awake.

"You guys didn't, like, get a quickie in or something first?"

"Christ, Chelsea, what the hell kind of question is that? No, we didn't. We came in, laid down, and she fell asleep." By the way his body shifts, I know he's likely checking on me.

"It really is more than just sex. Ew, sorry, that's weird for me to think about."

"I don't care. And yes, it is. Much more." He pauses, tensing under me.

"It's just...it's weird, seeing you guys like that. Like you can just touch her anywhere." She probably says that because his hand is on my ass.

"Okay, Chelsea, I'm going to say this one more time. Are you listening? I. Don't. Care. I don't care if it's uncomfortable or weird for you. And I'm going to make damn sure she doesn't either. And I *can* touch her anywhere; she's given me that permission." I have. Over and over. Forever.

"So you love her? Like *really* love her?"

"Fuck. Chelsea. Did you even listen when we talked? You spat it all back at her, but did you listen? Did you absorb any of it?" The exhaustion in his voice tells me he's trying *very* hard to remain quiet.

"I don't know, I guess, maybe I just thought you were saying what you thought you needed to. To convince me so I said it was okay or something. And honestly, I was just tired of seeing her so upset."

Lochlyn's chest rises and falls steeply. He's trying to keep himself calm.

"Do you understand what you did? You hurt two of the people you say you love most in the world. For what? Because we fell in love with each other? I'm sorry that we did it under your nose. I'm sorry that we kept it a secret. I can see how that would hurt you, but it never should have been an issue to begin with. We shouldn't need your permission."

"I already said I'm sorry."

"Yeah, well, maybe that's just not good enough."

"Loch, how long are you going to be mad at me?" Her voice sounds small. They may bicker and drive each other crazy, but Chelsea loves Lochlyn, looks up to him. Having him mad at her is going to be hard for her to deal with.

"I don't know. Maybe until you prove you're okay with this. You've said it, but you need to *prove* it. I won't let you tear us apart again." I want to tighten my arms around him. I want to snuggle close, so he knows I won't either. But I need to hear how this goes.

"I brought you back here, didn't I?"

"Yeah, after you'd finally had enough of seeing the girl you claim is your best friend in pieces. For weeks. *Weeks*, Chelsea. And for what? Your comfort?"

"I-I—"

I tighten my hand on Lochlyn's arm, causing him to look down at me. "Hey, baby girl. How are you?" Gently, he brushes his knuckles against my cheek. I missed every touch so much.

Snuggling my face into his chest, I give him a tiny kiss before sitting up.

I look between the two of them and breathe deep, making sure my voice is steady before I speak. "I don't want you two fighting over me. So this is what's going to happen."

While looking directly at Chelsea, I take Lochlyn's hand in mine, meeting her eyes with a fierceness I've never used on her before. Lochlyn pushes up to sit behind me, so his hand rests comfortably in my lap.

"Lochlyn and I are going to be together; we never should have been apart. We're happy together, and we love each other, a lot." His lips press gently to my shoulder. "I can understand that it may make you uncomfortable to see us together, so I promise we will do our best to keep anything beyond kissing out of this room. I don't want you to be afraid to be in your own space.

"But that means I'll be spending a lot of time at his apartment. We have a lot of time to make up for, thanks to you." I've never been so blunt with Chelsea. It feels good. "You should be happy for that, because it means you can have Brendan come up and stay in here, and you won't have to worry about being bothered." Lochlyn tenses behind me, but I ignore him. His feelings on Brendan don't matter right now.

"I'm going to pack a bag with some clothes and my books and stay at Loch's for a few days. I love you, Chels, but I'm hurt and I'm mad. I had nowhere else to go for a few weeks. Now I do. And I want to be with him right now. More than I want to be with you. I need time to heal, and we need time to put the pieces back together." Lochlyn has been resting his chin on my shoulder and tilts his head down to give me another kiss.

Chelsea looks at the ground and nods. I've never seen her upset before. At least not over anything I've said or done. "I'm sorry, guys. I really am. I understand, Shay. Go, spend the time you need. I'd even understand if you don't want to be my friend anymore." She's feeling vulnerable. It's a new look for her. And it's about damn time she showed some humility and take responsibility for her actions.

"Chelsea, I still want to be your friend. But you hurt me. You made me choose between the two of you. That wasn't right, and it wasn't fair. And I can promise you that it was not the easy choice you thought it was." I feel Lochlyn look up. He thought I chose her outright, that he had no chance. I never had the opportunity to tell him just how close I really was to choosing him. That I toiled over it for those days I asked him to give me space to think.

"I'm so sorry. I don't know how I could possibly begin to show you how truly sorry I am. I wish there was something I could—"

I hold my hand up to stop her. "It's not necessary." Besides, right now they're empty words. Like Lochlyn said, she needs to show us.

"Well, I don't know, babe," Lochlyn grumbles behind me.

I turn to look at him, putting my hand on his chest. "No, it's not important. It doesn't matter. We're together now, in the open, no more secrets, no more lies. We lost time, but we can get it back. We can make up for what we lost. No need to hold a grudge."

"You're too good of a person for me, Shay. I don't deserve you." He presses his forehead to mine.

"I agree," Chelsea says behind us. She's trying to make light of the situation, but he pulls away to glare at her. I know it's going take a lot longer for him to forgive her.

He opens his mouth to say something back, but I push my hand harder against his chest.

Sliding off the bed, I bend down to get a duffle bag out from under it. Lochlyn stands next to me, arms crossed against his chest, standing guard as he glares at Chelsea. By the time I'm done, they still haven't looked away from each other.

I put my hand on his cheek, turning his face to me, and pushing on my toes to give him a tiny kiss. "Hey, let it go." His arms fall to his side as he relaxes.

Turning around to face Chelsea, I read a sadness in her eyes. "This isn't goodbye, Chelsea. I just need some time, space. We"—I wave a hand between Lochlyn and myself—"need to be able to work through what happened. I chose you and turned him away, so we need to fix that."

Leaning down, he kisses my neck. "It's okay, Shay, I—"

"No." I turn to face him. "No, I need to explain myself. And I will." I lace my fingers through his, feeling invigorated not having to think about who's around and being able to do what I want. "Let's go."

Grabbing my bag, he throws it over his shoulder. He brings my hand to his lips and then lets go, roping his arm around my shoulders, pulling me against him. Before he leads me out the door, I turn back to say a quick bye to Chelsea. Lochlyn does not.

Once we're outside, he slides his arm down around my waist. We walk in silence to his car, where he tosses my bag in the trunk, not letting me leave his side. He opens my door for me, but before I can slide into the seat, he pushes me against the car, pressing tightly against me, his mouth on mine.

As his hand cups my chin, the world around us disappears. It's just Lochlyn and I, together again.

The apartment door is still closing when Lochlyn pushes me against it, one hand against my neck, thumb grazing over my lower lip, while the other slides to my hip. "I missed you."

His mouth closes over mine, hungrily and urgently.

"Babe," I try to say. "Loch."

"Loch." I try a little louder. "Lochlyn." I can barely get the words out around his hungry lips.

"What?" he asks as he moves to my neck.

"Loch, stop."

He pulls back, brows furrowed. "Why?"

"Because I want to talk to you."

"Really? After six weeks apart, you want to talk?"

"I do." There are a million things I want to do; some I *need* to do. And this conversation falls into the latter category.

"Why?"

"I think it's important."

He sighs and takes a step back, sliding his hands into mine as he pulls me toward the couch. As he sits, he tugs me down with him, sliding my legs over his.

Running his fingers over my skin, he looks at me expectantly. "I'm only going to give you so long before I'm tearing your clothes off."

I can't help but giggle. It's the first time I've laughed since Chelsea walked in on us. I take a deep breath before starting what I'm worried may be a difficult conversation.

"I feel like I need to explain why I chose Chelsea."

"You don't. It doesn't matter anymore, we're—"

"No I do. I need you to understand. It was the *hardest* thing I've ever had to do in my life, including delaying Cornell. I didn't get a chance to talk to you after that day, to explain myself."

If I don't continue, I'll never get the whole story out, and I need to. He needs to hear it.

"It was not an easy decision. I need you to know that. I toiled over it for days, barely sleeping in the process." I take another shaky breath, steadying myself and trying to stop the tears that are threatening. I haven't even looked at him. I can't.

"I'd longed for you for so many years. Finally being with you, it felt like a dream. I didn't want to lose you, so I tried to think of some sort of solution. You know me in ways she never can; there are things I've told you, even before we got together, that I've never told her. But after all Chelsea and I have been through, after she put her life on hold for me when my dad died, I had to choose her." I keep going, having to push through to get it all out.

"I love you, so much, but I've loved her longer. And it's different, of course, but I'd lived without you before. Those days without Chelsea were so hard. For sixteen years, she'd always been there, almost every day. I could turn to her for anything. And I had this one major crisis going on and she was the cause." Biting the inside of my cheek, I look away before I let the anger at the situation take over again.

"I talked to my mom before Chelsea caught us, which was a bad idea. I thought maybe, just maybe, she could be my mom again. But she said to always choose your friends over love, that love only leaves you broken-hearted. I know she's still so lost over my dad." Lochlyn swipes away the stray tears before I even realize they're falling. There have been so many lately I barely recognize them anymore. I still haven't looked at him, but clearly, he's watching me intently.

My lip trembles, knowing what I'm about to say may be the most heartbreaking. "I had to choose Chelsea, because I was worried. I was worried that someday, sooner or later, you'd realize you don't want to be with me. That if I chose you, I'd lose her and then eventually you'd come to resent me for turning away your sister and I'd lose you too. Then I wouldn't have her to turn to when my heart was broken."

The tears are flowing freely, so fast I can't swipe them away quickly enough and they patter against my legs. Lochlyn takes my chin in his fingers and tilts it up, pulling me in for a tender kiss. He swipes his thumbs under each eye slowly. When that doesn't help, he kisses one track of tears.

"Shay, I understand. I understand why you made the choice you did. I *hate* that we missed out on even a second of time together. But none of that is your fault. It's Chelsea's. You never should have had to make a decision like that. And I should have fought harder. I should have pushed against her more."

"No, there was no reasoning with her. I don't want your relationship to be harmed because of us. You've always been close." Initially, I *was* mad at him for not fighting harder. But it didn't take long for reality to set in that there was nothing he could have said or done to change things.

"It's too late for that. Chelsea already did that when she made you choose. But it took me all of three days to decide that I didn't care what Chelsea had to say. That nobody was going to determine our relationship except us. I was just biding my time to come back to you."

My pulse quickens at his words, and my eyes flick up to his, widening as I digest what he said. "You were? But it's been six weeks."

"I was trying to figure out the best way. I needed for Chelsea to not be around. I didn't think going home was the right place, so I had to wait until you moved on to campus. My plan was to learn your class schedule and conveniently bump into you one day."

"And you thought upon seeing you, I'd just fall romantically into your arms?" It's not the worst theory, because I certainly would be inclined to do just that.

He chuckles, and my whole body tingles at the sound that I've missed so much. "Well, I mean, I'd hoped. But I kind of figured I'd just work my way back, show Chelsea she was wrong."

I drop my gaze and twist my fingertips. "I had been kind of worried about seeing you around campus."

"Why?"

"I was afraid I'd see you with somebody else." It's so quiet I'm not sure he heard me. I almost hope he didn't.

But then he sighs. "Shay, I can promise you, if anything were to ever happen between us where we decided not to be together anymore, it would take *much* longer than six weeks for me to move on."

I chance a look at him. "Yeah?"

"I guarantee it." His lips are on mine in an instant, soft but forceful. I said what I needed to say, so now all that's left is wanting to be as close to Lochlyn as I can be. As I lace my hands around his neck, he slides an arm under my knees while the other wraps around my waist, lifting me as he stands.

He carries me to his bedroom, kicking the door closed behind us. Setting me gently on the bed, he slowly pulls my shoes off, dropping them to the floor with a thud. He runs his hands up my legs, fingers dipping under the waistband of my jeans and sliding to the button, flicking it open as he slowly pulls off my pants and panties.

His breath is shallow, his eyes trained on mine. I lean forward to reach for his jeans, but he pushes me back down on the bed.

"No." It comes out strained as he shakes his head.

He climbs out of his jeans, reaching over his shoulders and pulling off his shirt, tossing it to the corner. My breath catches at the sight of his chest, as it's just another thing I missed immensely and feared I'd never see again.

In only his boxers, he climbs up on the bed, straddling my legs. He slides his hands under my shirt, running slowly up my sides. Reaching behind my back, he unhooks my bra, slipping his hands under the band and around to the front, cupping my breasts, running his fingers over my nipples.

He smirks as I arch toward him. "I missed these."

Within seconds, my shirt and bra are on the floor as Lochlyn leans over me, hand running over my hair. "I missed you so much, Shay."

As his mouth closes over mine and his tongue slips between my lips, I take a moment and wonder why he never lets me answer. It's probably because he knows that I'll reciprocate the feeling, that he knows I missed him too. How could I not?

Six weeks of not feeling Lochlyn catches up to me. My lips turn hungry, my hands fly to the top of his boxers, pushing them down. He responds in kind, peeling them off and tossing them to the floor, hands grabbing tightly to my hips as he eases into me.

"Fuck, Shay," he exhales as his breath hitches, feeling my wanting, my *need*, for him.

I take his chin in my hand. "I missed you too."

His mouth crashes to mine as he starts moving slowly at first, then faster and faster until we're both breathing heavily and every exhale I make contains a whimper.

Nothing quite compares to the feelings of his body against mine. The firmness and warmth of his chest as it brushes my breasts as he moves over me, the tightness of his muscles under my hands. The feeling of him moving inside me, the way he fills me so completely.

As the pressure builds, he wraps his hand around the back of my head, hissing against my ear as I dig my nails into his back, tightening around him as one last loud moan releases from my chest. The sound of his throaty groan in my ear almost sends me into a tailspin.

He breathes heavily against me for a minute before kissing from my ear to the tip of my shoulder and rolling to his back. Before I even have a chance to move, he slides his arm under my neck and pulls me into him, kissing the top of my head as I lie on his chest.

Feeling his arms around me brings hot pricks to the back of my eyes. His hand stills on my hip. Even though no tears have dripped out, he knows.

"What's wrong, baby girl?"

"I was just so scared I'd never be this close to you again." It comes out barely above a whisper.

On some level, I know it's pathetic, overly emotional, and way too needy. But Lochlyn was all I wanted for years, a dream I thought I'd never have. And it wasn't just a situation where we gave it a shot and decided we weren't right together. It was us being torn apart under unfair circumstances.

He's not just my first boyfriend, or my first love. He's my forever. And if for any reason we end up not working out, I will still always have love for him.

He presses his hand into my hip and pulls me flush against him as his other arm wraps around me and his lips graze the top of my head. "I know. But we're here together. We won't let anything tear us apart again."

I nod, and his phone dings somewhere on the floor. Leaning over me, he grabs his pants, sliding his phone out of his pocket and sitting back next to me, resting on his elbow to read the message.

When he laughs, I sit up to look. "What's so funny?"

He shows me a message from Weston.

Wes: *Hey man. Just wanted to let you know I packed myself a bag and took off for Claire's for a few days. Figured I'd give you and Shay some alone time to get back together or whatever. I'll be back Sunday. Have fun!*

I look at him, brow furrowed, confused. "Why is he giving us the apartment? I mean, I appreciate it, but why? Did I do something?"

"Uh, not exactly. I think we may have scarred him last time you were here."

My eyes widen and heat flashes through my body as I drop my head to my hands and hide in Lochlyn's shoulder. "Ohmygod no. He heard us? That's so embarrassing."

It just makes him laugh harder and he kisses my temple. "I mean, it's kinda hard *not* to hear you."

I straighten and smack his chest. "No part of this is funny!"

"Are you kidding? It's hilarious!"

"It's humiliating."

"Nothing about having good sex is humiliating."

"Except the part where he *heard us.*"

He shrugs. "He wasn't that weirded out. He congratulated me after you left."

"Shut up, he did not." I slink down and bury myself under the covers. "Just leave me here to die of mortification."

Lochlyn just laughs next to me as he runs his hand up my body, over the sheet. "There's nothing wrong with letting people know you like it. You could tell me every so often."

I flip the sheet back to look at him. "Oh, so you want me to be *more* vocal?"

"Not necessarily what I mean. But every so often you could tell me you like something."

"I kind of figured you could tell by, ya know, the sounds."

Apparently, I'm just hilarious today as he laughs again, his hand resting on my stomach. "I guess it'd just be nice to hear you *say* it once in a while."

"I think I just feel so new at all this still. Like, I don't know what I'm doing. Even though it's been a few months."

"I don't think you give yourself enough credit. You're sexy as hell, Shay. It's not about knowing what to do, it's about what feels good. If you like it, tell me." He says it so matter-of-factly, like it's just that easy.

"That's the thing, though, I feel like I don't need to. It's like you just know. I mean, you've had a lot more experience, so I guess it makes sense."

"It's not about experience. It's about knowing you, reading you. And a lot of doing what I want to do with you, because I know you well enough to know that if you *don't* like it, you'll tell me. Like this?" He starts kissing along my collarbone. "I know you like this."

"Mhm."

"And this?" He slides his hands under the sheet to slip between my thighs as I stir. "I know you like this too."

"Yeah," I breathe.

"I'm pretty sure you're going to like this." He starts kissing down my stomach, lower and lower, until he gets to my hips. Licking down my tingling skin, he settles between my legs.

Even though I've been naked in front of Lochlyn well over a few dozen times by now, his face has never been so close to that part of me. I'm a little unsure, thinking of pulling away.

But the second his tongue touches me, any doubt disappears. *Everything* disappears but Lochlyn and his very talented mouth.

I pant and whimper as his tongue swirls around me. My hands tangle in his hair, pulling him closer as he wraps my legs over his shoulders. I'm sure it can't feel any better. Until he slides two fingers into me.

Bucking against him, gasping and moaning, I tug at his hair. "Ohmygod." It comes out as a whisper, but he hears and starts moving faster.

I shudder, about to let it all go when he stops, leaving me so close to coming it's almost mean.

Until he flips me to my stomach and lifts my hips, pushing into me as a quiet "fuck" leaves his mouth.

I'm so on edge that it takes all of two minutes before I'm screaming, gripping at the sheets, as I tighten around him. He slows but doesn't stop while I tremble, then once I'm still, he starts thrusting harder and faster until he's groaning and digging his fingers into my hips. He leans over my back, kissing between my shoulder blades, hands running up my sides, before pulling away and lying on his side, head propped on his hand.

I collapse, just a puddle of extremely content self. I can't even open my eyes. I feel like I'm floating.

Lochlyn brushes some hair behind my ear. "You okay over there?"

I shake my head, causing him to chuckle. My eyes flutter open to find him looking at me, a smile on his face. "You've been holding out on me."

"I suppose I have. I know we didn't exactly ease into things or take it step by step, so to speak, but you still seemed a little...nervous at times." He's right. I can still barely say the word "sex" even though at one point we were having it daily.

Right now, I'm thinking about reciprocating the favor. I know I should at least offer. But it's like my body is willing to do everything and anything he wants while my head and my mouth can't quite get there. I've obviously touched his cock, had it inside me. But for some reason, having it in my mouth seems like a little more than I'm ready for. Which makes guilt wrack through me.

"I don't...I don't expect anything, in return. Not until you feel ready, if ever. I'll never ask you for anything you're not ready to give, never ask you to do anything you're not ready to do." He hesitates for a minute, eyes flashing to my lips. "I didn't expect you to say yes that night. Part of me expected you to push me away or even slap me after I kissed you. Never, in a million years, did I think you'd say yes. But I had to ask. I had to take the chance."

"I'm really happy you did. I never would have known otherwise."

"Really? Not even after Thanksgiving?"

"Pfft, no. I was convinced you only kissed me because you felt pity for me. I was sitting there basically in tears about my sad, pathetic life and that I'd never kissed anybody."

"First of all, *if* I felt pity for you, I certainly wouldn't have kissed you like *that*. Or more than once. Secondly, you definitely don't see yourself clearly, and maybe that's from being in Chelsea's shadow for so long. You say I turn heads when we're out, but so do you, Shay. You're gorgeous. I know you don't see it, or maybe you don't believe me, but I see the heads turn. I watch the eyes follow you. And worst of all, I heard what the guys in high school would say." There's a tick in his jaw as he says it.

"Guys talked about me in high school?"

He rolls his eyes. "Out of all of that, what you took away was the guys talking about you in high school? Yes, they did. And let's just say it was not the sort of thing I'd repeat or ever want you to know about. It took a lot of strength to not beat the crap out of a few of them. Including Jay."

My eyes widen. "Jay?" I mean, sure, he was being creepy at that party over the summer, but I figured he was just drunk.

"Oh yeah. I won't repeat what he said, but I made it exceptionally clear that if I ever heard that he laid a finger on you, he'd live to regret it. To say he's jealous is an understatement. There were a few guys though who I worried about. Nice guys who just thought you were gorgeous and smart and sweet, who I thought maybe you'd give a chance and date. I never said anything, but part of me got a little nervous that you'd start dating someone and I'd miss my chance.

"I know you heard at least most, if not all, of my conversation with Chelsea. I could tell you were awake. And I know I've told you before, but it's worth saying again. I'm...a physical person. But if you were to say no more sex tomorrow, I'd be okay with that. It's you that I want, mind, soul, and yeah, body too. But I want everything. There's so much more than sex here, Shay. For me, at least."

I turn to my side and move to be right against him, pressing my lips to his. "For me too."

Chapter 19

Lochlyn has taken it upon himself to teach me how to cook.

"But why do I need to learn if I have you?" I whine at him. "What if you're hungry and I'm not here?"

"I'll starve."

"Exactly."

I can't really complain much, the lessons aren't so bad. He stands right behind me, chest pressed against my back, arms stretched the length of mine as he teaches me hand over hand. He's absolutely appalled that the most I can do is boil water and cook pasta, saying had he known my skills were so lacking, he would have made sure to do more with me over the summer.

On Saturday morning, Lochlyn's giving me another lesson. We haven't seen or spoken to Chelsea since we walked out four days ago. Weston is still giving us our space. Lochlyn's been taking me to classes, staying on campus to wait for me if he needs to. I wait for him at the library, where he'll find me and break my study trance by kissing my neck.

"I'm going to burn them!" My voice is slightly hysterical.

"You're not going to burn them." His voice is exceptionally calm.

"They're going to be undercooked! It's dangerous to eat undercooked eggs." Hysteria.

"You're not going to undercook them." Calm.

"Well, something's going to go wrong." Slightly calmer.

"Shay, they're just eggs."

I sigh and huff some hair out of my face when Lochlyn starts kissing along my neck. It's become a calming mechanism he uses on me when I'm spiraling. It always works.

"You need to relax, Shay. It's not as hard as you're making it out to be." Cooking may not be as hard as I think, but *something* certainly is and it's pressing into my back.

He's still kissing along my neck as one of his hands slides up my arm, down my side, and down the front of my pants. My head tips back against his shoulder as he slips along my wetness before pushing two fingers inside me. His other hand holds my throat, caging me against his body as I sigh and moan.

With a quick change of position, he spins me around to face him, hands grabbing under my thighs as he lifts me up, flipping off the burner and pushing the pan to the back of the stove.

"I think I burned my eggs," I say against his lips.

"I'll make you new ones." His mouth claims mine as he starts walking toward his room.

Lochlyn has his mouth around my nipple with my fingers tangled in his hair while we lie on the bed when my phone starts ringing.

"Ignore it," he says against my chest. I have no intentions of doing anything but just that.

My back arches and I squeak as he presses into me, his mouth latching onto my neck.

For the past four days and nights, he's alternated between slow and sensual, and hard and fast, bending and twisting my body to meet his desires. It doesn't matter to me; it all feels incredible.

As he moves inside me, slowly, my phone rings again. Lochlyn groans against my neck.

"Ignore it." It's my turn to say it, though more breathless than Lochlyn had been.

As his hand slides up my side, wrapping gently around my throat, he starts moving faster. His thumb presses against my chin as I try to tilt my head backward, moaning as the pressure builds.

"Look at me, Shay." The huskiness in his voice vibrates through my body. I could stay in this bed with him forever and it wouldn't be enough.

"God, Lochlyn," I breathe as the pressure peaks and my nails dig into his shoulders and I let out a scream. Slowing but not stopping, he continues to grind his hips against mine as I work through my trembles.

I lock my eyes with his, needing more of him, all of him. "Again." It's one simple word, but his lip quirks up before he leans down and presses his mouth to mine, kissing to my ear.

"Tell me what you want," he whispers against my ear before taking the sensitive skin between his teeth.

"More." It comes out harsh, forceful, especially as I have to work to say it around the hand pressing against my throat.

Leaning back on his knees, he takes one of my legs and puts it against his shoulder, wrapping the other around his waist. Bending forward, he rests his arms on either side of me. We've never had sex this long before, something I know Lochlyn does for me. I don't have to ask, and he doesn't have to explain. I know. Because I'm realizing everything he does, he does for me.

It doesn't take long until the familiar tingling takes over me again, and I'm about to come. I wrap my hands around his arms as I arch, digging my nails in as I whimper. His breath hitches as the hand by my head grabs at the sheets.

Releasing my leg and hovering above me, his thumb runs along my lower lip before he leans in and kisses me, rolling to his back, chest heaving.

When I regain my ability to think, I sit up, pulling the sheet around my chest before leaning down to find my phone somewhere on the floor.

Lochlyn grabs my bicep, trying to pull me toward him. "Lie down with me."

"I have to find my phone. Whoever it was, called twice."

"So what? It can wait ten more minutes."

"It could be my mom. I haven't talked to her in three weeks."

"You've only been here for about three weeks."

"Exactly."

He grumbles as he slides his hand down my back. Finding my phone under my shirt, I sit up.

"It was Chelsea." Immediately, I call her back.

"Don't." One corner of my mouth tips down, and I shoot him a glare. I needed the time away from her, but he won't even talk about her.

"Hey, Shay." Her voice on the other end of the line is hesitant.

"Hey, Chels. What's up?"

"Sorry to bother you. Were you busy? Actually, never mind. I don't want to think about what you were busy doing." Lochlyn, who's leaning close enough to hear, laughs lightly as he starts kissing along my shoulder.

"We were just making breakfast. What's up?"

"I just...I miss you, Shay. You're my best friend! I haven't seen you in four days. I'm wondering when you're coming back."

I look over at Lochlyn. He wants me to stay indefinitely, but I'm not sure it's the best idea. I'd chosen to room with Chelsea for a reason. And while I love him, I think some time apart every now and again will be healthy for our relationship. And I need to fix things with Chelsea too.

"I'm not sure yet, Chels. Lochlyn and I are still repairing things."

"That you broke," he says near the mouthpiece. With a flat hand, I push his face away, scowling at him.

"I know, I'm sorry. I just want to make it up to you. I want us to be okay again. I don't know how to do that if we're not talking and you're avoiding me."

"I'm not avoiding you, Chelsea. I'm just putting all my focus into Lochlyn right now. It needs to be that way for a little while." I hesitate. "I need to come get some more clothes."

"No, you don't," Lochlyn says against my shoulder, a smirk on his face.

"Maybe we can spend a few hours together when I do." It's a suggestion I'm not sure I actually want to follow through with, but I need to give her something.

"I'd really like that. Will it...will it be just you?"

"Is it a problem if it's not?" I wasn't planning to bring Lochlyn aside from dropping me off and picking me up. But I need her to be comfortable with us together and seeing us together, or things will never be better between her and I.

"No, I mean, I guess not. I was kind of hoping we could have some girl time. But if you want to bring him, that's fine. It just may be awkward because he's still not talking to me."

"Well, Chels, I haven't talked to you in four days either."

"Yeah, but we had all that time together. Aside from the day I went to his apartment to talk about you, I haven't spoken to him in over six weeks."

"It'll be just me." Lochlyn bites my shoulder. I turn my head to look at him and point my finger, mouthing, *No biting,* to which he smirks and takes my fingertip between his teeth.

"That'll be nice."

"Probably tomorrow."

"I'll make sure I'm around all day."

"Alright, Chels. I'll see you tomorrow."

"Okay. Bye, Shay. Oh, could you—"

I hang up before I hear what else she has to say. If she puts up an argument again, I won't be siding with her. I'd spent sixteen years living in her shadow, letting her take the lead, letting her tell me what to do and what not to do. It had almost cost me the person I love the most in the world. I'm not going to stand for it anymore.

Lochlyn lies down on his back, pulling me down against him.

"You're really going to go over there? And without me?"

"I do need you to drive me, but yes, we need some time, at least to talk without you around."

"Why can't you talk in front of me?"

"Because you're not exactly being nice to her right now."

"I'm still mad at her." He says the words very slowly and with enunciation on each one.

"She's still your sister, Lochlyn."

"I don't care. She cost us six weeks together. Six weeks."

I take a breath, putting my hand on his chest. "Are you planning to change your mind? Decide that this isn't what you want after all?"

"No. Of course not. I told you—"

"Then it doesn't matter in the grand scheme of things. Look, nobody can predict the future, but I'm not planning on not being with you. Ever. Six weeks will seem so minimal. Plus, how many years did you spend longing for me?"

He loops a curl behind my ear. "Many."

"Exactly. And I know, because I spent years longing for you too. Those six weeks, they were awful. I felt like my heart was ripped out when you stormed out that day." His arms tighten around me. "But we're here, we're together again. That's all that matters.

"Chelsea needs some time alone, to truly appreciate what she could have, maybe should have, lost. But we can't just shut her out forever. I don't want to. We'd all always been so close. I don't want that to change just because we're together. I think it'll be nice." I lean up, pointing at him. "And *you* have to figure out how to be nice and deal with Brendan."

Groaning, he asks, "Do I have to?"

"Yes, you do. Because she's happy with him. If we want her to be happy for us, you need to be happy for her. Listen, I don't care if you threaten him weekly; she *is* your sister, after all. But you have to find a way to at least be pleasant. If not for her, then for me."

"Well, if it's for you, I guess I'll have to find a way."

"Only because it's for me?"

"Yup." He pops the 'p' at the end of the word.

"Why not for Chelsea?"

"Because I wouldn't do anything for her. But I would do any-thing for you. Anything." My chest inflates as my heart flutters and his lips graze the spot on my neck where he can see my pulse.

"Anything? Really?"

"Really and truly."

"Okay then. There's something I need you to do for me."

He straightens and looks down into my eyes. "Oh yeah, and what's that?" There's a sultriness in his voice, and I know his mind has gone to a dirty place.

"Make me some breakfast?" My shoulders scrunch to my ears and a sheepish smile spreads across my face.

A chuckle rumbles from his throat as his head drops to my stomach. "Anything for you, baby girl."

Chapter 20

As the anniversary of Dad's death approaches, I start to withdraw into myself. Chelsea and Lochlyn are still barely talking, and seem to be fighting for my attention. She and I have worked our way back to a close friendship over the past two weeks, but to say things are strained when we're all together is an understatement.

While sitting in our room after class on Tuesday, the day before the anniversary, the two of them keep arguing over where I last spent the night. I've had enough.

"Would the two of you just fucking *stop* already? I can't take this shit anymore!" They both freeze and look at me. I still rarely curse, yell even less. "You're acting like children fighting over a toy. I'm not a thing; I'm a person."

"We know that, Shay. We just both want to spend time with you." Chelsea's being gentle. She's learned the hard way that if she pushes me too far, I'm not going to lie down and take it anymore.

Lochlyn doesn't say anything. He and I have already had this conversation, where he'd promised to be better, yet in front of Chelsea, he regresses to being a small child again.

"I'll make this simple. I'm going to spend time with who I want, when I want. We're all here together right now. If the two of you could get over your petty bullshit and make up already, then things would be easier. You both need to understand who the other person is and that they have a role in my life," I spit the words out angrily.

Lochlyn, who's been leaning up against the wall while sitting on my bed, slides forward so that I'm standing between his legs. He wraps an arm around my chest and kisses my neck. "What's wrong, baby?"

I shrug him off. "Nothing."

Chelsea looks at Lochlyn, the first glance I've seen between them that isn't filled with irritation and disdain. Instead, it's filled with worry.

"Are you having trouble in your classes?"

"No, Chelsea, that would be you." My rebuttal catches even me off guard.

"Wow, Shay. If you're mad at me about something, just say so."

"I'm not mad! Christ, can't you just see I'm tired of being talked about like an object rather than a damn person who has opinions and can make her own decisions about who she sees and what she does and when!"

Lochlyn hops off the bed and grabs my hand, dragging me out the door. He doesn't slow down or talk to me until we're outside, where he loosens his grip. I yank my hand from his and spin away from him.

He stands right behind me, so close that when he speaks, his breath tickles the nape of my neck. "Talk. Now."

Incapable of doing that, I move away from him. He follows, putting his hand around my bicep, pulling me toward him. I spin to face him, pushing against his chest and out of his grasp.

"Go away, Lochlyn! Leave me alone."

Both his hands land on my arms, tugging me closer. "Talk to me."

"I said, leave me *alone!*" I push against him, hard, almost tumbling backward as I force myself away from him.

Instead of listening, both of his hands latch completely around my biceps and he yanks me into his chest. He wraps his arms so tightly around me, I can't move. I thrash around, trying to break free. When that doesn't work, I smack his chest with open palms. After a minute like that, I fist my hands and hit him, but he doesn't relent.

"Let go of me!"

"No. Something is going on and you're going to talk to me." His words come out broken as I continue to wriggle, and he has to keep up with my movements.

"I said let go!" I scream. An outsider would think he's harming me with the way I'm flailing about and struggling.

"Shay. You need to talk to me. What the hell is going on with you? I know Chelsea and I can't possibly be pissing you off this much. There's something else and you're not telling me what it is."

Puffs of air leave my mouth instead of words, and I burst into tears, my thrashing turning into grasping fistfuls of his shirt. He supports me as my knees lose their balance, keeping his arms tight around me.

I don't know how long he holds me for, how long I just let the tears pour out of me without pause. He never asks me what's wrong, doesn't ask me to talk, just lets me sob uncontrollably into his chest outside my dorm.

As the tears start to subside, I'm left with just the shallow breathing and salt-stained cheeks. Lochlyn senses the calm and loosens his grip, hands cupping my cheeks as he wipes under my eyes. His face is full of worry.

"Baby, *what* is going on?"

"Tomorrow's...the anniversary...of..." I try to get it out between ragged breaths.

But I don't need to finish. "Your dad's death. Oh, baby girl, I'm so sorry. I wasn't paying attention to the date. Fuck."

Lochlyn looks up at the sky, and his jaw tightens as he pulls me back against him, wrapping his arms around my shoulders and head, boxing me into him. I take a few moments to just breathe him in, using his steady breathing to calm my own, feeling his heartbeat beneath my fingers to ground myself to him, and letting the sandalwood scent overwhelm me and allowing me to get lost in him.

When my breaths are no longer hitching, he lowers his hands, trailing my arms to take my hands in his. He leans his forehead against mine. It's the sweetest thing he does to me, making me feel so close to him.

"Are you okay to go inside? Or do you want to go back to my apartment?"

"Inside's fine."

"You sure?"

I nod silently.

Wrapping his arm around my waist, he leads me back upstairs to my room.

As soon as I'm through the door, Chelsea takes one look at me and rushes to envelop me in a hug. Lochlyn letting go of my waist. As much as I love Chelsea, I need him more, so I extend my hand back to find his.

When Chelsea pulls away, she opens her mouth to say something, but I raise my free hand to cut her off.

"I don't really want to talk about it."

"We're going to stay here tonight." Lochlyn speaks firmly, not allowing any room for Chelsea to argue. He hasn't slept here at all yet.

"Yeah, okay, that's fine."

I turn around to look at him. "Are you sure?"

He nods. "I think you need both of us right now." The way he sees me, knows me, understands me, will never cease to amaze me.

I smile as the tears threaten to fall again. Shaking my head, I chase them away. I hate being a blubbering mess, though; it's always happened a lot in Lochlyn's presence. It's something to do with the comfort I feel with him and how I can truly be myself.

Lochlyn closes up all the books on my bed, making a stack and putting them on my desk. He kicks off his shoes and climbs up, putting my pillows in the corner against the wall, leaning back and opening his arms to me.

Without hesitation or any exchange of words, I climb up and curl into him. "Let's watch a movie or something, yeah?" He wants to distract me. I nod, unable to find my voice. Chelsea hands him the remote immediately.

If she's at all uncomfortable with Lochlyn planning to stay, or the fact that his hand is comfortably in my back pocket, she knows better than to mention it.

I'm asleep before he even picks a movie.

When I wake up, it's dark outside. I shake as Lochlyn chuckles beneath me. *The Office* is on in the background—my favorite show. My stomach grumbles at the smell of Chinese food. I sit up slowly as Lochlyn slides his hand to my lower back, sitting up himself.

"Hey, baby. How'd you sleep?"

"Fine, I think. Sorry, I didn't mean to doze off." Grogginess slurs my words, and my eyelids are still weighed down.

"Don't apologize, you're fine."

"We got Chinese food!" Chelsea perks up behind me. I'd almost forgotten she was here when I fell asleep.

"It smells good. I'm actually pretty hungry."

"All right, let's eat."

Chelsea grabs sodas from the fridge and passes out the food. Lochlyn and I sit on my bed, our backs against the wall, while Chelsea sits on hers, facing us. We eat quietly; the only sounds being from the show and the scraping of forks and cans being set down on the wood of the bedframe. I'm feeling awkward, knowing their eyes are on me, worried.

"Thanks for getting food, guys."

"You're welcome," they say in unison. Chelsea had to have handled ordering and getting it from downstairs, but Lochlyn likely insisted on paying.

I glance at the TV and can tell we're almost in season two of the show. I've been asleep for at least two hours.

Lochlyn sighs heavily next to me but doesn't say anything.

I turn to him to find he's looking at his food, mouth tight. "What? Just spit it out."

"Do you want to go home? Do you want to be home tomorrow?" His eyes flip up to meet mine.

Though I haven't brought it up, I've already thought about it. I know if I were to ask, Lochlyn would drive me home, spend the night with me, and drive me back to school the next morning. Four hours each way and he wouldn't think twice or complain. He'd do it because he'd be doing it for me.

"No, I don't want to be home."

"But...What about your mom?" Chelsea either figured it out, or they talked while I slept.

I slowly release the breath I've been holding for days. "My mom. You know, I love her, she's my mom, but I think it's time she learns how to cope on her own. I put my whole life on hold for her. She was so bitter about the loss of my dad she asked me to put off my dream of being here, told me to give up on love.

I've barely seen her for almost two years. No, this is where I want to be. And you're who I want to be with. I need to do things for myself."

Chelsea nods and gives me a tight smile, while Lochlyn kisses my temple.

"If you change your mind—"

"I know. I won't. But I appreciate the thought. I just want to be here."

We finish eating in silence, with Lochlyn and Chelsea both giving me furtive glances.

They let me keep *The Office* on even though I've seen every episode over two dozen times. They're treating me with kid gloves, especially after my earlier meltdown, but I'm reveling in it, enjoying being in charge while in Chelsea's presence.

Chelsea gives us some privacy to get changed for bed. We'd had the forethought to keep some of Lochlyn's clothes in my dorm, more so for me to have on the few nights we don't spend together.

It was a compromise we had all come to. One night a week, I had to be in the dorm with Chelsea, alone, for girl time. But I have an early class three days a week, that's just easier for me to be in my dorm for. Most of the time. Many of those nights are spent together anyway. I just sleep better when Lochlyn's near me.

By the time Chelsea comes back in, we're sitting under the covers, our heads together, looking at recently announced concert tour dates, trying to decide if there's any we can go to and who we'd want to see.

"Uh, do you guys need like, any alone time or anything? I can disappear for a little bit if you need me to."

"No, Chels, that's not necessary." Heat prickles my back and cheeks that she even mentioned it.

But Lochlyn turns to me. "Well, I mean, if she's offering."

I elbow him in the ribs, causing him to wince and double over. "No, Chels, we're fine."

Lochlyn tucks some hair behind my ear, trailing his finger to the end and pulling the curl straight before watching it bounce back up. "You tired?"

"Yes and no. My eyes feel tired but not my mind, if that makes sense." Mostly, my eyes still feel puffy, which is making them feel tired.

"Do you want to try to sleep?"

"I don't think so. Maybe read?"

"Anything you want." Cupping my cheek, he rubs the pad of this thumb along my skin as I lean into his hand.

"What about you guys, though?" I look back and forth between them before settling back on Lochlyn.

"I doubt you have anything I'd read, so I'll study," he offers easily.

"Why would I have nothing you'd read?" Part of me is slightly offended. I have a variety of taste in books. Though, not necessarily his.

"I've taken you book shopping before, remember? And how many times have you complained about what's on my bookshelf and that there's nothing for you? I don't mind studying."

"Okay, point taken. Chels?" I turn to look at her.

"I'll just flip through a magazine. Don't worry about me."

I look between both of them again. "You guys sure? You don't have to baby me. I'm fine."

Lochlyn's shoulder lifts next to me, but I keep my eyes trained on Chelsea. She'll be the easier one to read if she's lying. And the one who will care more. Lochlyn likes to read and doesn't mind studying.

"I have a new stack of magazines I haven't checked out yet." She's trying really hard to be okay with it, but I pretend not to notice her hesitation.

I grab my book off the top of my desk. Lochlyn climbs over me, stopping while he's straddling me to give me a quick kiss, and grabs his books.

No more than ten minutes in, I realize I'm not going to be able to read. I've reread the same paragraph at least three times and still haven't absorbed it. Shutting my book and tossing it to my desk, I slide down with a huff, arms crossed against my chest. Lochlyn glances up at me but doesn't say anything, handing me the remote while he looks back at his textbook.

I flip on the TV and sink all the way down to lie on my side, pressing my back against Lochlyn. He puts his hand on my waist as he keeps reading.

"Oh, thank God," Chelsea says as she tosses her magazine to the floor.

I flip through the channels until I find a romcom just starting. I look back at Lochlyn in time to see his eyes flick to the TV and hear his groan. He hates this movie.

Sometime later, I wake up to Lochlyn carefully climbing over me. I watch silently as he quietly puts things away, throws away garbage, and puts my book back on the shelf with the others. He turns off the lights, climbing back over me and sliding under the covers. Knowing Chelsea likes to sleep with the TV on, he turns the volume down before putting the remote on my desk.

He wraps his arm around me and pulls me tight against him. "Good night, baby girl. I love you," he whispers against my hair.

"I love you too." He places the tiniest kiss behind my ear as I fall back to sleep.

The next morning, Chelsea had gone out early, bringing back muffins and coffees. But I can't really eat.

"Shay, are you sure? You should eat something."

"Chels, let it go." Lochlyn understands. It's just another one of the many things he knows that Chelsea doesn't. And something I told him well before we got together.

Lochlyn places his hand on my lower back, and that's all it takes for me to fall apart. He doesn't hesitate to pull me against him, leaning back into the pillows he's built up in the corner, anticipating my needs.

My hands twist in his shirt as I sob against him. His arms wrap around me, chin resting next to my forehead. The bed dips as Chelsea climbs up on the bed behind me and slides against my back, wrapping her arm around me to rest against my stomach. I reach one hand down to hold hers.

I sit there, bawling over the loss of my dad, for the first time since he died, surrounded by the two people I love and need most in the world.

Chapter 21

After the tears stop flowing and my breathing returns to normal, I sit up. Chelsea and Lochlyn are both still wrapped around me. When the tears were at their strongest, it felt like they were holding me together.

I take a long, deep breath, filling my lungs, and wipe at my face, feeling the dried saltiness, tasting it at the corners of my mouth.

"Chelsea, you should go to class. Both of you. I'm fine. I don't want you to miss classes because of me."

"I'm not going anywhere. Don't argue." Lochlyn's voice is low and firm. I know there's no way to convince him to leave, which is good because I don't actually want him to.

"I'm happy to stay, too."

"No, it's okay. You've already missed one class today. You need to go. I'll be fine. Loch's here."

"Are you sure?"

"I am. I'm really thankful you were here this morning, though. But please, go to class." Not only do I worry about her academic stability, but she wouldn't let me be if she were here. She'd constantly check in, offer things to do, and I just want peace today.

She looks at me for a minute, trying to read me, before looking over at Lochlyn. He nods slightly. "She'll be fine, Chels."

"If you change your mind, just text me and I'll come right back."

"I will."

"Promise?"

"I promise." Sure, I promise to message her *if* I change my mind. Which won't be happening. Lochlyn is all I need.

She points her finger at Lochlyn. "You take care of her."

He scowls at her but replies nicely. "I will."

Before whisking out the door, she pulls me into a hug. "I love you, Shay."

"I love you too, Chels. Now go, before you're late."

Once she's out the door, I let out a sigh, hanging my head over my lap.

Lochlyn runs a finger down my neck, causing me to look at him. "How are you?" He always asks the loaded questions.

"I'm...okay." It takes me a moment to take an inventory of my body, of my mind, to be able to answer him honestly.

"Are you hungry at all?"

"Maybe a little? I don't feel hungry, but I know I probably am. That I should eat."

"I think you should. At least try. If you don't want muffins, I can get something else."

Quickly and somewhat frantically, I grab for his hands. "Muffins are fine. I don't want you to leave."

Pulling his hands from mine, he folds me into him, kissing the top of my head. "I'm not going anywhere."

We eat our muffins, somewhat hard and dry, but the coffee is cold, rendering it utterly undrinkable. "Don't worry, I'm on it." Lochlyn pulls out his phone. Tilting toward me, he types out a message.

Lochlyn: *Yo Wes. Can you bring two coffees to Shay's? I'll hit you back tomorrow. It's an emergency.*

Wes: *No problem man. Everything ok? Didn't hear from you last night after saying you were staying at Shay's.*

Lochlyn: *Yeah, all's good. Except the coffee situation.*

Wes: *On it. See you in ten.*

"We're good."

A warm smile tilts up the corners of my mouth. "You just know how to handle everything."

He shrugs. "What my baby wants, my baby gets."

Ten minutes later, when there's a knock on the door, Lochlyn untangles himself from me and grabs the coffees from Wes, keeping the door mostly closed behind him, knowing I don't want to be seen. It makes my heart swell to see the little things Lochlyn does without me having to tell him, like shielding my puffy eyes and splotchy face from his roommate.

"Coffee crisis averted." He holds up two large cups, his straight white teeth on full display as he walks back over to me.

"My hero." My hands fly to my chest, and I flutter my eyelids.

"I try."

"No, I mean it. For everything, you've been there. I didn't really realize it at first, or notice the intentions behind it besides just being a good friend, but you've been there for me for so long. And this past year, you were strong when I wasn't. You were willing to fight for us when I wasn't. You were willing to give up your family for me. And then just today, and any time I'm upset. You never hesitate to fold me into you and hold me for hours. I just...thank you."

Gently, he takes my chin in his hand, bringing my lips to his. "I love you." He says it like it's the only thing I ever need to know, the all-encompassing reason. Maybe it is.

"I love you too."

We sit on my bed drinking our coffees in silence while I fiddle with the lid of my cup. His stare tingles the top of my head, but I can't look at him. The thoughts in my mind start swirling around again, my eyes burning.

Without a word, Lochlyn takes the cup out of my hands and sets it on the desk with his, pulling me against him as he lies back down.

I snuggle into his chest, my hand sliding up his shirt to trace the lyrics on his ribs. "My dad always liked you. He saw what a great guy you are. I think he knew I liked you, maybe even that you liked me. He'd hint at it at times, but I always just shrugged it off, said we were friends. Really more that we were friends and you're Chelsea's brother, that nothing could happen, and sure you weren't interested in me like that." Lochlyn starts trailing a hand down my hair as I keep running my fingers along the words scrawled on his skin. The repetitive motion allows the tension in my muscles to ooze out of me.

"I remember a few days before they told me he was sick, we had been talking about you. It was just before he said something about how I needed to live for myself. That I needed to stop letting other people make choices for me and do what *I* wanted to be happy, to make choices that would make me happy, not what would make other people happy. It took me until now to realize that he was talking about you, trying to help me link the two.

"He'd always tell me how you were kind and generous. That he could tell you took good care of the people you loved because of how often you had to take care of Chelsea when your parents were gone. When my mom freaked out about the tattoo, he said you were an adult, you handled a lot of what was thrown at you, and if you wanted to make that decision, he was sure you didn't come to it lightly."

Closing my eyes, I take a moment to listen to the steady rhythm of his heart, the one I've come to know so well.

"I guess it's just my very long-winded way of saying that I think my dad would be happy that we're dating. I think he knew all along we were meant to be together."

"Your dad was a great man. I really liked him and respected him. I know he'd be happy we're together."

"Yeah."

"No, Shay. I *know.*"

Slowly, I sit up to look at him with a furrowed brow, hand resting on his chest as I feel his heart pick up tempo. "What do you mean, you *know*?"

He closes his eyes and takes a deep breath. In that second, I know he's been keeping something from me. "Remember that barbeque we had that Fourth of July? It was just before your dad took a real turn."

I nod, unable to swallow around the lump in my throat.

"Well, your dad and I got to chatting. He wanted to know about Cornell and see if some things are still here or what's different. After we finished talking about Cornell, he called me out. He said that he could see the way I looked at you, the way I tried to be close to you. That he understood why I didn't just all out go for it, ask you to be my girlfriend, make a go of it. He respected it, my loyalty to Chelsea and her ridiculous wishes. His words, by the way. But he told me not to wait too long, that a girl like you wouldn't last, which I already knew.

"I was trying to figure out a way for us to be together despite Chelsea, when he took a turn. It didn't feel right after that. I just had to bide my time. Be near you, be there for you, and hope that some day you saw me the same way I'd always seen you." His eyes twinkle as he takes me in.

"Guess this time, it was father knows best." The realization that Dad had always known knocks the wind from my lungs. It would make sense that Dad knew, that he saw through me, through both of us. That's the type of person he was.

It makes my relationship with Lochlyn that much more perfect.

Taking his face in my hands, I crash my mouth to his, rolling him on top of me as my lips part for his, tongues meeting. He slips one hand to my hip, thumb rubbing along the bone.

I sink back into the pillow to meet his eyes. "I need to feel you inside me."

He groans as his lips trail along my throat. "What about Chelsea?"

I grab his wrist and pull it in front of my eyes. "She has class for three more hours."

That's all he needs to hear as his mouth closes over mine again, his hands quickly sliding down my pants and panties, lowering his. He sucks in steeply while my back arches as he pushes into me.

I always knew Lochlyn was smart, a quick and good study. But the way he has learned to read me is nothing short of amazing. Even slow and sensual, he has me gasping for breath, hands grabbing at his shirt to pull him closer within minutes. He just fills me so perfectly.

It was absolutely impossible to conjure up what sex with Lochlyn is like and there's nothing in the world that could ever compare to it.

As my breathing starts to pick up and tiny whines leave my lips with every thrust, Lochlyn shifts his weight, sliding a hand between our bodies. Using his thumb, he starts swirling around my clit, applying light pressure. It seems like every so many days since our reconciliation, he decides to try something new. Not that I'm complaining.

With every thrust and swirl, the pressure builds more and more until my head is tilting backward as Lochlyn latches on to my throat and a loud moan escapes my lips. A few more thrusts and he groans against my shoulder.

He presses his lips to my neck, sliding up and along my jaw to settle against mine briefly before pressing his forehead to mine.

"I love you so much, Shay."

I close my eyes and push back against his forehead. "You have no idea, Loch. No idea."

He rolls to his back, adjusting his pants as I do the same and curl into him, resting my cheek on his chest. Lying in Lochlyn's arms as he draws small circles on my lower back feels so right, so natural.

"Thank you for staying with me today. I feel bad that you missed class."

"There is absolutely nowhere else I would be. Not even for a second. I'm sorry I didn't realize it was coming up sooner. I was letting the situation with Chelsea distract me."

"It's okay. Really." How can I ever hold it against him? Especially when he's missing class to be with me today.

"No, it's not." There's a resoluteness in his voice, and I know he's going to hold this against himself for a while.

"You made up for it. Truly. You've been here for"—I quickly grab his wrist to check the time—"almost twenty-four hours, just sitting with me. It's all way more than necessary."

"Are you kidding? Baby, I would do anything for you. Truly anything. Being here? That's easy. Even with things being tense with Chelsea. When I asked you if you wanted to go home, I was ready to get in the car and drive you that very second. If it was what you wanted, I would have made it happen."

"I know you would have. Here, right here, is all I need. It's all I'll ever need."

He tightens his arms around me, squeezing me tightly.

"You know, I think it's why my dad liked you. He knew you were the type of guy to do anything for the people he loved. He knew you'd take care of me, do anything you needed to do for me. Like he always had."

Lochlyn starts twirling a curl around his finger as I fight back the tears. I'm starting to doze off when my stomach rumbles and I remember all I've had to eat today is a stale muffin and a few sips of coffee.

I shrink a little bit. Stomach rumbling isn't exactly sexy. But Lochlyn bypasses it, always saying the right thing. "I'm hungry too. What are you in the mood for?"

"Bacon, egg, and cheese."

"Mm, from that place by the high school?"

"Yeah."

"Well, I know I said I'd do anything for you, but I'm not sure a four-hour drive would be the best right now."

"Oh, well, then I guess that's it. You should probably go." I use my best neutral tone.

"You think that's funny, do you?" He slips his arm out from under me and straddles me, hands diving into my sides as I squeal and try to curl in on myself.

I'm thrashing under him, barely able to catch my breath between the incessant tickles. He stops momentarily and leans down to whisper in my ear. "Had enough?"

Doing that, he leaves himself exposed. My fingers jam into his upper rib cage, causing him to fall backward to the pillow, wincing as I lean over him, my hand pinching at his waist.

Leaning down, I give him the tiniest kiss. "My turn," I say breathlessly against his lips.

It lasts for all of two seconds before he has me on my back, hands pinned to the bed under his as he leans over me. His lips trail along my neck, stopping to hover against mine, our breath mingling in the small space between us.

The silliness quickly departs as our smiles fade, turning into something else, when Chelsea comes barging into the room.

"Oh! Sorry. Didn't mean to interrupt, uh, anything." Her eyes lower to the floor as awkwardness spreads across her face, a hint of pink tinging her cheeks.

Lochlyn leans in to give me a peck on the lips before flopping to his back. "You didn't."

"Lochlyn was just torturing me."

"Ah, tickles?"

"Yup." I'm notoriously overly ticklish. Lochlyn has taken advantage over the years, but never in what I saw as a sexual way. Though, it's possible I'm wrong.

"We were just talking about getting something to eat, Chels," Lochlyn chimes in nonchalantly. He's picking at his nails instead of looking at her.

"Oh. Any thoughts?"

They both look at me.

"Guys, I'm not made of glass. I won't break if you make a suggestion I don't like."

"Sure, but we can still do things that you *do* like. Food is food."

My eyes narrow at Chelsea. "Wait a second. Aren't you supposed to be in class? You should have two hours left."

She shrugs, lifting her hands to her shoulders. "Canceled?"

"Chelsea. You need to go to class."

"I felt like I needed to be here."

"You didn't. You don't. I'm fine."

"It's just one class." She persists as Lochlyn pushes up to sitting behind me.

"You missed another one this morning!"

"Relax, you're not my mom."

"No, I'm not, but somebody needs to keep you on track." She had managed to do well enough in school and on her SATs to get into Cornell, but I'm worried if she'll be able to keep her GPA up enough to *stay* at Cornell.

Lochlyn is staying unnervingly quiet. We've already talked about my concerns with Chelsea and how she's doing in school.

I turn around to look at him, but he's staring at his lap. "You could help, ya know."

His eyes flip up to me. "With what? I've done my part for Chelsea. If she wants to flunk out, let her."

"Nice, Loch." Chelsea shakes her head.

"Oh, I'm sorry, princess, did I not do enough for you when Mom and Dad decided they'd rather travel alone than spend time with their kids? Was making sure you went to school and cooking all your meals not enough?"

To calm the storm before it starts, I put my hand on Lochlyn's arm. He turns to me, eyes angry, but quickly softens.

"You okay if I leave to get us some food?" His voice is low, tight. I know he has to be extra irritated and in need of a breather if he's actually leaving me.

"Yeah, I'll be fine. You alright? Want me to come with you?" While I'd rather stay in his immediate vicinity, I know he needs some time to cool off.

"No, you stay. I'm good."

He slides off the bed and pulls his sneakers on, grabbing his phone, wallet and keys from my desk. Giving me a quick kiss on the temple, he walks out, ignoring Chelsea completely.

"What's his problem?" Thankfully, she waits until the door is shut to ask.

While I'm not entirely sure, I have a pretty good idea. "Chelsea, have you ever thanked him for everything he's done for you?"

"Thanked him? Are you serious?"

A bit dumbfounded, I stare at her. "He was a teenager, left in charge of another teenager. Who he had to watch out for and cook for and make sure you went to school."

"They were only gone for like a week at a time. And your parents were always checking in on us."

"Do you really not see how much he's sacrificed for you?" Irritation sweeps through my body at her complete blindness.

"Sacrificed for me? Are you serious? He still had fun, he still partied, he still slept around." There's a slight twinge of discomfort at the thought.

"So he had his life too, but he was there for you. I mean, did you starve? Did you not eat all week? I was there a lot, you'd eaten real, cooked meals. Somebody did that and it sure as hell wasn't you." My voice is stronger than it ever has been. Gone are the days I let Chelsea walk over me, and especially Lochlyn. He may shove it away, I won't anymore.

She shakes her head, nostrils flaring. "So, what, you guys start having sex and now you take his side on everything?"

"I always pointed out how much he did for you then too, how he was around and checking in on you and making sure you were taken care of. I'm trying to barter peace here. He's hurt, Chels. For a lot of things. Not recognizing what he did for you, it's just adding fuel to the fire. In the past few weeks, you've done a lot that's about you. Really, you always have, at least where Lochlyn's concerned."

"He's my brother." The way she says it is like her excuse for treating him like shit.

"You're right. He is. That doesn't mean he has to do everything for you. Bend over backwards and jump at your command. We both denied our happiness for *years* because of you. And we broke up because of you. Now, we're back together, we're happy, I've been able to move past it. But you've never apologized to him or thanked him. It's just one more thing you've been selfish about. I think he's just tired of it."

Chelsea doesn't say anything else, and we sit in silence until Lochlyn returns twenty minutes later.

"Now, I know it's not the deli by the high school, but this place has pretty decent bacon, egg, and cheeses. And I got fresh coffees." Balancing a bag in one hand and a coffee tray in the other, he walks in and kicks the door close, setting both down on my desk before pulling out a coffee and handing it to me.

"Here, Chels, I got you one too." He holds out a coffee with a sandwich balanced on top.

My eyes dart over to her with a look that I hope conveys 'see I told you so.'

"Thanks."

Climbing up onto my bed next to me, he takes a big bite of his sandwich, jutting his chin at me to eat mine.

It smells good. But the ones at the deli back home are legendary. He even gets one each time he's home for breaks. Slowly, I pull back the foil wrapper and take a tiny bite. It's not as good as back home, but pretty close.

I turn to Lochlyn and nod.

"Yeah?" he asks, pleased that he chose right.

"Oh, yeah." I put my hand over my mouth as I answer him, working a bite. His smile makes me warm from the inside out.

Slipping his arm behind my neck, he pulls me against him, kissing my head. "Glad I could make you happy."

I tilt my head to look up at him. "You always do." He leans down and gives me a tiny peck.

Grabbing the remote, he turns on the TV flipping through and finding *The Office* again.

After we eat and finish our coffee, I pack a bag. "Chelsea, we're going to spend the night at Lochlyn's."

"Yeah, sure, that makes sense. Um, sorry, Shay, I know this is your room, but could I talk to Loch alone for a minute?"

I look up at him to gauge his reaction, but can't tell what he's thinking. "Sure. Babe, I'll wait for you downstairs."

A few minutes later, Lochlyn walks out of the building, hands in his pockets, looking for me.

"Hey, what'd she—" He cuts me off, pulling me against him and closing his mouth over mine.

As he straightens, he wraps his arm around my waist and starts walking toward the parking lot, not saying a word.

"Okay, what happened up there?"

"She said thank you. And I know it's because you said something to her while I was out."

"She said thank you?" Shock doesn't even begin to describe how I'm feeling. To get Chelsea to see the error of her ways and get her to feel something about that feels like the biggest victory I could ever have.

"Yup. She gave me a hug and apologized for being a pain in the ass and again for splitting us up and thanked me for everything I did for her in high school, especially making sure she had real food to eat. That's always your sticking point. That I fed her lazy ass."

"It was way overdue. I knew you were upset when you left."

"I'm just happy you're finally calling her out on her bullshit."

"Also long overdue."

When we get back to his apartment, Weston is yelling into a headset at the TV. He quickly throws it off and jumps to his feet when we walk in.

"Oh, sorry guys, didn't know you were coming over."

"You're good, man. Hey, thanks for saving the day with the coffee this morning."

"Anytime. Everything okay?"

"Yeah. I think so." Lochlyn looks down at me.

"Yeah, everything's fine."

We hear yelling through the headset, and I can't help but laugh. "Go back to your game, Wes. Sorry if you weren't expecting me tonight."

"No, it's fine. You're always welcome, Shay." Before either of us can respond to him, he's back in video game world.

Lochlyn laughs, shaking his head and pulling me into his room. "So what do you want to do? Go to bed?"

"Not really. We've spent the better part of the day in bed."

"So, shower?" He quirks up an eyebrow. "Wes plays that game pretty loudly." He sidles over to me and wraps his arms around my waist, pulling me against him.

"Do you really think that's such a good idea after last time?"

"Okay, maybe not. It's whatever you want."

"I'm not picky. All I know is that whatever it is, I want to do it with you."

"Good thing I will always be here then."

"Promise?"

"Promise." To make sure it's a real one, he seals that promise with a kiss.

Chapter 22

Twisting his fingers into my hair, Lochlyn looks lovingly into my eyes. "Let's do something fun today."

"Lochlyn, I'm fine." It's been two weeks since the anniversary of Dad's death and I've been a little sullen. I don't need to burden him with my sadness. There are so many things he does for me on a daily basis, I don't need to add this to his plate of things to handle or worry about. I'll be okay.

We're lying so close to each other that I shift as he raises his shoulder. "We can have fun anyway. It doesn't have to be to cheer up a certain beautiful girl who's been wearing a frown more frequently than a smile as of late."

Despite the fact that it's been almost a year since we got together, I still get flutters in my chest every time he calls me beautiful. It makes the slightest of smiles grace my face. "What did you have in mind? Nothing crazy, I hope. Like skydiving or bungee jumping," I tease.

"Okay, I mentioned those things once, over a year ago. And I never expected you to go for it. I was just trying to get you to laugh a little, loosen up." His voice holds a touch of irritation, but mostly amusement.

"And for today?"

"How about apple picking?"

"Apple picking? Huh. I haven't been apple picking in...I don't know long. I'm sure I've gone; I just can't remember when." Narrowing my eyes, I lose focus of his face as I try to think back through the memories.

"We went together as kids once. A long time ago. But I think it will be fun. I mean, it's kind of quintessential New Yorker thing. We basically have to. There's a handful in Ithaca or just outside. We could even drive farther out if you want to make a real day of it."

"That actually does sound fun."

"Well, don't sound so surprised. I have good ideas sometimes."

Leaning in, I gently press my lips to his as my hand cups his cheek. "You always have good ideas. Should we invite Chelsea or Wes? Chelsea mentioned maybe having Brendan up this weekend since I told her I was planning to be here."

"No, let's go, just us." As he says this, his hand slides down my bare back.

"I like that plan better."

"Being alone with you is always my best idea." His mouth crashes to mine, tongue sliding in as he pulls me tighter against him.

Lochlyn's kisses have a way of making me fall into oblivion. It's my favorite destination.

As he glides over me, resting on his forearms, he deepens the kiss, cupping my chin with one hand while tangling his fingers in my hair with the other.

Suddenly, going apple picking doesn't sound as intriguing as spending the day in bed.

My body needs more of him, and I lift my pelvis to press against his. Taking the hint, he slides a hand between our bodies, feeling my wetness before pressing two fingers inside me. Arching toward him, my hands grip tightly at his back. His muscles shift below my fingertips as he moves his fingers deftly.

I'm whimpering and writhing beneath him as he kisses down my neck and across my collarbone.

"Loch, please." I need to feel him.

"What do you need, baby?"

"You."

A smirk plays across his lips as he hooks his fingers and my spine peels off the bed, a scream tearing from my throat. "You have me."

"I need you to fuck me." It's these vulnerable moments that Lochlyn has been able to get me to come out of my shell, to talk, to say what my deepest desires are.

He doesn't hesitate, removing his fingers and replacing them with his hard length as he slowly eases into me.

The tiniest squeak leaves my parted lips once he's all the way inside me. He stays still for a moment, pressing his forehead against mine, then he starts thrusting, slowly at first, but quickly picking up momentum.

Chelsea used to tell me that she'd break up with boys when the sex got old. I never understood what that meant, but she'd always tell me I would one day, when I finally had consistent sex, I'd get it. But Lochlyn and I have been together for almost a year now, having sex for almost ten of those months, and it's definitely not getting old. I can't even imagine that happening.

It's not just the physical connection we have, that every single time feels absolutely incredible. It's the passion. The way I can sense how much he loves me. It's how much I love him. I think that's what's always been missing for Chelsea.

Slowing, he draws my attention. "What's in your head? You seem distracted. Do you want to stop?" How is he not winded?

"No, I'm sorry. I was just thinking about how much I love you." I place a hand on his cheek and run my thumb over his temple, pulling him down for a kiss.

His tongue seeking mine, he intensifies the kiss and starts rocking against me in slow, even strokes. Trailing a stream of tiny kisses to my ear, his warm breath coming in bursts that shift my hair, he whispers, "I love you, Shay."

Pushing up, he starts thrusting harder and faster. I run my hands up his toned chest, wrapping one to his shoulder and the other to the nape of his neck, my fingers twisting into his hair.

I'm back to whimpering with every thrust, my nails digging into his back.

"Mmm, don't stop." After our conversation when we got back together, I've been trying to be more vocal.

"Feel good, baby girl?"

"*Yes.*" So damn good.

A few more thrusts and my head tips back, chest meeting his as I tighten around him, crying out, tugging at his hair as my nails scrape down his back.

He groans in response, sucking in sharply, giving two more quick pumps into me before he stops, resting his forehead against mine. It's still my favorite thing in the world. I haven't told him, but I'm almost certain he knows.

Rolling to his back, he slides his arm under my neck and draws me into him, tracing his fingers lightly along my arm.

Placing a gentle kiss on my forehead, he leaves his lips there. "I'm so Goddamn in love with you, Shay. I just need you to know that."

Rolling to my stomach to face him, I rest my chin on his chest. "I do. And I'm extremely in love with you, Lochlyn." Extremely doesn't even seem to cover it. It's all-encompassing. If I were to only know one thing, it would be my love for Lochlyn. And if I were to only feel one thing, it would be his love for me.

Two hours later, Lochlyn pulls into a grassy parking lot. We're surrounded by rows and rows of trees. It's the perfect fall day with gray skies, a crispness biting in the air, and the smell of campfires and baked goods floating on the breeze.

When Lochlyn walks around the car and wraps an arm around my shoulders, I curl into his side. I'm going to need to stay extra close to him as he's looking more attractive than usual today, though I was certain that was impossible. He bought some new fall shirts and the way the one he's wearing fits him is nothing short of perfection as it's taut against his toned chest. Even the Greek Gods would be jealous of his physique and the way he looks in that shirt.

I'd like to think it was just the double dose of sex we had this morning, but I know that's not it. Lochlyn's just that good-looking. I wrap my arms around his waist and squeeze, feeling lucky to have him.

With his hand slipping to my rib cage, he starts walking. "I see a small booth over there. I'd assume that's where we go."

"It's pretty here."

"Yeah, it's a perfect day. With my perfect girl."

I squeeze myself into him even more as a giant smile spreads across my face. Suddenly, he stops, resting his hands on my shoulders and pushing me back.

"Yup, I knew it. You're smiling. And we haven't even picked any apples yet."

"I'm *smiling* because you're just so sweet to me. It makes me happy."

"I'm glad, baby girl. Because I'll always be sweet to you."

When we get to the booth, we get options for a half bushel or a peck-sized bag. We look at each other in confusion and decide to go for the half bushel, the bigger one.

"We can always bake a pie or something. I don't know. We'll figure it out."

Having not gone apple picking in years, we don't know our favorite varieties and stand a little confused as we hold hands in the middle of the pathway. We're looking at the map and corresponding list of what's ready for picking.

"Maybe we should have picked a smaller orchard," Lochlyn mumbles under his breath.

"Don't lose your excitement! Let's just pick one and try it." To get him motivated again, I shake his arm.

"You choose."

"Hmm. I don't know. I don't want to get something we can eat any old time. Um, let's try these—Macouns. Am I saying that right? Ma-coon?" I look up at him, my nose scrunched up.

"Honestly, I have no idea. But Macouns it is!" He says it the same way I did, but it seems off. Maybe I'll ask before we leave.

We walk hand in hand, looking for the red and yellow striped ribbons on the trees to show the rows we're in search of. When we reach them, we look down the long aisles and shrug.

"You know, it's pretty private here. I'm sure if we wanted to, nobody would see us."

Playfully, I smack his arm with my free hand and, like a good boyfriend, he flinches even though it probably hurts me more than him. "That's not funny."

"Who said I was joking?"

Heat pricks at the back of my neck. "We're in public. And it's outside, so we wouldn't exactly hear somebody approaching."

"But if we could, you'd be interested?"

"That's not what I'm saying." He's making me antsy. When he chuckles, I know he realizes it.

"Relax, Shay, I'd never ask you to do anything that makes you uncomfortable. But maybe next year. I know we haven't picked any apples yet, but this is nice. We should make it a tradition."

My heart swells at the mention of next year and the future. I lean into him and encapsulate his hand in both of mine. I never could have dreamed that one person could make me so happy.

About halfway down the row, we stop and look at the trees. Some have many more apples on them than others, while the ground is littered with apples in various states of decomposition.

"Go for it, baby girl. You get to pick the first one."

"Oh, well, thank you for this lovely honor." I press my hand against my chest as I disentangle from Lochlyn and walk over to a tree. Inspecting the apples remaining, I find one that looks like it would fit in the palm of my hand and pull gently until it snaps free.

Walking back over to Lochlyn, I hold it out like it's a mysterious object. He takes it and pulls up the bottom of his shirt to rub it clean, revealing his toned abs and the V that sits at the top of his pants. It makes me rethink my position on sex in the apple orchard.

Handing the apple back to me, he raises his eyebrows. "Go ahead, you get first bite."

"Is it weird I'm nervous? What if it's gross?" Lochlyn has a strange effect on me. While I'm my most at ease around him, I'm also at my most self-conscious state, and usually about silly things, such as tasting apples. It's almost as though I don't want him to know I'm not as perfect as he thinks.

"Then you spit it out."

"Here goes nothing." I sink my teeth into the firm flesh of the apple. A juicy sweetness invades my mouth, and I can't contain the moan that rises from my chest.

"That good?"

I nod excitedly as my eyes widen and my hand flutters to my mouth. When Lochlyn holds his hand out to try it, I smack it away. "Get your own! This one's mine."

Chuckling as he walks past me to the tree, he smacks my ass, causing me to jump and yelp.

"Hey!"

"You get spanked for not sharing." He cleans the apple off, giving another surge to my hormones, and bites down. His reaction is similar to mine, eyes wide and a nod of his head. "You're right, these are good. Let's get a bunch."

I take a few more bites and toss my apple to the ground, brushing my hands on my pants as I walk to a new tree, picking a few and collecting them in my arm. When I walk back over to Lochlyn, he holds his apple in his teeth while opening the bag with two hands.

"Oo! Look at this one!" I hold it out in the palm of my hand, cheeks hurting at the smile on my face.

"Shay, that one's so tiny. We can't eat it."

"I know. But it's so cute! It's a baby apple."

"Fine, toss it in." He waves his hand in the air with a tone that says he gave in too easily. Which he does where I'm concerned.

I clap excitedly as I skip over to place it in the bag with the others. It looks even smaller in comparison.

He follows behind me as I keep picking and dropping. Since he's finished his snack, he stands with a hand in his pocket, smile on his face and glimmer in his eyes, as I flit from tree to tree, looking for what I feel are the best of the selection.

"Oh! I want that one, but I can't reach it. Will you get it for me?"

"I have a better idea." Lochlyn walks up right behind me and puts his hands on my waist, lifting me into the air. My hands fly to his and I shriek as he lifts me onto his shoulders. Once sitting, my fingers tangle in his hair for a moment while I get my bearings. "You good?"

"Mhm. Just wasn't expecting it." Holding my calves, he takes a step closer to the tree so I can reach out and grab the one I want. I'm almost taller than the tree now. They're not very large, but it's the perfect height to reach the apple I want, plus a few others that are on the other side, but I couldn't see from the bottom. "Okay."

"All set?"

"Yup."

"Okay, hold on to those. Ready?"

"As I'll ever be." Flying through the air, even secure in Lochlyn's grasp, isn't my favorite thing in the world. Placing his hands back on my waist, he lifts me and slowly sets me on my feet.

Before I can move, he pulls me against him, his hard chest against my back. Leaning in, he kisses down the side of my neck. "I love you," he murmurs against my ear.

Spinning to face him, my lips briefly meet his, easier in his bent over state. "I love you too."

Straightening up, Lochlyn holds the bag out. "Do we want to fill this with all the same kind, or we do want to try a few others?"

"I picked the first apple and the first variety, so you make the next decision."

"Alright. Let's see." Pulling the list back out, he glances over it. "How about Cortlands? The town isn't too far from here. And we know we like them."

"Sounds like as good a reason as any, if you ask me."

It doesn't take us long to find the rows of Cortland apples. When we get back to the same booth we started at, there's a line of people leaving. Lochlyn pulls me into his side, kissing the top of my head and running his hand up and down my arm.

My hair is blowing around my face as the wind picks up intensity. The sky is a darker and more ominous shade of gray, making me think rain isn't far off.

Once it's our turn to pay, Lochlyn makes small talk that I half listen to while staring up at the sky and the impending storm. Though I'm distracted, it registers with me that Lochlyn asks about pronouncing the name of the apple, and gets an answer that basically suggests, while there are some variations, the way we were saying it is, in fact, correct.

It's not until he grabs my hand that I draw my attention from the scenery and focus on him instead. We put the apples on the floor of the backseat to try to avoid spillage.

"Why don't we head over to the shop and get some treats?"

"They do smell good. And we should get cider. Hot cider is perfect on a day like today." Just the thought makes my mouth water.

"Cider it is." Holding his hand outstretched toward me, I take it, linking my fingers with his.

A light smile has been planted on my face since we started picking. As usual, Lochlyn knows just what I need. The fresh air doesn't hurt either.

The heavenly smell of fresh baked pastries of many varieties and brewing coffee greets us as we walk into the shop on the other side of the orchard. One wall has glass cases, filled with various baked goods. Another has more glass cases, but the contents look darker, like chocolate. There's a station with loose candy, an area in the far back that looks like collectables such as mugs and shirts. Right next to the checkout are three glass door refrigerators, stocked full with cider.

I'm not even sure where to start, and looking over at Lochlyn, he isn't either. Setting my sights on the pastries, I pull him behind me. Once I'm standing in front of the case, I can't decide. There are so many choices, and I'm not entirely sure what the difference is between them aside from the way it looks.

In the case in front of us, there are strudels, turnovers, and fritters, all apple. Plus, there are non-apple treats like various pies, bear claws, croissants, and cookies. I don't even know how to narrow it down. To make it even more difficult, they also make fresh cider donuts, which both look and smell amazing.

"Well, our choices here are to pick one or two things and then possibly miss out on something, or get everything and share." Lochlyn breaks it down logically as his chin moves against the top of my head and his thumbs hook into my front belt loops.

"Everything? That's a lot of food," I say absentmindedly.

"We don't really need more than one pie. And I think we can pick one type of cookie and share it. It'll be fun. We'll make a fresh pot of coffee. Oh, and we're definitely getting some donuts."

"I guess. I feel bad you're spending so much money. This isn't going to be cheap."

Flipping me to face him and putting his hands on my shoulders, he tilts down so he can catch my eye. "Shay, please don't ever worry about money when we're together. I would happily spend every penny I have on you. And I don't see that day ever happening because you're not materialistic and my parents have set me up just fine. Now, pick a cookie."

"Black and white." There's never any contest if black and white cookies are available.

Ordering one of everything, including a peach raspberry pie at my request, we walk back to the car with our arms full of treat bags and a half gallon of cider.

When the car is within sight, the heavens open, large droplets of water plunking against the ground, and pattering on our heads and clothes. We run toward the car, but a few feet away, I stop, Lochlyn putting the food inside and standing next to his open door.

"Shay! What are you doing?"

I'm standing in the parking lot, arms outstretched, with my face tilting toward the sky. The rain falls hard against my face, and I'm soaked from head to toe. But it refreshes me in a way nothing has in the past few weeks. Maybe it's the whole day combined.

A strong arm wraps around my waist while a hand cups my cheek and the most incredible lips meet mine. I loop my arms around Lochlyn's neck and my legs around his waist as his tongue slips across mine and he stands straighter, pulling me with him.

He carries me toward the car and I'm vaguely aware of the people running and yelling around us, trying to hurry to their cars to escape the deluge. But Lochlyn pushes me against the side of the car, hand still cupping my cheek while the other tangles in my sopping wet hair, no longer needing to support me.

When a shiver runs through me, Lochlyn pulls away and sets me on the ground. Popping the trunk, he pulls out a blue fleece blanket and wraps it around my shoulders, kissing my forehead as he opens my door.

Lochlyn cranks the heat, adjusting my vents so they blow right on me and flicking on my seat warmer.

I reach my hand out from under the blanket and link my fingers with his. Somehow, he's warm, my eternal space heater. "Thank you for a really great day. I had fun."

"I'm glad. And we're definitely making this a tradition. Every year. I'll even see what sort of strings I can pull with Mother Nature to make sure it rains."

"Oh, enjoyed that, did you?"

"Your shirt soaking wet and plastered to your body? Yeah, you could say I enjoyed that."

Looking out the window, my smile reflects in the glass. While I'm chilled to the bone, my heart feels warm. Happy feels better with Lochlyn.

Chapter 23

As Thanksgiving break approaches, we're all getting along better. Lochlyn and Chelsea are almost back to their normal relationship, including Chelsea being difficult, but she's toned it down a lot.

After much discussion, Lochlyn and I have decided not to go home for Thanksgiving. Chelsea's only going to see Brendan. Their parents won't be home and things with Mom, though somewhat better with phone calls a few times a week, are still relatively distant.

Which is why I'm shocked when two weeks before Thanksgiving, Mom calls me and invites all three of us to dinner at our house.

"Are you sure you're up for it, Mom?"

"Of course, sweetie, I'd love to have you all."

"It's a lot of work for you to do all on your own. Can we bring anything? Lochlyn's a really good cook." We're in his apartment and his eyes flash up from his books at the mention of his name. His brow furrows, shoulders rise, and he shakes his head, probably wondering what I'm talking about and especially volunteering him for.

Holding up a finger, I tune back in to Mom and turn away. I'd missed the earlier part of her reply. "...and Don's actually going to be doing a lot."

"I'm sorry, I must have missed something. Don? Who's Don?"

Lochlyn appears behind me, hand on my waist as he leans down to listen. I tip the phone slightly so he can hear.

"Oh, honey, I know you're busy with school, but I wish you'd listen when we talk. Don is the man I've been seeing."

Lochlyn and I look at each other with what I'm sure are the same shocked faces.

"Mom, I can assure you that you have never once mentioned Don, let alone any man, in any of our previous conversations." It's such a startling fact that I know for certain it would stick and would surely not be something I'd easily forget.

"I'm sure I would have mentioned him. We've been together for almost two months now." *Two months?*

"And you're hosting Thanksgiving dinner together?" Two months seems a little sudden for such a big to-do.

"Well, he'd like to meet you. And I haven't seen you in a while. Sweetheart, being with Don has made me realize how shut off I was for years, and I'm so sorry. I want you to come, if you'd like, to meet him and so we can maybe talk." Surprised is a massive understatement. Mom is seeing somebody, who's made her see her absence in my life. While I miss Dad, I'm glad Mom finally found some clarity. And hopefully happiness.

"Um, yeah, sure. I don't see why not. Chelsea's going down anyway."

"Oh wonderful, I'm so happy. Don's really looking forward to meeting you."

"Well, I guess I'm looking forward to meeting him as well."

That's how two weeks later, we find ourselves tossing packed duffle bags into the trunk of Lochlyn's car.

"Chelsea, you're in the back, no complaining about the music," Lochlyn says as he opens his door.

"Ugh, but why?"

"First of all"—he rests his forearms on the roof of the car before continuing—"my car, my rules. Second of all, we have a voting agreement and majority rules."

"Shay didn't even vote."

"She doesn't have to."

"Shay?" Chelsea should know better than to question Lochlyn about me, but she's desperate.

"Sorry, Chels."

"Ugh, fine," she grumbles as she climbs into the backseat, but Lochlyn and I just smile over the top of the car. We often joke that it's like we're her parents. In reality, it's not terribly different since we're both far more responsible and Lochlyn was fully in charge of her for a long time.

"You guys aren't going to, like, pull off somewhere and have crazy car sex or something, right?" This is the question we're greeted with as we shut our doors.

"I make no promises." Lochlyn laughs until I jab him in the ribs.

"No, Chelsea. Why would you even ask that?"

"We'll just save it for when we get home."

"Lochlyn!" I practically shriek. She's fully accepting of our relationship at this point. But she doesn't need to hear about the sexual aspect of it. I never wanted to hear about hers, and she doesn't need to hear about mine, especially since it's with her brother.

"Relax, Shay. I get it. You guys love each other, you have sex. I've come to accept it."

"Doesn't mean you have to hear about it."

"Ugh, Loch, do you *have* to use your phone? Can't you just listen to the radio? At least then I get commercial breaks."

"Sorry, Chels. We lose stations a few times. This way, no interruptions." As the phone syncs with the car, a Skillet song starts enthusiastically through the speakers. It's loud enough that I barely hear Chelsea groan behind me.

Four and a half hours, two coffee stops, and two bathroom breaks later, we're standing in front of my house. I'm staring at the door like it's the most foreign thing in the world. Chelsea and Lochlyn are silent behind me, until Lochlyn steps up to me, slipping his arm around my waist, pulling some curls behind my shoulder and kissing my neck. The calming mechanism still works.

Taking a deep breath, I open the door.

Dinner is actually nice and a lot of fun. Don is a really sweet guy, and it's very clear that he makes Mom happy. He has a fantastic sense of humor and keeps us laughing the whole time, including how he met Mom, which was by frequenting the store asking such ridiculous questions he said he was surprised she couldn't see through him.

My favorite is the one where he asked her if the pan could self-cook eggs. When she said yes, it could cook eggs, he clarified he meant by itself, without needing to pay attention, flip, or remove from the heat.

Lochlyn spends the whole dinner touching me, twirling my hair through his fingers, holding my hand, or resting his hand on my knee. I catch Mom smiling at us on more than one occasion.

After dinner, I'm helping her clean up and she has the first real conversation with me in over two years.

"You and Lochlyn seem very happy together."

"We are, Mom."

"And Chelsea? She's okay with all of it?"

"She is now. It was a hard six weeks apart, but Chelsea saw where she was wrong. It took a little while for all of us to get back to where we had been, but we did."

"I'm glad. Shay..." Something in her voice makes me stop and look at her. I almost cry, realizing she's looking at me, really looking *at* me instead of through or just around me, for the first time since Dad died. "I'm so sorry I told you that love wasn't worth fighting for. I know you two had those awful six weeks apart, and that they were so hard on you. I'm partially to blame for that, and I'm just...I'm sorry."

"It's okay, Mom." There's a waver in my voice that I try to fight, but can't.

"No, it's not. I haven't been a very good mother to you these past two years. And that's not fair. I'm just glad you've been able to find happiness despite that." She hesitates for a moment, looking pensive. "You know, your father would be happy. He always thought you and Lochlyn were meant to be together. He'd always joke after we spent time together, the two families, that he was going to have to write it on the walls for you two to realize you liked each other."

It's the first time in two years she's been able to talk about Dad without needing to stop and without crying. While I'd love to celebrate the tiny moment, I can't without throwing things off.

"I know. I don't know how I didn't see it. But then again, Lochlyn didn't either. All those years wasted. I'm glad Daddy would be happy. He had actually said something to Lochlyn, that last Fourth of July. But then...well, you know." I shake my head, chasing away the tears. I don't want to get upset; I don't want to ruin this time with Mom.

She smiles sadly at me and pushes some hair behind my shoulder. I'd received a lot of my looks from Dad. Mom has pin straight, very light brown hair, while Dad's had been dark and curly, like mine. She does something she hasn't done in over two years as she pulls me into a hug.

That's when the dam breaks. My shoulders shake violently as Mom holds me tight against her, a hand rubbing over my hair as she turns back and forth, like she's rocking me. It's been over two years since I've had any affection from her and it took a harder toll than I realized.

"I'm sorry, sweetheart. I'm so sorry. I love you, Shay."

"I love you too, Mom."

When we separate, there's a wet trail on her face as well. "Let's go back out to the living room, see what everybody else is doing. And before I forget, Don really likes Lochlyn."

Sniffling, I laugh. "How? He barely knows him."

"He said that he makes you happy, and it's clear as day the second you two are in room together how much that boy loves you. His eyes find you in an instant and brighten, like he's just seen the most beautiful sight in the world."

My heart swells hearing this. I see how Lochlyn looks at me, but hearing how it's seen through other people's eyes is amazing.

"I just want you to be with somebody who loves you, and it makes Don feel good to know that you are because I can rest easy."

If there was even a shred of doubt in Mom or Don, it's cleared up when she and I walk into the living room. Lochlyn's smile fades and he's in front of me in a second, cupping my chin in his hands and wiping his thumbs under my eyes before pulling me against him and kissing to top of my head.

"What's wrong?" he asks quietly as he holds me in his lap while we wait for the coffee to brew.

"Nothing, I'm fine."

"Shay. You were crying. What happened?"

"My mom hugged me."

"I like to think I've become the Shay whisperer in the past year or so, but you're going to have to connect the dots for me." The Shay whisperer. I like that.

"My mom hasn't hugged me since my dad died."

"Not even when you left for school? Or graduated?" Big moments where a daughter should have gotten a hug from her mother, but not this mother-daughter duo.

"Not since before the funeral."

"Oh, baby, I'm sorry. I didn't know that. I probably should have assumed, but I kind of figured at least with you leaving for school."

"It was just a lot at once. I didn't realize it was affecting me as much as it was until she hugged me and the floodgates opened."

"Have you always been a crier, or do you just save it for me?" He's teased me more than once about my crying. It all started as a joke when I went from crying to laughing one day, and he looked at me like I was crazy. I had to explain that before we were together, I rarely cried. That it has to be the comfort I feel with him that lets me feel like I can.

"Be nice or you're sleeping alone tonight." I push my shoulder into his.

"You'd never." He's right.

"Do you want to find out?"

"I'm sorry. You know I'm teasing. I like that you cry when you need to. That you feel comfortable and safe enough with me."

I snuggle into his chest as he wraps his arms around me. Even a few months ago, it would have been a crazy thought, worried about being caught. But now, I don't care who sees. Everybody knows we're together, we're happy. It's a freeing notion.

"I love you."

He kisses the top of my head before answering. "I love you too, baby girl."

We decide to spend the night at Lochlyn's. Mom looks at me with an expression I can't quite read, but I assume is something along the lines of whether or not she should allow me to go to Lochlyn's, knowing we'll be having sex.

Chelsea leaves as soon as we all get back to their house, heading over to Brendan's, and Lochlyn and I end up on the deck. He wants to spend a few minutes where it all started, one year ago. Just like the year before, he kisses me on the top step, under the stars. But instead of pulling apart and walking me home, he carries me upstairs, my legs wrapped around his waist.

Once in his room, he sets me down, closing the curtains.

"Brendan was kind enough to take Chelsea out of our hair for the night." There's a gravel to his tone as he walks back to me.

"Oh, so you like him now?"

He grabs me around the waist and pulls me against him. "Well, when he takes my sister out of the house so I can fuck my girlfriend wherever I want, then yeah, I guess I do."

"Oh, really? Wherever you want, huh? Does said girlfriend have any say in this?" I trail my finger along his collarbone, playing coy.

"I suppose she does. It is our one-year anniversary, after all." Lochlyn and I had many conversations about when our actual anniversary is, seeing as he's never officially asked me to be his girlfriend.

We agreed on two things for sure. The time apart was a break, not a *break-up*. Especially because it wasn't something either of us wanted. We also agreed that things between us had started a long time ago.

He argued Thanksgiving was when he made the first move, kissing me after dinner. I argued that I hadn't known it was more than pity, that it easily could have just stopped there, but after New Year's there was a positive change. With more promises of time.

What finally convinced me was his argument of all the time we'd spent denying ourselves and culminating in Thanksgiving night with our first kiss. To me, it doesn't really matter. All that matters is that I'm finally with Lochlyn, and allowing myself the happiness I had denied for so long.

That night, Lochlyn makes good on his word to fuck me anywhere he wants.

Chapter 24

For Christmas, we decide to stay in Ithaca. Mom is flying out to see Logan. They haven't seen each other since Logan moved west after the funeral. Lochlyn and Chelsea's parents decided they'd rather spend their Christmas on the Amalfi Coast, depositing substantial amounts of money in both their kids' accounts as an apology.

"I guess it's just you and me for Christmas this year." I kind of like it. If there's anybody I want to spend the holiday with, it's Lochlyn.

"This year and every year after."

It's two days before Christmas and we're snuggled against each other in Lochlyn's bed, arms around each other.

"Oh yeah? Every year? Don't think you'll get sick of me?" While it's mostly a joke, I do wonder if that's a concern in his mind.

"Never."

"I don't know, that's a pretty long time."

"Eternity wouldn't be long enough with you, Shay." He tangles his fingers in my hair before his lips meet mine, and my mouth parts for his.

His hand is sliding up my shirt when the door to the apartment slams shut and voices float into his room. We freeze, pulling away as we listen.

Giggles fill the apartment, then we hear a voice. "I want to give you your Christmas present." Our eyes lock on each other's and Lochlyn is hopping off the bed, jumping over me, and throwing open his door. I scramble out behind him to see for myself.

"What is going on here?" His voice is eerily calm but steely.

As I appear behind him, I see Weston and Chelsea jump apart as though a bomb is dropped between them. "Shit, Loch, I didn't know you guys were here. I thought you were going to our room to get Shay's stuff for break."

"Chelsea, what's going on?"

"Uh, well, Weston and I are, um..." She looks at Weston with questioning eyes.

"We're, um, dating?" Weston states hastily, as if he's at a loss for words.

I'm on my toes, peering over Lochlyn's shoulder, watching things unfold. He tenses, starting at his jaw, spreading through his body. By now, I know Lochlyn well, really well, and in this moment, I have absolutely no idea how he's going to react.

"What happened to Brendan?" His voice is still calm, but it comes through gritted teeth.

"We broke up."

"When? We were just home a month ago."

"Before we left to come back. I just couldn't do the distance anymore."

Lochlyn glances over his shoulder. I shake my head. I really had no idea. He sighs and looks back and forth between the two of them. Lochlyn and Weston are close friends, but Lochlyn can be intimidating when he wants to be.

"How long?"

Chelsea looks up at Weston and smiles. I recognize the look passing between them—the happiness. I recognize it because that's what I see in my own relationship. Every time Lochlyn looks at me, every time I see a picture of us.

"I don't know. Years, maybe? But we started seeing each other after we came back from Thanksgiving." Chelsea knew Weston before we came to Cornell. She'd met him when they helped moved Lochlyn into the dorm and a few times after.

As Lochlyn takes a deep breath, I run my hand down his back, tangling in the bottom of his shirt. I don't want him to be mad at them. The story is a little too familiar.

He relaxes under my touch. "You hurt my sister, I'll hunt you down," he says pointing, at Weston.

Weston holds his hands up. "I promise. I'll take good care of her. Besides, you know where I live."

"Guess we'll have to figure out some sort of schedule or something," Chelsea says, looking around the room.

Weston starts to laugh but looks at Lochlyn's face and stops. I don't need to see him to know he's not amused. When Lochlyn is in the room, he commands it. The only person who can challenge him is Chelsea. The only person who can make him pause is me.

I step forward, linking my fingers with his. "Loch was going to teach me how to cook a chicken and some other things for dinner. Why don't you stay? We have plenty of food."

He looks over at me, upset. "But, babe, if they're here, we can't—"

"Lochlyn," I growl.

He sighs. "Yeah, you guys should stay."

Chelsea and Weston look at each other quickly and shrug, walk over and settle on the couch, then flip on the TV and play whatever Christmas movie is on.

I walk into the kitchen after Lochlyn, where he wraps his arms around my waist and groans, resting his head on my shoulder.

"I had plans and intentions for tonight, baby girl."

I lean back in his arms to look at him. "Well, sometimes you have to adapt for family. That's what we are, you know. A pieced together family. Aside from you and Chelsea, of course. But you know Wes, you like him. He's one of your best friends."

"Apparently the same Wes who's dating my sister."

"Not all that different from us, wouldn't you say?" I run my finger along his collarbone.

"I guess not."

"I can only hope they'll end up as happy as we are."

He softens. "Okay, are you ready to touch raw chicken?"

My nose crinkles. "Do I have to?"

Lochlyn chuckles as we start cooking. He still works with me hand over hand, pressed up against me. It's easier to just be ourselves, not worry what anybody thinks, just seeing that we're deliriously happy.

Epilogue

Two days before my twentieth birthday, we're naked in Lochlyn's bed. My fingers roam his body, tracing his tattoos. Sometimes I use my tongue as I sit, straddling his lap.

We've been lying in bed all day. It's our weekend in the apartment and we're making the most of it.

I slide off and lay my head on his chest, swirling my finger along his muscles. "What do you think of girls with tattoos?"

"Girls in general, or one very specific, very sexy girl?" His fingers tickle along my lower back, grazing the top of my ass.

"Both, I guess?"

"It depends on the girl and the tattoo, but I think it'd suit you. Why, you thinking of getting one?"

Rolling my head to rest on my chin, I look up at him. "I was considering maybe getting one for my dad."

"I think that'd be a really nice gesture."

"One thing...I want to go for my birthday." There's a hesitation in my voice since it's only a few days away.

"Your birthday?"

"Yeah. That's the tradition, isn't it?"

I shake as he laughs. "Yeah, I guess it is. All right. I'll take you to my guy."

"Oh, your guy. I feel very in the loop now. How much does it cost?"

"Don't worry about it." With a shimmy of his shoulders as he sinks into the pillow, he closes his eyes, his fingers tracing along my spine.

"What do you mean, *don't worry about it?*" While I'm pretty sure I know *exactly* what he means, I need to hear it.

"I mean, I'll pay for it."

Yup. Exactly what I thought. "I can't let you do that."

Aside from feeding me regularly, Lochlyn buys me everything and anything I want, even surprising me with bouquets of flowers, new books he noticed me checking out, and notebooks for me to keep my notes about what I've read. He spoils me far too much.

"Of course you can. Shay, my parents show their affection by putting copious amounts of money into our bank accounts. Let me pay for your first tattoo." The way he says *first* is almost as though he expects there to be more. And who knows, maybe there will be.

"At least let it be my birthday present."

"No can do, already got you something." My heart skips a beat. Not so much because he bought me a present, but because my birthday is still a few weeks away.

"You did?"

He opens his eyes and looks at me, eyebrows furrowed. "Of course I did."

"You're too good to me," I say as I snuggle against him.

"And you're too good *for* me. I keep waiting for you to realize that."

"Lochlyn, you're an amazing person. I don't know how you don't see that. And I'm with you for as long as you'll have me."

"I guess it's forever, then."

"Forever it is."

On the evening of my twentieth birthday, Lochlyn takes me to his tattoo artist. I hold his hand tightly, nerves building.

"You'll be fine. I'll be right with you."

"But it's going to hurt." The thought makes me feel a little woozy.

"Yeah, it might. But the pain is temporary."

I take a deep breath as we walk through the door and are waved over to the artist's seat. Lochlyn pulls a chair over, spinning it so the back is facing me and straddling it, resting his arm across the back, chin on top.

"So, what are we doing today?" Steve, the tattoo artist, has a thick beard and dark green eyes, with hair pulled into a ponytail.

"Can I have something like this?" I hand him a picture of the design I have in mind.

"Yeah, no problem. Where do you want this?"

"Can I have it here?" I point to the area where I plan to get it done.

"No problem. First time?"

I nod nervously, and Steve laughs.

"Well, I'll make it as painless as possible. Should be pretty quick."

I inhale deeply and hold it to a count of three before releasing it through my mouth. Lochlyn takes my right hand in his as Steve starts with the stencil. Lochlyn had explained the process to me, and I know that I'll be waiting in anticipation of pain while the prep work is done.

"Ready?" Steve asks.

With mental force, I tear my eyes away from Lochlyn's to look at Steve, nodding.

As I hear the needle hum, I glue my eyes back on Lochlyn's blue and brilliant. He rubs the back of my hand as I try not to wince in pain, bringing it to his lips every few minutes. Every so often, he'll kiss the promise ring he surprised me with earlier today. It's two hearts, linked together, like ours. The design is similar to the diamond crusted infinity necklace he gave me for our anniversary.

We sit in silence, the only sound the tattoo needle marking my skin.

It's over faster than I thought it would be, and while it did hurt, it wasn't as bad as I'd built it up in my mind.

"Go ahead, take a look," Steve says as he starts cleaning up.

I pull my left hand to my face, looking at the inside of my wrist. There sits a perfect little skillet.

Lochlyn is suddenly behind me, looking over my shoulder. "Looks good, baby girl. I think your dad would love it."

"I think so, too." Lochlyn liked my idea of a frying pan as a memory of Dad. He understands the meaning behind it, the memories of the breakfasts he used to cook and, of course, the store. In a way, I feel like it also represents Lochlyn, because of all the meals he cooks and teaching me how to fend for myself a little. It's another tribute to Dad as well, since he saw us together long before either one of us did.

I chose the placement, because it's something I'll see regularly.

"Lochlyn, you'll help her keep on top of the care?"

"I got it, Steve."

"See ya next month?"

"Yup, appointment's all set."

"All right, see ya then. Nice to meet you, Shay."

"You too, Steve! Thank you."

Lochlyn throws his arm over my shoulder as he pays, and we leave the shop. He pulls me in and kisses the top of my head. "Your dad would be proud of you for doing something to make yourself happy."

He's right. Dad would be proud. He'd always told me to carve my own path. I'd spent so much time making other people happy that I hadn't realized what that meant. I always thought making people happy, doing what was expected of me was enough and that I'd have time for my happiness later.

Until Lochlyn kissed me.

That night, my whole world changed, and I have never been the same.

See more of Shay, Lochlyn, Chelsea, and Wes in Setting Limits.

Playlist

Since Lochlyn and Shay are big music fans, I wanted to include their playlist. You can find it here on Spotify.

Radiohead-All I Need
Yellowcard- Only One
Breaking Benjamin-Diary of Jane
Dashboard Confessional-Stolen
Lifehouse-You & Me
Allister-Don't Think Twice
Cage the Elephant-It's Just Forever
Coldplay-Yellow

Coming Soon

COMING December 2022

The following is an unedited preview and subject to change.

<h1 style="text-align:center">Setting Limits</h1>

C hapter 1

Things with Shay have been off all summer. For months if I really think about it. She's taken a lot more time off from the store, which I think is good for her, but what is she doing with that time? She's not spending it with me, that's for sure.

After getting annoyed with my boyfriend Brendan again, I decide it's time I find out.

Something feels amiss the moment I get to her house. Like there's some sort of unsettledness about the air giving my skin a prickly feeling.

I let myself into her house, like I've done for years, and immediately I know what the disturbance is.

Loud moans ring out from upstairs as well as deep grunts, clearly from a male. Shay's having sex. With who, I'm not sure, since I know she broke up with John months ago.

But I have an inkling, and it's been nagging at me for too long to let it be ignored.

Autopilot kicks in and I make my way upstairs, not even thinking about what's awaiting me behind the door as I throw it open.

The sight in front of me all but knocks me on my ass. Every molecule of air leaves my lungs and my blood crystalizes. Before my blood starts to boil as absolute rage takes over and explodes.

"What the fuck is going on here?!" The words erupt from my mouth as my brother finally stops fucking my best friend. And not only does he stop, but he lowers himself to cover her, to hide her, as though he could. We're in her house, so while he tries to shield her, it's not as though I wouldn't see her.

"Get out!" Lochlyn hollers at me, louder than I've ever heard before, and with a touch of something that seems like protection.

He's protecting her...from me. My blood boils as I stare him down, but turn on my heels and walk out the door, slamming it shut behind me.

While they may think I'm leaving, or going downstairs to hash this out, I'm not. I'm standing right fucking here and waiting for one of them to come out. To face me head on and tell me how long this has been going on.

This thing that I have been against, that I have made it very clear to them that I am against, for *years*.

How long has this been going on? How long have they been fucking behind my back?

Before I can ponder it too long, the door swings open and I turn around just as Lochlyn finishes pulling a shirt over his head and he jumps back.

"Fuck, Chels, you seriously just stood here?"

I brush right past him and into the middle of the room. It's a space I know so well, almost like my own, and yet right now it all feels off kilter, different, foreign. Frantically I look between the two of them, eyes wild, nostrils flaring. "*What* is going on here?"

Time is of the essence, and I don't give them any, turning on Lochlyn, finger in his face. "Are you fucking her? My *best friend?*"

Utterly out of control, I spin to Shay. "And you. How many times have I told you? Lochlyn's my fucking brother, Shay. My *brother*. You can have any guy you want, they all come around you. And you go after my brother?"

"Chels, I—" She doesn't get to finish, and I hold up my hand to stop her as my eyes fill to the brim, ready to spill over with the next blink. The sting of betrayal is so strong it tingles through my entire body.

"I've told you. I've told both of you, that *this*"—I wave my hands wildly between them—"was not something I was okay with. Not ever."

We all stand in silence. Nobody knows what to say to me. There are a million things running through my head but I have no idea where to start. I need something to take the focus off the pain.

"How long?" It's barely above a whisper, but I need to know.

They both turn their gaze my direction.

"Huh?

"How long?" I ask again, this time through gritted teeth.

Shay can't seem to figure out an answer, how to tell me what's surely only going to dig the knife in deeper.

"Since Thanksgiving," Lochlyn answers for them both.

Eyes searing, I turn on my brother. The one person I had left in my life who I knew would be there for me no matter what, the last blood member of my family I have left. "You've been hiding this from me since Thanksgiving? You've been screwing her since then?"

"No!" They both yell in unison.

This time, I turn to Shay, and I don't try to hide the pain etched on my face, in my words, or in my heart. "Shay, you've been lying to me for almost a year? How could you do that?"

"Leave her alone, Chels. I did this. I went after her." Of course he did, of course he went after her. That was never a question in my mind. Lochlyn wanted a new conquest, and who better than my virgin best friend?

With sheer exasperation and anger, I throw my hands in the air and spin to face him. "Oh, poor sweet Lochlyn. What, you couldn't get enough sluts at college? You had to turn my best friend into just another one of your conquests?"

Lochlyn tenses, hands balling into fists, as he points a finger at me. "Watch it," he says through gritted teeth.

"Really though, Loch, have you told her about all the girls at school?" Surely he hasn't told her about the steady stream of girls in and out of his room. Shay couldn't possibly be stupid enough to sleep with him if he had.

"I have not been with anybody since well before Thanksgiving. I have been faithful to Shay."

"Oh bullshit, Lochlyn. You couldn't keep it in your pants if a million dollars was on the line." I take a moment and shake my head. "It doesn't matter. I don't even care about that. I told both of you, time and time again, that I would never be okay if you two got together. I never thought I'd have to worry about it, you barely noticed each other. But I started seeing little things here and there this summer. I thought I was crazy. Guess not."

The party, the time he spent at the store and where she was sometimes gone too. It all felt off but stupidly I ignored it.

"Say what you want about me, Chelsea, but I have not, nor would I ever, cheat on Shay."

"To cheat on her, you'd have to be in a relationship, not just screwing around." The words angrily fly from my mouth.

When neither one of them say anything, their eyes locked on each other and it all becomes crystal clear. This is all so much more, so much worse, than I initially thought it was.

"Ohmygod. You're in a relationship? Like officially boyfriend and girlfriend?"   Something finally clicks into place and

I turn to Shay. "The messages. John. It was Lochlyn the whole time, wasn't it?" Shay must see the utter betrayal I feel because she can't meet my eye anymore. "That's why you never let me meet him. Because you were *lying* to me."

"Chelsea, I'm—" Shay starts quietly, but she doesn't get to apologize for this. This is beyond anything I ever could have dreamed of. The two people who I love most in this world have been sneaking around behind my back for more than half the year. I'm supposed to trust them, that they'll stick around for me like nobody else has. And then they go and do *this?* For months on end, they purposefully lied to me.

"You need to choose." The words tumble out of my mouth before I can stop them.

"What? I—What?" Shay sounds almost as stunned as I feel. Good.

"You need to choose. Me or him."

"Chelsea, cut the crap. You can't make her choose between us." Ultimately, he's right. I can't. I'm not foolish enough to think I actually have that kind of power.

I turn to him and tell him just one more truth on this whole day. "I can't be friends with somebody fucking my brother."

He glowers at me in response. I'd be scared if he wasn't my brother and I didn't know he'd fold like a lawn chair. "I won't let you do this."

Want to challenge me, brother? Fine. Challenge accepted. I turn to Shay to give her the news. "Here's the deal, Shay. I can't force you two to breakup. But I also don't have to keep talking to you. It's him or me."

It would be the complete destruction of my soul to never talk to her again. Shay is my absolute best friend, even though I know I don't always show it in return. To lose her? It would be devastating. But at least I'd be doing it on my terms, I'd be doing the ending. I wouldn't be the one getting dropped like last season's shirt style.

Sure, she could choose him, which would sting like nothing ever has before, but it would be by my hand, by my forcefulness, not her own free will.

I leave the room and storm down the steps, Lochlyn's voice bellowing after me. It's not until I slam the front door that I realize what I said up there, and the consequences.

"What have I done?"

Pre-order Setting Limits now, on Amazon. Releasing December 20, 2022

Acknowledgments

What an amazing journey it's been to get here. With that, comes many thanks.

To my amazing husband and children:

Another book, another thank you. I still cannot begin to truly show or explain my gratitude for all that you do and all the ways you continue to support me on this incredible journey.

I truly could not do a single aspect of this without you. Having you by my side every step of the way means so much to me.

I love you!

To my amazing trio; GC, AK, RL:

You three are my rock solid team. There for any question, any confusion, any help I need, I know you're there. It's amazing to have found not just great writing partners, but friends.

To my awesome PA, Jennifer Webb:

Thank you for being my biggest cheerleader! I could not do this without your constant support!

To my incredible street team:

Thank you all for you continued support of me and my work. It's amazing to have readers who enjoy my work enough to want to promote it for others to read. I'm truly thankful for you all.

To my amazing editors Zainab and Mackenzie:

This book would not be what it is without you and your input. Thank you for helping me learn how to be a better writer, adjusting my words, and most importantly, keeping my voice my own. And especially for your beautiful words as you read through it.

Thank you to the amazing **Coffin Print Designs** for my stunning cover!

To my ARC team: Your time and effort does not go unnoticed. Thank you for reading my novel before it hit the public and for your gracious reviews. I know it's not always easy to find the words, but it's all so appreciated.

And most importantly, to the readers:

Thank you for taking a chance on a small author like myself. I know it can be difficult to see a new name and say "hey let me try that" but it is so beyond appreciated, I cannot begin to find the words. I write because it's my passion, but I publish because I want to share my words with all of you. I hope you enjoyed reading it, as much as I enjoyed writing it.

About the Author

S hayna Astor is a romance author who loves writing sweet love stories, with a lot of spice. When she's not writing, she's probably watching The Office with a cup of coffee, spending time with her kids, or playing video games with her husband.

Stalk me for all the latest updates, teasers for upcoming novels, giveaways, and all the goods on what's coming next!

Instagram @shayna.astor.author

TikTok @shayna.astor.author

Facebook Group Shayna's Coffee Corner

Website www.shaynaastor.com